Blythe—Her dreams shattered by divorce, she escapes to England—and encounters a mysterious pair of lovers from the past and a secret that echoes down the centuries into her own life.

Ellie—Consumed with envy, she gets the ultimate revenge when she steals her sister's husband, Hollywood style.

Christopher—The talented, gorgeous Hollywood director always gets what he wants . . . and now he wants Blythe, the woman he betrayed.

Lucas—An Englishman, he can't resist the lovely American who agrees to help him save his estate and who, in the process, might save his jaded heart as well.

By Ciji Ware:

Fiction
ISLAND OF THE SWANS
WICKED COMPANY
A COTTAGE BY THE SEA*

Nonfiction
SHARING PARENTHOOD AFTER DIVORCE

**Published by Fawcett Gold Medal*

A COTTAGE BY THE SEA

Ciji Ware

FAWCETT GOLD MEDAL • NEW YORK

A Fawcett Gold Medal Book
Published by Ballantine Books
 Published in the United States by Ballantine Books, a division of Random House, Inc., New York, and simultaneously in Canada by Random House of Canada Limited, Toronto.

http://www.randomhouse.com

Library of Congress Catalog Card Number: 96-90722

ISBN 0-449-15039-9

Manufactured in the United States of America

First Edition: April 1997

10 9 8 7 6 5 4 3 2 1

Dedicated to my English cousins, Edd and Gay North, of Cornwall, who discovered "Barton Hall" and whose hospitality made researching and writing this novel a joyful experience.

In tribute to William Moffett, 1933–1995, director of the Huntington Library in San Marino, California —brave scholar, treasured friend, storyteller, mentor, and guardian of the written word.

In memory of novelist Daphne Du Maurier, 1907–1989, spinner of magical tales set in Cornwall that have inspired generations of writers and readers.

And, finally, with deep appreciation for The National Trust, savior of the Cornish coast and so much more.

Our birth is but a sleep and a forgetting:
The Soul that rises with us, our life's Star,
Hath had elsewhere its setting,
And cometh from afar . . .

William Wordsworth, 1770–1850

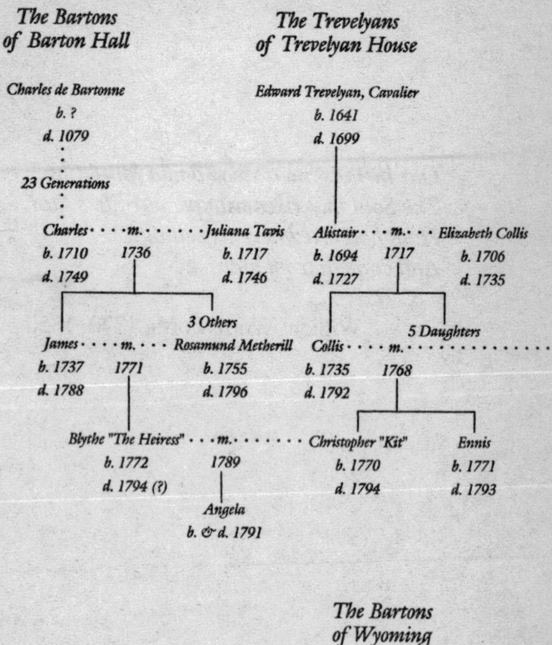
The Bartons of Barton Hall
Charles de Bartonne
b. ?
d. 1079
23 Generations
Charles
b. 1710
d. 1749
m.
1736
Juliana Tavis
b. 1717
d. 1746
3 Others
James
b. 1737
d. 1788
m.
1771
Rosamund Metherill
b. 1755
d. 1796
Blythe "The Heiress"
b. 1772
d. 1794 (?)
m.
1789
Angela
b. & d. 1791
The Trevelyans of Trevelyan House
Edward Trevelyan, Cavalier
b. 1641
d. 1699
Alistair
b. 1694
d. 1727
m.
1717
Elizabeth Collis
b. 1706
d. 1735
5 Daughters
Collis
b. 1735
d. 1792
m.
1768
Christopher "Kit"
b. 1770
d. 1794
Ennis
b. 1771
d. 1793

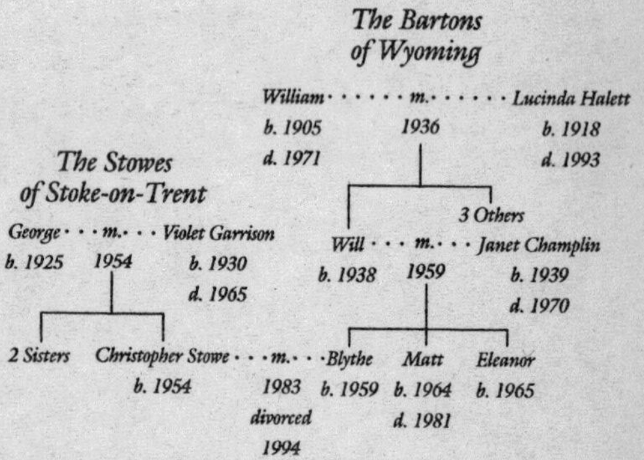
The Bartons of Wyoming
William
b. 1905
d. 1971
m.
1936
Lucinda Halett
b. 1918
d. 1993
3 Others
Will
b. 1938
m.
1959
Janet Champlin
b. 1939
d. 1970
Blythe
b. 1959
Matt
b. 1964
d. 1981
Eleanor
b. 1965
The Stowes of Stoke-on-Trent
George
b. 1925
m.
1954
Violet Garrison
b. 1930
d. 1965
2 Sisters
Christopher Stowe
b. 1954
m.
1983
divorced
1994

Barton–Trevelyan–Teague Genealogy

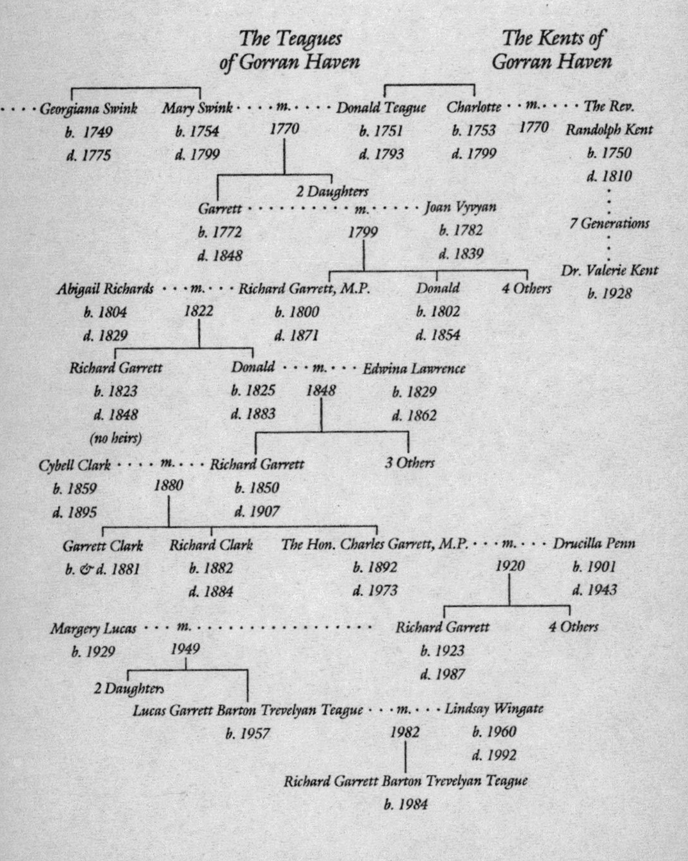

Chapter One

May 9, 1994

In Blythe Barton Stowe's considered opinion, justice would have been better served if the earthquake fault that ran under the Los Angeles County Courthouse had simply cracked open and swallowed her husband's vulgar white stretch limousine, passenger and all.

Instead, the showy vehicle that just last March had delivered its owner to the Dorothy Chandler Pavilion on Oscar night now inched through a platoon of hectoring paparazzi. Cameras clicked and camcorders whirled as Christopher Stowe's liveried chauffeur steered his behemoth to a halt in the handicapped zone at First and Hill Streets.

"Why don't the cops ever ticket those bastards?" muttered Blythe's companion, Lisa Spector, under her breath.

"Hey, gal," Blythe retorted, affecting her best Wyoming twang, "this here's Holly-weird. The guy just won an Oscar, remember? He can do anything he goddamn pleases in this town."

Instantly she regretted her display of bitter animosity, a reaction that too often surfaced at the slightest mention of Christopher Stowe. She inhaled deeply and slowly forced her breath out through her lips, hoping to clear her system of the corrosive hostility that had built up like rust on a barbed-wire fence. Meanwhile, she continued to stare down through the tinted windows in the judge's chambers that overlooked the media circus unfolding in the sultry May sunshine.

On the sidewalk below, the *National Enquirer*, not to mention television crews from *Hard Copy* and *Inside Edition*, had stringers with cell phones staking out every possible approach to the public building—the place where California residents, famous and otherwise, came to render their marriage contracts null and void.

Inside, Blythe, Lisa, and the rest of a small, subdued group continued to wait in the family law section of the courthouse for the most celebrated—and notorious—British film director in the world to make his tardy appearance.

As Blythe glanced around Judge Alan Hawkins's private chambers, her experienced eye told her that the book-lined room provided a well-appointed setting for the drama that would soon take place. Even the supporting cast members—including His Honor—were standing on their marks. The entire scene was a production designer's dream, except it was about to become this production designer's nightmare.

Oh, God, Christopher! Why would you do this to us?

Once again Blythe cast her eyes on the sidewalk theatrics through large tortoiseshell sunglasses that mercifully shielded her eyes. It almost felt like an out-of-body experience as she watched one of L.A.'s high-profile divorce attorneys emerge from Christopher's ludicrously long vehicle. Within seconds her handsome husband of eleven years, sporting his dark-blond "director's ponytail," stepped out too. The excited journalists pressed forward as the man of the hour leisurely unfolded his six-foot frame and stood to his full height.

Blythe watched with numb curiosity as the figure who had been her lover, mentor, husband, and business partner slowly surveyed the throng, almost as if he were calculating the best angle for filming his next scene.

It was just like an exterior shot from *Kramer vs. Kramer*, Blythe thought, only there was no six-year-old child for them to fight over.

Then she sighed with a mixture of exasperation and despair. Why did she keep seeing her life as if she were watching a film? she wondered. It was a ridiculous habit. However, she was incapable of pulling her gaze away from this real-life movie screen and continued to watch the award-winning director as he selected a leggy brunette on which to bestow a wistful smile and melancholy gaze from his arresting blue eyes. He paused curbside to speak earnestly to the striking woman coanchor of a nightly network news program as the cameras rolled. Here we had the sexy, "bankable" director, quizzed about his personal life by the easy-on-the-eyes news hen who had joined him for dinner once too often during the promo tour for his latest film. You stroke my back, I'll stroke yours, and everybody's happy. Well, not everybody, Blythe pondered silently.

"Blythe," Lisa said sotto voce, abruptly calling to a halt her client's unhealthy musings. "Come in here for a moment, would you?" urged the Armani-clad attorney, nodding in the direction of a small conference room adjacent to the judge's private chambers.

Blythe's lawyer closed the door and then placed her thick briefcase on top of the highly polished table where untold litigants had mediated their matrimonial breakdowns. Blythe and Christopher's agreement, however, was already a Done Deal, in Hollywood parlance, and Blythe wondered why Lisa had ushered her into the claustrophobic chamber.

Her attorney pulled a pile of colored newsprint from inside her attaché case.

"These aren't pleasant to look at, I realize," Lisa said crisply, "but I want your permission to use them today, in case we run into a snag during the final-settlement conference."

"I thought you said everything *is* settled," Blythe protested, apprehensively scanning the screaming headlines of a number of salacious tabloids that contained the unsavory details of her impending divorce.

"HEARTBROKEN BLYTHE!" one newspaper wailed at her.

Behind the large-type headlines was an unflattering photo of her clad in jeans and a sweatshirt captured by some low-life photographer who had lain in wait in the bushes behind her new condo. Blythe stared at the color picture, mesmerized by her own startled expression, which gave her the aspect of someone caught in a stealthy, underhanded act—in her case, depositing a bulging plastic bag filled with garbage in a large trash bin. Her curly, shoulder-length auburn hair looked wildly unkempt, as if she'd stuck her finger in an electric socket. Her brown eyes sported matching dark circles, indicating she hadn't slept for days—which she hadn't. The photograph, taken with a harsh flash at dawn's light when she erroneously thought it would be safe to leave her house, had transformed her tall, slender frame into a wraithlike specter—possibly an escapee from a women's prison camp. Definitely not a pretty picture.

The pull-quotes inside the article were cloyingly sympathetic, however, describing in riveting detail how Christopher Stowe's extramarital high jinks had triply cheated his talented American wife out of a handsome, wealthy husband; an award-winning business partner; and a father of the baby she had wanted to conceive—but hadn't.

"I doubt I'll have to bring any of these up," Lisa was saying, shuffling through the pile of tabloids, "but just in case they pull any tricks . . ."

Lisa allowed her sentence to trail off as she pointed a perfectly manicured vermilion nail at another headline that shouted "BLYTHE'S UNTOLD ANGUISH." The overheated subhead read: "Movie-Town Wife Rushes to Dying Grandmother's Side While Stowe Cavorts with Mystery Woman in Director's Trailer!" She glanced at the lead paragraph. "Left motherless at age eleven, production designer Blythe Barton Stowe raced against time to be near her beloved grandmother, Lucinda Barton, seventy-eight, who lay dying of a stroke in the pioneer family's log ranch house in Jackson Hole, Wyoming.

The tragedy unfolded while her husband, director of the box-office smash *Good Chemistry*, was—"

"What's the point?" Blythe said in a monotone, pushing from her mind an unspeakable memory. "Nobody believes this stuff."

"The point is that we know—and they know we know—that in this case most of it happens to be true," Lisa said patiently.

Blythe's gaze drifted to another edition of supermarket fare. This tabloid cried out "BLYTHE'S SECRET TRAGEDY." She sucked in her breath as she stared at a black-and-white photo of her brother's body being carried out on a gurney from the rodeo arena in Jackson. The image showed seventeen-year-old Matt Barton's neck canted at an odd angle. In the background of the photo sat a shadowy female figure on a horse.

"How in the world did they ever dig that up?" she murmured. Matt would have been thirty years old this year. She allowed herself an instant to consider what the engaging carrot-headed teenager would have been like in 1994.

"However disgusting these rags are, they speak of the way in which your husband has irreparably damaged you," Lisa said, bypassing Blythe's melancholy question. "If the other side suddenly decides to challenge the numbers today, I want to be able to show that you're a celebrity in your own right. I don't think they'll try to pull anything like that," she hastened to add, glancing at Blythe's stricken expression, "but I want to make clear, if they do, that you are not merely his wife . . . that you earned every cent of this settlement—both in your role as production designer on the five films, and as Chris's full partner in Stowe and Stowe Productions."

"But Chris knows all that!" Blythe insisted. "You don't think his lawyers would try to—"

"It's important to have ammunition at hand," Lisa interrupted tersely, "should we need to prove in court how much you stand to lose professionally—and emotionally—if this scandal results in your not being able to carry on with a reasonably normal life in this town."

"Gee . . . thanks for reminding me."

Like her hard-nosed attorney, Blythe had also been worried that potential employers in the film industry who weren't familiar with her work might assume she'd served as production designer on Chris's films due to nepotism. On the other hand, those who had worked with her might now fear to offend "The Great One," and decline to hire her.

What her lawyer didn't understand—what nobody in this glitzy, self-indulgent community would ever fathom—was that no job and no amount of money could ever put her family back together or bring Lucinda Barton back to life. A hundred-million-dollar divorce settlement couldn't make up for the loss of the woman who'd raised Blythe or the brother who'd shared her love of horses. What price tag would equal the pain of knowing that her father, his own heart battered by a series of losses, was thinking of selling the ranch that had been in the Barton family for generations?

Meanwhile, her husband had been cheerfully indulging in a long-term affair even as Blythe was flying back and forth to Jackson Hole, Wyoming, to witness a courageous old lady slowly surrender her life in the log bedroom at the Double Bar B.

Blythe reflected on the previous seven months with a bitterness so potent, she was prompted to open her purse and search for a Valium.

Christopher Stowe's Wife Number One was about to emerge from this meeting today with a couple of million dollars deposited in her bank in her own name. And Blythe was under no illusions that when that happened, no one in this town would waste a tear on her.

She could even predict that these same tabloids, spread out in garish profusion on the table in front of her, would in the future run breathless stories favorably chronicling the next chapter in Christopher Stowe's glamorous life.

"What's she crying about?" her so-called friends would say

behind her back. "She ended up with plenty of pocket change out of that divorce!"

Don't they get it? she wanted to scream. The truth was, unless people had been through the nightmare she had endured, they couldn't comprehend, as Blythe certainly did now, that there wasn't a figure you could name that could ease or erase the moment when . . .

Stop it!

She mustn't think about all that. She simply couldn't afford to relive the last time she'd laid eyes on Chris and his lover. If she did, she knew with absolute certainty that she was capable of murder.

"Look, Lisa," Blythe said curtly, pointing to the tabloids spread out on the conference table. "Do whatever you have to do. I just want this over with."

Returning to the judge's chambers, the two women watched through the window as several off-duty LAPD officers in the employ of Blythe's husband climbed down from their motorcycles and cleared a path through the crush of mass media vying for their sound bites from filmland's wunderkind.

Doesn't turning forty this year take you out of the Whiz Kid category? Blythe asked silently. Perhaps winning the Oscar put a director in the Permanent Genius pantheon so no one cared anymore how Christopher Stowe treated the "little people," including his wife. Ex-wife.

Blythe felt Lisa's shoulder gently nudge her own.

"Well, at least Chris's Grand Passion stayed at home," her attorney murmured, sounding relieved.

"You mean I should be thankful for small favors?" Blythe replied, feeling the knot that had resided in her stomach these last seven months turn over on itself.

"You are a citizen of the United Kingdom?" the judge inquired politely.

"I am."

"And you have permanent legal-resident status in the United States?"

"I do."

"And you have lived in the state of California as an alien legal resident for some ten years, is that correct?"

"It is."

Christopher Stowe offered quiet, authoritative answers regarding how he proposed he and his wife sort out the complicated skein that had become their personal and professional lives these last eleven years. His rounded British baritone was the product of voice lessons taken before he had dropped out of the Royal Academy of Dramatic Art fifteen years earlier.

Blythe's wooden chair was placed so near her husband's as they sat across the desk from the balding Judge Hawkins that their elbows nearly touched. She saw how the magistrate in charge of this "dissolution" nodded pleasantly each time the famous director answered a question. And with each response Christopher further established his right to end his marriage and boot her out of their illustrious independent production company under the no-fuss, no-muss divorce system in her adopted state.

Back in Wyoming, the way her husband had behaved, Blythe probably could've shot him in the heart and been acquitted.

"And do you attest that the documents I have before me represent any and all such financial holdings and real estate in the United States?" Judge Hawkins continued.

"I do."

"And you are prepared to divide them equally with your wife, as outlined in your proposed property settlement?"

"I am. More than equally."

On paper, Blythe knew, it appeared utterly fair. In fact, thanks to the Golden State's legendary community-property laws, the *Stowe vs. Stowe* financial settlement paid her liberally to walk away from her handsome British movie-mogul husband—if she would walk away quietly. The celebrated Mr.

Stowe was to remain in the five-thousand-square-foot house that his wife had designed and decorated on Bristol Drive in Brentwood. He also retained his pale-blue Bentley and, no doubt, their circle of powerful friends and acquaintances in the film industry. In other words, Blythe could reasonably assume that his life would stay exactly as it had been—and hers would be totally changed. Nicely furnished . . . but the pits.

Christopher hated colloquialisms like that, she remembered. "So common, darling!" he had chided her whenever she unwittingly revealed her origins as a child of the Wild West or fell into her "Wyoming slang-and-twang," as he called her more colorful speech patterns. "Remember . . . we speak the language of Shakespeare!"

In Stoke-on-Trent? she wondered. After all, her husband's father had been a kiln supervisor at the Royal Doulton chinaware factory.

Give it a rest, Chris, she thought savagely, and then felt as if her own venom were oozing directly into her veins. She took another deep breath and slowly exhaled again, wondering if it was possible to swallow another Valium without water.

Then she mentally shook herself. In the immortal words of Grandma Barton, it was time to Cowboy Up.

Stop your sniveling, gal, and get it together.

Her gaze fell on her husband's naked ring finger, and she wondered, suddenly, if it was true that unrelenting anger and longing for revenge could cause cancer or heart attacks. As Blythe's eyes moved up Chris's arm to the sleeve of his impeccably tailored silk-and-cashmere sport jacket, Judge Hawkins continued to recite the various aspects of their negotiated divorce and property settlement.

"There are no children of this marriage?" he inquired.

"Correct," Christopher said curtly.

Blythe shifted focus from Judge Hawkins's right hand as he ticked off the items that would determine her future. She looked directly at Christopher. Their eyes met briefly, and he looked away. During the last five years of their marriage, she had begged him to agree to start a family, but he'd argued persuasively that their Tinseltown lifestyle wasn't compatible with raising children.

"We work such bloody long hours, Blythe," Chris had countered with his customary wall of patient logic. "It wouldn't be fair to the child—plus it would complicate your life enormously!"

As she confronted him face-to-face for the first time in months—a woman of thirty-five whose biological clock had started to give off alarm bells—a grinding fury began to displace her grief over how they'd come to be in this place, at this time, taking these steps to end their marriage and their partnership.

For weeks now, she'd heard the rumors. Rumors that nearly choked the life out of her.

"Mr. and Mrs. Stowe," the judge was intoning as he removed his half glasses from the bridge of his nose and looked across his desk at them both. "Is there no possible avenue for reconciling this marriage?"

Blythe could see Christopher shifting uncomfortably in his chair. Then she heard the attorneys behind her rustling their file folders.

"I'm afraid a reconciliation is out of the question, Your Honor," replied Christopher gravely, his cultivated British accent interrupting the long silence. "You see, my fiancée and I are expecting a child and—"

"Then it's true?" Blythe exclaimed, swiveling in her oak chair to face the man she had taught to drive L.A.'s freeways when they were graduate students together at UCLA. "You made a baby! With my sister! And you wouldn't make one with me?" she asked, simultaneously incredulous and furious.

Her raw accusations reverberated through the judge's chambers. Both attorneys sprang to attention, responding to the possible meltdown of their carefully crafted divorce settlement. Chris's lawyer smoothly addressed Judge Hawkins.

"My client, unfortunately, finds himself irreconciled to this marriage. And, as you well know, Your Honor, California's no-fault system dictates that if one party sees no future for the marriage, it is, de facto, irreconcilable and may be legally dissolved."

Lisa Spector stood to reply to her adversary.

"If Mrs. Stowe wishes to review or contest various aspects of this proposed settlement in light of the punishing barrage of recent publicity garnered by this case, that is, of course, her right."

"If so, Your Honor," Christopher's legal representative replied belligerently, "we would move to bifurcate the proceedings, and go forward with the dissolution. We could, of course, withdraw our very generous property settlement and go to trial to adjudicate the financial issues. May I further point out—"

"Mrs. Stowe?" Judge Hawkins interrupted with a warning glance in the direction of both legal gladiators. He looked at her kindly. "What are your wishes in this matter?"

"I'll sign," Blythe replied, her voice barely above a whisper.

"What did you say?" Christopher asked tensely.

"I'll sign!" she shouted, slamming her handbag on the floor.

Her sister was pregnant. By Blythe's husband. Eleanor Barton might look like a fey, gamine artsy-craftsy type, but she'd certainly grown up—finally—and paid her older sister and grandmother back. Big time. And in a fashion only she could devise. This most recent sordid revelation also explained why the press was in such a feeding frenzy today. They had learned somehow that Blythe Barton Stowe's sister was pregnant with Christopher Stowe's child—and Blythe hadn't known. Not for sure.

Once again she felt herself floating in a surreal world, adrift in the emotional wreckage of the past half year's shocking events.

Lisa Spector rested a firm hand on her client's shoulder. Then she turned to address the judge. "As difficult emotionally as these unusual circumstances are for my client, Your Honor, she has thoroughly reviewed the terms of the settlement and is prepared to finalize the agreement. Aren't you, Blythe?" she added.

The Deal. Nothing was more important than The Deal in Hollywood, Blythe reflected, slowly nodding her assent.

Judge Hawkins turned the documents around on his desk and indicated a series of red *X*'s that were flagged by yellow Post-it notes. Accepting a pen from the judge's hand, Blythe mechanically wrote her triple-barreled signature where she was directed.

"And now you, Mr. Stowe."

Blythe watched as Christopher ended their marriage contract and their personal and professional relationship in the fashion she had witnessed him terminating so many other agreements: with a mere stroke of a pen—and millions in the bank. In the course of the five phenomenally successful movies he'd made with her as the production designer, Chris had invariably been the one to institute damage control when something went amiss. And other people were always the ones who got damaged.

Their exchange in open court was brief and businesslike. Then Blythe followed Lisa Spector out a side door without speaking to the man who had been the central figure in her life for more than a decade. A moment later she and her attorney were ushered down a deserted corridor. The bailiff politely held the elevator for them.

"Take this down to the judges' special parking area on Level B," he directed. "I confirmed on the two-way . . . your driver should be waiting for you."

An awkward silence hung in the air as the doors slid shut.

"Suitcases in the car?" Lisa asked with forced cheerfulness. "Got your passport?"

"Yes," Blythe murmured, wondering if she would always feel as dreadful as she did at this moment.

"Are you sure you're up to staying in Cornwall—alone?"

Lisa inquired carefully. "Isn't the place you're going awfully remote?"

"I hope it's as isolated as a mesa on the moon," Blythe replied.

"Well, yeah . . . ," Lisa agreed. "At least you'll be able to shake the press."

"That's why I picked the place," Blythe replied. "My grandmother always claimed the Bartons of Wyoming had owned an estate centuries ago in a remote section of the Cornish coast. Chris and I talked about going there to research the connection, but there was never time. Now time is what I've got plenty of."

"Now, where do you suppose the driver's got to?" Lisa said, obviously shying away from any further emotional entanglements with her fragile client. "Oh, there he is!" she exclaimed as the elevator doors parted, depositing them in the coolness of the concrete garage under the courthouse. "He's just caught sight of us too." Blythe was reassured to hear the familiar sound of her car's engine springing to life. "This should be just the escape you need, then," Lisa commented brightly. "Find your roots, just like Alex Haley!"

"Who knows if any of Lucinda's notions are true?" Blythe replied with a shrug. Her lawyer obviously wasn't interested in hearing about her client's recently deceased grandmother. Lisa Spector was the kind of woman who did not dwell on the past. "Cornwall seemed like a nice, obscure place for a rest cure," Blythe added with a touch of irony she assumed, correctly, would be lost on her attorney.

As the two women waited for Blythe's car to draw near, she wondered now if her own carefully plotted "getaway" would merely turn into a damp and miserable form of exile.

"Are there still Bartons living there?" Lisa inquired absently as they headed toward the Jaguar just nosing out of its preferred parking place some hundred yards distant.

"The place is currently owned by an offshoot of the Barton-Trevelyans . . . a family named Teague."

"It's still private? How did you persuade them to let you stay there?" Lisa queried, casting one eye toward Blythe's car, which was slowly making its way toward them.

"I won't be staying at the manor. I've leased a cottage on the estate for the month of May," Blythe disclosed, wondering silently if Lisa's description would prove to be closer to the mark than the tasteful brochure the owner, a man named Lucas Teague, had forwarded to her travel agent.

"Sounds cute," Lisa replied skeptically. "Did you rent a car for the month?"

"No. I can walk to the village."

"How quaint. But what if I have to fax you something over there?" her lawyer demanded, waving at the driver of Blythe's blue Jaguar.

"The cottage has no phone," Blythe replied, "but I figured that was the appeal," she added pointedly. Wasn't solitude what she wanted? Total privacy to lick her wounds? A chunk of time in which to figure out what she would do if she didn't do film production design anymore? A quiet, secluded place to gather her strength so she could begin to rebuild her life—and mend her heart. "Visitors can use the manor-house exchange as long as they don't abuse the privilege. I was told that his housekeeper is willing to take urgent messages. I left the number with your secretary," she finished, sensing a familiar weight of sadness settling in her chest.

"Well . . . I guess I could FedEx you in an emergency," Lisa considered doubtfully.

The sound of running footsteps interrupted their conversation.

"Oh, boy," groaned Lisa. "Here come the reptiles. Quick, get in the car!" she said, pointing to the dark-blue vehicle coming their way.

From around a concrete pillar a man with earphones clamped on his head and a tape recorder slung over his right shoulder suddenly bore down on them, shouting, "There she is! Mrs. Stowe! Mrs. Stowe! Can you tell us your reaction to today's divorce proceedings? Mrs. Stowe!"

Blythe stared, frozen to the spot, as the radio reporter thundered toward her. The microphone held in his outstretched hand was suddenly inches from her chin.

"What's your response to being two-timed by your own sister while you were looking after your dying grandmother?" he persisted, panting like an overheated dog after his dash across the cavernous garage. His shirttail dribbled below a waistline that bore the signs of too much booze and fast food. Several other reporters ran up behind him.

"How do you feel about her having a baby with your husband? Ex-husband, I mean," another journalist demanded, looking pleased at his stab at accuracy.

"Excuse me!" shouted the network anchorwoman who prided herself on still going out in the field to do breaking stories, and to whom Chris had been talking on the sidewalk in front of the courthouse. "Isn't it true that you're walking away from this marriage with a financial settlement in the seven figures?"

Blythe swallowed hard and blindly began to back toward her car.

"Oh, for God's sake, you creeps!" Lisa shouted. Then she flung open the left rear passenger door and practically shoved Blythe into the backseat. "Get in! Get in!"

Soon the phalanx of reporters had surrounded the sedan. Tungsten lights mounted on top of the television news cameras harshly illuminated the car's leather interior. Lisa, elbowing the disheveled radio reporter aside, rapped sharply on the chauffeur's window until the glass glided open.

"Just move forward, driver!" the tight-lipped attorney commanded. "They'll get out of the way if they see you mean business." Then, lowering her head, she whispered into the man's left ear, "Take her directly to LAX. British Airways."

Some twenty-one hours later Blythe felt like a hapless extra in *The Longest Day*. She groggily roused herself to attention in the backseat of the hired Volvo as the driver sped across an arched stone bridge spanning the River Tamar into Cornwall proper. The trip had followed hard on the heels of air-traffic delays on two continents and a numbing twelve-hour plane ride to London's Heathrow. Now the car's engine was slowing audibly as the vehicle labored down increasingly tortuous one-track roads that featured a few "lay-bys" here and there to solve the problem of face-to-face confrontations with approaching automobiles.

Each succeeding turn led to a narrower lane that was flanked on both sides by stone hedges. These six-foot-high "fences" were clad top to bottom in a wild profusion of lush greenery and hedgerow trees, which, at this late hour, rendered them gloomy and forbidding.

"You can't see a bloody thing!" Blythe muttered darkly, hopeful that her use of the British epithet, so favored by her former husband, would elicit a response from her hired driver, who had performed his services in silence the entire journey down from London.

There was no reply forthcoming as the car suddenly glided under a stone arch attached to a turreted gatekeeper's cottage. A discreet sign posted near the open gate announced BARTON HALL—PRIVATE RESIDENCE.

In the lingering twilight that foretold of the oncoming summer months, Blythe and her taciturn chauffeur drove nearly a mile down a leafy green tunnel bordered by sixty-foot larches whose top branches mingled overhead. The column of trees eventually let out on a circular gravel drive that led to the stone steps of a small-scaled castle. The crenellated round towers on each of the imposing structure's four corners looked to Blythe as if Richard Burton might suddenly materialize in tunic and hose bellowing, "Camelot!" The fairy-tale gray stone edifice boldly poked its parapets above a low-lying mist that boiled up from a narrow valley, bisected by a modest river burbling on Blythe's right. Lush green grass dotted with a profusion of bluebells and pink campion carpeted the banks of the meandering stream. The colorful sprinkling of flowers outlined the River Luney's path in the dusk as it flowed down to and across a narrow strip of beach and ultimately disappeared into the brooding waters of the English Channel.

Having stared for hours, semicomatose, at her copy of the ordnance survey map "Landranger Number 204—Truro, Falmouth, and Surrounding Area," Blythe determined that a grass-clad crescent called Dodman Point embraced the left side of the cove. In the distance on her right, the shadowy outline of mighty Nare Head must surely be the landmass that jutted its lava-laced cliffs into the sea.

Blythe gazed out her window at the only objects moving on the rural Cornish landscape—picturesque clusters of sheep, along with Highland cattle whose broad heads were crowned with formidable, curving horns. The large, shaggy carrot-colored beasts seemed somehow miscast in the quilted landscape of gentle, rolling hills and fields crosshatched by tall flower-encrusted stone and grass hedges.

Minutes later Blythe arrived at the three-thousand-acre seat of her supposed ancestors, the Barton-Trevelyans, only to be informed that her landlord, Lucas Teague, had already departed for dinner with friends in nearby Mevagissey. A glance at her watch told Blythe that she was more than three hours past the time of her estimated arrival. Even so, she felt unaccountably deflated by the news that the lord of the manor had not remained at home to greet her.

An elderly housekeeper in a navy-blue pleated skirt, white blouse, and gray cardigan who introduced herself as Mrs. Quiller had appeared at the front door the instant their car crunched to a stop at the gravel entrance. Lucas Teague's retainer—a small, neat woman with an exceedingly pleasant manner—promptly handed the visitor a large old-fashioned iron key and directed Blythe's chauffeur to proceed back up the drive, and down another twisting single-track road toward the sea, where they would find a wooden gate with a carved sign announcing PAINTER'S COTTAGE.

"Just mind to clo-ose the gate for the goin' in or comin' out," she cautioned in the soft, elongated manner of Cornish speech. "Us don't want to lose the few sheep that're still on the place," she added, exchanging her pronouns in the fashion typical of the locals. "I've left a pasty near the hob, if ya be of a mind for something fillin'. There's a fire laid, that'll give ya some extra heat if it's needin'."

By the time they bumped down a dirt track and reached a broad field flanking the sea, the swirling fog had turned into a driving rain. With lichen clinging to its slate roof, a small stone dwelling looked forlornly out across the English Channel. The cottage was illuminated only by a solitary lamp glowing in one of its deep-set windows. Facing north was a distinctive twelve-foot-by-eight-foot square-paned artist's window.

Blythe noted with some satisfaction that, as per the inviting prose in Lucas Teague's brochure that had accompanied the booking form and outlined the lodging's amenities, Painter's Cottage was, indeed, located thirty feet from a cliff near Dodman Point, a half mile from Barton Hall itself. However, at the moment, thanks to a steady downpour, she couldn't see five feet in front of the car.

It was close to eight by the time she found herself standing alone in the middle of the frigid cottage overlooking Veryan Bay—now completely shrouded in fog. As the hired car and uncommunicative driver disappeared into the deepening gloom, Blythe paused at the threshold, watching the taillights vanish into the mist.

Then suddenly she was overcome by a wave of loneliness so devastating that her breath caught, as if she'd been assaulted. Like a videotape endlessly replaying itself, her mind began to focus once again on the terrible sequence of events that had led up to the moment when she'd walked inside her husband's luxurious director's trailer.

Don't think about it . . . just don't think about it!

As she ventured farther into the deserted cottage, Blythe's eyes were drawn to the shadowy corners of the small chamber.

Try as she might, she couldn't seem to switch off the flood of memories regarding a scandal taking place half a world away.

Prior to her own shocking discovery of her husband's unorthodox infidelity, apparently everyone but she had been privy to all manner of gossip and innuendo. Those in the know whispered that Christopher Stowe, the brilliant filmmaker, had spent many a sultry afternoon at Ellie's artist's loft in Santa Monica, where she illustrated children's books, no less. It was real estate she, Blythe, had paid for, hoping her directionless younger sister would find a sense of purpose and some personal pride. And it had been there, during the last weeks of Grandma Barton's life, that Chris and Ellie had fallen into each other's arms with the doors locked, the blinds drawn, and the answering machine picking up on the first ring.

No good deed goes unpunished.

No kidding, Grandma, she thought bleakly.

For the thousandth time Blythe's mind scanned the details of the double betrayal, searching for some overlooked clue that might finally explain such sordid treachery.

"He was my husband!" she raged inside the dimly lit cottage, her fists clenched rigidly by her side. Her outburst was muted by the hand-hewn beams of her supposed place of refuge. "She was my sister, for God's sake!" And, perhaps worst of all, the furtive lovers had even brazenly claimed to be overwhelmed with work and had both remained in California the day Lucinda Barton was buried in the snow-choked cemetery that November afternoon.

Blythe began to pace in aimless circles around her luggage piled in the center of the room. With bitterness guaranteed to give her heartburn, she recalled racing to catch the last flight out of the minuscule airport nestled under the shadow of the Grand Tetons, desperately seeking solace in her husband's arms by nightfall. She could remember perfectly which parking space she'd chosen that day on the Paramount lot. She saw herself rushing across the pavement toward Chris's director's trailer stationed next to soundstage 27. Various members of the crew on their dinner break had watched her try the door, find it locked, and dig in her purse for her keys. Once she'd gotten it open, she merely stood on the trailer's threshold, staring inside. There, on the daybed, she beheld her husband—stark naked and sprawled across the tanned thighs of his twenty-nine-year-old sister-in-law. Both were fast asleep.

Blythe sat down on the largest piece of her luggage and closed her eyes.

If only she could cry, instead of think.

The story of the affair had been gossip too lurid, too juicy—and too valuable—not to have been sold to one of the sleazier television newsmagazine shows by someone on their film crew. Like a scalpel probing a wound, her mind once more conjured up the salacious tabloid headlines, the TV trucks from the networks and CNN parked in front of her condominium complex when the news of the incestuous tryst between the Oscar-winning director and his wife's sister became public.

All around Blythe in the small, dark room whose stone foundations burrowed into ancient Cornish soil, the evil specters of the last seven months seemed to rise and mock her vain attempt to escape the hurt and humiliation she'd endured.

What hope for the future could there be when the past was so ugly and would probably remain with her, wherever she went? Blythe stared at the relentless downpour slanting against the window and gripped the back of a Windsor chair to keep from fleeing into the night. Then, with a sudden sense of purpose, she rummaged inside her Vuitton suitcases and pulled out the bottle of duty-free Glenfiddich whiskey she'd impulsively purchased en route.

By midnight she'd drunk herself into oblivion.

The first sound Blythe became conscious of the following day was not the rhythmic surge of the surf a hundred feet below the cottage facing the sea. Nor was it the din of rain slapping against the slate roof above her head. What forced her to full consciousness was an irritating series of peremptory honks from a car horn that grew louder by the minute. The staccato beeping made the pounding in her head worse. This was soon followed by someone thumping on the thick oak door studded with heavy wrought-iron hinges and a large iron keyhole.

"Mrs. Stowe? Hello? Are you there?"

Blythe struggled to rise above the feather duvet smothering the double bed that was tucked under the eaves in the loft perched above the kitchen–sitting room downstairs. The square, European-style pillows supporting her neck did little to cushion her throbbing head, the unhappy result of downing half a bottle of single-malt whiskey.

And now, she thought, attempting to focus her bloodshot eyes on the rafters above her head, she was paying a very high price for achieving total insensibility. Her temples throbbed unmercifully as her stomach roiled in time with the fist thumping on her door.

Good God! That noise below was deafening!

"Hello . . . Mrs. Stowe? Anyone at home?" called a deep voice, accompanied by the incessant pounding that finally penetrated through her alcohol-induced haze.

For pity's sake, would someone have the decency to stop that infernal racket!

Blythe fumbled for her watch on the marble-topped night table beside her bed. The elegant roman numerals on the face stamped Cartier swam before her eyes. It was nearly one-thirty. In the afternoon!

"Mrs. Stowe!" the voice rumbled a third time.

Silence.

"Ah, well . . . ," someone muttered resignedly.

Soon she heard footsteps on the gravel path leading from the front door. Still in a drugged daze, she reached for her cotton dressing gown, shivering in the damp air. She stumbled down the steep, ladderlike stairway that connected the sleeping loft to the main floor of the cottage. Off to the side stood a two-burner cooker and a small microwave oven perched on top of a waist-high efficiency refrigerator. An ancient stone fireplace large enough for her to walk into—and where entire meals presumably had once been prepared—contained a neat stack of logs placed in readiness on its cold grate.

The dull day's light penetrated the cottage's dark corners, banishing most of the shadows that had cast such a melancholy spell over her the previous evening. Glancing hastily about the room, she spied an attractive folding screen, executed in needlepoint and placed around a claw-and-ball bathtub that faced a side window, offering a spectacular view of the jagged coastline. Through the "as advertised" floor-to-ceiling rain-spattered artist's window, she saw a hulking automobile that faintly resembled an army tank parked ten feet from her door.

Sprinting across the cold slate floor, she flung open the wooden portal. "Excuse me!" she called, gasping as the cold air swirled around her ankles and bare feet.

"Hello!" Then she sagged against the doorjamb for support, wincing in the anemic daylight filtering through the overcast skies above the cottage roof.

A man at least as tall as Christopher Stowe, in his late thirties, clad in tweeds and a well-worn stalking cap, paused at the door of a battered Land Rover. The oversize vehicle was painted the same shade of green as his knee-high rubber Wellington boots. Despite Blythe's unrelenting headache, she couldn't help noticing that her visitor could be a body double for some intriguing, nattily dressed British actor, familiar to American audiences through the auspices of *Masterpiece Theater* on public television. However, this man's superb bone structure and refined taste in chocolate-colored tweed jackets with leather patches on the elbows and tan moleskin trousers were somewhat offset by blue-black hair in need of a trim. Just short of shaggy, the glossy jet strands grazing his forehead and brushing his ears contributed to his faintly piratical appearance. Perhaps there was even a slight Latin cast to his features, as well. Hadn't a few members of the Spanish Armada washed up on Cornish shores in Elizabethan times? Surely the man seemed tanned and tall enough to have come from conquistador stock.

"Well, good morning, Mrs. Stowe," her visitor said with impeccable courtesy, although he was obviously trying not to stare at her disheveled state.

She imagined she looked a bit like a Skid Row derelict as she attempted to push her unruly mass of hair off her forehead. Fortunately, her polite visitor appeared determined to act as if everyone around these parts routinely slept till near teatime.

"H-hello . . . ," she croaked, her voice startlingly hoarse.

"Welcome to Cornwall. Pity about the weather," he added, glancing up at the dark clouds churning overhead. Judging from its ominous cast, the skies threatened to renew the downpour of a few minutes earlier. "Taking advantage of the dull day to overcome that dreadful jet lag, are you?" he inquired, his voice edged with amused irony.

Jet leg, my grandpa's spittoon, she groaned inwardly. What she had was a hangover brought to her in seventy millimeters and digital sound. She looked and felt a mess.

The intruder had retraced the cottage path to her door. He was close enough to her now that she could see his gaze had shifted from her face to beyond her left shoulder, where he was in a position to see the cold hearth and her suitcases still scattered in the middle of the room. Where in blazes had she discarded that bottle of Glenfiddich?

Her uninvited visitor was staring at her expectantly now. She knew that she should offer an introduction, but her brain was working in slow motion.

"Sorry to disturb you," he said at length. "I'm Lucas Teague."

"No. Really?" was all she could reply. She had incorrectly guessed that the stranger at her door might have been her landlord's property manager. Who else would force himself out in this disgusting weather to pay a visit to the recent arrival from America?

"Really, truly," he calmly assured her.

By now the hereditary owner of the castle perched on the hill behind them had reached the broad slate step abutting her door. Sheep in the field surrounding Painter's Cottage grazed in the background, their faint bleating nearly drowned out by the sound of the surf awash against the rocks at the bottom of the cliff.

Incongruously, she realized, the man dressed for a country outing was also carrying a slim briefcase. If I were designing this film, she thought suddenly, the scene would call for glorious sun to be shining down on that rakish black head of hair, and I would make sure the prop department found him a Purdey shotgun or a brace of pheasants to clutch in his gloved hand. I would also make him "Sir" Lucas Teague—a baronet, at least.

"Shall I come back later for you to sign the extension to your lease? Or better yet . . . perhaps you'd like to come up to the Hall today for tea?" he proposed in a tone of voice that had become entirely businesslike.

"Extension? Of my lease?" she echoed, mystified.

For the second time she attempted to tidy her auburn hair by running her fingers through its shoulder-length curls, made even more unruly by the moist air boiling up from the Channel. She groped for the open neck of her dressing gown and pulled at its flimsy fabric to veil her goose-pimpled flesh.

"Your solicitor—I mean lawyer—rang up late yesterday as I was about to leave for dinner. Said you were en route but would approve the new arrangement when you arrived."

Didn't one leave such lowly matters to an underling when one was lord of the manor? The owner of Barton Hall seemed to be a bit short on staff.

"That I would stay longer than a month?" she queried.

"Yes. Through September, she said," Teague confirmed patiently. "For a 'much deserved rest,' as she put it," he emphasized, regarding her even more closely.

The man had obviously concluded that his new tenant was a half-wit, Blythe thought with embarrassment. As she inadvertently met his gaze, she saw that he had blue eyes like Christopher's, only much darker and in wonderful harmony with his ebony hair. Then she silently scolded herself for making the comparison. He was her landlord, for God's sake, and he was undoubtedly wondering what in the world he had let himself in for by leasing this cottage to a whiskey-swilling American.

She blinked several times to clear her blurred vision. Spanish and Celtic, the man was, most probably, she concluded. An intriguing collision of cultures.

"Have you settled in all right?" he inquired, startling her from her thoughts.

"Ah . . . yes!" she blurted. "I mean . . . reasonably well, I'd say."

"You'll be able to stock up on food and supplies at Mevagissey or Gorran Haven, of course, a mile or so just down the road there. Have you had anything to eat?"

Blythe thought briefly of the bulging Cornish pasty, its half-moon pastry shell stuffed with congealed onion and braised beef, and nearly gagged. Once she had started on the whiskey, the housekeeper's offering had been utterly forgotten.

"Mrs. Quiller left me amply provided, thank you." Her mind was completely void of additional small talk, and she could think of nothing else to say. Instead, she stared over his shoulder at his green car. Several dents the size of pie plates creased the fenders of his long-suffering vehicle. No wonder he had honked so persistently to warn the sheep out of his way. He'd obviously learned that lesson the hard way.

"Well, then . . . shall we conclude our day's business around Mrs. Q's tea trolley?" he suggested, looking slightly grim.

"Oh . . . tea," she said vaguely. "That sounds nice."

She *was* a half-wit, she groaned. And Lucas Teague was a slightly disapproving Jeremy Irons in *Brideshead Revisited*!

"I can offer you a tour of the Hall and the gardens, if you like, and orient you to our bit of the Cornish coast. Perhaps you'd like to read over the extension of your lease then," he persisted.

The handsome Mr. Teague must need money, she concluded. Despite her obvious lack of promise as a sober, well-behaved tenant, Lucas Teague seemed positively anxious that she should sign on the dotted line to extend her lease by three months.

Here till September! Another media bombshell must have exploded in California, she reckoned, for Lisa to have committed her client without consultation to remain hidden in this remote outpost for such a long stretch.

"I am correct in understanding, aren't I," Teague persisted, "that you intend to let the cottage three more months? You haven't had a change of heart in the middle of the Atlantic, by chance?"

"Ah . . . no," she protested weakly. "Tea this afternoon sounds like a very sensible idea." A visit to the castle would allow her to call her attorney to discover what nameless horror was going on in La-La Land before she committed herself to such an extended exile. And, besides, she wagered that a strong cup of Darjeeling might be just the thing to counteract her hangover. Suddenly she shivered as the wind off the water once more blasted her bare ankles. "And do f-forgive my unkempt s-state," she added sheepishly, making a Herculean effort to stop her teeth from chattering. "I'm afraid I'm still on California time."

"I surmised it must be something like that when my rude pounding on your door didn't rouse you," he commented coolly.

"I crossed eight time zones or something . . . ," she apologized, wondering, suddenly, if he had concluded she was some crazed Hollywood drug addict. In truth, she hadn't suffered a hangover like this since she won the Barrel Racing Championships and took the Miss Wyoming Rodeo title her senior year in high school. "Is four o'clock okay?" she asked.

"Four-thirty would be more convenient," her landlord replied evenly. "We've a bit of a project under way up at the Hall. Take the path opposite the gate through the woods. It's a ten-minute walk. You'll come out near the stables. Follow the stone wall and you'll eventually arrive at the porte cochere."

When Blythe's hired driver had stopped to obtain the key to Painter's Cottage from Mrs. Quiller, she had duly noted that the granite canopy sported a crenellated top that matched Barton Hall's four round towers and the gatekeeper's cottage. From her studies in art design, she recalled that in centuries past, such arched entrances had shielded arriving coach passengers from inclement weather.

"Why is it called Barton Hall?" Blythe asked impulsively, letting her curiosity get the upper hand as the cold damp under her feet seeped into the marrow of her bones. "Why not Barton Castle?"

"That's all part of the Gold Star Tour I'll be giving you this afternoon," he said dryly. "In with you now, before you're frozen solid. Casual clothes are all we ever wear down here," he informed her, and she wondered if he thought his *très* gauche American tenant might mistakenly wear her prom dress to tea. "And may I suggest you don a jumper . . . or, rather, a sweater when you come up to the house?"

"You don't have heat?" Blythe suppressed a gasp.

"In the family rooms, yes," Lucas Teague replied with chilly courtesy. "I'm afraid we don't heat all fifty-seven chambers anymore. However, I thought you might like to have a look at more than just the castle's sitting room during your visit this afternoon." He nodded through her open door in the direction of the cottage's interior. "There's a fire laid with driftwood kindling. It should warm you up straightaway. And there should be plenty of hot water. It's quite pleasant when one sits in the bath and gazes out the window, or at those seascapes hanging on the walls."

Blythe looked blankly at the tanned, exceedingly attractive countenance of her urbane landlord.

"Seascapes? I don't think I even turned on a light before I crawled into bed last night," she admitted. His description of cozily bathing by the window overlooking the Channel, surrounded by marvelous art, had the ring of someone who had indulged in such decadent pleasures. Who with? she wondered. Mrs. Teague, one hoped—if there was such a person.

"Well, do have a look at them," Lucas advised briskly over his shoulder as he headed toward his dented Land Rover. "They were all painted by an eighteenth-century ancestor of mine . . . on the Trevelyan side. Not bad, for an amateur artist. The cottage was built for him by his brother in the early 1790s."

And before Blythe could shut the door against the biting wind, Lucas Teague fired up his lumbering four-wheeled vehicle and steered it up the winding track, honking his way through the cluster of sheep blocking his path.

Blythe turned, reentered the cottage, and gazed around the room at the series of paintings depicting the very same coastline that lay directly outside her windows. The artist had ably captured the distinctive jade-green light and crystal white that can sometimes illuminate the rolling surf just before it breaks onto shore.

Slowly she walked toward the largest painting framed above the massive fireplace. She noticed that all the seascapes had one thing in common: nary a person, nor a boat, nor even a seagull had been rendered by the artist who had pictured these lonely shores. Her studied gaze performed like a camera lens, zooming in on the thick swirls of color that this long-forgotten painter had slathered onto his canvas some two hundred years ago. Her scrutiny magnified the painting's whorls in such detail that she felt she could almost see their molecules.

Then the seafoam greens and jade hues began to swim before her eyes. Fighting a peculiar sense of dread, she extended her hand to touch the dried, corrugated oils so that she might somehow be grounded to the physical world and banish the light-headedness that threatened to blank her vision altogether.

She really must never, ever drink whiskey on an empty stomach, she advised herself sternly.

A rustling sound—or rather, the sense that there was some sort of *presence* lurking behind her—caused her to turn suddenly in place and stare at a wooden easel that she hadn't even noticed had been part of the cottage's decor. More than five feet high, it stood in a dim corner under the loft. For an instant she imagined that next to it she saw a shadowy hand holding an artist's brush saturated with green paint the color of jade. Just as quickly, she determined that there was only the stout wooden easel standing there picturesquely inside Painter's Cottage, and that, like the world evoked by the barren seascape hanging over the fireplace, she was very much alone.

Chapter Two

May 10, 1994

In typical Cornish fashion the weather had changed abruptly by midafternoon. The dark, rain-filled clouds that had greeted Blythe's arrival in the West Country quickly vanished and were replaced by benign puffs of white that drifted across a Wedgwood-blue sky.

Blythe set out for Barton Hall dressed in jeans and an ivory cable-knit turtleneck sweater. She walked along the public footpath that skirted the cliffside meadow, glancing back briefly at the sight of Painter's Cottage perched dramatically at its edge. She could hear the surf crashing on the narrow beach below, accompanied by friendly shrieks from gulls circling overhead. Wisps of smoke drifted from the chimney; the remnants of the crackling fire she'd carefully banked before her departure. Just as Lucas Teague suggested, she had soaked for an hour in piping-hot water while surveying the spectacular coastline in naked privacy.

A Bathtub with a View, she thought, smiling to herself as she reached the far corner of the grassy field. For the first time in months her spirits began to rise.

She shut the gate carefully, not wishing to be responsible for the escape of any of the sheep who were her new neighbors. Cautiously she looked in both directions for vehicles driving on the left side of the road.

"Do, please, avoid the Dead Yank syndrome, darling,"

Christopher had chided her on their first trip to England together. "The civilized world drives on the left."

Resolutely she darted across the narrow road that separated the coastline properties of Barton Hall from its principal holdings. Near a brambly hedge at the entrance to the next field, an iron sign enameled white and embossed with black letters beckoned her to follow another public pathway called, appropriately enough, Hall Walk.

She climbed gingerly over a wooden stile that consisted of four spiraling steps cleverly designed to allow humans access to the field while keeping four-legged animals from getting out on the road. A second metal sign directed her to make a right turn. Within moments she had plunged into a kind of leafy mine shaft, thick with English oak and dense underbrush, where dappled sunlight filtered through the trees that arched overhead. Enclosed in this cool, green, shadowed habitat, she suddenly had the giddy sensation that she was like the White Rabbit in the animated version of *Alice in Wonderland*, diving into an underground lair.

Then she halted in her tracks.

There I go again! she thought crossly. Everything in my life can't be a potential movie scene!

As usual, she was observing the world through a designer's eye, rather than simply living. It was an occupational hazard, she supposed. On some crucial level, however, she sensed that her habit of seeing daily events as fodder for some future film had a way of bleeding some of the joy and spontaneity out of her everyday life.

I'm in Cornwall, she lectured herself, I'm not scouting locations. I'm here. It's beautiful . . . and that's enough.

On her left, fifty yards down the path, the gnarled roots of an enormous oak had pushed up thick tentacles from the moist ground, forming a large hollow some three feet in diameter. She leaned forward to have a closer look, concluding that an Irish leprechaun or Cornish "pisky" would find this space a suitable abode. Or perhaps even the White Rabbit himself.

Old habits were hard to break, she mused.

Impulsively Blythe shed her indestructible dark-green Barbour jacket—another present from Chris that first trip—and placed it on the ground. Feeling like a mischievous five-year-old hiding from her nanny, she then squeezed inside the vaulted space that was blanketed with cozy moss so intensely green it seemed almost psychedelic. She had just enough room above her head to sit, legs crossed Indian style, like a happy Hobbit in a sheltering forest home.

This is a bit much, she thought, amused by her childish antics as she strafed her fingertips along the velvet-clad roots that formed her woodland cave. In this magical forest an uplifting harmony seemed to prevail—proof of a wholeness in the natural world that seemed to soothe and assuage her wounded soul. As if to confirm this hypothesis, a plump brown rabbit leaped across the path to her right, followed by a bounding gray squirrel who appeared to be not so much its pursuer as its playmate.

Reluctantly Blythe glanced at her watch. Twenty minutes past four. She pulled herself to her feet and dusted off her jacket. A gentle coolness enveloped her as her new walking shoes trod along the tufted emerald path that led through this enchanted wooded world of bright ferns, twisting vines, and ivy-cloaked tree trunks.

A thousand shades of green.

The phrase rang in her head, and the incredible beauty of her surroundings lifted her spirits another notch. As she slowly inhaled the soft Cornish afternoon air, the thought came to her that time spent here—with her feet planted in the soil of her probable forebears, her lungs filled with gentle breezes blowing off the sea—might purify the wells of bitterness and remorse she now realized ran deep.

As she peered ahead, her euphoria swiftly began to evaporate.

"It's always something, isn't it?" she exclaimed aloud.

The leafy tunnel, its shadows warmed every few feet by shafts of sage-green light, angled sharply upward. As far as

Blythe could determine, there appeared to be no way to avoid climbing the steep, challenging hill that stood between her and her destination, Barton Hall.

Lucas Teague kept his head down and sank his shovel into the shrinking pile of manure. He worked at an even clip, tossing his cargo into the wheelbarrow he'd parked at the entrance to the pony stalls.

He could only speculate what his former English tutor at Cambridge would think if he could see him mucking about like a field hand. His palms now were thickly callused—certainly not a "gentleman's hands" any longer. Half an hour earlier he had even shed his work shirt, reveling in the season's first gloriously warm day. The languorous sensation of the sun's rays beating down on his bare back made him think of the sun-drenched beach on the island of Corfu, in Greece, where he and Lindsay . . .

He brought himself up short and pitched the shovel deep into the remnants of the dung heap as he heard his three remaining Cornish ponies snorting in their stalls. The necessity of becoming physically involved in the running of the estate had its good points, he reminded himself wryly. It kept him reasonably fit and his mind off the sorry state of his personal life. Furthermore, he had discovered during these last years that he actually enjoyed the physical labor of chores like these quite as much as he did calculating hay yields, supervising the sheep and cattle production, and attending meetings of the local council of neighboring landowners.

Now, if only he could somehow sort out his fiscal worries and find a practical solution to getting Barton Hall back on sound financial footing in the wake of higher taxes and the great gale of 1990 that had wreaked havoc throughout his estate and the entire Duchy of Cornwall. His patchwork attempts to reduce staff and depend on summer lets to keep the place afloat were clearly becoming untenable.

Damn the Inland Revenue! he cursed silently. One simply accepted the weather.

His thoughts drifted to his first glimpse of his new tenant, Blythe Stowe. The rent she paid for Painter's Cottage would at least improve his cash flow. From the very first he had been curious about the woman. After all, from the information he'd had at hand, she sounded highly intriguing, and Lord knew, he was due for a little excitement.

However, Luke's prospects for pleasant female companionship had been severely diminished by the sight of his tenant's unruly mass of auburn hair and her tousled appearance when she stood at the door of the old cottage that morning. Nice, coltish figure, he remembered appreciatively, but he hoped to Christ she didn't turn out to be a problem. He would have sworn that the woman was suffering from a monumental hangover! If she turned out to be a bit of a boozer, that certainly would be a disappointment.

Deep in thought, Luke gazed toward the sea. Life in the West Country was picturesque, to be sure, but that it was frightfully devoid of home-grown females of his age and stage in life was an understatement. He'd been overjoyed to be informed that morning from the businesslike Ms. Spector that her client would be staying the entire summer. His hopes had been that while the American's rents would replenish his coffers, her person might provide some pleasant company after the depressing last years he'd endured as the impecunious heir to a faltering estate.

Suddenly he smiled at the notion of his summer tenant at Painter's Cottage making small talk during tea with the London houseguest he had invited to visit Barton Hall in a few weeks' time. This patrician family friend of long standing was nothing if not patient and had been a veritable brick when it came to dealing with certain domestic matters. Surely they both recognized that the time was upon them when they either would take their relationship to a higher level—or call it quits.

Luke tossed his shovel aside and resolutely pushed the

barrow in the direction of the walled garden where old Quiller was laboriously hoeing the few vegetable beds committed to this year's kitchen garden.

As Luke rounded the corner of the stone stables, he halted, mesmerized by the sight of first one long jeans-clad leg, and then another, extending provocatively over the wooden stile that led from the end of Hall Walk.

The mysterious Mrs. Stowe's hair had magically been tamed and tucked up beneath a dark-green baseball cap. Surprisingly, he found himself feeling deflated not to see those auburn tresses billowing about her shoulders. Her skin was smooth and clear and slightly flushed from the exertion of striding up the steep path. Her dark eyes were subdued, but as soon as she caught sight of him, she smiled and waved—both gestures conveying a sense of accomplishment for having scaled the hill to the castle grounds and successfully arriving at her destination precisely at four-thirty.

He, on the other hand, was a bare-chested, sweat-soaked mess.

"I'm so sorry," he shouted across the stable yard with an embarrassed grin. "The time got away from me."

Her generous lips broke into a wide smile, as if she were amused to find him in the same disorderly state she had been in earlier that day. He noticed she wore lightweight hiking boots and an expensive-looking Irish cable-knit pullover with a high neck underneath a dark-green Barbour coat, the sensible soul. All in all, she had accoutred herself in an utterly appropriate fashion.

"No problem," she laughed, glancing around at her surroundings with a satisfied air.

"Hold on a tick, can you?" He waved back and parked the wheelbarrow just inside the walled kitchen garden. He quickly donned the blue cotton shirt that he'd hung on the gate and pointed toward a path across from the stables that led to the rhododendron and azalea plots. "Why not have a ten-minute stroll down that way while I have a quick shower and catch up with you," he said, narrowing the thirty-foot distance that separated them. "Is that all right?"

His houseguest gazed with shining eyes toward the rose-encrusted bower that marked the entrance to the formal flower gardens.

"Oh . . . please . . . don't worry about me," she assured him happily as she headed off with a confident, leggy stride in the direction he'd indicated. "Take your time. I'll be in heaven."

He sensed suddenly that perhaps Blythe Stowe wasn't going to be a problem tenant after all.

"Holy cow! These can't be rhododendrons!" Blythe exclaimed, staring at a mass of vibrant pink blossoms that towered above her head. "These bushes are thirty feet tall! In California we're lucky if they grow as high as a neighbor's hedge."

"In Cornwall these plants can be as large as trees," the dark-haired owner of Barton Hall explained. Blythe felt inordinately pleased to see that Lucas Teague was wearing a forest-green Barbour jacket made of the same waxed cotton as her own. "Except for the occasional hurricane, like the one we had in 1990, the climate in these parts doesn't produce as hard a frost or as steep changes in temperature as the rest of Britain." He pulled a pair of garden clippers he called secateurs from the pocket of his coat and snipped off a branch studded with a generous cluster of lush pink flowers. Nearby, two Labradors—one black and one yellow—sniffed ecstatically in the underbrush. "Barton Hall's gardens are modest, compared to the neighboring estate," he added.

"Caerhays Castle?" Blythe asked, remembering a large tan area stamped on Ordnance Map Number 204 that bordered Lucas Teague's "modest" three-thousand-acre holding.

"They have fifty-five acres of gardens, compared to our twenty-five of rhododendrons, camellias, and azaleas," he replied. "Caerhays even grows magnolias, and when they open to the public, they draw garden fanatics from around the world."

"When is that?" Blythe asked eagerly.

"For two weeks in late March and early April. Part of a local charity event. Unfortunately, you've just missed it."

She and her new landlord had tramped for some twenty minutes across fields and meadows dotted with trees bursting with blooms in every imaginable hue. A lush profusion of bluebells carpeted the undergrowth. To her right another giant rhododendron cloaked in vivid scarlet demanded to be admired. Next to it were equally impressive specimens in shades of rose, shell-pink, mauve, snowflake-white, and saffron. In the distance she gazed in awe at the gently undulating hills that were sprinkled with other flowering trees and bushes in arresting hues of violet, salmon, and canary-yellow.

As she and Lucas Teague continued to meander through Barton Hall's magnificent gardens, Blythe eagerly leaned forward to read the names on the small metal plaques that identified each variety: " 'Countess of Haddington' . . . 'Surrey Heath' . . . 'Veryan Bay' . . . 'Winsome.' Look at this! 'Rebecca'!" She glanced up at her amused host. "I adored that old film . . . Laurence Olivier . . . Joan Fontaine . . . and remember Judith Anderson as the sinister housekeeper, Mrs. Danvers?"

"I enjoyed the book," Lucas replied dryly. "Its author, Daphne du Maurier, lived not far from Barton Hall, you know . . . about ten miles northeast of here, near Fowey. Her house, Menabilly, was the setting for Manderley in that story." Again he pulled out his secateurs and snipped off a branch of the vibrant scarlet blooms. "These are hybrids. My father and grandfather spent years crossbreeding to achieve this shade. To my mind the red color's a bit tarty, but it'll brighten your cottage," he said, cheerfully ignoring Blythe's protests that her arms were already laden with his generous offerings.

Blythe heaved a contented sigh.

"It's mind-boggling . . . that's what it is," she allowed, turning in a complete circle as she inhaled the faint perfume that floated on the shafts of sunshine filtering through the vegetation above their heads. She buried her nose in the blossoms she held clutched in her hands. "My grandmother would have lost her mind here."

Without warning a sudden, overwhelming sense of loss invaded Blythe's chest. She briefly closed her eyes and felt her lashes brush softly against the scarlet blooms. How Lucinda Barton would have reveled in this flamboyant beauty, she thought, battling a wave of sadness so piercing, she had difficulty breathing.

"I take it your grandmother was a keen gardener?" Teague asked, gesturing with his tall walking stick in the direction of a path that led back toward Barton Hall and the tea table that awaited them.

"A fanatic," Blythe replied, looking up from her armful of flowers. She was strangely thankful for the opportunity to speak of the woman whose kindness, pluck, and wisdom had served as beacons throughout Blythe's life. "Among other things, she ran a small nursery business on our ranch in Wyoming," Blythe explained, following alongside her tour guide. "She was one of the first in the West to specialize in cultivating Alpine wildflowers. I was inspired to get a master's degree in landscape design because of her," she continued in a slightly rueful tone. She thought, suddenly, of the hours she'd worked by the side of Grandma Barton, whose father, Emory Halett, had also been a rancher with a spread outside Jackson Hole. Every spring and summer of Blythe's childhood she and Lucinda had gathered a riotous bounty of blooms growing in the rolling, flower-carpeted foothills that stretched below the magnificent Grand Tetons in the Rockies. Most of their neighbors had considered her grandmother daft to be harvesting seeds so carefully from plants that every native in Wyoming considered to be weeds. However, even as a little girl, Blythe had admired the flinty old woman's dogged determination to make a success of her mail-order wildflower seed business.

"I had understood that you were involved in the motion-picture industry," the owner of Barton Hall said as he gestured toward another bush with his staghorn staff. The lofty plant virtually dripped with purplish-blue rhododendrons. "A production designer, I think my estate agent told me. Did he get it wrong?"

"Soon after I earned my degree, I began to design stage sets instead of landscapes." Blythe shrugged, her sudden burst of enthusiasm for the sights and smells of the enchanting garden abruptly diminishing. "One thing led to another, and eventually I ended up in the film business."

It had been Christopher who had wheedled and cajoled her into using her drafting abilities to help him plan his first student film. Once more she stared at the garden's colorful panorama, deliberately drinking in its abundant array of colors this warm May afternoon. It felt almost as if her surroundings could provide a kind of mental medicine for what ailed her. She wondered how she could have strayed so far from her passion for growing things.

"What exactly does a production designer do?" her host inquired.

"She mediates between the studio executives, who want to save money, and the director, who wants to spend it," Blythe answered flatly.

"Rather puts one in the middle, doesn't it?" he commented as he chose the left fork on the narrow path she assumed was a shortcut that led back to the house.

"Yep. Right between the proverbial rock and a hard place."

Again she discerned the bitter tone bubbling beneath the surface of her flippant response. The sense of peace and well-being she'd experienced during her magical wooded walk to Barton Hall had begun to dissipate. It was too fragile an antidote to have much of an effect on truly calming the emotional cauldron that had become her life.

Her gaze drank in the sight of an azalea bush whose branches were laden with electric-pink blossoms. All this beauty had been sprouting and maturing during the very same spring that she had been awash in the grim legal machinations of her divorce as it wound its way through the courts in Los Angeles. Now that all that was behind her, it was definitely time for her to make a shift away from the negative self-absorption that had gripped her for so long. Despite the blows she had endured, other things—wondrous things—were going on in the world. If only her grandmother were still here to share the sight of this amazing garden with her.

Blythe suppressed a small sigh and redoubled her efforts to sound cheerful for the benefit of her amiable host.

"Production design involves supervising the building of the sets, the dressing of locations indoors and out . . . overseeing the costumes . . . basically creating the whole 'look' of the film, if you will," she explained.

She paused to stroke the smooth heads of Derek and Beryl, who had trotted obediently beside their master each time Blythe and Lucas Teague had set off to view another section of the garden. The dogs had been named, she had learned upon inquiry, for Barton Hall's celebrated—and now retired—head gardener and his wife.

"Movies like *Blade Runner, Bonnie and Clyde,* even *Batman*, will be remembered for their visual impact as much as for their storyline." She cast a sidelong glance at her questioner and heaved an ironic shrug. "However, most of the time it's a sort of 'we don't get no respect' situation. The majority of the kudos go to the film's director when the movie's a box-office hit."

"That may be so, but what you do sounds like fascinating and important work," he observed as they arrived at the circular drive leading up to the porte cochere.

"Only if everyone on the film agrees on what that 'look' should be," she replied, following along as he pushed against the enormous wooden front door and guided her into a foyer paved in slate.

"Stay there, chaps," Teague directed his two dogs firmly, who gazed at him beseechingly from just outside the front door. "I expect you'll get your tea soon enough." Hiding a smile, Blythe turned to her right into a small chamber that was cluttered with an assortment of tweed coats with elbow patches like the dark-brown herringbone jacket that her host had worn earlier in the day. Next to them were several hooded windbreakers—anoraks, Chris had always called them—hanging on pegs. Lucas Teague, playing the obliging butler, helped her shed her Barbour and hung it next to his own larger version. The two jackets looked as if they might indulge in a friendly chat while their owners were having tea.

Nearby, several pairs of gardening boots and thigh-high rubber waders in graduated sizes were lined up on the floor. Fishing poles and umbrellas leaned against one corner, while numerous rain hats, woolen caps, and down vests decorated a hall tree that stood in the other. Noting with pleasure the cluster of gardening gloves neatly assembled on a small wooden chest next to the wall, Blythe volunteered thoughtfully, "You know, I often wonder if I wouldn't have been better off sticking with landscape design."

Lucas Teague arched a dark eyebrow but made no further comment as he led the way down a wide wood-paneled hallway. Beneath her feet lay a frayed Persian carpet, and above her head large, dust-laden family portraits observed their progress toward a small sitting room. Inside, a bright fire glowing on the hearth put to rest Blythe's fear that the castle would have no heat. She welcomed its warmth, thanks to the temperature in the garden having grown increasingly chilly as the afternoon sun slid behind the hills that stretched toward Land's End in the west.

"Good afternoon, Mrs. Quiller," the lord of the manor said to his housekeeper, who stood in attendance beside a tea trolley loaded with all manner of scones, tea cakes, finger sandwiches, and shortbread.

"Good afternoon, sir," the servant said, beaming. "You'll be wantin' a vase for those flowers," she noted, pointing to a waiting glass container filled with water. The housekeeper must have spotted her employer and his guest through the window and noted the masses of blooms Blythe had been carrying. As Mrs. Quiller retrieved the fragrant bounty, she cast a friendly look in the visitor's direction. No Mrs. Danvers here, Blythe reflected, as she watched the older woman place the flowers in the tall receptacle and arrange them expertly. "So 'appy ya kin sample our Cornish cream tea, ma'am," she added cheerfully.

Blythe sat down on a faded chintz love seat and gazed at the teatime delicacies. Then she surreptitiously glanced around the room, noting the shabby-chic quality of the antique furnishings and faded damask wall-coverings. Watermarks discoloring the ceiling in several places confirmed the presence of old leaks in the roof. But despite this, and the sixties-era television set sitting in the corner that added to the frozen-in-time aspect of the place, Blythe felt remarkably comfortable. Even so, she would judge that Barton Hall had seen far better days.

Her gaze returned to the abundant tea table as she watched Mrs. Quiller place generous portions of her homemade specialties on their plates. Blythe had noticed that afternoon that she had a bit of a scratchy throat—no doubt due to her long flight in the air-conditioned jetliner—and eagerly looked forward to a soothing cup of tea. The queasy stomach that had plagued her earlier in the day had magically disappeared, and now she was ravenously hungry.

"You'll eat dinner after such a feast?" she asked, glancing at a handsome enameled clock ticking loudly on the mantelpiece. It was fifteen minutes past the hour of five. Christopher's family in the Midlands, she recalled suddenly, had dispensed with such hallowed English traditions as afternoon tea and preferred coffee at meals. This was certainly not the case at Barton Hall.

Only two teacups stood in readiness next to a plump teapot that was muffled in a large quilted "cozy" to keep its contents scalding hot. Was there not a lady of the house?

"Thank you, Mrs. Q," Lucas was saying to his housekeeper. "We can manage from here, I think."

"Yes, sir," the gray-haired woman murmured. Taking a step backward, she pushed against what appeared to be a built-in bookcase. The rectangle magically turned sideways, allowing Mrs. Quiller to retreat into a small pantry beyond. Instantly the book-lined panel slid back into place.

"That must have made for marvelous games of hide-and-seek when you were young," Blythe commented, watching her host prepare to do the honors with the teapot. Lucas Teague had donned his tanned moleskin trousers once again, topped by a garnet-colored turtleneck, complete with leather patches on the elbows. Very tweedy and certainly a handsome contrast to his blue-black hair, she concluded silently.

"The secret bookcase? It did indeed," he laughed, first putting a splash of milk into the fine bone-china cups, followed by a stream of steaming amber-colored liquid poured through an ornate silver tea strainer. He expertly filled each cup to exactly half an inch beneath its gilded rim.

Blythe settled contentedly against the sofa's overstuffed cushions, noting with silent amusement that a thin sprinkling of dog hairs dusted most of the furniture. Mrs. Quiller obviously favored cooking over housecleaning.

"Mrs. Stowe—"

"Please. Call me Blythe," she urged, savoring the sinful dollop of Cornish cream topped by a spoonful of raspberry jam that Mrs. Quiller had spread over her scone.

"Lucas—or Luke—will do as well," he agreed genially. "Well, Blythe, then . . . I must say I am quite delighted that you have determined you'd like to stay with us at Painter's Cottage all summer because . . ." He hesitated, his black brows furrowed under the roguish shock of dark hair spilling over his forehead. "I wonder if you'd be willing to give me your professional opinion about something."

Blythe was startled by his request and took time to chew slowly on her scone and swallow.

"I'll certainly try, if my profession could possibly be of any use so far away from Hollywood," she replied with a rueful smile.

"Very much so," he responded quietly. "You see . . . well . . . in the last few years I've begun to face an inevitable situation here at Barton Hall." He inhaled slowly, as if to keep some emotion in check.

"Which is?"

"That summer lets, constant economies, and reducing my sheep and cattle herds will not ward off the ravages of the Inland Revenue's devouring an ancient family seat like this."

"You mean the income-tax people?" she said sympathetically.

"I do, indeed."

Having been married to an Englishman, Blythe had heard quite a lot about Britain's crushing death duties and confiscatory taxes that people of wealth and the landed gentry had faced since the Second World War. The Inland Revenue's dogged quest of the Almighty Pound was the principal reason the ambitious Christopher Stowe had pursued his directing career in America. As a married couple earning two incomes, the Stowes had paid their fair share of taxes to Uncle Sam, but Chris had probably made and saved a couple of million by becoming a legal resident in the United States instead of plying his trade in the British film industry and paying up. In fact, her husband's only holding in Britain had been an investment they had made in a reforestry scheme near some Highland moor in Scotland that neither of them had ever visited. "Splendid tax dodge," Chris had proclaimed smugly. "And perfectly legal!"

"Barton Hall has become a greater burden every year," Lucas continued. "I've reduced my staff to the bare minimum, which is terribly unfortunate for those who live in the village. Even so, I still find that the costs of maintaining the house and keeping up the gardens you've so admired are becoming prohibitive. The death duties at the time my father passed away have made it nearly impossible to carry on . . . unless a drastic change of course can be found."

Blythe was astonished that a member of the English upper classes would speak so candidly about his financial woes to a relative stranger. Conditions at Barton Hall must be dire indeed, she reflected. Her thoughts drifted to the remarkable sight of the man of the house, stripped to the waist, mucking out his own horse stalls. If Mrs. Quiller was the only house servant in Lucas Teague's employ, no wonder there were dog hairs on the furniture. How could the poor woman possibly cope with keeping fifty-seven rooms in perfect order? Was there no Mrs. Teague or a "significant other" to assist this attractive creature in solving his domestic woes? Blythe nibbled at her scone and looked at her host expectantly.

"So . . . ," he continued, apparently choosing his words with care, "I've been thinking of turning Barton Hall into some sort of posh country hotel." He was staring into his teacup, as if a final confirmation as to the wisdom of his plan might be found in the few leaves floating at the bottom. "You know . . . first-rate service . . . Mrs. Quiller's glorious food . . . the bedrooms done up à la Laura Ashley—that sort of thing. In the long run it might prevent my having to sell the place, although I haven't the faintest idea how to execute such a scheme, or to judge if it would be successful, so far off the beaten path." He set his cup down on a side table with a clatter and met her gaze. "I simply cannot bear the thought that after eight hundred years of Barton Hall having been part of my family, I am to be the descendant who sells it to some German industrialist."

"Or to an American movie star?" Blythe couldn't resist adding.

Luke had the grace to flush under his bronzed countenance. Then his dark-blue eyes fixed on hers intently.

"Would you be willing to have a thorough look around and give me your honest opinion?" he queried earnestly. "Could it work? It seems clear that I shall be forced to make some decisions before the summer is out, so I'd consider it a very great kindness if you'd offer a candid appraisal of the notion," he finished, masking some emotion Blythe couldn't quite define by retrieving his cold cup of tea and sipping it slowly.

She gave the sitting room another cursory glance. Despite the manor's down-at-the-heels appearance, her practiced eye saw a host of possibilities. She reflected on the fairy-tale spell that the Barton estate's rounded castle walls had cast upon her when her car had driven down the stately, tree-shrouded entrance. Modernized and glamorized inside, it was just the kind of place that would appeal to wealthy Americans on vacation, especially those seeking the elegance and romance of a bygone era.

Her glance was drawn to the antiquated electrical outlets and well-worn furnishings. There was little doubt, however, that bringing it up to five-star standards could cost a fortune. And despite Mrs. Quiller's glorious scones, the woman was obviously getting on in years and could hardly be expected to dish up eighty to a hundred meals a day.

Barton Hall's glorious gardens, on the other hand, offered some very interesting commercial opportunities, she mused. Then Blythe pulled herself up short.

"And is Mrs. Teague keen on the idea?" she asked quietly.

"She was, actually. I lost her eighteen months ago . . . to cancer."

"Oh, I'm terribly sorry. . . ."

Blythe's host accepted her embarrassed condolences with a brief nod. Then, once again, he solicited her professional opinion on the merit of his proposal.

"Well . . . perhaps this is the moment to conduct me on the Gold Star Tour?" She smiled, avoiding giving him a direct answer until she had a thorough look around.

"Not before I get you to sign your lease, Ms. Barton-Stowe," Lucas announced firmly, conferring on her a hyphenated double-barreled surname in the English manner. Blythe watched as her host crossed to a small desk tucked in a rounded alcove that was surely the ground-floor section of one of the stone turrets outside. "Can't have my adviser slipping away."

He pulled a legal-looking document from the desk drawer. "I noticed your middle name—Barton—in the letter from your travel agent when she first contacted me. Are you aware that the Barton-Trevelyans were the original owners of the house? You must have a look at my genealogical chart in the library and see where your American branch might fit in."

"It was probably just a fancy of my grandmother's," Blythe replied briskly, "but her stories that we originally came from this part of Cornwall were what prompted my decision to spend some time in this area."

That, and the fact that my husband jilted me for my sister, she added silently.

"Your curiosity is my good fortune, then." Lucas Teague grinned, transforming his slightly forbidding features into those of a man possibly possessing a very potent measure of charm.

Charm. It had been the quality she'd grown to like least in Christopher Stowe.

Lucas Teague indicated the sheet of paper lying on his desk. "This is merely an addendum to your original lease for the cottage."

Blythe glanced at the one-page document and then looked longingly at the telephone perched on the desktop. Perhaps Lisa had overreacted to whatever had happened in Los Angeles. Blythe couldn't imagine what could have prompted her lawyer to arrange for such a prolonged stay in this remote part of Cornwall. In fact, she realized suddenly, the woman's high-handedness annoyed her quite substantially.

Meanwhile, Lucas was holding out a silver-plated fountain pen that was probably manufactured at the turn of the last century. Still Blythe hesitated. She shifted her gaze to a seascape hanging above the mantelpiece and its magnificent enameled clock. The picture was executed in the same style as those that hung in Painter's Cottage.

If I want to leave before September . . . I'll just leave! she thought, reassuring herself that she wasn't signing up for a stint in the Royal Army. After all . . . some might consider her quite a wealthy woman now. She could do anything she wished.

As she continued to stare at the oil painting executed by Luke's eighteenth-century ancestor, an inexplicable feeling of gloom seemed to close in around her.

"I-I really must first touch base with my attorney in Los Angeles," she said in a low voice, struggling to control the strange tightness gripping her throat. "Could I impose on you to use your telephone before we tour the house?"

Lucas's puzzled look signaled that he sensed a distinct change in the atmosphere. However, he merely pointed to the old-fashioned instrument on his desk.

"Certainly. Help yourself. Let me just have a word with Mrs. Quiller so she can tidy up in ten minutes or so, and you can have some privacy."

"Thanks . . . ," Blythe replied faintly. "I'll use my calling card, of course."

Without considering what time it was in California, she laboriously dialed 0101 to reach the international operator, feeling annoyed, suddenly, by the lack of a touch-tone phone. Fortunately, her call was quickly put through.

Lisa's receptionist answered. It was nearly ten in the morning in Los Angeles, and Blythe was informed that her lawyer was just leaving for a deposition across town.

A curt voice came on the line.

"Yes . . . ?"

"Oh, Jesus, Lisa . . . I'm sorry," Blythe blurted. "I got your message about remaining here in Cornwall through September, and I wanted to know why you thought it necessary."

"Where are you now?" Lisa asked abruptly. "Is anybody with you?"

"Well, there's the lord of Barton Manor, of course . . . in another room somewhere in this drafty pile," Blythe replied in a voice edged with sarcasm. Was she just another bothersome client to Lisa Spector, now that the lawyer had been paid her fat fee?

"Is it awful?" Lisa asked, sounding as if any problems that Blythe might be having in far-off Cornwall would be an unwelcome addition to whatever else had landed on her desk that day.

"No . . . as a matter of fact, it's quite wonderful," Blythe replied tartly, "but four months of pastoral pleasures may be just too much for a recovering cowgirl like me."

"Blythe . . . there's a good reason you should stay there," Lisa said in her most lawyerly tones.

"Four months?" she demanded. Then, attempting to sound utterly in control of her emotions while, at the same time, making a revelation that surprised even her, she added, "Look, Lisa . . . I've been having these odd bouts of what I guess is depression since the moment I arrived. Nothing to do with the scenery or the natives, really, but the thought of spending four months completely out of touch with everything I—"

"Your sister and Christopher got married . . . right after his courthouse appearance," Lisa interrupted.

Blythe gripped the edge of Luke's desk with her free hand.

"The white stretch limo," she blurted. "He took her to a church in it?"

"He took her to the airport in it," her lawyer replied evenly. "Right behind you, apparently. They flew to Mexico. Presto! Mrs. Christopher Barton-Stowe the Second."

Blythe was sickeningly aware of the generous portions of Cornish clotted cream churning in her stomach.

"Blythe? Are you there? I knew this would come as a shock . . . but it was inevitable. The bambino and all that . . . Blythe! Say something."

"I'll be all right," she murmured, feeling as if she were speaking underwater.

Fact was, nothing between Ellie and her had been right for years . . . way before she'd walked in on her husband getting it on with her own flesh and blood on the Kreiss sofa bed in his director's trailer. There were some things in life that simply defied fixing. Unfortunately, as events had shown over the years, Eleanor Barton specialized in making things worse. "I just can't stand it that Ellie actually got him to marry her!" Blythe added in a rush. "It wasn't enough that she fucked my husband and knocked herself up with my baby? Now she's even got my name!"

"With a little help from old Mr. Midlife Crisis himself," Lisa added caustically. "As you can imagine, every tabloid in the universe managed to cover the nuptials. CNN has gone with the story big-time. The bride looked like a blimp, of course, which made their reporting even juicier. The cooing newly-weds left today for Africa. *In Kenya* starts filming there on a closed set next week. That leaves the Fourth Estate in L.A. with no pictures of them, so the TV trucks are back in front of your house, and everyone's calling here, trying to find you and—"

"Okay, okay, I get the picture . . . ," snapped Blythe. She swallowed hard. There was silence on the line as Lisa gave her time to absorb the details of this latest revelation. As reality sank in, Blythe felt as if she were rolling naked in a bed of nettles. The pain was sharp and the exposure complete. "I suppose Cornwall's as good a spot for exile as anyplace else," she added dully. "Thanks, Lisa, for arranging for the extension on the lease. You'd better get on to your deposition." Hooking the earpiece onto the ancient black telephone, she gently hung up.

She leaned back in Lucas Teague's leather desk chair and stared blankly into space. Not into space, she realized absently, but at the desolate seascape that hung above the mantelpiece, a near twin to the one over the fireplace in her own cottage. The sweep of vacant sand, lacking footprints or even seaweed, for that matter, seemed as empty as she felt inside. Nothing growing, nothing living, a barren landscape of sharp, treeless cliffs where—

Blythe closed her eyes and then opened them, to confirm whether the figure standing suddenly etched against the remote, brooding promontory was, in fact, human. Tall, and leaning heavily against a staghorn walking stick, the dark-haired man stared disconsolately down at the churning waters of Veryan Bay, his gaze riveted on an overturned dinghy that bobbed forlornly on the sea.

Blythe didn't hear the knock reverberating lightly on the sitting-room door.

"Ready?" Lucas said cheerfully, and then paused at the threshold, gazing at the stricken look on Blythe's face.

"What's happened?" he asked, shutting the door behind him. "You've had some bad news." It was a statement, not a question. "Something back in the States, is it?"

"You couldn't possibly understand," she said in a tight voice. To her astonishment the painted seascape was once more devoid of any sign of life. And so was she.

"Understand loss?" he asked evenly. "Yes, I think I can."

"Not my kind of loss," she said, startled from her near-catatonic state by a sharp stab of galvanizing anger. Luke's wife had died. To be sure, it must have been a tragic, poignant finish, but the late Mrs. Teague, whoever she might have been, didn't betray her husband with his—

"I have some idea what you've been put through," Luke said quietly.

"No, you don't!" she cried, slamming her fist against Luke's desktop, unable to prevent the angry outburst that had been boiling just beneath the surface.

"Blythe," Lucas said, crossing quickly to the desk that stood between them. "Did you notice that satellite dish the size of a dinner plate attached to Mrs. Quiller's kitchen window? We watch CNN even in this remote part of the world, you know—and then there're those dreadful tabloids whose headlines scream at one in the food shops. So I do have some notion of what you've been subjected to." He perched one hip on his desk and leaned forward toward the chair where Blythe sat utterly still. "Your former husband's films are splendid, of course, but his behavior has been appalling."

"Well, can you beat that?" she drawled sarcastically, feeling a mild form of hysteria rising in her throat. "A Cornish guy with his boots on the right feet!"

Looking puzzled, Luke suggested uncertainly, "I suppose he felt compelled to marry so soon because of the child. . . ."

The child . . . the child . . . My child . . .

"So I gather you caught that CNN broadcast about the ever-so-talented Christopher Stowe marrying Ellie Barton, whose talents are mostly limited to those she can perform on her back!" she declared, her eyes drawn with loathing toward the antique TV set that stared blankly back at her from the corner. "You Brits are all so discreet," she added acidly. "All this time you knew who I was and what had happened in my life, but you never mentioned it, of course!" She wondered if humiliation was a disease you could die from.

"I assumed that what you'd come here for was anonymity—and a long rest," he replied quietly.

"I came here to escape!" she cried. "To hide out . . . to try to forget that my husband screwed my sister, up close and personal, on a couch I special-ordered for his director's trailer!" Moisture bathed her cheeks, and her voice sank to a raw whisper. "I came here to mourn my grandmother . . . and to get as far away from those two monsters as I possibly cou—"

Her voice cracked and she was finally speechless. She shifted her gaze to the damask walls that seemed to pulse in concert with the pounding in her chest. She could see that Lucas was earnestly speaking to her, but for some reason she couldn't actually hear what he was saying. That was because she couldn't think coherently. Instead, she began to weep. Not a ladylike whimpering, but a wounded animal's keening cries that were so shrill, they made her throat sting. Her loud, attenuated wails were not at all the response that a paying guest should be making in front of her well-meaning host.

Blindly she rose from her chair to make her escape but was halted midway to the sitting-room door. She fought the stranger's arms that were suddenly wrapped tightly around her shoulders, but Lucas Teague's grip was too strong and his determination to comfort her too great.

"I'm so sorry . . . I'm so sorry," he kept repeating.

"He married her . . . he *married* her!" she shouted, her voice reaching a frenzied pitch as the weight of the double betrayal bore down on her.

Then she gave herself up to deep, racking sobs and stopped struggling, allowing Lucas Teague to rock her in his arms.

"You'll sleep here tonight," he announced softly, "in the guest wing."

The following morning—spent from her ordeal, and embarrassed by her unrestrained outburst in front of her well-mannered host—Blythe woke up in a cheerful yellow guest bedroom and promptly began to weep again. Between bouts of sobs and attempts to get a grip on her emotions, she wondered where she would go next.

By the time Mrs. Quiller bustled in with a breakfast tray, Blythe also faced another problem: She had a raging sore throat. Her bones had begun to ache, and the crisp linen sheets brushing against her body felt as if they might peel off her skin.

"All right if I be puttin' yer tea on the bedside cabinet?" the housekeeper inquired.

Blythe could only produce a strangled croaking sound when she attempted to reply, "Fine . . . thank you."

"Oh, dearie dear," Mrs. Quiller clucked. She carefully set the tray down and immediately marched over to the windows. With the hand of a professional she flung back the heavy drapes that had shut out the light in Blythe's large, but rather threadbare, guest quarters. "Let's have a look at you."

Blythe winced as bright sunshine flooded the room. The older woman approached the side of the bed and scrutinized her houseguest's flushed face.

"We'll be callin' the doctor straightaway," she announced in a firm manner that brooked no dissent and recalled for Blythe Lucinda Barton's fierce, motherly ministrations whenever someone on the ranch was shown to be genuinely ill. However, malingerers at the Double Bar B were another matter, she remembered ruefully.

"No! Please . . . ," Blythe rasped, and then was consumed by a fit of coughing. Her fervent wish was simply to crawl back to Painter's Cottage and disappear under the goose-down duvet—forever, if possible. However, when she struggled to sit upright, she soon flopped back onto her pillow and cried weakly, "Ooh . . ." She suspected that during her fitful night's sleep some raging bull had kicked her in the head.

"You poor dear," Mrs. Quiller sympathized, helping Blythe to find a comfortable position among the piles of feather pillows. "Just you be tryin' to get some rest and I'll ring Dr. Vickery."

Blythe retained no clear memory of the ensuing twenty-four hours, other than recollecting that a stranger with bushy eyebrows in his early fifties who she assumed was a medical doctor injected her in the bottom with some drug. Following that, she had a dim recollection that Mrs. Quiller handed her antibiotics every six hours, around the clock.

By the second day of her massive indisposition, Blythe's fever broke, but her throat still felt like a fired-up barbecue pit. She found herself, when not giving in to drugged sleep, unable to refrain from weeping for more than twenty minutes at a time.

Cowboy up! some voice whispered in the back of her mind.

"I can't!" she wailed, and buried her head beneath a pile of pillows so no one could hear her sobs. The Barton family motto had lost its power to conquer the despair that literally held her by the throat.

The lanky, balding Dr. Simon Vickery reappeared one morning clad in tweeds appropriate for playing a round of golf, as he explained cheerfully. He peered down her gullet and directed Mrs. Quiller to continue her duties as impromptu nurse and carry on with the medical regimen of sleep, soup, and prescription medications.

Later that evening Blythe heard the sound of the dumbwaiter creaking to a halt down the hall from her bedroom door. She made a lunge for the box of tissues perched on the nightstand beside her bed. She barely had time to wipe her eyes before the housekeeper opened the door to deliver her dinner tray. However, Blythe assumed that the balled-up tissues already littering her bedspread gave some clue to her mental state.

"Feelin' a bit better, are we?" The housekeeper smiled as her charge struggled to sit up so that the wicker bed tray would fit across her knees. This night's bill of fare featured Mrs. Q's interpretation of minestrone, delicately laced with fresh vegetables from the castle's own kitchen garden.

On Blythe's fourth day as a recovering invalid, Mrs. Quiller disclosed that she and her husband, John, the undergardener, were, indeed, Luke's last remaining employees. Neither the kindly older woman nor the recuperating visitor referred to Blythe's continuing emotional crisis.

For his part Lucas Teague kept his distance, to both Blythe's relief and her mortification. However, Mrs. Quiller brought a vase of fresh rhododendrons every morning, along with several novels by Daphne du Maurier—all set in Cornwall—that the housekeeper presented to her on her meal trays. The books, Mrs. Q informed her charge proudly, were courtesy of her employer's extensive library.

As if it were an assignment that would give Blythe a reason to keep breathing, she became determined to devour the author's novels in the order they had been written. *The Loving Spirit*, first published in 1931, was one she'd never read, and she plunged into the story that spanned three generations of a Cornish family whose fate was tied to the sea. Each day her sore throat improved and her respect for du Maurier's magical storytelling increased. And each day she rediscovered the deep pleasure she had once enjoyed indulging in the sheer act of losing herself in the world of fiction—an activity that Christopher had found utterly alien to his world of manufacturing visual images.

However, in the hours before dawn on the fifth morning of her unscheduled stay at Barton Hall, she awoke with the oppressive sense that the four walls of her lonely bedchamber were closing in on her. Clad only in a sheer batiste nightgown that she assumed belonged to Lucas's deceased wife, she set out in search of another du Maurier novel to distract her.

The long hallway leading to the landing was several degrees chillier than her room. Hurrying along the corridor, Blythe had a brief vision of herself as some updated version of Cathy in *Wuthering Heights*, flitting downstairs at Barton Hall in a filmy peignoir "on a dark and stormy night." Only the Cornish sky had remained remarkably cloudless all day, even at dusk.

Will you cut it out? she reprimanded herself sharply. Where do you think you are, Gothic City?

Nevertheless, Blythe could not shake the eerie sense that she knew exactly where Lucas's library was located. Sure enough, at the bottom of the broad staircase she turned toward a door to the right of the lower landing.

Silvery beams of moonlight were streaming into the room through two tall windows, flooding the wall behind Lucas's desk where an impressively framed parchment sheet, decorated with colorful family crests, hung against the mahogany paneling. The other walls were covered with floor-to-ceiling bookshelves crammed with leather-bound volumes and tattered paperbacks.

Flipping on the desk-lamp switch, Blythe padded softly around the leather wing chair to have a closer look at the huge genealogy chart that loomed on the wall nearby. She stared up at the myriad branches of the Barton-Trevelyan-Teague family tree. Filled with a clandestine curiosity about Lucas Teague, she began to trace her finger along the line that commenced with her landlord's name and date of birth: November 23, 1957.

He was nearly thirty-seven and a widower, as he had disclosed to her, for the chart noted that Lindsay Wingate Teague had died in February 1992. Obviously the ornate document had been carefully kept up-to-date for hundreds of years.

In the section chronicling a cluster of Luke's eighteenth-century relatives, a line ended with the name Garrett Teague sketched in elegant calligraphy. From there the line veered to the left and led to the names of Garrett's first cousins, Ennis Trevelyan and his elder brother, Christopher "Kit" Trevelyan.

Blythe's hand began to tremble as she realized that this ancestor of Lucas Teague's, Christopher Trevelyan—a man with the same first name as her former husband—had married a woman named Blythe Barton in 1789!

No wonder Lucas had urged her to have a look at his family's genealogical records. Perhaps her grandmother's fanciful dynastic claims were correct. Her American Bartons might, indeed, be descendants of the people who had held this land for hundreds of years. Who was to say what specific ancestor was the link between her family and her landlord's, but certainly Lucas Teague could actually be a distant cousin, many generations removed.

Mesmerized by the swirling pattern of the chart's old-fashioned lettering, she continued to stare fixedly at the four names: Christopher, Ennis, Garrett, and Blythe. Once again she extended her forefinger, this time brushing it against the letters spelling Christopher "Kit" Trevelyan.

"Christopher . . . ," she breathed aloud, the sound of her ex-husband's name echoing in her throat.

As soon as she touched the glass that protected the framed genealogy chart, a strange force began pulling at her arm. The bizarre undertow then spread to her shoulders. In an instant it had invaded her entire body, as if she were being sucked into a violent whirlpool on the mighty Snake River in Wyoming that bordered the Double Bar B ranch.

The next thing she knew, a door slammed behind her, startling her nearly witless.

"Ah . . . here you are, you damnable bitch!" a voice growled menacingly.

Blythe whirled around, and there, in front of the paneled entrance to the book-lined chamber, stood a man with a thunderous expression etched upon his face and a heavy broadsword clutched in his hand.

"And just what do you plan to have inscribed on that parchment of yours in a few months' time?" he demanded, gesturing angrily with his sword at the chart chronicling her ancestors. "My name? Or that of Brother Ennis? A Trevelyan in either case—is that your damnable scheme?"

The intruder's dark-blond hair was fastened haphazardly at the nape of his neck, periwig style. His sweat-stained cotton shirt fell loosely from the waistband of soiled, buff-colored breeches, and his knee-high leather riding boots were covered with mud. In similar disarray, an elaborate lace neckcloth lay limp and torn beneath the blunt features of his smooth-shaven face, pitted mercilessly by a rash of deep, disfiguring smallpox scars. The man standing in the library of Barton Hall this moonlit night brandishing his sword was distraught and disheveled and dangerously close to committing violence.

As anyone could see, the mere sight of Blythe Barton Trevelyan had provoked her husband to a murderous rage.

Chapter Three

February 5, 1793

"For the love of St. Goran, will you calm down!" said Blythe, practically shouting. Sleet was beating against the window, and she could feel a draft swooping down the chimney.

"Don't you dare to patronize me, wife!" Kit barked back. "Not that you've ever acted as a proper helpmate, you damnable jade! Like it or not, you married me, Kit Trevelyan—not Ennis—and I shan't hesitate an instant to run that scoundrel through if he ever sets foot in Cornwall again!"

Moisture had started to fill his eyes, belying his bellicose words. His shoulders began to heave as he slowly lowered his fighting arm in defeat, the glittering weapon thumping heavily against his muscular thigh.

"I loved you, Blythe, you harlot!" he cried brokenly. "You are my wife! Ennis is my brother! The whole village must have known! How in the name of Christ could you do such a thing?"

"Christopher—K-Kit—" Blythe ventured in a low voice. "I—" She hesitated, fearing to antagonize him further. She glanced at the half-empty brandy decanter.

"Don't say another word, you reckless slut!" Christopher Trevelyan whispered hoarsely, his voice laced with sorrow and disgust. He jabbed his finger roughly at his wife's midsection. "In your lust, could you think of no one else? Not even the fate of that babe you carry in your womb?"

A bulge round as a melon protruded from under Blythe's

swollen breasts. She ran her fingertips down the thick folds of the boned brocade gown and continued to stare at her bloated belly. She felt a fluttering of butterfly wings that could only be her baby stirring inside.

"I knew you never loved me, you lying trollop! But to dishonor both the Barton name and mine in such a vile—"

Kit's eyes blazed with mounting fury, and once again he raised his sword. Blythe grasped the back of a chair to steady herself, prepared for an attack. However, her enraged accuser stormed past, flinging open the library door. He charged toward a framed oil canvas hanging in the reception hall.

"You bastard!" Kit screamed. "Bastard . . . bastard . . . bastard!"

With murderous force he began to rip deep gashes in the portrait of the stylishly attired young man, his brother, who had fathered the baby Blythe was carrying.

Kit continued to stab at the face in the picture with his weapon until he had reduced the artwork to shreds. At length he whirled around, exhausted from his outburst. His pitted cheeks were glistening with tears as he slowly advanced toward the open door to the library.

"And you . . . my lady wife," he said in a ragged whisper as he reentered the room, slamming the door behind him. "What . . . punishment . . . fits . . . your . . . crime?" he asked, slowly advancing toward her.

Then, as the raging laird of Barton Hall moved ever closer, Blythe Barton Trevelyan emitted an ear-piercing scream and began to run.

Lucas Teague was awakened from a dreamless sleep by the unearthly sound of a woman's shrieks. Thanks to his lifelong habit of sleeping in the nude, his navy-blue cashmere dressing gown was in its usual place at the bottom of the massive "Barton Bed," the outsize canopied four-poster that had witnessed the births, wedding nights, and deaths of generations of his ancestors. The screams continued as he bolted down the broad staircase, two steps at a time.

By the time he reached the closed library door, however, the terror-filled cries echoing from the other side had ceased. Once inside, he saw a single small lamp glowing on his desk. Otherwise, the chamber was suffused by an almost unearthly silver light that poured through the south windows. A three-quarter moon outside the castle's walls illuminated the rolling hills that tapered down to the Channel, whose waters glistened in the distance with a metallic sheen.

Lucas was alarmed to find his American houseguest, clad only in a sheer cotton nightgown, standing with her back to the genealogy chart and staring right through him with unseeing eyes. He was beginning to think the poor woman needed professional care, considering her precarious emotional state. Yet his heart went out to her in ways he knew would not be possible had he not suffered his own bout of anguish.

"Blythe? Blythe!" he said sharply.

She flinched and then turned to stare at him, dazed.

"I—" she began, and then fell silent. Next she inhaled and blew her breath through her lips while blinking her eyes several times, as if she were trying to wake up.

"Blythe . . . what can I do?" Luke asked urgently. When she didn't respond, he cautiously moved closer and touched her shoulder lightly. "Here . . . let me help you. We'll get you back to bed. . . . Come now. . . ."

He wrapped his arms around her shoulders to give her support just at the moment that her legs seemed to give way. He eased them both into the large leather winged chair that faced his desk. As if it were the most natural thing in the world, he settled this woman who was a virtual stranger into his lap and began rather awkwardly to stroke her curly mass of shoulder-length auburn hair. As his fingers tangled in its luxuriant strands, he suddenly had a vision of Blythe Stowe stepping out of her shower and shaking this unruly mane to allow it to dry, like some sort of naked twentieth-century Botticelli.

Her curls might be Botticelli-like, he corrected himself silently, but her slim, long-legged body and the perfectly proportioned thighs that were pressed against his legs were straight out of *Vogue* magazine. Not so, however, her lovely, rounded breasts. Now, they—

His hand paused, midcaress. His wandering thoughts were fast congealing into full-blown lust! His chest tightened at the sight of the moonlight pooled around their chair, and he had the unearthly sense that he might still be alone in that enormous four-poster upstairs, having an erotic dream. If so, he thought recklessly, why not make the most of it? He slid his right hand down the silken sheen of Blythe's hair once again and gently began to massage the muscles in her neck. Her skin was smooth and felt strangely familiar.

With a rapid intake of breath, he abruptly stopped stroking Blythe's neck. Such provocative behavior on his part, he realized with sudden embarrassment, was totally out of character. But, then, so was hers. This highly intelligent young woman hadn't expressed a coherent thought since he'd entered the room. Instead, her expressive brown eyes merely gazed at him with alarm.

"Now, tell me . . . what's got you into such a state?" he inquired gently. "No thumps in the attic or rattling of chains has brought this on, I should hope?" he added in an attempt to lighten the atmosphere and channel his thoughts in new, safer directions.

Blythe seemed almost to recoil at his words.

"This is crazy . . . ," she replied, refusing to look at him. "I . . . just now, I . . . ," she stammered. However, instead of jumping to her feet, she slumped against his chest once again and gazed with a bewildered look at the ornate family tree framed on the wall to their right.

Involuntarily Luke's arms tightened around her. His senses were being dangerously stimulated by the delicate texture of the thin batiste nightdress cloaking Blythe's fragrant skin. Mrs. Q had sensibly provided it to this unexpected houseguest, but the sheer sensation of the fabric against the palms of his hands brought Lindsay's image softly into focus.

Oddly, he felt no guilt that this stranger nestled against his chest was wearing such an intimate item of apparel that had once been owned by his deceased wife. Their marriage had been a comfortable, altogether suitable match. In the course of it he had gained a deepening respect for Lindsay Wingate as he watched her grapple valiantly with the more horrifying aspects of her illness. The sweet, accommodating young debutante he had married had been transformed by the onslaught of breast cancer into a courageous, dignified woman as she quietly met her fate. He, on the other hand, had felt the underpinnings of his life give way as he witnessed her die by inches. The process was a punishing one in which he grew to love and value her more each day while she agonizingly slipped away.

Blythe hadn't moved a muscle and lay quietly against his shoulder, as if she were an empty vessel.

"I'm sorry," she whispered against his neck. "You and Mrs. Quiller have been incredibly nice to me the whole time I've been here and . . ."

Her voice trailed off, and he realized, with a jolt of surprise and compassion, that here was a woman who wasn't accustomed to many people being kind. He absently stroked her wonderfully lustrous, springy hair and was unnerved to discover himself becoming physically aroused by her nearness.

Was it only this, the long absence of normal sexuality in his life, he mused, or was this emotionally fragile young American the first human in recent memory who had summoned any kind of response in him since Lindsay had died? His late wife had been a pretty, kindhearted girl. Blythe Barton, he had concluded after this short acquaintance, was all woman—and a complicated, wounded one at that.

"You're not crazy," Luke consoled her. Inhaling Blythe's warm, soap-scrubbed scent, he felt a stirring in his groin. "I expect that each of us is perfectly normal," he added wryly.

Oblivious to his double meaning, Blythe pointed in the direction of the framed record of their shared ancestry. Slowly she rose to her feet and gestured toward the names inscribed on the central section of the genealogy chart.

"Did you realize . . . ," she began, pausing to take a deep breath, "that a woman named Blythe Barton married a man named Christopher Trevelyan and—"

"Ah . . . on the genealogy chart," he interrupted. "Christopher and Blythe . . . yes, of course . . . Seeing those names up there gave you a turn, did it?" She was still in love with her husband, he realized with regret, or at least the bastard continued to have tremendous power to hurt her. He pointed at the elaborate listing of his ancestors. "The coincidence of that pair up there struck me right away as well, when your travel agent first contacted me and gave me your full name," he continued, trying to reassure her. "She mentioned that you'd told her your family might have emigrated from these parts. There must be thousands of Christophers in England, but Blythe is a fairly unusual Christian name. Presumably you Yankee Bartons could have descended from that eighteenth-century Cornish hellcat of mine." He smiled, hoping to take her mind off her troubles with diverting stories about his—and perhaps her—obstreperous ancestors. "The gene pool hatched by that Barton heiress probably rendered members of her line reckless enough to make the treacherous journey across the sea."

"The name Blythe was always given to the eldest daughter in my family," Blythe explained, her dark-brown eyes widening. "Lucinda Barton—the grandmother I was telling you about? She had married into the family, of course, and was very proud of her husband's claim to being a descendant of 'English landed gentry,' as she termed it."

"And quite right, too!" Luke chuckled, encouraged to see that this ill-used young woman seemed much calmer as she spoke of her family residing in America.

"Grandma Barton made a huge fuss with my mother and father until they gave in and named me Blythe as well," she continued softly. "My mother worried that with a handle like that, I was destined to become some silly dink—Noël Coward's play *Blithe Spirit* and all that. As it turned out, the role of dink was assigned to my sister."

" 'Handle'? 'Dink'?" Luke repeated with an amused smile, ignoring her disparaging reference to Eleanor Barton. "You Americans do make a hash of our mother tongue."

Blythe grimaced apologetically.

" 'Handle,' you probably know . . . and 'dink' is Wyoming for a shirker . . . a ditz. My husband was forever telling me I fractured the King's English." Blythe shrugged. Apparently in better command of her emotions now, she asked him earnestly, "What do you know about my namesake? The woman you described as such a hellion?"

Luke rose from his chair and stood beside her in front of the wide expanse of the gilt-edged genealogy chart. Their shoulders were just inches apart. He suddenly had the absurd desire to turn and kiss the generous mouth that posed such odd questions at this late hour.

"I don't know an awful lot of the story, really," he admitted, grateful for the opportunity to divert his lecherous thoughts by relating bits and pieces of Barton-Trevelyan-Teague family lore. "I do know from what's noted in the family Bible that at age seventeen, the first Blythe Barton had been betrothed for purely dynastic reasons to the eldest Trevelyan son . . . Christopher—known as Kit."

"And?" Blythe pressed.

"Everyone in both families was perfectly aware that the poor girl had been infatuated since childhood with the younger Trevelyan brother, Ennis here," he continued, tracing his finger above the line linking the two brothers.

"Don't touch the glass!" Blythe blurted, grabbing his arm. Her face had grown even paler. "It might make a smudge," she amended sheepishly.

"Well . . . right . . . ," Luke replied, assuming her skittishness was part and parcel of her recent emotional upset. "Kit's younger brother, Ennis Trevelyan, was a dashing bloke, consumed by a passion for art. By all accounts, your eighteenth-century namesake was quite vocal in her opposition to forced marriage to the eldest brother, heir to the Trevelyan lands."

He pointed to a framed modern ordnance survey that hung on the wall next to the genealogy chart.

"Here's the cause of poor Blythe Barton's thwarted passion," he explained.

The highly magnified version of a map of the Dodman Point region of Cornwall showed in minute detail every farmstead, caravan and camping site, ancient burial mound, and sewage works in the area. A hand-drawn line etched in bright-red ink outlined the boundaries of his family's three-thousand-acre estate.

"See this bit?" he continued. "These were the original Barton holdings that abutted the Trevelyan lands and shared the coastline hereabouts where smugglers made a tidy fortune bringing ashore French brandy . . . silk . . . lace . . . all sorts of luxuries that the Royal Revenue Men wanted to get their hands on in order to collect the necessary taxes due. It's no secret that the Bartons and Trevelyans, like virtually everyone else in Cornwall in those days, added to their profits on sheep and grain with a little contraband trade from time to time."

"And your Blythe Barton . . . ?"

"She was an heiress—no males ahead of her to inherit the land." Lucas shrugged. "Probably some male chauvinists in both families thought, 'What a good idea if the Barton heiress married the Trevelyans' eldest son! Then the lands could be joined and the smugglers could carry on at this secluded cove,' here," he continued, pointing to an area on the map named Hemmick Beach, a stretch of land immediately adjacent to Painter's Cottage and shaded a beige color to indicate sand. "Situated in the middle of the contiguous properties and honeycombed with natural caves, it was an ideal spot for smugglers to land their goods away from the prying eyes of the king's men." Impulsively Luke gripped Blythe's cold hand in his. "Here . . . let me show you something else."

Blythe allowed him to lead her into the reception hall, where he gestured in the direction of several portraits.

"These were painted in the early 1790s by young Ennis Trevelyan, my ancestor, who also produced those seascapes you've seen on the walls in your cottage," he explained.

Before Luke could individually identify any of the long-dead players in the drama they had been discussing, Blythe pointed to the framed oil closest to her.

"That's Christopher Trevelyan, isn't it?" she confirmed in a low voice. "Kit. Only his skin is unscarred."

Luke was amazed that his American houseguest could so easily identify Ennis's rendering of his older brother, Kit, the first and only Trevelyan laird of Barton Hall.

"Harelips, pockmarks, scars . . . you rarely see them on family portraits like these, no matter who the artist is," Luke explained. "It wouldn't do for a painter to offend his patron by rendering him warts and all, now, would it?" He shifted his gaze from the painting to Blythe's face, which had drained of its color. "Are you sure you're all right?" he asked. Blythe had an odd, haunted look about her.

"I think so," she replied.

"Positive? You seem so—"

He couldn't quite describe the peculiar aura of sadness and regret that surrounded his night-prowling guest.

"It's just . . . seeing my own name linked on that chart with another Christopher was . . . unsettling," she explained.

"I can certainly understand how it would be," he replied. "As I said before, I was struck by the coincidence myself."

Luke sensed there was more to her muted distress than that she'd spotted her name coupled with that of another Christopher. However, she was obviously reluctant to disclose intimate details of the emotional roller coaster she'd been on since her arrival from California—if Mrs. Quiller's anxious description of their guest's tormented state of mind was any guide.

Blythe pointed to another spot on the wall.

"There's no portrait of Ennis?"

"There was one . . . a self-portrait. It's up in the attic or out in the stable loft somewhere. The picture's got a terrible lot of gashes in it. I've been meaning to have it restored, but the cost, you know—"

"H-how was it damaged?" she interrupted.

Luke gestured at the elder Trevelyan's portrait.

"Family lore has it that old Kit here was rather displeased with his brother, for some reason or other. One night he apparently drew a ceremonial sword off the wall and slashed the canvas to ribbons. In his cups, probably."

"And is she my namesake?" Blythe inquired, nodding in the direction of the woman's portrait positioned next to that of Christopher Trevelyan.

Like some spectator at Wimbledon, Luke shifted his gaze several times between the flesh-and-blood Blythe Barton Stowe and his distant forebear, Blythe Barton Trevelyan. Then he emitted a low whistle.

"I haven't really had a good look at her since your arrival," he said, impressed by the apparent similarities between the two. "Your bone structure is like hers, don't you think? You don't have those almond-shaped eyes, and your hair's auburn, of course—hers is brunette—but I see the resemblance, don't you?"

"What eventually happened?" Blythe asked, ignoring his question. "Did Blythe Barton ever make her peace with her family's prohibition on marrying Ennis . . . the b-brother she loved?" she stammered.

"No one knows, exactly," Luke replied, escorting her back into his study and reaching for a decanter of brandy. "At some point during this family drama, Blythe Barton disappeared, died, or ran off. At least we know she's not buried in the family plot at St. Goran's churchyard. A grandfather of mine said that his grandfather declared that Kit's wife was a harridan and utterly to blame for the lack of legitimate Trevelyan heirs."

"Typical!" Blythe interjected shortly.

Lucas allowed her predictably American response to pass without comment.

"Even my late father referred to Blythe Barton's apparently scandalous behavior toward her lawful husband in hushed tones, but I'm not sure he even knew exactly what our ancestress had done to earn such a shameful reputation." He pointed once again at the genealogy chart and indicated the line that extended from Kit's name several inches to the right. "See . . . here's where we Teague cousins came into the picture when the Trevelyan-Barton line petered out. . . . This is my many-times-great-grandfather, Garrett Teague, the Trevelyan brothers' first cousin. Garrett's mother and the mother of the Trevelyan boys were sisters with the unfortunate surname of Swink."

Blythe was looking at him oddly as she asked, "Did this Garrett Teague figure into the story in any way? Is there a portrait of him?"

"Yes." Luke nodded. "It's at the other end of the reception hall. All I know is that he and his family were booksellers," Luke disclosed, pointing at the book-lined walls filled with moldering two-hundred-year-old leather volumes, their bindings sorely in need of restoration. "Garrett's father, Donald Teague, and the former Mistress Swink lived above their shop in Gorran Haven, in the next village. Poor as a church mouse, Garrett was, when the estate came to him."

"Is there no record of what ultimately happened to Kit's wife?" Blythe insisted.

"Your namesake? I've never come across any. Whatever supporting letters or diaries that may have existed have been lost or misplaced after all this time. . . ."

"Or were destroyed . . . ," Blythe murmured absently.

"Possibly," Luke agreed. "My wife, Lindsay, was always struck by the mystery of how the house came into my branch. She insisted on christening our son Richard Garrett Barton Trevelyan Teague, saddling the poor lad with the same collection of surnames that I have strung after mine." He paused briefly, lost in thought. "I thought it a rather sweet attempt, really, to reunite the family—if only in name."

"You have a son?" Blythe exclaimed, glancing over at Luke's family tree. "Oh! Of course . . . there he is . . . listed at the very bottom. You never mentioned him. How old is he?"

Her incredulous gaze was an uncomfortable reminder that Luke had maintained a decidedly distant relationship with his only child these last two years.

"He'll be ten soon," he replied evenly. "He's due home from school for the summer holidays in a few weeks' time."

Blythe placed her brandy snifter on Luke's desk and prepared to return to bed.

"It's always been amazing to me how you Brits still pack your children off to boarding school at such a tender age," she said wearily, looking as if she were fatigued to her very marrow. "It's absolutely Dickensian."

Then she turned to face him suddenly and appeared conscience-stricken.

"What a rude thing to say," she apologized. "It's just that it's so different in America. I grew up on a ranch in Wyoming. I helped my dad feed our cattle with a team of horses and a sled throughout the winter . . . and spent the summers on horseback, chasing lost cows in the hills."

"And your mother?" Luke asked curiously. "Did she ride too?"

"Not after my sister was born," Blythe disclosed quietly. "She was twenty-six when she had Ellie, and died of a blood clot in the brain about five years later. So, you see . . . ," she concluded, as if she were embarrassed to have offered such a lengthy account of her various relations, "from the time I was eleven, my grandmother, my brother, and I all competed in the local rodeo—a kind of gymkhana, I think you call it here. I loved Jackson Hole. I never wanted to leave my family—or my home."

"So you're a genuine cowgirl," Luke laughed admiringly, tacitly accepting her apology and grateful that the conversation had veered away from the subject of his young son. "We must go riding on the moor while you're here."

"Retired cowgirl," Blythe corrected him.

With a small sigh she turned toward the library door. Luke strode across the room and escorted her up the wide oaken staircase. As they reached the landing, he suppressed a desire to guide her farther down the corridor on the right into his own bedroom.

The woman's an emotional mess, he chided himself silently. *You, of all people, should understand what that's like.*

Turning to his left, Luke walked her to her bedroom door. Smiling faintly, he said, "You'll be all right, will you, cousin? Not afraid of any ghosts?"

"Wouldn't that be something?" Then she added hastily, "Our being distant cousins, I mean?"

"Hands across the sea, and all that?" He grinned. "I think it would be splendid."

Instead of clasping her hands to emphasize just how splendid he thought their potential kinship could be, the current owner of the threadbare Barton-Trevelyan-Teague estate politely bade her good night and quickly retraced his steps to the landing. And before his houseguest had stepped into the sanctuary of her own bedroom, Lucas Teague had marched resolutely into the shadows of the opposite hallway that led to the castle's master suite.

Blythe gently closed the door to the yellow guest bedroom and slumped against the wood paneling. She took a deep breath to try to steady her nerves, wondering if she had finally, completely, lost her sanity.

Who was that raving lunatic storming around the castle waving his sword, and why was he clothed as if he were playing some down-at-the-heels Sir Percy Blakeney in *The Scarlet Pimpernel*? She glanced down at her trim waistline, cloaked, as before she'd descended the stairs into Luke's library, by her cotton nightgown. She was at a loss to explain how its sheer material had been replaced earlier by the thick folds of the boned gown that had pressed painfully against her bulging stomach.

Whose bulging stomach? she wondered, utterly bewildered. Whose child? And was that woman named Blythe herself? It was as if she'd been in a dream and watching a dream at the same time.

However, thanks to her extensive training in theatrical makeup and costume, Blythe hazarded a guess that the clothes and unpowdered hairstyle worn by the sword-wielding, breeches-clad, pockmarked apparition dated toward the end of the 1700s.

As for the portrait of Kit's brother—it had seemed genuine enough before it had been obliterated by Trevelyan's rapier thrusts. As far as Ennis's portrait of the first Blythe Barton herself—the resemblance was close enough to be unsettling.

She walked unsteadily to her bed and sank onto the mattress, her mind reeling. The genealogy chart had behaved as if it were a TV screen in some kind of Cornish "virtual reality" video arcade! To Blythe the anguished words uttered by Christopher "Kit" Trevelyan had reverberated across the book-lined chamber, across time, across the centuries, across oceans and continents. The agonized sound of his voice echoed, almost word for word, the phrases she'd shrieked at her husband that ghastly day when she had found him with Ellie.

I loved you. . . . Everyone else must have known. . . . How could you . . . ?

But was any of it real, or had she recently experienced some sort of weird hallucination—a vestige of the raging fever that had plagued her these last few days? How in the world could Luke's genealogy chart have provided such a world-class paranormal peep show—one that had offered a glimpse into the tumultuous lives of ancestors who, perhaps, had sired her branch of the American Bartons?

Blythe ran the palm of her hand along her flat abdomen and mulled over several other possible explanations for the phantasmagoric display she had seen. The likeliest answer to these eerie developments, she concluded, was that she was simply having a nervous breakdown.

And with that Blythe gulped down her antibiotics, plus two extra-strength headache tablets, and fell into bed.

A gentle knock roused her from a deep sleep that had been blessedly free of dreams—a remarkable feat in itself, she thought drowsily, considering her bizarre experience in Lucas Teague's study the previous night.

The bedroom door opened a few discreet inches.

"Morning tea, mum," Mrs. Quiller announced softly. "Shall I put it on the table beside your bed?"

"That would be lovely," Blythe replied, struggling to sit up and arrange herself comfortably against the plump bed cushions. Barton Hall's housekeeper set the tea tray on the nightstand and immediately crossed the bedchamber to fling aside the heavy drapes. Brilliant morning sunshine flooded the room, and Blythe felt reassured that her strange encounters in Luke's library had, indeed, been only imagined.

"And could I be bringin' you a poached egg, or perhaps you'd fancy a bit of kippers this morning for breakfast?"

"That's so kind of you, Mrs. Q," Blythe replied. "I'd love to try the kippers, if it wouldn't be too much trouble. It reminds me of when my father and I used to eat trout for breakfast in cow camp in the Rockies when I was a child."

"Cow camp, mum?" Mrs. Q asked with a puzzled smile.

"In the summer in Wyoming, we moved our herd up to the foothills onto the summer range so we could use the lower range to grow and harvest our hay for winter. We'd catch our breakfast in the icy creeks feeding the Snake River." She threw aside her bed linen and reached for her dressing gown flung carelessly across the bottom of the bed. "Which reminds me that I've lazed around a lot lately," she noted wryly. "I am definitely on the mend, so it's about time I had breakfast downstairs and let you get on with your usual duties."

"Ah . . . 'tis no trouble, either way, so suit yerself, but you must show me where Wyoming be in the atlas, if you would, miss." Mrs. Quiller laughed in her easy manner that always seemed to erase any awkwardness between them. After all, the woman probably watched CNN, right along with her employer. "Mr. Teague was tellin' me you rode horses there as a girl, despite your bein' from Hollywood and all. Must be your Cornish roots, he says."

So Lucas Teague was already up this morning and had presumably had a friendly chat about her with his housekeeper in the early hours. Blythe recalled, suddenly, that she'd revealed a hint of her "cowgirl" past to Luke last night in the library, so that part of the evening's events was true, at least. But what of her host's rampaging ancestor—the one sporting the wickedly sharp sword? She fervently hoped that that peculiar phenomenon, experienced in the dead of night, might simply be an untoward reaction to the terrible stress of her ordeal in faraway California.

Deciding that this conclusion was as likely an explanation as any, Blythe smiled warmly at Luke's housekeeper.

"My Cornish roots tell me I've been a terrible layabout," she said with sudden decisiveness. "It's time I moved back into my own cottage and left you in peace."

Obviously pleased to see that her "patient" was much improved, Mrs. Quiller departed downstairs to prepare the kippers while Blythe bathed and dressed in the jeans and turtleneck sweater she'd worn to tea at Barton Hall five days earlier.

As she descended the broad staircase en route to locating the breakfast room, her gaze was irresistibly drawn toward the library door. It stood open. On Luke's desk sat the Waterford crystal brandy decanter and two glasses—one empty, and one that remained a quarter full, just as Blythe had left it four or five hours earlier.

Bright May sunlight shone through the casement windows, bathing the rows of books and mahogany paneling in a rich, warm glow. The enormous genealogy chart was also illuminated by shafts of light, and its swirling black calligraphy and colorfully gilded family crests were dazzling.

Drawn magnetically into the room, Blythe gingerly approached the framed parchment. Like the biblical Lot's wife who had been unable to resist glancing back at the wicked city of Sodom, she extended her hand and cautiously traced the delicate lettering that spelled "Blythe Barton b. 1772 m. 1789 d. 1794 (?)."

The placement of a question mark apparently denoted that her namesake's date of death was uncertain. As Luke had mentioned—family lore had it that the eighteenth-century heiress had "disappeared."

As if conducting an experiment, Blythe rested her forefinger lightly on the glass that protected the genealogy chart itself. Then she whispered aloud her own name. Immediately she felt the same strange force as before beginning to pull at her, almost as if she were hurtling down a steep incline on a roller-coaster ride that was traveling at a hundred miles an hour.

"No!" Blythe reacted sharply, her outburst filling the book-filled chamber. Frantically she pushed a second time against her name etched on the chart beneath the glass covering, and to her relief, her world instantly returned to normal.

Good God! she thought. The chart did seem to act like some interactive video screen.

Blythe was reminded of her first encounter with the make-your-own-greeting-card machine at her local pharmacy. One Saturday, as several other customers looked on curiously, she pushed her fingers as instructed against the smooth glass surface of what appeared to be a television screen. Laughingly she chose pictures and typed messages according to directions that had magically appeared on the screen to guide her. Her actions had instantly produced all sorts of images that ultimately became a tailor-made thank-you card for Lisa Spector in appreciation for the lawyer's hospitality on a weekend strategy session they'd shared at Lisa's second home in Santa Barbara. She had seen similar TV screens at airports and shopping malls dispensing interactive local information to inquiring customers.

But this was totally insane, Blythe chided herself. Had she really felt a gravitational pull when she'd touched the chart? Or was her overstressed mind converting Luke's family tree into some sort of *Back to the Future* carnival ride?

My life is not a movie, she reminded herself for the nth time.

However, Blythe found herself studying the name of Lucas Teague's eighteenth-century forebear—the "poor church mouse" who had inherited Barton Hall. To put to rest once and for all any demented notions she might harbor about the "supernatural" events of the previous night, she warily pushed a fingertip against the chart and defiantly pronounced, "Garrett Teague."

Once again a potent jolt of energy began to shoot up her arm, succeeded by the now familiar sensation that she was being hurtled like a NASA rocket through uncharted space.

"Oh, Jesus!" Blythe groaned into the vortex whirling around her. "Shhh-it!"

A second later a youthful voice behind her shoulder whispered loudly, "Psst! Blythe! In here. Behind the secret bookcase. Quickly, now, beauty, or Kit and Ennis might find us and tell their da!"

Chapter Four

September 2, 1789

Blythe Barton was among the select few who knew that the Hall had not just one, but *two,* secret bookcases. Even so, she was startled when, without warning, a section of the library wall suddenly pivoted inward in the same fashion as the book-lined panel that provided access to the kitchen pantry from the small sitting room.

Kit Trevelyan's cousin, Garrett Teague, emerged from the shadows like some agitated apparition, gesturing frantically.

"Blythe, come quickly! Kit and his father are on their way here! Follow me," he said urgently. "I'll explain everything!"

The lanky seventeen-year-old whose black hair fell across his forehead to the arches of his ebony brows stood before her in the narrow opening between the movable bookcase and a corner of the library.

"Zounds, but you'll addle my brain with such fool trickery!" she gasped. "How did you know—?"

"You're not the only one who knows this hidey-hole, missy." The young man smiled mischievously. "Kit said Uncle Collis supplied the wood to line the inner chamber and then shared the cost with your da of expanding that cave down by Hemmick Beach."

Blythe surveyed her childhood companion's plain brown breeches and matching cuffed coat, which were devoid of decoration. Garrett Teague and his Trevelyan cousins and she had kept company throughout their youth, but sadly, this engaging bookseller's son could not afford the luxury of fine clothes. The dark hue of the lad's jacket collar only served to emphasize his bronzed complexion. Local gossips whispered that Garrett inherited its faintly Latin cast from a survivor of the Spanish Armada in the time of Queen Elizabeth, two centuries earlier. The waterlogged sailor had been given shelter by a Gorran Haven man with a hot-blooded daughter. After rather hasty nuptials, so the story went, a girl child was born to this unlikely union, and 'twas she who married into the Teague family. From that day forward Teague descendants were distinguished by their romantic temperaments and swarthy skin tones.

Garrett suddenly cocked his head and listened intently. Footsteps could be heard in the hallway, coming in their direction. The sound of voices—one a woman's, and the other loud and insistent and obviously male—was growing louder by the second.

"Jesu, Blythe," he hissed. " 'Tis bound to be my uncle Collis. I came to warn you that—"

"Warn me?" Blythe echoed. "About what?"

"Quickly!" her rescuer cried. "Or they'll find us out!"

He dashed across the chamber and grabbed Blythe's arm by the ruffled cuff that encircled her wrist. She wore a light muslin frock featuring a pointed, boned bodice and scooped neck with additional ruffles sewn around its edge. Her feet were shod in dainty slippers made of soft leather dyed pale pink. Despite her stylish appearance, Garrett Teague unceremoniously dragged her across the room and into the gaping black hole behind the bookcase. "Kit told me about this secret door in Barton Hall," the boy whispered in the darkness. " 'Tis best if we head for the stables!"

"Garrett!" Blythe protested into the surrounding blackness.

"What?" he grunted, pushing the secret bookcase back in place.

"Pray, what is going on?" she demanded.

"According to your guardian, there's to be no more waiting," Garrett replied testily. "You're to be betrothed to my cousin without delay," he added, his adolescent voice cracking under the weight of his announcement. "Now, stop prattling while I try to find the spring latch that will open the door into the walled garden."

Shocked by the suddenness of this revelation, Blythe stood stock-still as she heard Garrett knocking softly against the sides of the hidden closet.

"Has Ennis come with them?" she asked in a muted voice.

There was silence and then she heard Garrett sigh.

"Give it up, Blythe. As we both know full well, 'tis the eldest son who's come to claim your hand."

"Guardian or no, 'tis daft for your uncle Collis to think I'd accept that pockmarked dolt who rarely has the wit to say a word to me," Blythe replied disdainfully. Cautiously she took a step forward and felt her toe collide with something solid. Her hands shot out to prevent her falling, and she clutched at a curved wooden object that appeared to be a barrel among a stack stored next to the wall.

She groped her way along in the dark and sniffed the air. The sweetish smell that met her nostrils confirmed her suspicion that several casks of spirits had recently found a hiding place in the bowels of Barton Hall. Her father had had this secret room constructed after Blythe had gone up to London two years ago to visit her aunt. Her mother had warned her not to ask questions about the muffled sounds they sometimes heard in the dead of night, but Blythe assumed the noises were caused by the delivery of contraband goods stored in barrels like the ones stacked at her feet.

Garrett seized her by the wrist once more.

"I am an eldest son," he proclaimed suddenly, the earnestness in his voice harsh in her ear. "If I had wealth and land, would you marry me?"

"Before Kit Trevelyan? Of course," she laughed. "You're my friend."

"Then we must hide, till we can make an escape."

"Escape?" she asked, alarmed by the ferociousness in Garrett's voice. "To where?"

"Plymouth!" Garrett answered promptly. "And thence to America, if you truly wish to avoid this match."

"And how, my fine adventurer, do you propose we pay for passage and keep ourselves once we get there?" she demanded, snatching her hand away as the seriousness of the situation began to penetrate her consciousness.

"We'll hide in the stable loft," Garrett whispered back, "and when the coast is clear, you'll gather together as much Barton family silver as we can carry."

"And then?" Blythe asked, dumbfounded by his audacity.

"I only just learned this morning of Uncle Collis's intentions to post the banns before your father's year of mourning has elapsed," Garrett replied, continuing to search for the door that led outside the castle walls. "However, with a silver candlestick or two, perhaps we could coax an owner of a village sloop to take us to Plymouth, or if we must, we could nick two ponies from your stable and ride there by cover of night."

"Thirty-five miles? Are you mad?" Blythe felt a knot of cold dread nestle in the pit of her stomach. "Besides, how could we possibly escape without someone stopping us?" she said, stretching out her hands to see if she could assist in Garrett's search for the secret catch to the outside door. "Would Ennis come?"

"He knows naught of this scheme," Garrett replied grimly, "nor would he risk his fine neckcloth to help, I can assure you! He stands to gain only if this match with Kit comes to pass."

" 'Tis not true!" Blythe protested, thinking of a series of brief, stolen kisses they'd shared recently in the shadow of the cliff at Dodman Point.

"Ennis's one true love is art, Blythe Barton, and 'tis time you saw the truth of that. If Kit Trevelyan marries you, your wedding portion will be more than ample to send Ennis in fine style to Italy, where his only desire is to study with the master painters there." Just then the muted sound of shouting suddenly grew louder on the other side of the bookcase. "Aha!" Garrett announced triumphantly as a dim shaft of light penetrated their lair. "I've found the door to the outside! Come, now, let's make a dash for it."

Blythe allowed her young companion to guide her swiftly down a path that bisected a kitchen garden enclosed by three high stone walls near the back door of the turreted mansion. Garrett fumbled to open the gate's latch, and the pair ran through a wooden arch encrusted with flowering purple clematis. He pointed in the direction of a path that veered off to her right, turning his back on the trail that headed left toward the sea.

Within minutes they arrived, panting with exertion, inside the musty-smelling stone building filled with fat ponies stirring restlessly in their stalls. Garrett and Blythe scrambled up a steep ladder and dived into a pile of straw. The silence in the stable was broken only by the ponies pawing and snorting below the loft. " 'Tis not Kit's fault . . . all of this . . . ," Garrett ventured quietly, peering at her through heaps of hay.

"Lud! What a fool you are sometimes!" scoffed Blythe, burrowing deeper in the straw and praying she wouldn't commence a fit of sneezing that would give them away. "Just because he's been ill, I suppose you feel sorry for your surly cousin?"

"Ill?" Garrett protested. "The smallpox nearly killed the poor chap. And can you imagine your disposition if pockmarks had marred your pretty face?"

"A pity it didn't kill him," she opined. "Then Ennis would be the eldest and I could marry . . ."

The seventeen-year-old Barton heiress had the grace not to finish her sentence. She knew if she disclosed to Garrett the depths to which she desired to be wife to Ennis and Ennis alone, she would greatly wound his feelings. But everyone from Dodman Point to Nare Head, including Garrett Teague, knew full well that she had never made a secret of her single-minded affection for Ennis Trevelyan, Garrett's handsome, beguiling cousin. But neither her guardian nor her late father—truth be known—gave a farthing for her happiness. Not a whit, she thought morosely.

"Blythe, you're a fool if you—" Garrett began in a low voice.

"I know perfectly well why Collis Trevelyan has stormed over here," she interrupted in a hoarse whisper. "He's protecting an investment, pure and simple—and the soundest way to do that was to order me to marry his eldest son without delay. Well, I'll have none of it!"

"Brave talk, m'girl," Garrett whispered back, "but then your only way out of this coil is to flee! You're key to the whole damnable scheme!"

The truth of Garrett's words smothered Blythe's imminent retort. For years now the Trevelyans and the Bartons together had traded their locally raised wool to the Frenchies in exchange for contraband brandy and lace. These were items that, if one avoided paying the exorbitant taxes required by the Crown, fetched other needed goods and hard cash from Cornish landowners who lived farther inland and above all despised paying customs duties.

In fact, Blythe had realized in the months since her father had died that she was merely a pawn in the game of "free trade" played by nearly everyone in Cornwall. The entire region was sick of paying for such foolhardy wars as the recently concluded fiasco in the American colonies. As a consequence, fishermen provided the smacks and wherries for transporting goods across the Channel. Farm laborers served as "bat men" to beat off any challengers when the wares were ferried from ship to shore into cellars, attics, and assorted hidey-holes near Gorran Haven and Mevagissey. The linchpin in the entire enterprise was landowners like the Bartons and Trevelyans who supplied the woolen goods for export and, later, provided strings of ponies needed to cart the foreign luxury goods inland to waiting customers.

"If members of the clergy like the Reverend Randolph Kent didn't dance to Collis Trevelyan's tune, I might not be in such a coil!" Blythe hissed. Kent and his fellow men of the cloth had filled their flasks with free brandy by allowing contraband kegs of spirits and ropes of tobacco to be stored in coffins and buried in their churchyards in the dead of night under the collective noses of the harried customs officials. As far as Blythe could determine, everyone in Cornwall benefited from the illicit enterprise except her!

"The government's taxation of the West Country is wholly unfair, and you know it!" Garrett rasped, defending his mild-mannered relative. "Uncle Randolph says that the Trade keeps the poorer folk from starving when gales ruin the crops or the fishing's poor or the tin mines play out. But then, I don't suppose m'lady ever considered such calamities in her pampered world—brat!"

Stung, she glared back at him and retorted, "Well, perhaps there's truth to some of that, but the king's men are taking aim at the gentry now, as well, and your two uncles put us all in danger—not just the small fish like you, Garrett Teague!"

Both of them knew full well that smuggling had become so widespread on the west coast, as the eighteenth century drew to its close, that red-coated king's men had taken to keeping an eye on even the most prominent local families like the Edgecumbes, Bartons, and Trevelyans. As recently as the previous day, a clutch of soldiers had made an unwelcome and totally unexpected visit to Barton Hall at the precise hour that goods on a French ship were due to be off-loaded and stored in the library's hidey-hole. Fortunately, the Bartons' stable boy had had the wit to run to Hemmick Beach and signal the vessel away, but everyone involved in the business—and especially Blythe's widowed mother—had been rattled by such a close call.

With the Barton-Trevelyan coastal properties joined through the bond of marriage, Blythe knew that the Preventive Service would have a difficult time guarding against illegal shipments of brandy, tea, and lace landing on Hemmick Beach. Barton-Trevelyan lookouts posted along the estates' boundaries to warn of the approach on land and sea of such nosy "visitors" would make it impossible for a Revenue Service spyglass to gather any proof of the movement of goods from ship to shore. Indeed, if Blythe Barton was wed to Christopher Trevelyan, the customs men would be forced to keep scores of smacks and sloops patrolling the coast from Plymouth to Land's End. Even those fool functionaries sent down from London town knew that the weather in these parts was often too foul for that!

But did Collis Trevelyan and his accomplices realize that she would absolutely refuse to marry Kit, that tongue-tied simpleton? Blythe wondered silently, declining to debate Garrett any further. And when it came to Kit's dashing younger brother, did any of them—including Garrett lying moodily beside her in the hayloft—have any idea how seriously she intended that Ennis should be her bridegroom instead?

Blythe seized a blade of straw between her fingers and stared at it, deep in thought. Perhaps if she was very clever, a bargain could be struck with an avaricious man like her guardian. She turned and glanced sideways at her would-be rescuer. It was very dear of Garrett to play her knight in shining armor, but she had no intention of abandoning Barton Hall. She would retain her homestead and acquire the husband of her choice!

"Blythe Barton, you impertinent chit!" a voice bellowed from outside the castle wall at the far end of the stable yard. "Where are you? Come inside the house this instant!"

"God's eyeballs!" Blythe whispered hoarsely, tossing another layer of hay on top of them both. "I fear they've caught us out!"

"Shhh! Lie still!" Garrett hissed. He flung one arm across her bosom to prevent her from making the slightest movement that might give them away. She felt a stab of fear as she recognized the voice shouting for her attention. Her game of hide-and-seek had suddenly turned deadly serious. Collis Trevelyan was demanding to know where his ward had hidden herself, and woe betide anyone who was interfering with his mission. "How did you know old Collis would call the question today?" she asked in a low voice.

"He was at the bookshop this morning," Garrett murmured, referring to the small establishment run by his father on a narrow street in Gorran Haven.

"And was my guardian bragging to your father about his intention to increase his estate at my expense?" she demanded.

"That he was," Garrett answered glumly.

Both Blythe and Garrett were woefully aware that such intimate confidences took place only because Collis Trevelyan and Donald Teague had both married Swink sisters, rendering them brothers-in-law. Thanks to such twisted branches in the Teague family tree, this coupling with the Swink clan had condemned Garrett and the rest of the family to play the role of "poor relation" to one of the largest landowners in Cornwall.

"I heard Uncle Collis say that he intends to have your wedding banns read at St. Goran's Church within the month," Garrett revealed gruffly. "Either we flee, or you are destined to be Kit's bride."

Those damnable Revenue Men! Blythe fumed. If it weren't for their prying eyes and repeated fleecing of Cornwall to pay for their misbegotten wars and adventurers, Collis Trevelyan wouldn't be in such a lather to consummate this match.

Suddenly another angry outburst interrupted Blythe's seething reverie.

"Blythe!" Collis Trevelyan shouted, causing her to wonder if the voluble man wouldn't one day fall dead in an apoplectic fit.

"There must be something I can do, short of fleeing the country!" Blythe protested.

"Well, there's not!" Garrett shot back. "Be still or he'll hear us!"

"So that's where you are!" a second, softer voice now

exclaimed below their loft. "Oh, Blythie, my darling, are you ever in the soup! I'm coming up there to protect you from the wrath of my da."

The sounds of someone scrambling up the ladder were followed by the sight of a dark-blond head peering into the gloomy hayloft.

"I've seen to that, Ennis," Garrett declared hotly as his uncle Collis burst forth with a string of epithets in the stable yard below.

Ennis Trevelyan crawled across the loft to where they both still lay covered in straw.

"Blast and bother, Ennis!" Garrett declared. He sat up and attempted to brush the stubble from his hair and clothes. "You'll give us away!"

"I fear my father plays no games this day," Ennis said, suddenly serious. "You'd both best come down before he finds you here lying in the hay."

"No!" Garrett insisted in a hoarse whisper.

"Really now, Blythe," Ennis coaxed, switching tactics to address her in his customary teasing tone, "I know you can't stand the sight of dear brother Kit, but I've always assumed you were bewitched by me, not my bookish cuz here!"

He had come to rest on his haunches beside them, looking like a well-satisfied pasha. His riding breeches were pristine and clung impressively to his well-formed thighs. The eighteen-year-old's fashionably cut burgundy-colored coat was immaculate. As Blythe gazed into his face, she judged it extraordinarily handsome by virtue of his straight nose, perfectly rounded chin, and a mouth whose engaging smile was as much due to a small scar received in some childhood romp as to his strong, even teeth. A worm of doubt began to eat at her. Would she never be his bride? Could his father actually force her to the altar of St. Goran's and compel her to wed Kit instead of Ennis? Would her mother stand by and permit it?

"Garrett says your father schemes to—" Blythe began.

"Who's up there?" an angry voice demanded from below. "I want whoever's in that loft to come down here immediately!"

Finally the trio gave up. They descended the ladder and stood sheepishly in the stable in front of a supremely agitated Collis Trevelyan, looking like guilty five-year-olds rather than the confident young adults they had become.

"Ennis, where's your brother?" Collis snapped.

"Here I am, Father," a voice replied.

Christopher Trevelyan, having recently celebrated his nineteenth birthday fighting for his life against the smallpox, stood in the stable door. Blythe assumed he had been drawn to the scene by the sound of his sire's fulminations. The dim light cast a merciful shadow over the deep scars that pitted a face which, under happier circumstances, might have pleased some young ladies she knew, though certainly not to the same extent his talented, charming younger brother did.

Blythe could see that Kit looked as miserable to be summoned to this revolting parley as she was. She judged that the eldest Trevelyan son habitually held himself apart out of simple shyness and in reaction to an overbearing father who dominated every room he entered. Kit's dark-blond hair was the same shade as that of his fellow Trevelyans, but it was already thinning at the temples and lacked the sheen of good health. The heir to his family's estate wore the modest attire of a farmer. His clothing was more mundane, even, than the plain-cut breeches and coat that their hotheaded, impecunious cousin Garrett was forced to don by virtue of his family's limited financial circumstances.

Giving Christopher his due, Blythe reflected, poor old Kit would one day make a fine landowner when he inherited his father's holdings. The young man actually enjoyed supervising both fieldwork and sheep raising—and dressed accordingly.

"Blythe Barton, look at you!" Collis said grimly. Next his angry stare fell on Garrett and Ennis. "There's been no slap-and-tickle going on, has there?" he thundered. "I should hope you've not turned the chit into damaged goods?"

Blythe's neck and face flushed scarlet in response to her guardian's accusations. Ennis merely grinned, and Garrett stared sullenly at his boot tops, while Kit pursed his lips into a thin line.

"No, Father," Ennis said with a deprecating laugh. "We were just having a bit of fun, like the old days—"

"Well, you're not children anymore," Collis barked, "and I would thank you all to remember that!" He glared at Blythe. "And I don't appreciate your disappearing, missy, the moment we come to call. Blythe . . . Kit . . . you shall come inside with me." Collis Trevelyan's fit of temper had mottled his face various shades of crimson. He waved a dismissive hand toward Garrett. "Aren't you needed in your father's shop, boy?" Then his glowering gaze absorbed Blythe and Garrett's disheveled appearance. Meanwhile Ennis had somehow managed to remove all traces of his sojourn in the straw. "Be gone with you, Garrett, as your manners are so lacking! As for you, Ennis . . . ," he added.

In the midst of this tirade Ennis had pulled out a small sketching pad and was drawing the contours of Collis's livid countenance, which served only to make his father more incensed.

"Put away that useless nonsense and wait for us in the sitting room until I have finished with this business."

The dispirited bunch trooped out of the stable and scattered in all directions. Blythe watched Garrett stalk along a narrow path leading toward the village. Then, in what was clearly a meaningless act of rebellion, the seventeen-year-old turned his back on Gorran Haven and headed toward the coastline path that bordered the sea. As for Blythe, she already felt like the prisoner she would soon become if she didn't follow Garrett's advice and run away. She soon found herself being herded into Barton Hall alongside the cheerless, pockmarked soul whom her guardian decreed would be her mate for life.

* * *

"You will wait here until we summon you, minx," Collis commanded, pointing to a straight-backed chair outside the library that had once served as her father's inner sanctum.

As soon as the paneled door had closed behind her purple-faced guardian and his hapless son, Blythe stealthily tiptoed toward the keyhole. Squatting on her heels in a most unladylike fashion, she squinted through the narrow gap. Unfortunately, her view was blocked by the wide expanse of Collis Trevelyan's high-collared blue coat. However, she could hear the conversation with unnerving clarity.

"James will have been in the ground a year this November, Rosamund," Collis was saying. "Why not unite the two families immediately and let the mourners be damned!"

In point of fact, Blythe's mother, Rosamund, had no legal standing in the question of whom her daughter would marry. However, the elder Trevelyan apparently thought it politic to seek the widow Barton's endorsement of his plans. Even so, the unhappy truth was that Blythe was now Collis's legal ward, to be dispatched as he saw fit. Then, once she was wed, her mother could either remarry or end her days in the drafty dower house at the bottom of the garden.

"But would the vicar countenance such hasty nuptials?" Blythe heard her mother say calmly, detecting in Rosamund Barton's inflection her customary irony. The thirty-four-year-old woman had been a bride at sixteen, a mother at seventeen, and widowed the previous autumn. "I'll grant you, we've dispensed with full mourning attire," she allowed in the distinctive husky voice that, along with her striking figure, had won her late husband's heart, "but 'tis only September, Collis, and a squally month for a wedding."

"Bah!" Collis spat. "A pox on the blasted weather!" he exclaimed, followed by, "Ah—begging your pardon, Kit, my boy!" He wagged a finger at her mother. "You allowed those Revenue Men to nose around here good and proper, I'll be bound. 'Twas only the hidey-hole here that kept us all safe from being hauled off and locked up."

"Mrs. Barton's a woman alone, Father," Kit ventured cautiously. "I thought she coped admirably with those blighters when they came here uninvited."

"My point exactly!" Collis exclaimed. "There's nothing you can do, Rosamund, alone here at the Hall when those bastards come snooping about. What you need is a good, strapping son-in-law like Kit here, and stout men, answerable only to us, to be on the lookout for such meddlesome scoundrels. We shan't waste another moment! I've left it to Donald Teague to convince the vicar. He'll see to it that his brother-in-law adjusts his scruples by a couple of months."

"Who shall tell Blythe?" Kit asked in a low voice.

"Why, the randy bridegroom, of course!" Collis replied roguishly, slapping his son on the back and sending the recovering invalid into paroxysms of coughing.

"She won't like it," Kit said, gasping to catch his breath. " 'Tis Ennis she fancies."

"I don't care if she fancies a merino ram!" Collis exploded. "You'll tell her and you'll bed her—before the wedding, if necessary!"

"Collis!" Rosamund interjected sharply. "My daughter has a right to her tastes in suitors, whomever she may eventually marry. I shall tell her!"

"Well, I hope that you inform her that she could do a far sight worse than Kit here," Collis grumbled.

During this conversation Kit's face had flushed an unbecoming shade akin to the hue of pomegranate juice. Squinting through the keyhole, Blythe wondered if there could possibly be a more unsightly looking bridegroom in all of Cornwall.

" 'Tis plain she wants Ennis," Kit said stubbornly. "She's always favored him, even before—"

"Nonsense, lad!" Trevelyan said gruffly. "I've always known you've had tender feelings for the chit, though she's bound to be a handful," he added, with a look of asperity cast in Rosamund's direction. "You must woo her, that's all . . . show her you're not the rascal your brother is . . . convince her she's got the best of the bargain in the long run. 'Twas what I did with your mother when she thought she wanted to marry Edward Grieve over at Mevagissey." Kit's father chuckled slyly. "My acres bordering the coast were far more valuable than landlocked Grieve Manor, and my dexterity in the feathers was far more to her liking—or so she says. . . ."

"Must you?" Rosamund interrupted disdainfully.

Collis shrugged.

"A jest, Rosamund . . ."

"Ah . . . I see." Blythe's mother smiled faintly, her eyes narrowing. "A bit of levity in the face of Kit's concern he won't be able to entice his virginal bride into the marriage bed?"

"From what I saw around here today, 'twill be fortunate for Kit if she is a virgin, my dear," Collis retorted icily. Ignoring Rosamund's indignant gasp, he turned to his son and added, "If you must beat her into obedience, so be it. A thump on the backside can prove a great persuader, my boy."

By this time Blythe was palpitating with fury. She leaned her forehead against the cool metal doorknob and inhaled long, even breaths to calm herself. It was all she could do to keep from bursting into the chamber to tell those damned scoundrels she absolutely refused to be treated as so much chattel. Yet at seventeen years old, and female, she was forced to admit she was chattel . . . worse than chattel, except for her value as a brood mare.

The sound of footsteps coming down the hallway prompted Blythe to pull her eye away from the keyhole.

"Had your fill of commerce?" Ennis called softly from the opposite end of the dim corridor. "Surely your fate has been decided by now. Come have your tea. . . . It grows cold in the sitting room."

"Much you care," Blythe hissed. Still, she thought, walking toward him, at least Ennis was attempting to raise her spirits.

"Ah . . . Blythie," he crooned, reaching out and placing his hand behind her neck with a gentle touch. "You wound me, my darling." He smiled down at her while gently rubbing her nape with his thumb. "You've always been my favorite, my pretty one, and well you know it! No one but you fires me with such a desire to create . . . to paint."

She felt his glance sweep her frame from head to toe. In the last year her slender figure had filled out admirably, and lately Ennis had been showering her with compliments, even asking her to do him the honor of allowing him to paint her portrait. He had pictured the perfect setting, he'd told her, and his description sent delicious tremors down her spine: he would place her in dappled light amid the emerald woods that led down to the sea near Hemmick Cove.

"When will you sit for me?" he urged her once again, gently shoving her against the paneled wall and pressing his thighs provocatively against her. "Would you permit me to draw you without your—"

"Lud, Ennis!" Blythe protested in a low voice. "Don't you understand? I'm to marry Kit! And soon! Probably before my father's proper mourning has ended—"

"Then there's so little time . . . ," he murmured, pulling her closer. "I've nearly persuaded my father to allow me to travel to Italy to study art with the masters when Kit is settled. If I do go, he's agreed to allow cousin Garrett to accompany me in the role of valet and traveling companion."

"Ah . . . I see," Blythe said cuttingly, pushing hard against his chest. "So once Kit and your father get their hands on my wedding portion and can afford to send you away, off you'll go!"

She stared accusingly into his pale-blue eyes, which, as always, remained unreadable. She wondered if any stab of guilt rankled his conscience. Garrett was right, she thought bleakly. If the Barton-Trevelyan match was finalized, there would be the funds, at last, to finance Ennis's sojourn abroad.

"Ah, Blythie, dear heart," Ennis soothed. "Fond of you as I am, 'tis always been the plan—"

"But don't you care if I'm taken to bed and owned, body and

soul, by your brother?" Blythe demanded. "Doesn't the thought of our lying together in that wretched Barton Bed upstairs bother you at all?"

Despite her youth, Blythe had learned that, when it came to men, there was often a way to turn a proper key in the lock. She had observed her mother, often enough, beguile her father, either with flattery or with stony looks. As Blythe stared at Ennis, her chin raised in defiance, she sensed she had stirred some spark in him. Was it because of his competition with his brother—or was it mere lust? Either way, perhaps his response could be employed to rescue her from her current predicament.

"Ennis, I can't bear the thought of Kit touching me . . . not as you have," she whispered softly, and though she was deliberately coaxing tears into her eyes, she knew the sentiment to be true.

"He'll not have you first!" Ennis growled.

"He will, unless you do," Blythe retorted. "But if you get me with child, then they'd have to let us marry, wouldn't they?"

"Ah . . . so you know something practical concerning the wages of sin. . . ."

"Is it sin to love someone?" she exclaimed. "To want—"

But Ennis wasn't really listening. He fastened his mouth on hers, and instead of nibbling around the corner of her lips in his usual, teasing fashion, coaxing her awkward ardor to respond to his fervid lust, he took care this time to kiss her properly. Like a man. Like the rake he had become, thanks to the doxies in Gorran Haven and Mevagissey who were only too happy to satisfy the sexual appetites of the younger son of one of the region's most prominent landowners. She'd heard the tittle-tattle whispered in the castle hallways and on the servants' stairs.

As she sank into Ennis's embrace, she acknowledged silently that the younger Trevelyan brother had always held a fascination for her. The two of them had evaded their elders many times over the years, sharing the same restless desire to escape the prison of village life in the prescribed worlds of

Gorran Haven and Mevagissey. On clear days, when they sat side by side on Dodman Point and talked of France across the Channel, they told each other stories of the exotic places they might find there.

She felt a delicious warmth radiate toward her throat as Ennis slipped the palm of his left hand between the two of them to gain free access to her breasts. The fingers of his right hand continued to cradle her neck as he deliberately deepened their kiss. Blythe gave a little moan and pressed herself with abandon against the length of his body.

Giving herself up to the astonishing array of sensations provoked by Ennis's knowing touch, she realized that it had always been the two of them, joined in a conspiracy to outwit their kin. This had been especially true when it came to Kit. Instinctively she and Ennis had combined forces to tease him and play him for the fool, even though he was the eldest and should have commanded their respect.

Yet, in the end, she feared that Ennis had been made to understand and accept the inevitable: that the eldest son always won the prize. By the time he was fourteen, she could see that Collis Trevelyan's younger son had determined he must seek something that was within his grasp, and that something had become his passion for art.

"I'll pose for you . . . ," she murmured, deliberately pressing her midsection firmly into his pelvis, signaling in this unmistakable fashion that she was acutely aware of his being aroused.

"Blythe," Ennis groaned, and buried his lips at the hollow of her throat.

"We can run away," she whispered, cupping his head between her hands and frantically kissing his hair. To her amazement, shrewd calculation on her part had given way to physical feelings so powerful, her legs felt as rubbery as seaweed. Ennis clutched at the back of her skirt, his fingers bunching up the fabric of her gown. Cool air kissed the tops of her silk stockings.

"Come," he mumbled. "Let us find a place where—"

"I'll sail with you to Italy," she cried softly, tightening her arms around his waist. "Please, Ennis, don't leave me! Just promise me—"

A door rattled at the end of the hallway. The couple jolted apart.

"Blythe? Now, where's that baggage got to now?" Collis Trevelyan said with exasperation. "Ah, there you are!" he exclaimed, squinting nearsightedly down the dim hallway. Blythe whirled around to face her guardian, and the hem of her skirt fell discreetly to the floor. Collis had poked his head farther out the library door. "At least you weren't spying through the keyhole. Come, everyone," he called over his shoulder to his companions inside the book-lined chamber. "The widow Barton has insisted we all stay for tea."

"As I think I made clear earlier, Collis," Blythe's mother was saying testily, "a wedding as early as September would cause a scandal. As it is, October is appalling enough, though I suppose we could manage. . . ." The mistress of Barton Hall glanced around the room. "You do realize, however, that such unseemly haste will have the gossips in Gorran Haven saying Blythe's enceinte and—"

"All the better if she is, as long as it's by Kit here," Collis said gruffly, behaving as if his ward were absent from the chamber. "I'll wager 'twon't be the first time some reckless lass stood at the altar full-in-the-belly."

Trevelyan's two sons exchanged embarrassed glances, while Blythe set her cup down with a clatter.

"Mama," she said, biting her lip to bolster her courage. She realized, now, that if she was ever to carry Ennis's child, she would need to play for time. "Father's not been in his grave a year. Surely you wouldn't wish us to show his memory such little regard. . . ."

" 'Tis not a matter of regard," Rosamund interrupted curtly. " 'Tis a matter of survival, my dear. We shall all be quite unhappy if the king's men ever garner proof of what we do along these shores in the dead of night. Unhappy—and impoverished, I'm sorry to say."

Blythe was stunned into silence. Her mother had practically promised that she would put Collis Trevelyan off for another year. But that was before the recent visit by the Revenue Men. Apparently the encounter had badly frightened Rosamund Barton.

Blythe glanced quickly over at Ennis, whose slender fingers drummed lightly against the arm of his chair. Either he was bored or he was eager to escape from the sitting room with sketchbook and charcoal in hand.

But what about me?

As if he had heard her silent cry, Ennis turned his patrician head and smiled faintly, as if to say that he, too, was defeated by the machinations of their elders. Then Blythe looked over at Kit Trevelyan, and her spirits sank even further. His visage was like a low tide on Dodman Point that laid bare treacherous shoals and dead fish best not seen in the cold light of day.

Before his illness Kit had seemed merely an earnest lad without much wit or charm, in contrast to his brother, Ennis. The older Trevelyan son could talk halfway intelligently about farming and inclement weather, but as far as Blythe had ever witnessed, if the skies turned fair, Collis's son and heir became utterly tongue-tied. Since the smallpox had ravaged his complexion, Kit had become even more withdrawn. In fact, Blythe thought morosely, her proposed betrothed was behaving like a bloody mute!

I couldn't kiss him, she told herself glumly.

And if she couldn't kiss him, how could she possibly—

"I will not marry Kit Trevelyan," Blythe blurted suddenly to his father. "I'll marry Ennis, if you wish, so you can join your precious lands with ours."

"Hold your tongue, wench!" Collis barked.

"Let Kit give over his inheritance to his brother," she boldly proposed, "and I will consent—"

"How dare you utter such outrages in front of my eldest son!" thundered Trevelyan. "They are not interchangeable, you stupid cow! Kit is my heir, and as such, he takes his duties seriously. As for his brother here, he'd like to flit around the Continent, painting naked women—"

"Father!" Ennis protested heatedly. "Italy is where all the great artists have studied! 'Tis not some frivolous scheme!"

Collis ignored the protests of his younger son and heaved his corpulent frame from the settee. He turned to address Blythe's mother.

"Rest assured, madam, that the Reverend Mr. Kent will marry this trollop to my son before the month is out. I charge you with making it plain that she'll pay a high price if she doesn't act the proper wife to him!"

"Collis, calm yourself," Rosamund admonished in her husky voice. "Let us handle this sensibly—"

"I will not marry Kit!" Blythe shouted, jumping to her feet. The elder Trevelyan brother sank deeper into his chair while Ennis suppressed a smile. "I'd rather *die*!" she cried, and bolted for the door.

Rosamund rose to try to prevent her daughter's departure.

"Let her go," Collis intoned. "The saucebox will be back beside your hearth soon enough," he added, casting a look of contempt at his deceased neighbor's wife. As much as anything, he blamed the mother's indulgent behavior for the daughter's revolting deportment.

As Blythe sped along the path that led to Dodman Point, she realized her pink kid shoes would have to be discarded. They were entirely covered with mud. And now that her left heel had sheared off, she was forced to hobble along like a wounded sand crab.

But what did it matter? she thought, stumbling forward blindly. She wouldn't need shoes. She wouldn't need anything.

They don't care about me, she cried out silently. None of them care about anything but the land . . . the bloody land! Even my mother. She's young. She'll marry again . . . she'll marry anyone who'll make her mistress of a house. Why doesn't she marry Kit, for God's sake? I'm nothing to her! Nothing to anybody! Not even Ennis . . .

Her thoughts careened like a woman gone mad as she charged up the grassy verge that led to the headlands, now sharpened to a point by raging gales and pounding surf. At the crest a slender figure stood etched against the pewter sky. Blythe pulled up shortly and promptly stumbled on the heel of her damaged shoe. Her body thumped against the soggy ground as a sharp stone bordering the edge of the path ripped her sleeve and slashed her arm.

"Blythe? Blythe!" a voice shouted against the wind.

Dazed, she rolled herself into a ball, gasping with pain that surged like a broadsword through her right arm. Someone grasped her shoulder, and she screamed with anguish. It was Garrett Teague, stumbling to his knees and calling her name.

"I won't marry him . . . I won't," she sobbed.

"I'm so sorry . . . I'm so sorry," Garrett kept repeating. His determination to be of comfort was in violent opposition to her need to be left alone. "I tried to keep you away from them . . . I tried—" he said, attempting to gather her into his arms. "I'll see that no harm comes to you, Blythe, I swear it! We'll escape from here, just as soon as—"

"Let me go!" Blythe shouted against the gusts that whipped her curled coiffure into a rat's nest. "Ennis!" she wailed. "I want *Ennis*!"

Her keening cries were as potent as her intense shame, for there could be no denying that the man who had kissed her with such ferocious passion had remained silent in front of his father, forgoing the chance to claim her for his own.

Blythe struggled to her knees, fighting Garrett's smothering embrace with all her strength. She threw herself forward against the wind. There was only a yard or two farther to reach the edge of Dodman Point. Grit and grass wedged beneath her fingernails as her hand curled around the granite cliff.

"Let me go!" she screamed. *"Let me go!"*

Chapter Five

May 15, 1994

Luke's genealogy chart swam before Blythe's eyes. She stumbled toward his desk and slumped into a wing-backed chair. Feeling dizzy, she cradled her head on her forearms on top of its tooled leather surface.

Where the hell had she been just now?

Twice her unwitting experiments had proved that, by merely touching the parchment on the chart and reading aloud a particular name, she could call up, at will, past events involving specific members of the Barton-Trevelyan-Teague families.

Surely the oddest component of these two experiences was the fact that her own observations and judgment seemed to be suspended as she became caught up in the life of her namesake. This time, much to her astonishment, she had felt like a seventeen-year-old . . . rebellious, half in love with Ennis Trevelyan, convinced that no one truly understood the unfolding events from her point of view. Somehow she had slipped into the skin of the original Blythe Barton, and while wearing it, she felt perfectly normal!

And something else was totally bizarre about this latest sojourn. From the perspective of a woman born in the twentieth century, she assessed Garrett Teague to be the kind of suitor she would find most appealing among his clan. He had dash and daring and had genuinely appeared to care about her namesake's well-being. Yet during Blythe's strange journey among Luke's eighteenth-century ancestors, Ennis was the man she had kissed with abandon—the person with whom the first Blythe Barton had later committed adultery, at least according to Kit Trevelyan.

Should she assume she was reliving some past life here, she wondered, or had she somehow witnessed the ultimate time travel? Either way, the experience was downright hair-raising.

For an instant she imagined the feat of describing the bizarre phenomenon to Christopher. Would he be struck, as she certainly was, by the astounding coincidence that a woman with her own name had betrayed her husband—also named Christopher—with his brother? Surely he would be astonished to learn that there might have existed an eighteenth-century version of their unholy triangle, turned upside down?

No, she thought grimly. Chris wouldn't be astonished at all. Rather, he'd be convinced of the necessity to have her committed to an institution for the mentally deranged.

Blythe's glance drifted to the bookcase that had pivoted sideways to admit the apparition of Luke's ancestor into the library. Warily she rose from her chair and approached the rows of shelves where the secret door had swung open. She pushed against it. Nothing. She pushed harder. Still nothing. Then she raised her hand, prepared to run her fingers along the wood to feel for a hidden catch.

What am I doing? she chastised herself. She was behaving as if she thought these phantoms were real!

A hefty Bible caught Blythe's eye. Its binding was cracked, and its leather covers were gouged with scuff marks. She pulled the heavy volume out of its slot and scanned through its end papers, where she confirmed that the dates chronicling the births and deaths of family members—written in a variety of colored inks—matched many of those specified on the chart.

On a lower shelf stood a series of estate ledgers whose dates went back, year by year, to the late seventeenth century. Skimming her fingertips along the shelf, she selected one volume labeled 1789.

"The year of Blythe and Kit's wedding . . . and the fall of the Bastille in France," Blythe murmured. "How appropriate." Like every other movie buff with a VCR, she'd seen Charles Dickens's *Tale of Two Cities*.

Flipping through the ledger's pages, she saw that they were written in an elegant hand. Suddenly Blythe's breath caught in her throat. There upon the yellowed document, written in bark-brown ink, were entries detailing the names of European cities, along with notations referring to the costs of art instruction, art supplies, and lodgings.

Ennis's grand tour!

Then something else caught her eye. Wedged behind the row of ledgers was a worn-looking diary written in flowing penmanship and brimming with detailed descriptions of the sights and scenes of Italy.

Had Lucas ever seen this? Blythe wondered excitedly.

Toward the conclusion of this daybook were passages that revealed that the journal must have been the property of Garrett Teague, his cousin Ennis's traveling companion.

> *August 11, 1791*
> *A letter from my father confirms my fears for his health. The musty books and dusty shelves make breathing in the shop intolerable for him, he writes, and urges me to return. Ennis also has received a missive from Uncle Collis that caught up with us in Naples. In it he counseled greater frugality on our part and discloses that Blythe is with child "at last." I was so severely affected by the news, I absented myself for several days from Ennis's eternal carousing. I care not for the sights or company any longer in this hot, excessive country. I crave Cornwall's clear air, knowing that if Blythe is at least nearby, I can be somewhat content. . . .*

"Blythe?"

Startled, she glanced up from the diary and discovered that her host was smiling at her from the library doorway.

"Feeling better?"

"Ah . . . hello . . . I mean, good morning, Luke," she replied, wondering if he now considered her an utter lunatic after their rendezvous in this very room during the wee hours. "Absolutely better. I . . . ah . . . I hope you don't mind my browsing your bookshelves? After spotting my name on your genealogy chart last night, I thought I'd have a good look at it in the light of day."

"Not at all," he assured her, approaching the desk. "Perhaps you'll find a clue in these old ledgers to explain the connection between our two families."

"You've caught me out." She laughed nervously, patting the tome. "I was, in actual fact, blatantly snooping, trying to see where—or if—my Bartons fit in."

"Please . . . be my guest," he said, smiling. "I haven't had the patience to wade through them page by page myself, so by all means, have at them anytime. But for now, madam," he added with mock seriousness, "your kippers await, and if you don't eat them while they're hot, Mrs. Quiller will think you don't like them and her feelings will be profoundly wounded."

Blythe quickly closed Garrett's diary and replaced it on the shelf.

"That," she said, smiling in return, "would be intolerable."

To her relief Lucas made no further reference to their nocturnal encounter. As they walked down the hallway toward the breakfast room, a thousand questions crowded Blythe's mind.

The Barton-Trevelyans had produced no heirs, so what had happened to Blythe's unborn child? Had the rebellious heiress had an affair with Garrett Teague as well? Could Chris and Ellie's recent betrayal of her be some sort of cosmic payback for the amorous misdeeds of her eighteenth-century counterpart? What if the key to her own peace of mind lay in uncovering what had happened in the family's tangled past?

This is absurd.

What would Luke think of her mental state if she advanced some theory about a two-hundred-year-old love triangle as the possible link between their two families? Good God, he'd probably evict her!

No, the likeliest explanation for what had transpired since her arrival was that she was experiencing some sort of psychosomatic reaction, triggered by the shocking events of Christopher's adultery and their subsequent breakup—a world-class version of post-traumatic stress syndrome.

Forget the past, she counseled herself, and for God's sake, keep your distance from that bizarre genealogy chart! Focus on the future.

Meanwhile, Luke had escorted her to a sun-splashed breakfast room painted a pale shade of blue. Its coved ceiling was decorated with molded white plasterwork shaped like clamshells and feathery scrolls.

"A bit peckish, I hope?" Luke asked as he removed the silver hood from an exquisite Wedgwood breakfast service that had kept her food warm on the sideboard.

"You mean hungry?" She smiled, recalling that Chris's use of that odd expression used to confuse her. "Peckish" had always sounded to her as if a person *wasn't* hungry and was merely pecking at his food. In fact, the word meant "empty." "Pardner," she drawled, "at this moment I could eat half a hog and the platter it came on."

Luke exploded with laughter.

This Englishman liked her jokes, she marveled. Perhaps she had unfairly damned an entire nation.

"Now, that is a hungry lady!" Luke replied, still chuckling. "And will you be fortified enough after this substantial repast, madam, to then proceed into Gorran Haven to secure your supplies and get the lay of the land?" he inquired with mock formality. "Mrs. Q tells me you plan to abandon us for your cottage today."

Blythe nodded, her mouth full of delicious kippers.

His smile faded, and his glance was suddenly filled with concern.

"Are you sure you're completely on the mend? You won't be too . . . isolated at the cottage?"

"I'll be fine," she assured him.

They exchanged looks, and Blythe had a strangely comforting sense that this man whom she had known a mere five days understood her better than almost anyone she could think of. Furthermore, her host and Mrs. Quiller had shown her more consideration since this nightmare began than all the people she'd left behind in California—combined. She smiled and felt some small stirring of—what? Good cheer? Perhaps it was merely a tiny flicker of happiness after inhabiting such a dark, lonely tunnel of misery this past year.

"I know you must think I'm an emotional basket case," she began as a startled reaction flickered across his face, "but I'm hoping that the worst is behind me. I may seem like I'm the hysterical type, but actually I'm not."

"I don't think you're the hysterical type at all," Luke said slowly. "When one is dealt a body blow, one needs time for the bruises to heal."

"I think that's it, exactly." She nodded. "Thank you for understanding. And thanks for everything you and Mrs. Q have done to make me feel . . . better. And welcome," she added softly. She took another bite of kippers and added with a smile she intended to be a bit flirtatious, "And if you think that ugly green tank of yours can make it into Gorran Haven, I'd love a lift."

During the next few weeks, whenever Blythe accepted Luke's open-ended invitation to four-o'clock tea at the Hall, she scrupulously avoided the library and its Barton-Trevelyan-Teague genealogy chart. Likewise, she tried hard not to stare at the stark seascapes hung on the walls of her cottage. Gradually they became merely part of the furnishings.

For the first time in her adult life, Blythe read far into the night, slept late, and went on long treks along the coastline paths that were maintained in a pristine condition by The National Trust.

Before long she had devoured Daphne du Maurier's 1936 novel *Jamaica Inn*, a full-bodied romance featuring lonely moors, Cornish smugglers, and an inn of evil repute. In early June, Luke drove her over to the Fowey Estuary region, less than an hour away, to catch a glimpse through the trees of the manor house and estate at Menabilly, the setting for the mysterious house Manderley in du Maurier's classic tale, *Rebecca.* When Blythe returned to her cottage, she read the novel far into the early hours. At its riveting conclusion she closed the book with a snap and almost blurted out her thoughts: It was better than the movie!

Movies . . . She mustn't think about the movies, she cautioned herself.

She was deeply thankful, she acknowledged as she smoothed the palm of her hand over the leather binding of the du Maurier novel, that she had neither the occasion nor the opportunity to see films or television during her first weeks in Cornwall. She was certain that such things would inevitably remind her of Chris and Ellie. And the mere thought of Chris and Ellie and the infant that would soon be born to them was enough to cause a setback in her "recovery" campaign, as she had begun to think of her simple life during the soft summer days that were floating by.

As time went on, Blythe's erratic sleeping habits, along with the soporific sea air, made her so drowsy by late afternoon that most days she stretched out on a chintz chaise facing the coastline and dozed for an hour or two.

One morning three weeks after Blythe's arrival in Cornwall, Luke stopped by the cottage to deliver a letter postmarked "Jackson, Wyoming."

"I thought it might be important," he said, preparing to set off in the direction of his car, which was parked in the grassy field next to her abode.

"Hold on a sec," Blythe said quickly, ripping open the envelope. "If nothing else, I owe you a cup of tea. C'mon in." She glanced at the first few lines of the letter and suddenly sagged against the doorjamb.

"What is it?" Luke asked quietly. "Bad news?"

Blythe continued to stare at the familiar scrawl. Finally she said, "My father's getting married again," and walked back into the cottage.

"Ah . . . well . . . that can sometimes be very tricky business, can't it?" he sympathized, following her through the door.

" 'To a real-estate lady in Jackson named Bertha Pyle,' " she quoted from the letter. Her eyes scanned the bottom of the page and she blurted incredulously, "He's actually done what he threatened—put the ranch up for sale. He's moving into town for good!"

"Selling up . . . after all those years the place has been in your family. What a shame."

Blythe pointed to the top of the second page. "He says he's deeding ten acres to me and ten acres to my sister 'on opposite sides of the Snake River,' " she read, and gave a short, sarcastic laugh. Then her eyes glued to one sentence as her mouth settled into a grim line. Next, she glanced at her watch and then looked over at Luke. "After we have a cup of tea, would you let me use your telephone?"

"Dad? This is Blythe! In Cornwall. England. I got your letter."

There was a long pause on the other end of the line. She imagined her father covering the phone and mouthing her name to the "real-estate lady from Jackson" who had obviously been the one to suggest her sixty-two-year-old father sell the ranch.

"Blythe!" The senior Barton sounded happy to hear from her. "How's it goin'?"

How's it goin'?

As far as Blythe was concerned, the past year was one for the record books! Her grandmother died, her husband left her for her sister, and now her childhood home was on the auction block and her father was acting like an idiot over some slick-talking saleswoman, anxious to parcel out the Double Bar B into ranchettes!

"I'm fine," she answered calmly. "Congratulations are in order, I see."

"That's right," he replied. "We eloped last Friday. To Mexico."

"Wow . . . ," Blythe breathed. She wondered if Ellie had steered the happy couple toward the same wedding chapel that she and Chris had used. "Well . . . congratulations again to you and your bride."

"Well . . . thank you. I'll pass that along to Bertha."

Pause.

"Look, Dad," Blythe said crisply, "I thought before anything out there was a done deal, I'd offer to buy the ranch myself. Thanks to my sister, I'm pretty rich these days."

"Too late," her father said cheerfully. "Signed the papers yesterday."

"You did?" she gasped, barely keeping her response from sounding like a coyote's wail.

"Yep. You got any objections?"

"Well . . . I-I just wanted to discuss a few things with you . . . you know . . . before everything was final. . . ."

"It's final. Already filed at the county seat. Your deed and Ellie's too."

"Oh."

"You got the parcel at the bend in the river . . . where we buried Mom and Matt . . . and Grandma, okay?"

Blythe felt tears sting her eyelids.

"That's very sweet of you, Dad," she managed to say. "That was my favorite spot."

With the portion of her brain that wasn't feeling like an abandoned child, Blythe knew that her father had every right to do as he pleased at this stage of his life. He'd been a slave to the Double Bar B all his adulthood, doing his level best to continue as a rancher in a vastly changing economy. Herding dudes instead of cattle just wasn't Will Barton's thing. A widower for the last twenty-four years, he earned whatever rest and joy he could get. If Bertha Pyle had helped him achieve it—so be it.

"Well, then . . . ," her father said after an uncomfortably long pause, "I guess that's about it. This call's costin' you a mighty mint."

"As I said before, I can afford it."

"Look, Blythe," Will Barton said gruffly, "I'm . . . I'm sorry for the fix you're in. But just remember one thing. You're a lot stronger'n Ellie. You gotta take that into account."

Why? Blythe wanted to scream.

And before he could say anything else or she could burst into tears, she bade farewell.

"You take care now. My regards to your new wife."

Soon after this conversation Luke began to make a habit of swinging by the cottage several times a week around noon in his battered Land Rover with the offer of a lift into Gorran Haven or Mevagissey for lunch and various shopping expeditions. Blythe invariably accepted his invitations, grateful for any activity that kept her occupied.

Once a week, at least, he would choose a coastal village to show her.

"Are you of a mind for crab sandwiches today?" he inquired one morning before whisking her off to Polperro, a fishing hamlet that clung to a rocky cliff and was steeped in smuggling lore.

The owner of Barton Hall kept a fourteen-foot sailboat on a trailer rig behind the pony stable and, on sunny days, took her to Portholland and Portloe, tiny seaside villages whose harbors were so small and treacherous, even motor crafts had to wait for calm seas before trying to pass the jetties.

On one of their weekly outings Blythe summoned the nerve to ask Luke why his Land Rover had so many dents crimping all four fenders.

"Mother," he pronounced with an amused smile. "Before

she left to live with my sister in Canada, she ran the estate for a few years after my father passed away. To her exceedingly genteel way of thinking, it was impolite to constantly sound one's horn, so I'm afraid her method of creeping forward to make her way through a knot of sheep put rather a lot of wear and tear on our car. Ah! Here we are," he announced, pointing through the windshield at the entrance to Trelissick, an immense garden adjacent to the charming King Harry Ferry river crossing and maintained by The National Trust. "Tea first?"

As the mild summer days drifted by, Blythe was amazed to discover that her existence in Cornwall had become a total reversal of the way she and Christopher had lived, especially when they had been working together.

During those brutal months of full-scale production, she had hardly slept for days at a time. She was usually up before dawn, seeing to it that the interior sets were in place, or that the exterior shots were properly "dressed" before shooting began in the early-morning hours. There were wardrobes to coordinate, sketches to be made, workers to supervise, plus the constant pressure of anticipating total disasters, or at the very least, major changes in the shooting schedule due to bad weather, script revisions, or temperamental actors.

As she thought back on those years, she realized that her job as Chris's wife included an equal number of responsibilities off the set.

"Darling, have the car pick me up at five-thirty, will you?"

"You said you wanted the driver at five."

"Well, I've changed my mind."

As usual, she had reached for the phone.

"Where's my bloody shirt?"

"What shirt?"

"The one I wear with my bloody tuxedo!"

"I had it delivered yesterday. It's in your closet."

"Well, I can't find it in my closet!"

"Have you looked?"

"Could you look, darling? I'm having a bath."

She had donned her robe and let Chris sink into the waiting tub.

"Did you get the airline tickets?"

"I put them in your briefcase."

"Am I on the aisle?"

"I requested it."

"Well, did I get it?"

"Look on your boarding pass."

"I can't find it. I've got to call Michael. Be an angel. . . ."

She had, of course, found the tickets where he'd stashed them in his desk drawer. He was on the aisle. In first class.

Finding time to get a haircut herself, or to slip away for lunch with her women friends, became nearly impossible. Eventually the friends had fallen by the wayside, and she kept her hair shoulder length to eliminate frequent trips to Joseph Martin Salon on Rodeo Drive.

When she allowed herself to consider the sexual component of their marriage, Blythe's musings had a tendency to put her in a deep funk. On many days in her first weeks in Painter's Cottage, she stared for hours at the English Channel outside her windows. As she sipped a mug of tea, she sometimes allowed her thoughts to recall the marathon of carnal exploits Chris had apparently committed in his director's trailer on the studio's back lot, to say nothing of Ellie's Santa Monica loft.

During the last year of her marriage Chris and her love life had been erratic, to put it mildly. For months now she had tried to identify the moment when it had all begun to change. She recalled those grueling trips, flying back and forth from Los Angeles to Jackson . . . her fatigue and worry about Grandma Barton's agonizing decline . . . Chris's total absorption with preproduction for *In Kenya*. And later . . . his affair with Ellie. Why hadn't she figured out what was going on much sooner?

Was there something wrong with her . . . some terrible lack? Blythe wondered, gazing out to sea. Were Ellie's legs that much trimmer than hers? Was her sister's matching 36-C bust somehow more enticing than hers? Or was the second Mrs. Barton-Stowe's chatter about illustrating bunnies and balloons and "little engines that could" more scintillating than the conversations she'd had with Chris about multimillion-dollar film budgets and the nefarious habits of studio executives?

Granted, Ellie's most recent series of children's books had been moderately successful, and her long-term future in her field had finally shown some promise. However, the fact that Blythe's career as a production designer in the glamorous world of feature films was a soaring success had only stoked the fires of her sister's perpetual discontent. Ellie's successes were never enough, in her view, and her resentment of Blythe had been palpable for years.

When Blythe's thoughts careened in these unhealthy directions, her antidote during the first month she spent in her coastal retreat had been to undertake another hike along the cliffs.

And as she began truly to rest and relax, a weight that she could only identify as the "It's Always Something Reflex" simply melted away.

"I tramped seven miles yesterday," she announced proudly to Luke as she climbed into the front passenger seat of his wheezing four-wheel-drive vehicle late one morning on a day in mid-June. "I did the shorter National Trust walk along the South Coast Path from Hemmick Beach, around Dodman Point, and on to Gorran Haven. From there I took the road back to the cottage through Boswinger."

"Good heavens!" he said admirably. "You should be more than fit enough by now for that pony trek I proposed a while back."

"Different muscles," she replied, and immediately changed the subject. "What's our itinerary today?"

"Just a jaunt into Mevagissey, I'm afraid," he replied. "I'd like to be back home by noon before my son arrives from boarding school. Would you join us for luncheon?"

"Richard? He'll be here today?" Blythe exclaimed. Her incredulous tone disclosed her amazement that Luke hadn't mentioned his son's expected return before this. "How wonderful for you," she added. She gazed through the windshield at the sparkling blue-green sea as thundering waves rolled toward shore in frothy white sequence. "What a heavenly place for a child to spend his summers. What plans have you two made?"

"Oh, there are lots of things a ten-year-old can find to amuse himself with around the Hall," Luke said with a shrug.

Blythe looked at her companion quizzically. "But what kinds of things do you two enjoy doing together? Sailing? Hikes?"

Her host, who had been amazingly sensitive to her fragile emotional state when she'd first arrived at Barton Hall, pursed his lips in a line that obviously indicated annoyance with her probing.

"We'll decide those things as we go along, I expect," he said evenly.

None of your business, was the way Blythe heard his response.

His unexpectedly curt reaction elicited an unwelcome memory of Christopher Stowe, who had a similar habit of distancing himself from anyone who asked him to confront something unpleasant.

"I expect you will," Blythe replied quietly. She turned her head away from Luke to stare out the car window.

Clearly she was treading on dangerous ground. She'd asked a perfectly normal question and had felt a proverbial steel door close. Maybe there was some problem with the boy. Lindsay's death had to have been traumatic for both of them. Perhaps . . .

Englishmen! she thought with sudden exasperation. Hadn't she learned yet that they were genetically incapable of declaring what they felt? In the old days Blythe's full-time occupation had become making the attempt to figure out what was bothering Christopher at any particular moment. As she and Luke rode along in silence, she continued to stare through the windshield and silently vowed that she wasn't ever going to take on the role of Mind Reader again.

"What's wrong, darling?" she used to query Chris when his lips would flatten into a straight line as Luke's were doing now. "Tell me what's going on."

"What do you mean?" Chris would reply.

Let me guess!

That was what it boiled down to: a guessing game wherein she always turned out to be the one with The Problem. As Blythe looked back on eleven years with Christopher Stowe, it dawned on her that she'd always been the one to do the emotional heavy lifting.

Well, not anymore.

"No point in ridin' the same ornery horse," a voice rang in her head. The expression had been one of Grandma Barton's favorites. But why in heaven was Blythe attracted by the sophistication and urbanity of British men, while repelled by the closed-off way they dealt with what went on in their heads and hearts?

"Richard's birthday is in three weeks' time," Luke said at length, breaking the silence that had followed their tense exchange. "We're having a few of the local children over and will celebrate by taking them to the village fete in Gorran Haven. Any chance you could be there to lend Mrs. Q and me some moral support? I've not had much practice with the preadolescent set."

"Neither have I," Blythe replied coolly.

Silence.

"Blythe . . . I'm sorry . . . it's just . . ."

"What?"

She turned to gaze at his profile. Luke stared ahead at the road. He appeared to be struggling to say something that would explain his odd behavior.

"I just thought . . . you might enjoy seeing the village fete . . . a bit of local color and all that."

He had struggled—and failed. Well, at least the man was trying to make amends for his testiness, she thought grudgingly. Offering a helping hand with his son's birthday party was the least she could do after his kindnesses to her the previous month. She reached across the armrest between them and placed her palm lightly on his sleeve.

"Look, Luke . . . I'd be glad to do what I can to give you a hand," she said quietly. "But I hope you won't expect a Hollywood production."

As soon as they completed their errands in Mevagissey, they returned to Barton Hall and, at a quarter to twelve, retired to the small sitting room, glasses in hand, to wait for Richard's arrival.

Every few minutes Luke glanced at his watch nervously as he sipped his sherry.

"Ten more minutes to go before you can declare him late for lunch." Blythe smiled teasingly. "How far away is his boarding school from here?"

"A couple of hours' drive . . . Shelby Hall is on the east side of Dartmoor, in the county of Devon."

Blythe wondered silently why Luke hadn't made the trip to fetch his son.

"As we're waiting," he said, taking another sip from a glass shaped like a large crystal thimble, "perhaps you can give me your thoughts about my idea of converting Barton Hall into a country hotel."

"I *have* been thinking about it, actually. . . ."

She hesitated. She could simply give him her professional view of the enormous task involved in turning this breathtakingly beautiful but decrepit castle into a working hostelry for discriminating guests. Or she could advance an idea she'd had that would be much more likely to succeed commercially, require far less capital to launch, and might plunge the two of them up to their necks in a project that both excited and petrified her.

"And?" Luke pressed.

"Well . . . ," Blythe started slowly. "Remember how you told me the reason Barton Hall was a hall instead of a castle, even though in this incarnation it is a castle—if you follow me so far?"

"Sort of," he laughed.

"You explained that, centuries ago, 'Barton' meant 'farm.' 'Menabilly Barton,' as you pointed out, means 'the farm at Menabilly,' next to the manor house. And this Barton, near Dodman Point, was just a farm during the days of William the Conqueror, correct?"

"Ten sixty-six and all that. Yes, go on."

"Well," Blythe said, inhaling deeply and feeling as if she were about to pitch a film idea to the Paramount suits, "Barton Hall could be a farm again . . . a very profitable farm . . . a flower farm."

"You mean raise tulips and hollyhocks and such?" Luke asked skeptically.

"No . . . not that!" Blythe corrected him excitedly. "You've got your stock already in place. . . . You can sell plants, seedlings, and seeds for some of the most beautiful rhododendrons, azaleas, and camellias I've ever seen. A mail-order business! You know, ordering goods by post!"

She could see she'd gotten Luke's attention.

"Postal shopping?" Luke said with a thoughtful expression. "You mean you think we could make a go of selling what we grow in the garden here?"

"That's part of my plan, yes," Blythe replied. "And the beauty of it is, you won't have to have hordes of tourists invading your private household. You and Mrs. Q won't have to run yourselves ragged trying to please forty finicky hotel guests at a crack."

She took another deep breath.

"One of my ideas would be to convert the pony stable into a school for avid gardeners. Perhaps these very few special visitors could come to Barton Hall for a fortnight, take classes from really knowledgeable gardening experts and landscape designers, while paying to stay in Painter's Cottage or in a few rooms in the castle's guest wing, done up à la Laura Ashley, as you suggested. I think you could charge a fortune," she added.

Luke cocked his head and nodded thoughtfully.

"You mean that Mrs. Q would manage a small B-and-B-type arrangement?"

"An elegant bed and a scrumptious breakfast for a select—and wealthy—few. You could play the genial host the way you do so well." She smiled mischievously.

"And do you think we could really make it pay?" Luke wondered, a muted look of hope beginning to dawn on his face.

"Yes!" she said enthusiastically, as if the L.A. Lakers had just won a big one. "And I have another idea for this scheme," she ventured.

"Good heavens," Luke laughed. "Our Cornish air has really charged your brain cells."

Just then a horn sounded outside their window. Luke's housekeeper stuck her head through the movable bookcase.

"They're here!" Mrs. Quiller said excitedly.

"Let's talk about this later," Luke said, rising from his chair. "It all sounds quite intriguing."

Such a response, spoken by an Englishman, could mean either "It's a brilliant idea" or "It will never work, you silly woman." Blythe had had too much experience with True Brits of the male persuasion not to wonder which sentiment the owner of Barton Hall had really been expressing.

Meanwhile, he exited the sitting room, strode to the heavy front door, and opened it. From inside the hallway, Blythe watched with surprise as a striking young woman with flawless skin and golden hair twisted into a chic chignon at the nape of her swanlike neck stepped out of a Jaguar she'd parked in the gravel driveway. The car was of the very same midnight-blue as Blythe's model, now stored on blocks in the garage of her new condo in Brentwood, California.

From the visitor's choice in automobiles to her camel-colored cashmere sweater and matching skirt, the lady had taste. In fact, the stunning-looking creature appeared to possess the perfect features and impeccable grooming of a Princess Diana, coupled with the self-conscious voluptuousness of a *Penthouse* pet.

Blythe also noted that the blond beauty had ignored Luke's recommendation that visitors dress casually in Cornwall. Blythe's jeans suddenly seemed woefully inappropriate for a luncheon celebrating Richard's homecoming.

"Chloe . . . welcome . . . and thank you so much for fetching Richard for me," Luke said heartily.

"A godmother's work is never done," the woman replied with a warm smile for the father of her young charge. From Blythe's vantage point the visitor seemed somehow to be standing closer to Luke than he was to her.

Luke turned to face the youngster who stood stiffly beside the car. The lad looked small and pinched in his blue blazer and school tie. His light-brown hair was carefully combed, and his pale face, unlike Luke's tanned countenance, undoubtedly made him his mother's child.

"Hello, son," his father said, extending his hand formally.

"Hello, Father," Richard Teague mumbled shyly, shaking his hand.

They both then fell silent as Richard gazed down at his shining shoe tops. Blythe thought she detected in Luke's expression a look of fatherly concern tempered by British restraint. It appeared to her as if he'd like to give his child a hug, so why didn't he? Instead, he assumed his role of perfect host.

"Mrs. Quiller has lunch waiting," he said smoothly, "and I want you both to meet our guest who's staying at Painter's Cottage."

"The summer let?" Chloe wondered aloud. She cast a languid glance in Blythe's direction. A small frown suddenly creased her forehead. "You've invited her to lunch?"

Would you like me to eat in the kitchen? Blythe wondered silently.

The new arrival surveyed Blythe from head to toe. "How delightful that you could join us," the woman added, smiling faintly.

"Blythe, may I introduce Richard's godmother and a family friend of long standing, Chloe Acton-Scott, who lives in London. Chloe, this is Blythe Stowe."

"Ah . . . from America," Chloe replied before Blythe could respond. "You're in the motion-picture industry, aren't you?" she asked. Her cool green eyes continued to gaze at Blythe appraisingly. "I expect you've been appreciating Cornwall's isolation. Such a lovely place to get away from it all."

Does everyone in Cornwall watch CNN? Blythe wondered. Perhaps she could plead a "mee-grain," as Chloe would undoubtedly pronounce it, and head back to her cottage before lunch. However, at that moment Luke's housekeeper appeared in the open front door.

"Hello, Mrs. Acton-Scott," Mrs. Q said politely. "Welcome home, young man!" she added, and then threw her arms around the lad. "Come, in with you now, and let's be washin' your hands." To Luke she advised, "Luncheon is on the sideboard, sir, so just help yourselves. Young Richard and I'll just be checkin' on the summer puddin', won't we, Dicken, my boy?"

"Dicken?" Blythe repeated. "Is that your nickname?"

"It's what Mrs. Q likes to call me," Richard replied, smiling bashfully.

Blythe smiled back. "I like it, too."

Mrs. Quiller and her employer's son walked arm in arm ahead of the trio, who were left standing at the entrance to Barton Hall chatting aimlessly about the fine weather Cornwall was thus far enjoying in June.

"Well . . . ah . . . shall we go in to lunch?" Luke asked abruptly.

"I'll just get my cases," Chloe said with a smile reserved exclusively for her host.

"Here, let me," Luke intervened quickly, and followed Chloe to the rear of the Jaguar. Blythe watched silently as he lifted the visitor's elegant luggage out of the car and proceeded into the house. "Perhaps you'd like to freshen up before we sit down?"

"In the blue bedroom?" Chloe inquired expectantly. By this time she and Luke had mounted the grand staircase while Blythe remained standing at the front door. "I'm looking forward to a new view of the Channel."

The lord of the manor—doing double duty as the butler—hesitated on the carpeted landing.

"Mrs. Quiller's made up the yellow room in the guest wing . . . out of habit, I'm afraid," he said over his shoulder. Then he continued up the stairway, adding, "I hope you don't mind?"

Blythe had convalesced in that sunny chamber, she remembered with a start. She had stared for hours at every inch of those wall coverings that age had mellowed to a warm, buttery color. As she continued to gaze at Luke's and Chloe's retreating backs, she wondered how close to the master suite the blue room might be located.

"At least I won't run into the furniture at night," Chloe assured her host as she followed in his wake. However, her tone of voice had gone from sultry to Arctic Circle. "I rather expect there to be a plaque with my name on the entrance to the yellow room by now, Lucas."

To Blythe's surprise it was Richard who ultimately ate his lunch in the kitchen. And considering Chloe Acton-Scott's interminable and content-free exchange with Luke about people Blythe had never met, she concluded that (a) the woman was certainly beautiful to look at; (b) she was no rocket scientist; and (c) most men would never notice that fact. As far as Blythe was concerned, she would have vastly preferred joining Master Teague and Mrs. Q in the servants' quarters.

* * *

Mrs. Acton-Scott, a divorcée with no children, remained a guest at Barton Hall for several days. One morning Luke and she arrived at Painter's Cottage with an invitation to join them for luncheon at the Old Ferry Inn in Bodinnick, near Fowey.

Chloe's shoulder-length honey-colored hair had been allowed to escape from its sophisticated chignon and, today, was held back sleekly by a smart black velvet headband. She had donned an elegant pair of gray gabardine trousers and a forest-green cashmere pullover that enhanced both her come-hither figure and her sea-green eyes.

Blythe, in contrast, still had on the first thing she'd slipped into after rising from bed: a faded pink running suit she preferred to wear when she sat down alone to do some sketching.

"Ah . . . ," Christopher was wont to comment whenever he perceived his wife choosing comfort over style, "I see Minnie Rag Bag's with us today."

Six thousand miles from Hollywood, this same item of clothing had somehow acquired a blotch of tea absentmindedly spilled on the fabric between her breasts during her morning's labors. Holding her sketch pad under her chin, Blythe politely declined her English host's invitation to lunch, explaining that she was deeply engrossed in du Maurier's *Frenchman's Creek* and was sure they'd forgive her if she begged off.

"It takes a foreigner, doesn't it, Luke, to make us appreciate our own authors?" Chloe said cheerfully. "Although personally I find du Maurier's writing a bit swoony."

"Well," Blythe replied, "you know how sappy Americans can be." Then she added sweetly, "I'm loving every word. Enjoy your lunch."

Bitch.

The woman made her feel like a clod, Blythe thought indignantly.

She managed to maintain a polite smile plastered on her lips until Luke had put the Land Rover in reverse and headed down the dirt track that led away from her cliffside abode.

An hour later Blythe was still in a foul mood. The billowing clouds of midmorning had congealed into an overcast sky, and the wind was starting to whip the waves into whitecaps across Veryan Bay. The Old Ferry Inn would be gloomy indeed on a day like this, she concluded with satisfaction.

Blythe changed into jeans and a sweater, donned her green Barbour jacket, and struck out toward Hall Walk, sketchbook in hand. She and Luke had not had an opportunity to further discuss her proposal to parlay his estate's magnificent gardens into a paying attraction. Meanwhile, she hoped to complete her blueprint outlining places on the estate where propagation and growing areas, plant stock storage, and the office and sales points might be situated on his property with a minimum of disruption to life at the Hall itself.

The leafy coolness along the shaded path served to remind Blythe once again how grateful she was to have found such a soothing refuge in Cornwall. She shifted her sketchbook from one hand to another, preparing to make the final ascent to the castle itself. Her new project with Luke, she realized thankfully, was the kind of all-consuming enterprise that would serve both to keep her from dwelling on the past, and provide her with a means of reentering the world of floral and landscape design.

And most important, Blythe thought with a sudden, overwhelming sense of her own isolation, she needed to be connected to something!

The opportunity to create Barton Hall Nurseries here in enchanted Cornwall was certainly the most appealing way she could think of to avoid the people and places in California that reminded her of Chris and Ellie and the scandal that had blown her life apart.

As Blythe emerged from the "White Rabbit's Tunnel," as she had come to call the path leading from her cottage to the Hall, she noticed a gate near the stable yard with a rickety trellis arching above it. Suddenly she was reminded of the walled kitchen garden into which the hidden door leading from the library's secret storeroom had opened when Garrett Teague had—

She peered through the gate's wooden slats. Sure enough, greeting her gaze was a weed-strewn vegetable garden, and beyond, a window in the castle's stone wall through which she glimpsed rows of leather-bound books. Where would that hidden door have been? she wondered.

Just forget it! she admonished herself sternly.

Now that she had a better view of the area, she could see that, in fact, Luke and John Quiller had put about one quarter of the walled garden in cultivation this year. The small patch provided enough vegetables, Blythe supposed, to meet the needs of Luke's reduced household. The stooped old man, accompanied by young Richard Teague, was hoeing weeds. Mrs. Q's husband expertly dug into the soil with a hand spade, assisted by Luke's son, who gamely yanked the unwanted vegetation out of the ground and threw it into an ancient wooden wheelbarrow.

"Good morning, Mr. Quiller," Blythe called. "Hello, Richard. Mind if I make a few sketches while you work?"

"Not t'all, miss," Quiller replied, his unshaven face bristling a welcoming smile. "Dicken and me wouldn't mind a bit a company, would we, now, lad?"

"Hello, Mrs. Stowe," Richard mumbled, and looked down at his pint-sized rubber gardening boots.

"Please . . . call me Blythe," she replied, approaching the edge of the section where they were working. "Don't let me disturb you."

She sat down on a wooden bench placed against the castle wall near the library window and began to sketch a proposed design for a vegetable and herb garden. Her mind was fired with ideas that bubbled up from her recollection of a similar plan that her grandmother had once devised.

"Impulse items," Lucinda Barton had explained, pointing to clusters of rosemary, lemon basil, and thyme. Vacationers heading south on Highway 89 out of Yellowstone Park had been seduced into stopping at the small plant-filled lean-to positioned at the entrance of the Double Bar B ranch, nine miles outside Jackson. The potted varieties were arranged attractively near the cash register. "If you display herb plants where the customers pay for their seed packets and flowers, you're bound to make a sale," she advised. "Then they take along a catalog while they're there, and the next thing y'know, they've placed a nice big order by mail."

Inspired by her grandmother's innate business acumen, Blythe quickly put the finishing touches on her design for an ambitious kitchen garden. Her thoughts drifted to pleasant memories of late-summer days spent with her grandmother gathering wilted wildflowers in the shadow of the Grand Tetons. Both she and Grandma Barton had fitted themselves out with long woven-wicker baskets shaped like a quiver for arrows. When they returned from these arduous expeditions, they dumped their harvest onto newspaper spread out on the long hand-hewn kitchen table. Then they'd carefully shake the seeds from their pods, identifying each type with a brief notation before twisting their bounty into small squares of paper, which they later sold to tourists driving down from Yellowstone.

Suddenly Blythe recalled a vision of Ellie, alone outside the kitchen window, sitting forlornly on the swing made from an old rubber tire that their father, Will, had attached to a branch of a lone pine tree. Her sister must have been around six years old, which meant Blythe would have been twelve. The previous year their mother had crumpled to the ground on a windy spring day while she was hanging out the family laundry—felled instantly by a blood clot that traveled from her heart to her brain. After that event Ellie had never wanted to help with gathering seeds.

It was often during these hours Blythe spent with Lucinda that the old lady reminisced about her pioneer forebears and her girlhood growing up on a neighboring ranch. She delighted in telling stories and repeating sayings that always seemed, to the impressionable preteenager Blythe had been, chock-full of rustic wisdom.

"As your ol' granddad used to say, cowgirl," Grandma Barton concluded most seed-harvesting sessions, "ask no more—and give no less—than honesty, courage, loyalty, generosity, and fairness. Stand by this Barton Code, m'girl, and it'll stand by you."

The reward for an afternoon of such sustained effort was a cup of tea and a scone made from a recipe Lucinda swore had been handed down, generation to generation, from the original Barton Cornish ancestor—whoever that might be.

Blythe was startled from her reverie by the presence of someone looking over her shoulder.

"That doesn't look much like our garden!" Luke's ten-year-old son scowled, pointing at the precise schematic Blythe had been making.

"It doesn't, does it?" she agreed cheerfully. "It's a plan for how the garden could be if your dad and Mr. Quiller decided to go whole hog."

"Whole what?" Richard asked, confused.

"Really put this garden back in shape," she translated. "Got any ideas where a nice big parsley patch could go?"

"There!" the boy responded emphatically, pointing to a section of open ground in the middle of her drawing. "That part of the garden gets lots of sun . . . at least when it bothers to shine," he amended, glancing overhead at the dark clouds scudding across the sky.

Blythe burst out laughing, and Richard allowed himself to smile, pleased with the little joke he had inadvertently made.

"Teatime!" Mrs. Q called from the kitchen door. "Oh, Mrs. Stowe, how nice to see you. Perhaps I should be layin' tea in the sitting room?"

"Naw . . . ," Blythe responded in her best Wyoming accent. "I reckon your cozy kitchen sounds much more invitin', don'cha think so, Dicken?"

"Yes, ma'am," he agreed, only for politeness' sake, Blythe

realized instantly. After all, he was being educated in a British boarding school, where manners counted for a lot.

Young Richard Teague was neither rude nor friendly. Rather, he seemed . . . watchful. Like Blythe and Ellie, he had lost his mother at a tragically early age, and she suddenly had an overwhelming urge to put her arms around him right there in the middle of the kitchen garden.

Instead, Blythe ruffled his chestnut hair that was many shades lighter than Luke's dark mane. Richard shot her a startled look, as if such casual physical contact was definitely not what he was used to.

"You sound kinda like the Wyoming cowboys where I grew up," she commented as they trooped into Mrs. Quiller's domain. "Except they all say it this way: 'Yesss, may-yam!' " she drawled.

"Yesss, may-yam!" Richard mimicked her, and everybody laughed.

They sipped their tea sitting around the trestle table that was positioned near a wall at the far end of the large rectangular kitchen that had served the household when the castle's fifty-seven rooms had been fully occupied. A platoon of copper pots in a myriad of sizes hung from iron hooks overhead, along with large metal skewers, chestnut roasters, and quaint kitchen implements whose functions had long been superseded in most modern households by toasters, waffle irons, and Cuisinarts. An enormous cast-iron Aga cooker, stoked now by an oil furnace, not only served as a stove, but heated the room as well.

Blythe glanced out the kitchen window and was startled to see Luke loading suitcases into the trunk of Chloe's Jaguar parked to the rear of the castle. The striking blond woman had donned a beige Burberry trench coat lined in a muted tan-and-burgundy-colored tartan. Her hair had returned to its sophisticated chignon, and she looked like a member of the royal family about to return to Kensington Palace after a weekend at Balmoral.

Blythe gazed down at her blue jeans. The cuffs were ringed with mud.

Meanwhile, Luke's two Labradors padded in anxious circles around Chloe's car. Blythe caught Mrs. Quiller's eye as she shifted her attention back to their snug little group.

"Mrs. Acton-Scott will have rain on the trip up to London this evenin', I'm afeard," Mrs. Q commented in her elongated Cornish speech.

"Perhaps she'll be stayin' over to St. Austell, with her parents, afore she go up-country," her husband suggested.

"No . . . she's a-headed back to her flat, I know that," the housekeeper asserted sagely. "She'd always rather be stayin' here than with her parents." She put a gentle hand on Richard's shoulder. "Be a fine gentleman, and run out to say your good-byes, there's a good lad."

Reluctantly Richard rose and tramped loudly down the servants' hallway and out the rear door, banging his hand against the wooden wainscoting every few feet.

Blythe couldn't resist witnessing the departure of Richard's godmother. She watched the boy emerge from the back door and dutifully kiss Chloe's cheek. Luke did likewise and handed his houseguest into the driver's side of the car. Father and son stood side by side and waved as the Jaguar rolled past Barton Hall's rounded west turret and headed down the shaded drive.

Then Blythe watched as Richard slipped his hand into his father's. He began to talk to him excitedly. More than a little curious, Blythe continued to observe their exchange, oddly gratified to see that Luke had paused to give his son his full attention. He nodded several times, and then the pair disappeared inside the door. Soon Blythe could hear them, along with the two dogs, approaching the kitchen.

"Have you saved a cup for me?" Luke asked, smiling at the congenial group sitting around Mrs. Quiller's table. Derek and Beryl wagged their tails enthusiastically to punctuate their master's request.

"I've just put the kettle back on, sir," responded his housekeeper. "Let me get you a cup."

"Would it be too much trouble to bring it through to the sitting room?"

"Of course not," Mrs. Q replied cheerfully, reaching for a small tray.

"Blythe . . . do you have a minute to continue our chat about the garden? I want to hear about the rest of your scheme."

"She's made some drawings, Father," Richard volunteered.

"Yes, you mentioned that," Luke said, glancing at the sketch pad resting on the table near Blythe's teacup. "Well, I'd very much like to see what this world-famous landscape designer has been up to."

"World-famous?" Blythe laughed. "The only two things I designed professionally before I went into the movie business were a cactus garden and a fish pond for friends. Hold your praise until you see what I can do."

"I want to come too!" Richard demanded.

"Dicken has had some awfully good ideas about where to put the parsley," Blythe put in quickly.

For an instant Luke hesitated. The expression on his face at first seemed to welcome the notion of allowing his son to participate in their discussion. Then a look of resolve invaded his features, and he directed Richard to remain with the Quillers while he, Blythe, and his two dogs decamped for the sitting room.

Chapter Six

June 20, 1994

"Another cup?" Luke asked Blythe as Mrs. Q did her vanishing act with her tray, exiting into the pantry behind the movable bookcase.

"No, thanks . . . ," she replied, watching as Luke poured himself some tea.

Blythe couldn't get over Richard's crestfallen look when Luke refused his request to allow the boy to join them. She was continually amazed how this surprisingly easygoing Englishman would suddenly assume the stance that his son was better seen than heard. On the other hand, the companionship of his dogs, Beryl and Derek, was always welcome. At the moment the Labradors were curled up in front of the fireplace, snoring.

"So?" her host was saying, smiling wryly. "What's the rest of the scheme you were about to tell me when you first proposed we turn this hallowed family legacy into a commercial nursery?"

"We're talking about just the gardens themselves, and the adjacent properties," Blythe corrected him.

"And the pony stables . . . for the gardening classes."

"You only keep three ponies there," Blythe replied dryly. "Can't you stash them in the old piggery?"

"Done!" Luke snapped his fingers, his eyes alight with humor. He really could be quite charming, she thought, as he tilted his head against the wing-backed chair and looked at her with an amused expression. He pointed at her sketchbook and grinned engagingly, saying, "Why do I think, Ms. Barton-Stowe, that you've got something else up your sleeve?"

"Because I do," she said matter-of-factly. She whipped open her pad and showed him her blueprint for the entire proposed operation. "Barton Hall Nurseries—"

"Nurseries?" he interrupted. "Plural?"

"I'll get to that in a minute," she replied. "What I propose," she announced, pausing for emphasis, "is a combined commercial enterprise, educational center, and cultural institute. If we can pull this off, Luke, the Inland Revenue will eventually get off your back."

"Well, that would be a blessing."

"You sound skeptical, but hear me out."

He took a long, scalding sip of tea and shook his head ruefully.

"No wonder you Bartons made such a success of it in America. You've got such amazing optimism and energy. . . ."

"Quiet," she commanded. "I'm serious. You use the existing plants and shrubs in your twenty-five acres as your basic growing stock and your showroom, so to speak. Customers can wander the grounds with a shopping list that we provide them, ticking off the types of plants they would like to have in their own gardens." She pointed to a series of areas shaded lavender that she'd drawn next to the existing garden. "Over here are the growing areas: A, B, C, D, away from the public's eye. That's where the smaller plants you sell are raised." She pointed to another section of her master plan, shaded green. "No one goes beyond this hedge, here, guaranteeing the privacy of the castle itself. Next to the growing areas is a rockery, plus a section for sales to the trade—other nurseries and large public gardens like the ones at Trelissick and Glendurgan."

"Don't they already have flowers?" Luke asked blandly.

"They don't have Rebecca, do they? You told me that your father and grandfather developed that rhododendron just for their amusement. And you can bet those National Trust gardens will want examples of the sexy new varieties you develop: Jamaica Inn . . . Frenchman's Creek. . . . Why not make Barton Hall Nurseries and their world-famous rhododendrons, azaleas, and camellias a tribute to the local heroine and sell du Maurier's novels at the gift shop—along with fabulous gardening books, great gardening gloves, locally crafted garden pottery, top-of-the-line spades, hoes, pitchforks, hand tools, Wellington boots, how-to videos, seed packets . . . the works!"

Luke leaned forward to have a closer look at her sketch pad. "A gift shop . . . where?"

"In one of the old sheep sheds."

"Of course."

"You can sell large-sized items like statuary, paving stones, and garden furniture in the exercise barn. Your mail-order—I mean 'postal shopping'—division could be housed in the old coach house, here, and the potting sheds and additional display beds would go there." She pointed to an area near the sales shed, which she'd placed in the former icehouse. "The walled kitchen garden at the back of the castle will become primarily an herb garden, and the parsley will be planted exactly there, where your son thinks it should go," she added with measured emphasis. "At Barton Hall Nurseries," she continued in her best salesperson manner, "the merchandise is labeled 'Plants for Shady Areas' or 'Plants for Sandy Soils,' and so forth, so the untutored customer won't be overwhelmed. You want to attract both the gardening expert and people who love gardens but perhaps know nothing about how to create their own little jewel and want to begin their education with you."

"Me?" Luke protested. "I'll be too busy pulling weeds or hauling manure to serve as the plant professor. That shall be your job."

"I don't mean you personally," she assured him, "but your staff . . . Quiller, and the guys you recruit locally who have gardening knowledge and believe in what you're trying to do here. Plus, I suspect they'll be grateful for a job."

"The villagers," Luke said thoughtfully.

"Right!"

By this time Blythe was nearly breathless. She leaned back against the chintz-covered love seat and immediately felt a dog hair settle on her nose. It was not surprising, since Beryl had rolled over in her sleep and was now resting her muzzle on Blythe's toe.

Crikey! she thought. This was tougher than taking a meeting with the suits at the studios.

"Any other ideas?" Luke asked, deadpan.

"As a matter of fact, yesss!"

He really was an extraordinarily attractive man, Blythe thought suddenly as she felt caught in the playful mood that had bloomed between them. She'd bet her last pair of cowboy boots that the man sitting opposite her in his moth-eaten green Shetland sweater possessed enormous telegenic charm, which he could put to excellent use in a gardening equivalent of the old Barbara Woodhouse dog-training videos.

"Don't keep me in suspense," Luke demanded, his dark-blue eyes narrowing in mock solemnity. "Let's hear about this latest terrifying scheme of yours."

"What about the idea of inviting world-renowned gardening experts for weekend seminars? Ecology types, rosarians, the National Trust folks, the prizewinners from the Chelsea Flower Show? You give them a free weekend in the lap of luxury at Barton Hall in exchange for their dog and pony show—"

"Their what?" Luke interrupted.

"Public lectures and question-and-answer sessions," she explained. "They'll present their little talks in the large sitting room, and we'll charge a little fee. Not too much, mind you, so the locals will come, but enough to make our customers think, and rightly so, that the event is important. After the talks, Mrs. Q will serve her drop-dead cream teas, buffet style, in the formal dining room or, on sunny days, out on the terrace facing the sea. That way, you'll get media coverage. . . ."

"You mean in the *Mevagissey Post* and the *Gorran Haven Gossip*?"

"More like the *London Times* and *House and Garden*!" she retorted.

"I take it that this is the 'Cultural Center' part of your plan?" Luke smiled. "But tell me this: How do we entice hordes to come down to our Cornish outpost?"

"It will take time," Blythe acknowledged grudgingly. "But one way to get the word out would be to lease a field on the main highway near St. Austell and have a strictly commercial enterprise there with just the stuff Sunday gardeners need—"

"Ah . . . now I see . . . Barton Hall Nurseries—plural."

"—with lots of your leaflets and brochures posted all over the place, telling about what's going on down here. Plus, after we start our national and international advertising campaign, a steady increase in your postal-shopping business should do the trick," she finished, ignoring his teasing.

Luke set down his teacup and looked at her steadily.

"There's just one problem," he said. "How do I get the capital to launch this Royal Botannicum?"

"Well, now . . . ," she said with a wide grin. She turned the page of her sketch pad and pointed to a long column of numbers. "I have one . . . more . . . idea."

"How did I know that?" Luke asked dryly. "Fire away."

"How would you like a business partner? A silent investor?"

"You?" he asked with an astonished expression.

"We could structure it like a movie deal," she proposed. "I'll provide the up-front money and take points on the back end."

"Points?" he echoed, confused.

"A nice percentage of the profits if the project is in the black within three years. If it doesn't fly, you won't have to pay me back my initial investment . . . but you will have to deed me Painter's Cottage and the acre it sits on." She folded her hands in her lap and met his glance steadily. "We'd put everything in writing. Why don't you take a couple of days to think about it?"

Luke remained very still. Then, one by one, he held up the collection of drawings Blythe had submitted to him.

"You're a very creative woman," he said finally, "and an even more impressive negotiator . . . but I expect you learned all that in Hollywood."

"I learned it when I was eighteen playing poker with Otis McCafferty behind a rodeo arena," she retorted coolly. "And if my proposal doesn't seem fair—"

"Actually," Luke interrupted, appearing to sense, correctly, that he had offended her, "it's more than fair. If my last remarks sounded churlish, I apologize." Blythe merely raised an eyebrow in agreement. "I was expressing myself poorly," he continued, shaking his head in a gesture of frustration. "It's just that I've debated the fate of Barton Hall for such a long time, perhaps I feel a bit muddleheaded for not having thought of such a sensible and rather obvious solution myself." He glanced out the window in the direction of the towering rhododendrons. "But what you're proposing sounds awfully ambitious. . . . It's much more than a mere nursery scheme. . . ."

"Much more," Blythe agreed calmly.

"We'd have to get permission from the County Council . . . ," Luke murmured.

"Obviously we'd have a number of hurdles to overcome," she said, nodding in agreement, "but I'll bet the enterprise will probably qualify for a government grant or two if you train people in the nursery business and provide them employment."

As she watched his gaze shift back to the drawings she had made, she wondered suddenly if she hadn't foolishly allowed herself to be carried away with enthusiasm for a venture that entailed a host of critical unknowns, most important of which was her own willingness to remain in Cornwall for the foreseeable future. Then there was the issue of Luke's ability—or desire—to accept a woman as his full-fledged business partner. After all, this was Britain, she thought ruefully.

However, Luke carefully placed her sketches on the table beside his chair and extended his hand, callused from having taken on so many of the duties that had belonged to the retired head gardener.

"What can I lose that I won't lose by doing nothing?" he mused. "And how often is one offered the opportunity to go into business with such an accomplished professional?" Then the hereditary owner of Barton Hall seized her hand and said in a reasonable imitation of John Wayne's western drawl, "Put'er there!"

As Blythe shook his hand, it was her turn to wonder what in the world she had let herself in for.

Blythe and Lucas kept the financial details of their written contract simple: She agreed to deposit funds from her American bank into a joint account in a St. Austell building society. The sum there equaled the cost of the estimated renovation on existing buildings and the purchase of equipment and additional plant stock. Each partner was required to sign all checks, and Blythe had veto power over any expenditure she deemed unrealistic or excessive.

Fortunately, the new partners found themselves in agreement over most practical and design issues. One point they didn't agree on, however, was the matter of Blythe's rent for Painter's Cottage.

"I absolutely insist that I continue to pay you like a good little tenant," she said firmly, after a spirited discussion one morning. She knew full well that the cash generated by Luke's summer leases paid for extras like Mrs. Quiller's salary.

"Perhaps you're not the brilliant negotiator I'd credited you for," Luke protested as he reluctantly accepted the check for July's rent. "If I ever sign over the deed for the cottage, you'll have paid for it twice!"

"You should be praying that you never have to sign the deed over to me," Blythe reminded him mildly, "since that will mean we will have failed with Barton Hall Nurseries—plural."

"We mustn't . . . ," Luke replied, suddenly in dead earnest. "We simply mustn't fail."

"We're going to be a huge hit!" she exclaimed, closing her checkbook.

"That's a deal," Lucas replied, holding out his hand.

"Please don't use that word," Blythe replied fervently. "It reminds me of Hollywood."

"Agreed then . . . that we'll make this a smashing success?" he corrected himself, his hand still extended toward her.

"Agreed." She smiled, enjoying the warmth of his fingers as they encased her own. She sat down at his desk and quickly inserted the few agreed-upon changes into the document she'd typed on the computer. The six-pound laptop that had been so essential when she was employed as a production designer had been air-expressed to Cornwall from California by a friend the previous week. Despite the castle's antiquated wiring, a voltage converter had put the machine in perfect working order.

"If this had been a movie deal," she laughed as the edited document spit out the front end of her portable printer, "this contract would have been a hundred twenty-seven pages long!"

"Whatever for?" Luke asked, mesmerized by the sight of their amended agreement magically emerging from Blythe's machine.

"Funeral clauses and antifuneral funeral clauses."

"How grim. What do funeral clauses in a film contract do, exactly?"

"All the contingency clauses are put in there in case someone later changes his mind and wants to get out of the deal. In La-La Land they're called the 'what if' clauses. What if I grow to hate you? What if your work stinks? What if I get a better deal?"

"But a contract's a contract," he protested. "At least it is in England."

"I'm very glad to hear that," she replied.

Luke seized his antique silver-plated fountain pen and signed his name to their homemade document. Then he handed the pen to Blythe, who signed her triple-barreled signature with a flourish.

"This is going to be fun," she laughed. "I'm going to play 'producer' for a change, and I can't wait for the day I have to tell you that you simply cannot purchase one more hoe."

The next morning, however, tormented by her own sense of mild panic, Blythe awakened at four-thirty. Waves cracked rhythmically on the beach below as a group of insomniac seagulls cried out in concert with the sound of sheep bleating in the nearby field, roused by the summer's early-rising sun. Try as she might to use this Cornish symphony to lull her back to sleep, a thousand thoughts about the project crowded her brain.

Alone in her bed under the eaves, she watched the anemic sunlight as it slanted through the tall artist's window and cast gloomy shadows across the cottage walls. As the sun continued to rise behind a solid bank of clouds in the east, her thoughts dwelled upon the impulsive way she had signed a legally binding document—without a shred of legal advice—to fund Barton Hall Nurseries. Glumly she imagined the harshness with which her attorney would severely chastise her for such foolhardy behavior.

At last, pulling herself out of bed, Blythe reached the decision that she at least owed lawyer Lisa Spector a call to tell her about her impetuous actions. Perhaps the hardheaded Ms. Spector would refer Blythe to a solicitor in London who could go over the written agreement she and Luke had created together, as well as advise her as the project went along. By six o'clock on that Friday morning, Blythe donned a goose-down vest and her Barbour coat and trudged along the road to Penare. Passing Lamledra Farm on her left, she headed up the hill to Canton Road, which ran next to the Gorran Haven post office. There she passed the village public telephone housed in a familiar red call box. Fortunately, British Telecom had not yet replaced this charming antique with one of its nondescript modern equivalents made of vandal-resistant acrylic that was such a blight on the landscape.

She slid an icy 10p coin into the slot. After listening to a dozen peremptory pips, she eventually reached the international operator and dutifully recited her calling-card number. It was still Thursday in California, just past nine o'clock in the evening. Even during the worst moments of the divorce proceedings, Blythe had refrained from contacting her attorney outside office hours. However, her full-blown anxiety before dawn's light concerning her hasty decision to become partners with Lucas Teague had prompted her to plod up the hill to the village and put the call through to Lisa's home number.

Now, shivering within the confines of the frigid telephone booth, Blythe suddenly hoped that Lisa's answering machine would pick up, allowing her merely to leave a message asking her lawyer to forward the names of recommended legal counsel in London. That way she could avoid a discussion about the recent developments in Cornwall.

The familiar, curt voice cut across ten thousand miles of satellite transmission.

"Have you gone bananas?" Lisa demanded as soon as she heard the details of Blythe's intentions. "I can't believe you signed a business deal without having me go over it first . . . and with a guy you've known for all of one month!"

"Almost two months," Blythe corrected her.

"Jesus, Blythe! What are you doing? Wasn't one English bastard enough for you in this life?"

"I know it all must sound a little crazy," Blythe admitted, feeling like the fool she knew Lisa thought she was, "but I got so totally charged by the amazing possibilities in this gorgeous place, I just had to give it a try. Finally I'll be back in the field I should never have left and—"

"Are you really ready to give up the film business, with all the contacts it's taken you ten years to build, to stay in England for three years?" Lisa boiled. "You do realize, don't you, that you're about to invest a substantial chunk of change—not to mention emotional and creative energy—half a world away from everything you've ever known?"

"Nothing is forever," Blythe replied, pushing aside her residual doubts as she rallied to defend her joint venture. "And I think Lucas Teague and I could really make a success out of this. I like the fact that it has nothing to do with the movie business—or with movie people."

"I can't believe you're telling me that you're willing to completely forsake your friends and your entire profession to grow a few rhodo . . . rhodo-whatchamacallits in Cornwall!" Lisa exclaimed.

"Rho-do-den-drons," she prompted helpfully.

"Christ, Blythe!" Lisa exploded over the wire. "You said yourself last time we talked that you were depressed. It sounds to me as if you're going off the deep—"

The wind off the bay was whistling through a broken windowpane near her ankles, rendering the telephone booth frigid. Just then a large vehicle rumbled by, making conversation almost impossible.

"Hold it, Lisa," Blythe shouted. "I can't hear you. . . . Let this lorry pass by."

"This what? Where the hell are you?" Lisa yelled.

"At a public phone in Gorran Haven," Blythe answered. "I wanted some privacy," she added sheepishly.

"Well, explain to me, then," Lisa said more calmly when the truck had turned the corner into Rattle Alley, "how a sufficient number of customers are going to find you in a backwater like Cornwall—where even telephones are apparently rationed commodities?" Blythe herself had worried from the first whether customers from St. Austell and environs would drive an extra ten miles out of their way merely to shop in a castle garden. Historic houses were a dime a dozen as far as the British were concerned.

"That's a reasonable issue to raise," Blythe agreed, attempting to sound centered and thoroughly prepared to answer any objection Lisa might throw her way. It was a technique she had learned from Chris when they had run up against skepticism, or even outright contempt, for their ideas in the Hollywood executive suites. "However, twenty-five acres of gardens with rhododendron trees forty feet high are pretty spectacular, Lisa. People come from around the world to see them in bloom."

"What happens when it isn't spring?" Lisa snapped, assuming her most lawyerly tone. "Look, Blythe, I, for one, don't even know what a rhododendron looks like. What I do know is that you'll probably need to recruit an army of skilled carpenters, plumbers, roofers, and gardening gurus to transform that pile into a going concern. Where do you propose to find qualified people in the sticks? And whose little checkbook will be called upon to ante up if Rhododendron-land turns out to cost a lot more than you've budgeted? Not Lord What's-his-name, certainly. Why else would he need *you* for a partner? I just hope you haven't fallen for the oldest con in the world: 'Distraught divorcée falls for slick dude with a fancy title and a leaky roof.' "

"He's a plain 'mister,' and besides, I was the one who proposed this thing to Lucas, not the other way around," Blythe retorted heatedly. "And I've set it up so that I have to approve every expenditure."

"In your state of mind, that's what concerns me," Lisa shot back. Then she added, "Be honest, Blythe. You haven't gone squishy over this Lord of the Manor guy, have you? Are you sure that you're not just on the proverbial rebound?"

"Don't be ridiculous!" Blythe replied testily. Lisa was treating her as if she were a half-wit. "This is just a business deal," she said coldly. "A very good business deal, I think. I merely called you to let you know what I'd decided to do."

"Well . . . if somewhere down the road you wind up knee-deep in shit, find yourself a phone booth on the moor somewhere and give me a call. I'll do what I can to get you out of it."

"I don't want to get out of it," Blythe protested. "Why do

people in Los Angeles assume the world is out to rob them blind?"

"Because it is," Lisa pronounced. Then she picked up her previous theme. "If the deal with this Teague character blows up in your face, I'll just say that the stress of your divorce impaired your judgment . . . or that you didn't understand British law . . . or that—"

"I don't want to get out of it!" Blythe repeated sharply. "And, in fact, I'm due at Barton Hall right now. . . . We're cleaning out the loft above the pony stalls today."

"Just you? Or is the other CEO wielding a broom as well?" Lisa retorted sarcastically.

"Drop me a note with the names of a couple of solicitors in London as soon as you can, will you?" Blythe asked, ignoring her lawyer's derisive comment. "And make sure you charge me for your time."

"Will do," Lisa said curtly. She was obviously a woman who didn't appreciate her advice being ignored.

"Thanks," Blythe answered. "Well . . . I'll let you go. You probably want to turn in pretty soon. Isn't it amazing?" she added, trying to sign off with a show that she hadn't taken Lisa's crustiness personally. "You're about to go to bed and I'm about to have breakfast . . . at a darling little place called Toasties. Cheerio," she joked in a deliberate "jolly-hockey-sticks" tone of voice.

She quickly hung up the receiver and took a deep breath, leaning against the inside of the telephone booth. The conversation with Lisa had made her feel as if she'd done something extremely naughty and had been unfairly chastised by higher authority.

But what if Lisa was right?

Blythe knew—in the part of her character that was not the dreamy artist—that many of the objections her lawyer had raised were perfectly sensible. She wondered, having heard them articulated in the cold light of day, if she had, in fact, gotten herself in way over her head.

Blythe heaved open the heavy red metal door and was blasted in the face by the stiff breeze swooping off the bay. Was she truly ready to cut all of her ties to Hollywood in exchange for at least three years in a place she hardly knew, a "backwater," as Lisa so delicately put it, populated by people whose customs and language she didn't fully understand? Had she actually given serious thought to becoming an expatriate?

And where was her relationship with her new partner heading? Perhaps she had been blatantly fooling herself. Perhaps she'd been hoping, unconsciously, that in one easy business negotiation she and this attractive widower would fall madly in love, magically filling the hole in her heart left by the breakup with Christopher.

God knew she could use a bit of an ego boost. The state of her sexual relationship with her husband the year before their divorce should have been a major clue that something disastrous was brewing. Truth to tell, she had been too exhausted and Chris had been too busy for much lovemaking last year, what with her trips to visit Grandma Barton in Wyoming, not to mention coping with a brutal production schedule. And then, of course, during the last months of their marriage, Chris and Ellie had been—

And what about Luke? she wondered, forcing her thoughts to veer off in a more appealing direction. More to the point, what about Chloe Acton-Scott's permanent claim on the yellow room in the castle's guest quarters? Blythe suddenly wondered if any secret doors were to be found up there. Obviously Richard's godmother had filled some sort of void since Luke's wife had died. The question was, how big a void?

Jesus, Blythe!

It was nearly two years since Luke's wife, Lindsay, had died. He might very well have been ready for love, or even a pleasant roll in the hay, but Blythe certainly wasn't.

Unsettled by these musings, along with her recent exchange with her cynical attorney, Blythe discovered that she had walked two hundred yards beyond Toasties. She had also lost her appetite and made an abrupt decision to keep trudging on ahead.

As she climbed over the stile that led to the public footpath en route to Barton Hall, the leaden skies overhead began to spit rain. She pulled the strings of the hood of her Barbour tightly around her chin and tried to ignore the foul weather, concentrating, instead, on the chores facing her this day.

And then a comforting thought occurred to her. If she found herself out of her depth with Barton Hall Nurseries—or even in her relationship with Luke—she'd simply pull the plug. She'd seen Christopher initiate "damage control" many a time, and she could do it too—if she had to.

Blythe bent forward, braving the rising wind. She wondered where in remote Cornwall a person could purchase hundreds of yards of polyurethane. Grateful for the diversion, she mentally began to design the inexpensive hothouses she planned to erect until they were sure the business would succeed and the partnership could afford to build permanent structures made of wood and glass.

However, in one corner of her mind she chewed on the fact that, undeniably, she and Luke were confronted with a daunting number of decisions and concerns. And lurking behind everything was the matter of secret bookcases and uninvited eighteenth-century ancestors materializing in and around the estate when least expected. It was a situation best left unexplored, yet it always lingered on the edge of Blythe's thoughts.

Fortunately, as soon as she walked into the stable yard at Barton Hall, her worries faded into the background and the day flew by in a blur of activity and hard physical labor.

One warm July day, not long after the conversation with Lisa Spector, Luke climbed the ladder to the stable loft looking for Blythe.

"I am pleased to announce that the ponies are delighted with their cozy new quarters in the piggery behind the walled garden," he said with a flourish, as if he were the town crier. "They said to thank you for liberating them from this stone hovel."

But Blythe didn't respond with her usual good cheer. She was sitting on an old leather trunk, staring fixedly at the wall opposite.

"The self-portrait of Ennis Trevelyan . . . ," she said in a low voice, and pointed at a dust-laden canvas defiled by vicious gashes that disfigured the handsome face of Luke's long-deceased ancestor.

"Ah . . . so that's where it's got to," Luke replied, drawing near to have a closer look at the damaged painting that leaned against a stone wall blanketed with cobwebs.

"Do you have a flashlight on that rig you're wearing?" Blythe asked quietly, referring to his leather carpenter's belt full of pouches and straps for carrying a small storehouse of tools.

"A torch, you mean?" he replied. "Yes . . . here," he added, handing it to her.

Blythe shone the light on the vandalized portrait. One slash of the attacker's blade had savaged Ennis's face from eye to ear. Another had cut his throat as brutally as a professional assassin.

"If, in fact, your ancestor Christopher Trevelyan did this, he obviously was very angry," she said in a subdued tone of voice.

"Well, as far as we know, brother Ennis wasn't murdered by Kit," Luke assured her. He gestured toward the painting. "This fracas was probably just the result of two drunken siblings squabbling."

Blythe's memory flashed to her glimpse of the standing figure that had materialized briefly on the cliff of Ennis's seascape that hung in Luke's sitting room. The person who had appeared suddenly in that painting had been staring down disconsolately at a capsized dinghy that bobbed forlornly in the cove. Who had been in that boat? Blythe wondered. And why was the boat floating upside down in the water? Had someone been killed in an accident? Or had a murder been made to look like an accident? The dark-haired young man had been leaning on a staghorn walking stick that was identical to one currently stored in the castle's mudroom—that is, when the distinctive staff was not in use by Garrett Teague's descendant, whose own head was crowned with a similar blue-black mane. Had Luke's forebear somehow been involved in the quarrel between the Trevelyan brothers?

Don't start! she told herself fiercely, and purged the image from her mind.

"Blythe? Are you all right?" Luke asked. He retrieved the lighted flashlight that was dangling uselessly against the pant leg of her jeans. "Not spooked by shredded ancestral portraits or long-forgotten family quarrels, are you?"

"Well, that picture is a bit creepy, don't you think?" she replied, trying to laugh.

"It certainly is," Luke agreed cheerfully. He seized the painting by its dusty gilt frame. "Look at it this way. If our venture goes at all successfully this year, I intend to send it up to Christie's in London and see about having poor Ennis here restored to his former roguish glory. Meanwhile, I'll clean it off and store it in the pantry cupboard in the Hall."

"Good," she replied, relieved to have the damaged portrait out of her sight. "Where's Richard this morning?"

"Helping Mrs. Q pack our picnic. It's too glorious a day to spend all of it in this dusty loft. Luncheon will be served today at Hemmick Beach, m'lady—if that meets your approval?"

"Right on, Loretta!" she laughed. "But we have to get back by two o'clock. The roof men are coming to give us their estimate."

"Then I'd better be sure the wine's been packed," he responded grimly, and backed down the ladder. "I hope to be completely numb when they tell us their bill of quality."

"You mean how much they'll charge? Their price?" she asked in one of her frequent attempts to confirm they both were speaking the same language.

Luke nodded and then paused halfway down the steps. "Oh, and, Blythe . . . guess what I found at the back of the big toolshed this morning. James Barton's drawings for the expansion of the Hall in the late 1780s. There's a sketch of another secret room behind a bookcase in the library. Come . . . quickly, before we go. Let's have a look to see if it's still there."

Blythe hesitated near the library door as Luke and Richard, consulting a roll of drawings now yellowed with age, surveyed the bookcases from every angle.

"Now, let's see . . . ," Luke murmured, "which case could it be?"

"What about this one, Daddy?" Richard ventured, using a less formal address for his father while pointing to the bookcase nearest the corner. "See that square? On the drawing it looks as if the secret room is—"

"You're right, son," Luke interrupted. "It looks as if it might come out right about . . ."

Blythe realized she was holding her breath as Luke's fingers probed behind the carved molding that fronted the shelves. A click resounded in the room, but the bookcase didn't move.

"Perhaps if you just push inward with your shoulder on the left side of the bookcase," she suggested quietly. "The hinges are probably rusty."

Luke took her advice, with young Richard following suit. The bookcase retreated inward an inch while making a loud splintering sound.

"Something moved!" Richard said excitedly.

"All right, son . . . let's try again. One, two, three . . ."

And just as Blythe knew it would, the bookcase pivoted to the side, exposing a black, gaping hole beyond. The door's movement also resulted in a flurry of scurrying sounds that were probably produced by rodents who had found a home in Barton Hall's eighteenth-century smuggler's lair.

Luke whipped out his flashlight and shone it inside.

"Good heavens!" he exclaimed.

"What, Daddy?" Richard piped.

Blythe inched forward into the library chamber. "Brandy barrels?" she called.

"Stacked to the ceiling," came Luke's muffled reply. "This stuff's either poison or worth a fortune!" She heard a knocking sound. Then, "Oh, blast!"

"What's the matter?" Blythe said, crossing to the bookcase and peering inside.

"These sound pretty hollow. I think most of the barrels are empty, or everything's evaporated. It's very drafty in here. I'm guessing there must be a door to the outside. . . . Ah . . . yes . . . it's been boarded up. Probably bricked over on the other side."

"Yes . . . ," Blythe murmured. "I expect so."

She sank into Luke's leather desk chair as the memory of Garrett Teague's unexpected appearance outside the library's hidey-hole crowded her thoughts. That event, at least, hadn't merely been in her imagination. Nor was the existence of the self-portrait of Ennis shredded by an enraged Kit Trevelyan. Had the other visions she'd experienced since her arrival in Cornwall actually taken place two hundred years ago? Was Ennis, indeed, the father of her namesake's child? Did Blythe Barton's baby die? That would certainly explain why there were no Barton-Trevelyan heirs. And what about that sorrowful figure Blythe had seen gazing down from the cliff at the overturned dinghy in Hemmick Cove? How—and why—had all this been revealed to her?

Many born-and-bred Californians might believe in this bizarre paranormal stuff, she thought defiantly, but not she—not Miss Rodeo Wyoming 1976, ol' Feet-on-the-Ground Blythe Barton of Jackson Hole!

I just can't deal with this now. . . .

Blythe straightened her spine and placed both fists on Luke's desk. She simply wouldn't deal with it, she decided firmly. Perhaps these apparitions had really happened. She had no idea. But she was ready to get on with her life. And, besides, she definitely had no desire to explore what all these bizarre occurrences might have to do with her.

"All this is very exciting," she called to Luke and Richard, "but I'm starving and the roofers will be here in an hour."

"No time for a beach picnic, then, I'm afraid," Luke said, emerging with Richard from behind the bookcase and dusting off his hands. He gestured toward Blythe, perched on the edge of his leather chair. "Good heavens, Richard, my boy. If we don't feed this woman immediately, I fear she'll eat the picnic basket too. Shall we quickly have our lunch on the terrace, instead?"

Richard giggled and ran to tell Mrs. Q about their change of plans.

Blythe and Lucas eventually had their picnic at the beach, but without young Richard. A week after Luke's discovery of the second movable bookcase in Barton Hall, Chloe Acton-Scott arrived unannounced, declaring that she intended to drive her godson to Plymouth, an hour and a half away, for a fitting of the still-growing boy's new school uniform.

"Really, Chloe, this is very kind of you, but there was no need for you to come down all this way," Luke assured her as he and Blythe climbed down the ladder from the loft in the pony stable. "I was going to get around to it one day soon."

Both he and Blythe were covered with grime after a morning's efforts sorting through the last of the debris stored overhead for generations. Chloe, on the other hand, was immaculate in beige gabardine pleated trousers and a matching silk blouse. Blythe quickly wiped her soiled hands on her pants legs as their stylish visitor cast a critical eye at the crowded loft. Broken household appliances, an antique brass daybed covered with a plastic dust sheet, as well as an old traveling trunk, waited to be dealt with before the workmen could begin tearing off the roof and replacing rotting rafters and broken slate.

"Well, I realized as soon as you told me about this new garden scheme of yours that you and Mrs. Stowe would have your hands full with this project," Chloe replied, smiling faintly in Blythe's direction, "and I thought I might make myself useful."

"That's awfully generous of you, isn't it, Richard?" Luke said. The boy nodded politely but appeared less than enthusiastic about leaving the scene of excitement and activity that currently reigned at Barton Hall.

"Besides, darling," Chloe added, with a smile directed only at Luke, "you promised to escort me to that boring drinks party at the Strattons' in Mevagissey tomorrow night, remember? I thought afterward I'd take you to dinner at that lovely little restaurant on the water in Fowey, and you can thank me then."

"Well, that sounds as if it might make a pretty full day," Luke replied slowly. He glanced apologetically in Blythe's direction. He was clearly uncomfortable to be arranging his social calendar in public. "Saturday's Richard's birthday party. We'll be taking the children to the village fete in Gorran Haven all afternoon."

"Couldn't be simpler," Chloe laughed reassuringly. "I'll give you a hand with all that, and then we can just drive on to Mevagissey afterward. Perhaps Mrs. Stowe would be willing to bring the children back here for their parents to collect? Can you drive on the left, Mrs. Stowe?"

"Not yet," Blythe replied.

"It's not much of a walk," Chloe responded with a pointed look in the direction of Blythe's scuffed sneakers. "Lovely, then. Saturday's settled. Come, Richard, dear. We'd best be off, so we shall be back in time for some of Mrs. Quiller's delicious scones at teatime. I've had her take my bags up to my room. I hope that's all right with you, Luke?"

Blue room or yellow room? Blythe wondered.

Before Chloe and Richard had climbed into her Jaguar, Blythe had turned and retreated up the ladder into the stable loft. By the time Luke had caught up with her, she had grabbed the handle of the heavy leather trunk that had been wedged in a corner. She was pulling on it with all her might.

"Here, let me help you move that," he said, reaching for one of the handles. "Good God! This thing weighs a ton. Let's get it over to the window and see if it's been haboring rocks all these years."

Blythe straightened up and put both hands on her hips. "Better yet, let's break for lunch. I need a good, brisk walk. The 'sunny intervals' seem to be holding. Shall we take our sandwiches down to the beach?"

Luke carried the wicker picnic hamper on his shoulder while Blythe transported a tartan car blanket under her arm. To his surprise, she headed off ahead of him, not in the direction of Hemmick Beach, but down a steep, grass-strewn incline directly below Painter's Cottage.

"Too many holiday makers at Hemmick by this hour," she called back. "I've discovered there's a marvelous spot down here when the tide's out."

"You're getting to sound like a native," he laughed, amused at her substitution of the term "holiday makers" for tourists. The locals couldn't survive if visitors didn't flock to Cornwall in the summer, but they didn't much like it and would climb down cliffs, regardless how treacherous, to find a bit of the coast they could enjoy in solitude.

Ten minutes later they had spread the dark-green plaid blanket onto a thin stretch of sand directly below Blythe's abode. Luke watched contentedly as she unpacked the delicious repast prepared by Mrs. Q. Thick ploughman's sandwiches chock-full of cheddar and lettuce, and spiced with mustard, were followed by ramekins of creamed potato salad, bottles of lager, and, finally, squares of his housekeeper's ten-alarm chocolate cake and a vacuum flask full of hot tea.

"Ohhh . . . ," Blythe groaned, flopping down onto her back. "I'm exercising my veto. No more afternoon chores. I'm taking a nap."

She immediately closed her eyes, and Luke wondered if she had, indeed, dozed off. Her lovely face was etched in profile against the rocks burrowed into the sand behind them. She seemed utterly relaxed, and her wide, generous mouth curved upward, making it look as if she might break into a smile at any moment. The moist air had swirled her shoulder-length auburn hair into a tangle of luxuriant curls that spread out in riotous disarray against the forest-green blanket. Her denim work shirt was unbuttoned at the throat. Since her eyes remained shut, Luke allowed his gaze to leisurely survey her flat stomach and long jeans-clad legs. Then his gaze came back and focused on her breasts. They rose and fell in concert with Blythe's slow, even breaths.

Although Luke had just eaten his fill of Mrs. Q's picnic lunch, an odd pang akin to hunger seized him with a ferocious craving. As he continued to stare at Blythe's prone form, the thought came to him that it would require very little effort on his part simply to roll over once and, in an instant, cover the length of Blythe's body with his own. At the very least he could reach an arm's length and touch the denim stretched tautly over her right breast.

A wave broke onshore suddenly, and the bottom of their blanket was immediately drenched in seawater. Blythe gave a little yelp and sprang to her feet.

"I'll get the hamper," Luke cried, "you get the rest!"

Together they scrambled to gather up their possessions in a confusion of laughter and curses.

"Quick! Back here!" Blythe called, scampering toward the dark-gray rocks that jutted out from the cliff overhead. Luke followed her into a dim, narrow cave carpeted with sand that felt dry on his bare feet. "The fissure goes back thirty feet or so," she shouted over her shoulder. "Mr. Quiller told Richard and me that the tide never comes in here very far during the summer months." They leaned against the rocky walls to catch their breath after their hasty departure from their picnic site. "Well!" she laughed. "What a rude awakening."

Luke set the wicker picnic basket on the sand and fingered an edge of the blanket Blythe still clutched against her chest. Their gazes locked, and he sensed that she was as aware as he of the emotional currents crackling between them. Her lips parted slightly, as if something puzzled her.

"You looked so peaceful, lying there," Luke said softly.

"I was feeling peaceful," she replied at length, looking up at him steadily.

"And lovely . . . you looked lovely taking your nap."

"I did?"

Her question echoed off the cave's weeping slate walls and hung in the moist air.

Kiss me.

Was it his own lecherous thought, or had she said something?

"With pleasure," he said aloud, not caring if she thought him daft. Gently he cupped his hands on either side of her face. The blanket wedged between their bodies slid down to the sand. He experienced an odd sense of relief when Blythe pressed her lithe form against his own and willingly melted into his embrace. He felt her arms encircling his back and gloried in the incredible sensation of her breasts pressing against his chest.

She was taller than Lindsay had been, and her limbs were considerably leaner than his wife's after she'd given birth to Richard. It felt strange to have a woman in his arms whose smooth, firm musculature reflected a youth spent riding in the Jackson Hole Rodeo. But in seconds Luke gave himself up to savoring the sensations of those full lips and her wonderful hair that seemed to wrap itself around his hands like spun sugar.

She's lovely . . . lovely for you. . . .

That thought gave him both comfort and courage, almost as if some invisible force urged him to continue with the extraordinary adventure of kissing this woman. Her lips parted even wider, offering him an unambiguous invitation to indulge in more than a moment's flirtation. Her tongue tasted of chocolate, sweet and seductive, and he realized that kissing her like this could lead to a serious addiction, just like his uncontrollable craving for Mrs. Q's celebrated devil's food cake, which they'd eaten at lunch.

Blythe was most definitely kissing him back. He found himself in the grip of a sudden surge of emotion, as if the sea were about to come crashing into their cave. Finally, to save himself from drowning, he tore his lips away and began to nuzzle a soft, fragrant spot just beneath Blythe's left ear. Next, he explored the hollow of her throat conveniently exposed by the open neckline of her denim shirt.

"So sweet . . . ," he mumbled.

"Better than chocolate cake . . . ?" she murmured.

His answer was to slide his hands down her back to her jeans-clad derriere and to pull her even closer to him. He wanted her to feel his arousal, to know how he had been waiting these weeks to take her in his arms.

At length Blythe broke their kiss and leaned her head back, inhaling deeply.

"For a genteel, mannerly sort of Brit, that was . . . amazing," she said shakily.

"I'm woefully out of practice, but thank you," he replied as a lightness filled his soul—a sensation that had been missing from his life for a long time. Blythe looked at him skeptically but remained silent. "Did you mean it about chucking the afternoon's chores?" he ventured hopefully.

In response Blythe stooped to retrieve their picnic blanket and began folding it into neat squares. He could almost hear the wheels in her head turning recent events over in her mind. Chloe Acton-Scott had reappeared today. What role did she play in Luke's life? she was wondering. He was wondering about that himself.

"It's definitely tempting to knock off for the day," she replied, smiling wryly. Then she glanced up at him through her long eyelashes in a manner that he could swear was deliberately flirtatious. "But . . . no. I think we shouldn't give in to such poor work habits quite so soon . . . don't you agree?" He grinned apologetically but said nothing, waiting for her to make the next move. Unfortunately, it was a friendly checkmate. "I'm not up to coping with that old heavy traveling trunk today," she announced. She headed toward daylight at the end of the cave. Then, framed by its opening, she turned to face him. "But what do you say if we spend what's left of the afternoon pitching out that bit of junk in the icehouse and sweeping the place?"

While she talked, the sunlight shining outside the cave was creating a golden nimbus around her glorious auburn curls. She shifted her weight onto one hip and hooked her thumb into the belt loop of her faded blue jeans.

"Quite the risk taker, your little American adventuress," Chloe had commented the day she had pressed Luke on the telephone from London for details about the new business enterprise that he and his summer tenant had embarked upon. "Obviously Christopher Stowe's ex-wife is willing to gamble that her investment in Barton Hall will eventually be . . . profitable."

Botticelli angel or daring American cowgirl . . . which was she? Luke asked himself as he gazed at Blythe, who was waiting for him to join her at the entrance to the cave. The choices were formidable and definitely not what he was accustomed to.

"You pitch the stuff," he suggested, "because you'll be ruthless—and I'll sweep." Chloe was wrong, he thought. Blythe wasn't ready for real-life adventure. She was close, but she wasn't there yet.

And suddenly he wondered if he was ready himself.

Chapter Seven

July 16, 1994

Seven children, most of them the same age as the newly minted ten-year-old Richard Teague, piled into Luke's Land Rover, primed for their friend's birthday celebration.

Central casting. Blythe smiled to herself as her gaze rested on the cherubic faces of this boisterous gang.

To her the freckled, rosy-cheeked youngsters looked straight out of a scene from *Goodbye, Mr. Chips*. As if on cue, they squealed and shoved each other good-naturedly as they scrambled to find seats among the boxes and hampers Mrs. Q had stored in the back of her employer's overburdened vehicle. Luke and Blythe had devised a plan wherein the children would be taken on a brief tour of the sheepshearing operations in progress at the holding pens a mile or so away from the Hall itself. Meanwhile, Mr. and Mrs. Quiller would proceed to the site of the village fete to see that everything was ready for Richard's party.

Blythe found herself mildly irritated, however, when Chloe proceeded to climb into Luke's car, taking the seat of honor beside the father of the birthday boy. Blythe immediately turned heel, strode across the stable yard, and sat next to the food cooler that perched on the backseat of the Quillers' trim Ford Fiesta. There she quietly fumed while the Land Rover's engine finally coughed to life.

The yearly event to raise funds for the Royal National

Lifeboat Institution was to take place on the outskirts of Gorran Haven in a large, flat field that had been lent by the owners of nearby Lamledra Farm. Already the festival grounds were packed with local residents preparing for the grand opening at two o'clock.

"Oh, look!" Blythe exclaimed as they came to a halt in the car park. "Donkeys!" The doe-eyed beasts with shaggy ears and presumably stubborn dispositions were being harnessed in one corner of the field in anticipation of an onslaught of eager riders.

"Oh, it's a grand event," Mrs. Q agreed. "The worse those animals behave, the better the children like them. And see . . . we're to have a proper Punch-and-Judy puppet show this year." She pointed to a puppet theater that was in the process of being assembled on a knoll across from the spot where—thanks to a modest donation—Luke had arranged with the president of the local Lifeboat chapter to hold Richard's party.

"And look at that tent!" Blythe said, gesturing toward a large white canvas structure, its support poles decorated with colorful streamers. "Will there be a circus too?"

"Oh, goodness me, no," Mr. Quiller chuckled. "It's just the 'Tea Pavilion,' " he informed her, pointing to a line of catering trucks that were backing up to the enormous tent to deliver trays piled with dozens of scones and cakes.

As they climbed out of the Ford parked on the edge of the field nearest the area assigned to the Teague party, Blythe noticed a display of color photos set on easels that depicted the local lifeboat brigade in action. The pictures bore witness to the fact that the organization had an impressive record of rescuing everyone from fishermen to the pale-skinned bathers who trooped down from London each year only to risk their lives in the churning sea.

Before long Blythe, along with Mr. and Mrs. Quiller, was flushed from inflating scores of balloons, which they had tied to stakes bedecked with crepe paper. More crepe paper, strung from stake to stake, created a colorful enclosure where Richard and his young guests would enjoy birthday cake and ice cream at the appropriate moment.

Blythe suddenly was swept up by a memory of the parties Grandma Barton organized at the ranch when she and her sister were growing up. Instead of offering Pin the Tail on the Donkey, the flinty old woman had saddled up two of the gentlest ponies in the stable and supervised spoon-and-egg contests. The winner who had the fastest time riding around the corral while balancing an egg on a large soupspoon won a second scoop of ice cream.

"You don't think the ice cream will melt, do you, Mrs. Q?" Blythe asked anxiously. What a contrast these lush, green fields were to that dusty corral at the ranch, she thought. Yet the children's excitement was the same as hers at their age.

"Don't you be a-worryin'." Mrs. Q smiled with the same reassuring complacency Lucinda had displayed at family gatherings. "This cooler's the best a body can buy. . . . Mrs. Teague saw to that. She loved celebrations like this. Dicken's first birthday was as grand as this, even though he was just a babe. . . . The lad will be pleased as a button with all the fuss."

"He does seem to be having a nice summer," Blythe ventured.

"Enjoys bein' part of the plans and doings, tha-at's for certain," Mrs. Q's husband said, nodding approvingly.

Luke's housekeeper met Blythe's gaze with eyes that seemed to exude the wisdom of a woman who, during her long life in remote Cornwall, had watched all manner of triumph and tragedy unfold.

"You kin see by the boy, healin' takes time, now, doesn't it?" she said kindly. "Just when things seem a-like they'll never sort themselves out—"

Their conversation was interrupted by the peremptory honking of Luke's Land Rover. The children tumbled out of the vehicle as though rehearsing for a Chinese fire drill and immediately clamored for tickets to the donkey rides. Luke held up both hands.

"Ah . . . hold on, chaps. . . . Let's have a little order here. . . ."

Blythe could see that the children were essentially well mannered. They soon settled down but continued to fidget with excitement. "Here's two tickets each," Luke announced. "As soon as you've had a go once or twice, come back straightaway for the Punch-and-Judy show over there!"

He pointed in the direction of the puppet theater that now stood in readiness. A sign leaning against its red velvet curtain promised, First Performance, 2:30 P.M.

"Thank you! Thank you!" the children cried before scampering across the field.

"This all looks wonderful," Luke said in a grateful voice. "For a minute there I wasn't sure we'd make it."

"A noisy drive over?" Blythe laughed.

"Positively deafening," Chloe pronounced, emerging from the Land Rover dressed in gray glen-plaid slacks and a cranberry sweater set. Then she turned to Mrs. Quiller. "Relieve my troubled mind, Mrs. Q. You did bring some sensible refreshments for the adults, didn't you?"

Mrs. Q appeared uncharacteristically flustered.

"Well, there be lemonade . . . and milk. . . . I—"

"Don't think a thing about it," Chloe interrupted, and cast Luke a beseeching look. "I see a tent over there with a Guinness sign. Luke, darling . . . do you suppose you'd repay me for my composure under fire and stake me to a lager? The children will be occupied for a while, and I'm sure the Quillers would be kind enough to cope if someone ends up with a bloody nose or something."

Luke addressed Blythe. "Will you join us?"

Chloe shot her a proprietary look.

"No . . . ," Blythe replied slowly. "I think I'll just have a look around . . . local color and all that," she added pointedly for Luke's benefit.

"Oh, there's lots to see," Chloe offered. "There's always the rose exhibit. Surely you and Quiller should enjoy that. Come, darling, I'm fainting with thirst."

"I think I will have a look at the roses," Blythe said to the Quillers as Chloe made a beeline for the Guinness tent with Luke in tow. Blythe suddenly felt she had to excuse herself from polite company or she might let fly with one of Grandma Barton's legendary expletives. "Why don't you two put your feet up and enjoy your last moments of peace?"

"Don't mind if I do," the leather-faced undergardener replied. "I've seen enough roses to last a lifetime."

So have I, Blythe fumed silently, and headed in the opposite direction from where Chloe was inveigling Lucas Teague to buy her a beer.

Stay out of it! Stay clear! Don't get involved! Just stick to business!

And don't be a damned fool, she added to her litany of silent self-invective.

A kiss is just a kiss . . . a sigh is just a sigh. . . .

The lyrics from the song in *Casablanca* suddenly floated through her mind as she rifled through the memory of Luke's extraordinary embrace the previous day.

The man's merely randy, she told herself in the next breath, feeling as if she'd like to shoot someone in the feet. He'd obviously been waiting until a decent interval elapsed before allowing himself to be "darlinged" into a permanent relationship with his deceased wife's best friend.

And while he was waiting, she, Blythe, had been conveniently available. The good-looking tweed-clad widower exuded an understated but highly subversive brand of sex appeal and had simply grabbed for the nearest female who happened to be standing in a dark place! And, besides, Blythe seethed, Chloe was the perfect woman for Lucas Teague, Lord of the Manor. She was cool and self-contained and liked to give orders to the help—and she was more than willing to abdicate most of the parenting chores, as was he!

But most important, Blythe thought, as old psychic wounds

smarted afresh, Luke and Chloe, like a certain director of her acquaintance, were English with a capital E. Don't say what you mean. Say the *opposite* of what you mean. And smile politely when you slip that knife between the ribs!

God! That sort of behavior drove her insane! She'd just gotten out of one agonizing relationship with a Brit. Why in the world would she want to be snared in yet another? Ever?

Because Lucas Teague was wickedly attractive? Because she hadn't been to bed with a man in ages? Because they both adored rhododendrons? Because—

By this time Blythe had tramped halfway across the field and was out of breath. She glowered at the tent sporting the Guinness sign and drew up short.

I came here to mend my heart, not get it broken again!

There it was, boiled down to its monstrous simplicity. Why would this Englishman be any different from the one who had left her bleeding from every pore? A suffocating sense of inadequacy was now smothering the fledgling spirit of well-being that had begun to blossom in Blythe like a tender hothouse plant. The mere sight of young Richard's stunning, yet coolly sexy, godmother might make most other women momentarily doubt their own appeal. For some reason Chloe Acton-Scott made Blythe feel like an unmitigated frump!

Why couldn't she just face facts? In the end Chris had preferred Ellie, and Luke was sure to find Chloe a more suitable companion for a man to the manner born.

But there was no getting around one fact, Blythe concluded, indignant. His Horniness, Lucas Garrett Barton Trevelyan Teague, was a sensational kisser . . . the bastard.

Blythe resumed her march across the field with no particular destination in mind. As she strode through the grass, she looked down at her feet. The moist air boiling off the Channel was now blowing a fine mist across the fields, and her walking shoes were soaked. If the mist turned to rain, the rest of her clothes would be rendered a soggy mess as well. She wished she owned a pair of Wellington boots like Luke's.

Luke.

Oh, God! He was her business partner now! Suddenly she recalled the ghastly day the movers had arrived at her new condo, grunting under the weight of her metal filing cabinets—the ones that had been dispatched from Stowe and Stowe Productions after she'd agreed to resign from the company she and Chris had founded.

"I've been there . . . done that," she mumbled savagely.

Then a frightening possibility struck her.

What if her emotional bereavement and the attraction she'd admittedly been feeling toward Luke lately were the key factors behind her proposal to launch a business together, and not her purported desire to make a career midcourse correction?

Even if she'd unconsciously done such a monumentally stupid thing, her lawyer, Lisa Spector, would have every right to have her committed to the nearest loony bin.

At that moment Blythe pulled up short to avoid colliding with a small tent displaying a sign that said CRYSTAL BALL GAZING. Below the sign was a poster that touted the virtues of supporting the Search and Rescue Team, a Gorran Haven organization that was "proud to work in concert with the Royal National Lifeboat Institution." Next to it was another handmade sign that read Valerie Kent, Ph.D. Psychology. Readings: One Pound.

Blythe couldn't resist peeking inside the tent. She was interested in seeing what a local gypsy looked like, especially one who both touted an advanced degree in psychology and dutifully supported local civic groups.

What met Blythe's gaze was a heavyset woman in her mid-sixties with a shock of black and silver hair poking from beneath an outlandish scarlet turban that sat on her head at a dangerously rakish angle. Like a plump, broody hen, she was roosting on a folding chair in front of a glistening crystal sphere the size of a baseball. The round table it rested on, topped with a fringed tablecloth, was positioned on a small Persian carpet that covered the grass.

"Welcome . . . madam," the presumed psychic greeted Blythe in mock sepulchral tones. "May I look into your future in my crystal ball? All for a good cause, you know. . . . All for a good cause."

"Oh . . . hello," Blythe said tentatively.

"Do come in . . . ," she trilled in a singsong voice that obviously reflected the woman's best efforts to sound genuinely gypsylike. "My crystal ball awaits. . . ."

"Oh, thank you . . . but—"

"You'll be my first customer," the gypsy implored her. "I promised myself I simply couldn't indulge in a cup of tea unless I'd told at least one person's fortune. I must do my bit for my colleagues, you know."

"Are you a member of the Search and Rescue Team?" Blythe asked skeptically. She couldn't quite imagine the rotund Dr. Kent rappelling down a cliff to save some stranded soul.

"I help people afterward . . . to talk about the trauma and that sort of thing."

"Oh . . . well, then." Blythe shrugged, ducking her head to enter the woman's inner sanctum. "You certainly deserve a nice cup of tea."

Why not help the poor woman do her civic duty? Blythe thought. At least it might prove an amusing way to pass the time before the birthday boy cut his cake. That way Blythe could avoid the Hostess with the Mostest. In any event, it was unlikely that Dr. Kent could produce anything more fantastical than what Blythe herself had conjured up when she had pushed her finger against the glass on Luke's genealogy chart.

"You're American," said the stout turban-clad woman hovering over her crystal globe. "You must be Luke's summer let. From Hollywood, are you?"

"Hmm. Gorran Haven must be a very small village indeed," Blythe replied with a resigned smile.

"Welcome to Cornwall, Mrs. Barton-Stowe," Dr. Kent continued brightly. "Luke told me at dinner the other night that he's delighted you'll be staying all summer."

"He did?" Blythe replied, surprised to learn that this unlikely pair broke bread together.

"He's my cousin . . . once or twice removed," Dr. Kent laughed. "Most of us whose families have lived here a long time are related one way or another, way back."

Blythe wondered if that made this exotic-looking woman a cousin of hers as well.

"I understand you may be kin to us both," the psychologist said, startling Blythe by practically reading her mind. "Blythe Barton is a name not easily forgotten in these parts, I assure you!" the woman added, laughing.

"So I gather," Blythe answered. "And do you do crystal-ball gazing as a sideline to your work as a psychologist?"

Valerie Kent looked at her visitor intently. "I took early retirement as a school psychologist. I still practice at the local clinic in the village two days a week. Except for my time at university, however, I've lived in Cornwall all my life."

"Do you have children yourself, Dr. Kent?" Blythe inquired politely.

"Never married. Do call me Valerie. . . . May I call you Blythe?" she prattled on cheerfully. "Good. I suppose my diminutive patients became my children. Now that I'm an empty nester, as you say in the States, I have plenty of time to read. I study all manner of wonderful subjects like piskies and knackers and the myths connected with Cornish folklore." She smiled broadly at Blythe and lowered her voice to a whisper. "I also find myself exploring all the exciting parts of my profession that were taboo when I was working in the state school system."

"Such as crystal-ball gazing?" Blythe smiled, raising an eyebrow in the direction of Valerie's transparent sphere.

"Scrying, it's called in the trade," she answered with manifest dignity. "It's the art of gazing into any clear surface in order to conjure visions within."

Blythe was taken aback.

"You mean, people claim to have seen visions in shiny surfaces *other* than crystal balls?"

"Oh, my goodness, yes. Mirrors, polished stones, glassy lakes . . . even pools of blood!" she added with relish. "Scrying's a very ancient technique, you know, used by the Chinese and the Egyptians and your Native Americans. . . . All sorts of spiritual leaders have employed it to forecast future events."

"A-And to look into the past as well?" Blythe said hesitantly.

"Have you not heard of past-life therapy in America?" Valerie Kent asked excitedly. "I thought everyone in California was interested in that sort of thing."

"Oh, of course . . . I've heard of it." Blythe nodded. "But I was born in Wyoming, so I must say, I haven't paid much attention to the subject."

"Wyoming? How fascinating. What state is that in?"

"It *is* a state," Blythe laughed. "In the Rocky Mountains . . . part of the Old West . . . cattle ranches . . . cowboys . . . that sort of thing. Like the movies."

"Well," Valerie barreled straight ahead, "I read in a professional journal recently that there are some eight hundred hypnotherapists in your country, and many of them specialize in exploring past lives with their patients. Others, I hear, are looking into the possibility that we may have genetically based memory or an ancestral component to our genes. Who knows?" she pondered with a zealous gleam in her eye. "Perhaps traces of past events that were significant or traumatic in the lives of one's ancestors may somehow be etched on one's own DNA."

"I-I don't understand," Blythe said, shaking her head.

"Encoded messages engraved on the genes," Valerie replied, as if she were stating an accepted fact. "Why do some people cry when they hear bagpipes and others, like me, plug their ears? Or why do travelers swear they've been in a particular castle or Buddhist temple before? It's because they have been—or because some ancestor was the chief priest and was murdered by a cabal or something."

"But wait," Blythe protested. "How is that possible? How could the traumas of war in one generation, for instance, possibly be remembered four or five generations down the line?"

Valerie leaned forward, tapping her forefinger to her skull.

"Trauma can change the brain and body chemistry," she pronounced solemnly. "That's been very well established by scientists these days, you know. And a change in body chemistry could alter some cells, which, in turn, might conceivably change the DNA—or notch a gene with information that future descendants inherit and might be able to access under hypnosis."

"Hypnosis . . . as in a trance?" Blythe asked slowly. "And you use your crystal ball to—"

"The crystal ball helps subjects focus their attention," she interrupted eagerly. "I've discovered over the years they can be hypnotized far more easily. Once they're in an altered state of consciousness, recalling one's past lives is rather like pushing the correct key on that computer of yours—the one Luke was telling me about—and then pulling up a long-lost file from your hard disk!"

"Luke mentioned my computer . . . ?" she asked, wondering in what context.

"The other lives one may have lived," Valerie continued, waving her hand airily as if her cousin's comments were not particularly relevant to their conversation, "or the memory of one's ancestors encoded on one's genes, may merely be 'files' that have never been retrieved by the brain until hypnosis is used to push the right key!" Then she smiled brightly and demanded, "Now, I ask you: Aren't past-life recollections and the theory of genetic memory intriguing notions? You Yanks have done such marvelous, open-minded research on these subjects. America's such a wonderfully go-ahead country!" By this time Dr. Valerie Kent was breathless with enthusiasm.

"Eight hundred past-life therapists in the United States!"

Blythe repeated with astonishment, reacting to the first of Dr. Kent's many startling statements. "Holy cow."

"My sentiments precisely, my dear." Valerie nodded emphatically, with near disastrous results to her turban. "I've read scores of books on the subject published in America . . . *Life after Life* . . . *Reunions* . . . *Closer to the Light* . . . *Saved by the Light*. All these dear people coming forward who've had near-death experiences or past-life adventures, or have seen into the past, or dared to look into the future. They are bravely telling their stories to the world. So courageous! So absolutely fascinating, don't you agree?"

"I-I had no idea . . . ," Blythe stammered. "And these past-life therapists ask their patients to stare into mirrors and such? What about glass-covered pictures or paintings and the like? Would . . . ah . . . that kind of thing induce a trancelike state?"

"You'd be simply amazed to read in the literature the variety of surfaces that have initiated an altered state of consciousness in people," Valerie volunteered enthusiastically. "Personally, I think," she added in a hushed tone of voice, "that it has more to do with hypnosis, the sensitivity of the subject in the trance, and what might be engraved on their genes than the particular shining surface involved—but that, of course, is mere conjecture on my part."

"But aren't you and others involved in this held up to ridicule by your more conservative colleagues?"

"Constantly," Valerie acknowledged with another airy wave of a hand bedecked with an extraordinarily tasteless collection of costume jewelry. "But not to worry. It's such exciting work . . . it's worth being ridiculed in the name of science," she added dramatically. Then she raised her arms and settled her turban more firmly on her head. "You know the old story . . . 'A prophet has no honor in his own country.' " She sighed. "But," she continued cheerfully, "I have my pension now, so what do I care?" Then, as if to bolster the arguments supporting the merit of pursuing her eccentric hobby, she disclosed conspiratorially, "Even Queen Elizabeth the First employed a wizard with an obsidian 'shewing stone,' he called it. She asked him to divine what might happen to the Spanish Armada."

"Amazing," Blythe murmured politely. She dug into her jeans pocket for a five-pound note and placed it on the table, prepared to pave her escape by making a contribution to Valerie's favorite charity.

"I'm a bit disappointed you can't tell me more about crystal gazers in California," the pseudogypsy sighed. "Well, no matter. Thank you for this," she said crisply, tucking it into her ample bosom. "The Search and Rescue Team appreciates every penny, I assure you." With that she leaned forward, and the palms of her hands hovered above her crystal ball. "Now," she said in a most professional manner, "I want you to begin to breathe very deeply . . . in and out . . . in and out. . . ."

"Oh, I-I don't think I want—"

"Come, come, Blythe," Valerie hushed her. "I've never had the opportunity to hypnotize an American. You must allow me to have a go. That's it . . . sit down! Now, breathe from your diaphragm . . . in and out . . . in and out . . . that's better . . . just breathe deeply . . . in and out. I want you to relax completely . . . just let your mind go blank, and . . ."

Blythe didn't reply. In fact, in the next few minutes she hardly heard Dr. Valerie Kent's voice at all. Instead, she stared, transfixed, at the sight of the ersatz conjurer's crystal ball. Inside the translucent sphere floated the vision of a baby. It appeared before Blythe's gaze like a tiny astronaut, adrift in infinite space, and utterly alone in its pink perfection.

"Blythe? Do you see something?"

"A child . . . ," she murmured. "I see a child. . . ."

"What else do you see?" Dr. Kent asked quietly.

"I-I think it hasn't been born yet."

"Why do you say that?"

Silence. And then Blythe answered in a labored whisper, "The baby . . . is still attached . . . to the umbilical cord."

"Who is its mother?"

"The baby's lost . . . and the mother . . ." Blythe paused, her voice choked with emotion. "The mother's crying."

"Why?" asked the psychologist gently.

In response to the hypnotist's previous question, Blythe herself began to weep.

After a few moments Valerie inquired gently, "What is it about this baby that makes you so melancholy, my dear?"

But Blythe didn't answer. She continued to stare at the crystal ball on the table in front of her and began to shake her head. The vision of the infant slowly disappeared, and with it her understanding as to the reason tears of despair had coursed down her cheeks.

"Blythe?" Valerie said softly. "I see you're back. How do you feel?"

"Sad."

"Do you remember why?"

"The baby was lost . . . it couldn't . . ." Blythe furrowed her brow, attempting to make sense of the memory.

"Were you that baby?" Valerie asked.

"No," she replied firmly, and then wondered why she felt so certain of this.

"Can you think who the child could be . . . or could represent?"

"I haven't a clue," Blythe replied tersely, wiping her cheeks with the back of her hand. "And now, I-I really must get back," she added, and stood up abruptly. A sense of despondency that was almost palpable had settled in her chest, and she was close to tears again, although she couldn't have explained the reason to anyone.

"I'm available if you'd like to explore this further," Valerie said gently.

"No, thanks," Blythe replied.

"Just ring, or drop by the clinic in Gorran Haven on Tuesdays or Thursdays," Valerie added, ignoring her visitor's curt reply. "I share space with the local GP in rooms above the shipwright's shop at the bottom of Rattle Alley."

Blythe sensed the psychologist's genuine concern and was sorry she'd been so short with her.

"Look, Valerie . . . it's very nice of you to offer, but I think I'll leave matters where they are." She turned toward the opening of the tent to make her escape. "It was a very . . . interesting . . . experience—both meeting you and gazing into your crystal ball."

"Likewise," Dr. Kent replied, pulling her scarlet turban from her head and setting it to one side. "Be well."

By the time Blythe emerged from the gypsy tent, it was nearly four o'clock. Still shaken by what she'd glimpsed in the crystal sphere, she set off toward Richard's birthday party in full swing on the other side of the open field.

As she tramped through the dewy grass past the donkey rides, she realized that her longing for motherhood had not waned one iota, and that she unconsciously had been blocking her awareness that, very soon now, her former husband and her sister would be holding an infant in their arms—a child by Chris that Blythe had desperately wanted herself. The mere thought of Ellie having a baby that was half her ex-husband's flesh and blood was enough to make her head throb and her pulse pound. Was it any wonder, then, that under hypnosis she conjured the sight of an unborn baby, when she dreamed of babies often in her sleep?

Blythe heaved a sigh of resignation, vowing yet again to work harder at accepting what was past and moving forward on a path of her choosing. However, the image of that child, floating like a cloud in an empty sky, haunted her.

She approached the balloon-and-crepe-paper-festooned enclosure just as Chloe Acton-Scott was sharply clapping her hands and calling for silence.

"Shall we all sing the 'Happy Birthday' song now?" the sleek blonde asked the tableful of children gathered around Mrs. Quiller's celebrated chocolate cake. Blythe looked on from the sidelines, unnoticed, as the moist air filled with the sounds of ten-year-olds bellowing the familiar tune. Richard's godmother promptly handed the cake cutter to Mrs. Quiller and picked up her glass of Guinness. Then she gazed up at Luke for a congratulatory kiss. Blythe's landlord obligingly bent down and brushed Chloe on the lips as the children tucked into their cake and ice cream with relish.

A kiss is just a kiss . . . a sigh is just a sigh. . . .

Blythe gratefully accepted a plateful of cake and a mug of tea from Mrs. Q and sat down on a camp stool.

"Oh . . . there you are!" Luke exclaimed, stepping away from Chloe. "We wondered where you'd got to. You missed Richard's big moment."

"I was here," Blythe corrected him quietly.

"The cake is marvelous, isn't it?" Luke asked, watching her take her first bite.

"Delicious," she agreed without looking up.

Was he thinking, as she was, of their beach picnic, where she'd first sampled Mrs. Q's extraordinary chocolate confection? Had he given much thought to what had happened after that? Probably not. As far as she could tell, when it came to Luke, a kiss was just a kiss, and nothing more.

Or, as Grandma Barton used to say, "You can warm yer socks in the oven, m'girl, but that don't make 'em biscuits!"

Chloe drifted over to where Luke and Blythe were engaged in desultory conversation and laid a well-manicured hand on his shoulder.

"Shouldn't we think about making our escape, darling?"

Blythe promptly stood up and announced, "If you two'll excuse me, I'm just going to give a hand to Mrs. Q."

Thankful for the diversion, she began the chore of packing the party paraphernalia into the hampers and coolers for transport back to Barton Hall.

"Truly, darling, we'd best be off," Chloe persisted, just as Richard declared that his friends wished to play a round of charades before it was time to leave. "Best to do that at the Hall, dear," she said decisively. "I'm sure Mrs. Stowe would be an excellent referee. . . . She's from Hollywood, where they make all the films," she proclaimed brightly for the children's benefit. She turned to Blythe and added, "You wouldn't mind taking over from here, would you? Luke and I were due at the Strattons' for drinks half an hour ago. I had Quiller bring round the Jag."

Blythe merely nodded. She was amazed the woman had the gall to ask a seventy-year-old man to walk a mile and a half back to Barton Hall in order to drive her car over to the fete.

"Are you sure you don't mind?" Luke asked Blythe quickly.

"No problem," she replied coolly. "I like children." Then she turned to the covey of Richard's friends, who gazed up at her expectantly.

"Who all is brave enough here to get in a car with me while I drive on the left side of the road for the first time?" she demanded.

"I am!" chorused the boys in unison.

"But I get to sit next to her," Richard announced excitedly, "because it's my birthday, right, Blythe?"

"Right you are, buckaroo." She grinned. "Last one in the Land Rover's a bowlegged cowpoke!"

"Are you sure you'll be able to navigate all right driving back to the Hall?" Luke asked with a worried frown as his son's boisterous friends piled into his car, laughing and shouting.

"Watch me," she challenged, holding out her hand, palm up, to receive his car keys.

"What about driving on the left? No qualms?" he persisted, handing her the keys.

"What difference will another dent or two make on the green monster?" She shrugged. "We'll all survive. See ya."

And without a backward glance she climbed into the driver's seat and flawlessly put Luke's car in gear. She'd driven hay balers trickier than this, she thought grimly.

She watched Luke through her rearview mirror monitoring their retreat as his scarred vehicle packed with noisy, happy children rolled across the field and headed toward Dodman Point.

Then, for absolutely no reason she could think of, a motto from her high-school days came to mind: When a cowboy gives you the keys to his truck, you know you're close to winnin' his heart.

"Oh, get real!" Blythe muttered to herself as she efficiently released the four-wheel-drive mechanism and took to the paved roadway. "It's just business."

Chapter Eight

July 17–31, 1994

As the summer wore on, Blythe kept strictly to her pledge that, when it came to her new business partner, she would conduct herself in a purely professional manner. To her surprise, so did Luke.

She gauged his cool-down was because he found Chloe's obvious attraction to him flattering and in typical English fashion opted for the choice that offered him the least emotional investment and the most emotional safety. In any event, Blythe figured after the year she'd been through, she wasn't in the market for a man, period. It was just a kiss, for God's sake!

She was more convinced than ever that her extraordinary response to Luke's ardor had been part of her attempt to compensate for Christopher's wounding behavior. She was persuaded that a great deal of time would have to elapse before she could trust her own judgment when it came to men. Yet, having come to this logical conclusion, Blythe couldn't deny her absurd sense of disappointment every time she recalled Luke's bending down to bestow that kiss on Chloe's lips.

As for Chloe herself, Richard's godmother arrived without fail every Friday evening, a refugee, as she described it, from her "beastly" job as an executive secretary in a London public-relations firm that specialized in touting pharmaceuticals worldwide. She invariably stayed until after high tea Sunday evening, with the result that Blythe found a way to busy herself revising sketches or reviewing work orders in her cottage.

When Luke was out of earshot, Chloe made it abundantly clear that she considered Barton Hall Nurseries an endeavor that was—in her words—"rather NQOCD." When Blythe requested a translation from Mrs. Quiller, the housekeeper flushed and revealed that it was a Sloane Ranger abbreviation that stood for "Not Quite Our Class, Dear."

Not long after this conversation, Blythe set out along the cliff walk in an increasingly unsettled state of mind. As she stared out to sea, she made a vow. Whenever she felt the slightest unwelcome spark flash between herself and Luke, she pledged to herself she would summon the memory of Chloe casting cow eyes at her swain during Richard's party, and Luke's kissing her in response. On the lips. Blythe and the dark-haired Mr. Teague were business partners and nothing more.

If you're fixin' to get yourself a good stallion, don't go lookin' in the donkey corral.

Damn, Grandma, Blythe thought irritably. She wasn't fixin' to get herself anything but a pile of work on her desk and potting soil under her fingernails!

Meanwhile, the stable's slate roof had been completely renewed at shocking expense. By the last week in July, Blythe began designing the raised beds where herbs would be planted in season in the walled garden. To her delight she found an able helper in young Richard.

"Hold that string for me, will you, Dicken?" she called, driving a small stake into the moist earth to mark the boundaries of the large patch of parsley they'd plant when the time was right. "After all, pardner, this section is being installed in your honor."

The ten-year-old had exhibited remarkable patience, working beside Blythe in the garden for hours at a time. He willingly fetched tools, dug long furrows with his hand trowel, carried small batches of old bricks destined to be used in a variety of low walls they were going to build, and generally made himself useful.

In contrast, Chloe had taken one look at the latest raft of repair projects and decamped for London, promising that she'd be down to see how they were getting on "some weekend soon."

Luke, meanwhile, began to master Blythe's computer, teaching himself how to set up spreadsheets so that they might better keep track of their inventories and, eventually, install a payroll system for their future workers.

Not surprisingly, word had leaked out in Mevagissey and Gorran Haven that Barton Hall Nurseries would soon be offering employment to locals with suitably green thumbs. Every day someone rang up or drove into the gravel entrance, volunteering to help out with large projects as a way of showing interest in coming to work permanently when the enterprise was in full operation.

One Saturday afternoon toward the end of July, Blythe urged Richard to accept an invitation to attend a beach picnic at Hemmick Cove with the family of one of the boys who'd come to his birthday party.

"You've done more than your fair share this week, Dicken, ol' bean," Blythe said with a smile, ruffling his hair. "It's a perfect day for the beach, so get moving!"

"Absolutely, son," Luke agreed. "Blythe and I can't put off any longer going through the last bits and bobs up in the stable loft, and you can't really help us with that."

Mrs. Quiller chauffeured her charge to the rendezvous point in her Ford Fiesta, announcing that she would then go on to Mevagissey to visit with friends for the rest of the afternoon.

"I say, Blythe, are you up to tackling a general tidying up so the electricians can install the new lighting grid next week?" Luke inquired as they watched Mrs. Q's car disappear up the shaded drive. "It might take us until dinnertime."

"I certainly don't have to rush anywhere tonight, do you?" she replied, and then flushed with embarrassment. She didn't mean to sound as if she were fishing for information about Luke's social life. She didn't give a damn if Chloe might be coming down from London this weekend, but her reply made it sound as if she did.

"I have no plans," he disclosed.

"Then let's have at it," she agreed.

It was nearly three in the afternoon by the time Blythe and Luke had worked their way through the last cartons that had been stored for decades under the eaves in the stable loft, where the warm air still smelled of loamy hay. An old pier glass stood upright on gilded legs—a legacy from the Victorian Age. Nearby, an eighteenth-century brass daybed had been pushed against one wall. Its two ancient feather mattresses had miraculously survived under a dust sheet. Beside it stood the large, unwieldy leather traveling trunk whose contents they had been ignoring for weeks.

Luke used a crowbar to force open the rusted lock.

"Oh, wow . . . ," Blythe breathed, awed by the sight of fine lawn shirts, silk cravats, and an ivory shoehorn neatly stowed in the trunk's upper compartments, just as they had probably been packed away by some well-trained valet untold years before. "Look how perfectly preserved everything is!" she exclaimed. What lay before her in remarkably good order was a costumer's treasure trove. "Who do you suppose these belonged to?"

Luke carefully lifted out the top tray and set it to one side. The next level contained men's sleepwear and shaving gear. Scrutinizing their design, Blythe could date the items as coming from the last quarter of the eighteenth century. A small leather-bound journal next to a pair of silver shoe buckles peeked from under a pile of silk hose.

"This must have been Ennis Trevelyan's . . . ," Luke declared, carefully turning the pages of the two-hundred-year-old volume. "It's written during the period he was traveling abroad to study painting in Italy and France. See?" he added, pointing to the date 1789 scrawled in brown ink at the top of one entry. He flipped through a few more pages. "This is from March 1790, in Paris," he read. " 'Last year the street rabble reduced the old prison to mere mortar and stone. People riot in the streets here for want of bread.' "

"The fall of the Bastille . . . ," Blythe said softly, remembering Garrett Teague's diary filed away behind the ledgers in Luke's library. Garrett's journal had been written during the same general time, when the two cousins had been traveling together on the Continent. "Storming the Bastille happened a few months earlier, didn't it? July . . . 1789 . . . am I right?"

"Correct. Because of the unrest in Paris," Luke murmured, tilting the diary so that the light filtering through the small window in the loft illuminated the yellowed pages. "Ennis writes that he and his cousin decided to continue on to Italy . . . Venice, in fact, where Ennis painted his self-portrait." Luke glanced sideways at her and added, "When I cleaned all the dust off, I realized that he was standing in front of the Doge's Palace on the Grand Canal." He rifled through a few more pages.

"Does it say there that they traveled farther south?" Blythe asked casually, remembering in Garrett's account that he'd had word in Naples that Blythe Barton Trevelyan was pregnant and that the news greatly upset him.

"Rome . . . Siena . . . Sorrento . . . ," Luke mumbled, thumbing through the pages. "Capri . . . Naples. Oh, dear," he chuckled.

"What?"

"It's just a single page. Ennis writes here: 'Father refuses to advance further funds and insists we return home. . . .' "

"Is that all?" Blythe asked.

Luke turned the page and then said more seriously, "No. There's another short entry. . . . Ennis received word a bit later that his father had died."

"Collis Trevelyan?"

"How did you know his name?" he asked, amazed.

"I . . . I saw it on your genealogy chart," Blythe replied, avoiding his quizzical glance. Her gaze fell on a stack of letters nestled beneath a neatly folded linen neckcloth and tied with a ribbon the color of faded roses. The clear, bold handwriting identified the cache as posted from Cornwall.

"Oh, my God . . . ," Blythe murmured as she began to peruse the sheaf of brittle stationery she had taken from the top of the pile. "It's from Blythe . . . my namesake . . . to Ennis . . . written in July of 1790."

"What does it say?" Luke asked, making room for her by the window so she would have better reading light. "Here, let me take the dust cover off the daybed and let's sit down."

With the stack of old letters resting in her lap, Blythe silently scanned the parchment she held between her fingers and tried to keep them from trembling.

> *It is of you I think when the candles are lit and dusk falls . . . a time when we two should be adrift in the great Barton Bed, the curtains drawn, the wind and rains held at bay, and I should have you in my arms to cosset you and kiss you and show you, as I did that very day of my foul wedding, that I was born to marry the younger Trevelyan brother, and not the man who claims me as his wife!*

"Read it aloud," Luke protested.

She looked at him, embarrassed to give voice to her namesake's two-hundred-year-old lust for Ennis Trevelyan. Then she shrugged.

"I can take it if you can," she said. "Stand by, O Laird of Barton Hall. But I'm warning you . . . this is pret-ty spicy stuff."

As she began to read to him from the beginning of the letter, her words took on the cadence of another age. When she reached the second page of Blythe Barton's highly erotic expression of thwarted passion, her voice sank to barely above a whisper.

> *When I am forced to submit to those wifely duties I so abhor, I can only stomach the task if I dream of your embrace. . . . I remember that afternoon in the wooded copse where we lay on the velvet moss and your hands traced the shape of my body before I would permit you to sketch my form with your chalk. Would that those contours were with you now, sinew and bone, flesh against flesh, so that you might recall the touch of my thigh, the taste of my lips, the—*

Blythe raised her eyes from the yellowed pages, unable to continue, and locked glances with Luke, who was staring at her with an intensity that totally unnerved her. After a few moments of electrifying silence, he pulled another letter from the pile and scanned it.

"Oh, Christ . . ."

"What?"

"She's pregnant," Luke reported, "and longing for it to be Ennis's child. . . ."

Poor Garrett Teague, Blythe thought suddenly. How heartbroken he would have been if he had ever stumbled upon these letters! He had loved Blythe Barton steadfastly, according to what she knew of the story, but had he and she ever—?

She glanced over at Luke and felt an odd sensation: Here she was, sitting beside the descendant of these people who had been caught in such tangled relationships so many years ago.

And what of sad, benighted Kit, whose own brother had betrayed him? His relationship with his wife in the bedroom had probably been hell.

And the wretched bride herself, Blythe thought morosely, a woman longing for what she could not have . . . a mere pawn of her elders' machinations. She must have been terribly lonely as the mistress of Barton Hall, living each and every day with a man she had been forced to marry who physically repelled her.

Each of them saw their dilemma from their own vantage point, she reflected soberly. Thinking back to the debacle in her own life—and the unholy triangle with Chris and Ellie—perhaps there was some lesson to be gained in this observation.

Her thoughts harked back to the accusations of neglect Christopher had hurled at her when she had gone to visit her ailing grandmother during the last year of their marriage. She recalled her bewilderment when Ellie categorically refused to accompany her on those trips, or to bear any of the burden of dealing with Lucinda Barton's lingering illness.

"If you want to play Florence Nightingale to the old bat, go ahead," Ellie had announced resentfully. "She always liked you best. Be my guest."

Undoubtedly Chris and Ellie felt like the injured parties, or at least they found a way to justify their reprehensible behavior in the same way the eighteenth-century members of the Barton and Trevelyan families rationalized their actions.

Meanwhile, Luke had begun to read a third letter aloud.

"Good God!" he exclaimed, reading from the missive that spoke candidly of Blythe's highly unsatisfactory marriage to Kit and described in explicit and immodest detail the young woman's carnal craving for Ennis to return to Cornwall.

"She paints a pretty vivid verbal picture of her physical longings, I'd say," Blythe commented. She was secretly embarrassed to discover how stimulating she found the first Blythe Barton's words, and awed by the sheer intensity of the letters.

"The Victorians may have been a repressed lot, but apparently not everybody in the Georgian Era was a prude, if this is any indication," Luke agreed as his eyes remained glued to the last paragraph of the letter he held in his hand.

"We're talking hot tamales for the ol' eighteenth century, wouldn't you say?" she drawled, drawing a deep breath as she allowed the letter she'd read to drop limply into her lap.

Luke retrieved it and reread the second page. " 'Would that those contours were with you now . . . ,' " he recited aloud, and then shot her another unsettling look. " 'Sinew and bone . . . flesh to flesh . . . so that you might recall the touch of my thigh . . . the taste of my lips . . .' " He shifted his gaze to meet hers and held it steadily.

His continuing silence charged the air as if lightning were about to crackle overhead. Blythe's nervous laugh finally broke into the heavy atmosphere.

"W-well—as my sainted Grandma Barton used to say—'a lot of what a man knows, a woman knows better.' "

Luke slowly shook his head, his eyes shifting briefly to stare at her hair and then back to her face as if he were trying to fathom some mystery concealed behind her expression. "I don't agree," he said quietly. "This letter reminds me of me, Blythe . . . when I was in the cave with you. How it was for me that day. What it's been like . . . whenever I've thought about you since."

"Oh, Luke," she began, "I really don't think we should—"

"The taste of you . . . ," he murmured, as if he were putting together the pieces of a puzzle, "so hot . . . so sweet and laced with chocolate." He smiled faintly, ignoring her feeble protest that they should avoid the subject of what had transpired between them during their picnic at the beach. "When I touched your marvelous hair . . . and took the measure of those beautiful long legs . . ." He raised one hand and threaded his fingers through her curls, resting the callused heel of his palm lightly at the base of her throat. Here was a member of the British gentry who had the hands of a Wyoming wrangler, no less, she thought distractedly. It was crazy.

Lucas Teague had stopped talking now, but his eyes glided brazenly down the length of her jeans.

"Luke . . . ," Blythe protested weakly, "you're supposed to be a repressed Englishman, remember?"

"Shall I let you in on a secret?" he asked with a dangerous glint in his eye. "I confess that for quite some time now I've been plagued by impure thoughts. In fact," he confided in a conspiratorial whisper, "I feel quite the libertine when it comes to you."

"You could've fooled me!" Blythe retorted, and then bit her bottom lip with vexation for having so imprudently displayed her cards.

"Ah . . . then the waiting worked." He smiled roguishly.

"You dog!" she shot back. Then she met his gaze head-on, her eyes troubled. "The timing's all wrong, Luke," she began, but he stilled her words by brushing his thumb across her lips.

"Shhh . . . ," he hushed her gently. "No, it's not. Both our hearts are sore, I grant you that, but—"

"More to the point," she interrupted, "we both know we should keep this venture together strictly professional. What's happening here is . . . it's . . . well . . . we've both been deprived of a normal . . ." She halted in frustration. "It's just the letters," she blurted. She felt herself increasingly stymied—unable to think clearly or express herself adequately. "They're very—"

"Provocative?" Luke suggested.

"Hot," she replied, nodding emphatically.

"Extremely stimulating," he agreed.

"Hmmm . . ." was all she could answer.

"After our picnic," Luke said, taking her left hand in his and examining the diamond ring she wore on one finger, "I could tell that you thought it was probably best to keep our relationship on the level of business." He turned her palm upright and lightly began chafing his thumb along the inside of her wrist. "It did seem the wisest, safest thing to do. But like our mutual ancestor, I'm afraid, Blythe, that I couldn't forget the touch . . . or the taste of you."

"Our ancestor?" she protested in a strangled voice. "We don't know for sure. . . ." She felt edgy and aroused, almost as if the Blythe of ages past had magically become encased in her skin, as if the woman's pent-up passion that had spilled upon these pages were dangerously close to overflowing right here, right now, in the loft above the deserted pony stalls. And it was definitely not Ennis Trevelyan who was putting Blythe's emotions in such turmoil. "Oh, Luke . . . ?"

It was a question and a plea, for she had found that she was unable to take her eyes off the sight of his thumb drawing gentle circles on her wrist. She felt as if she had begun to travel at Mach 2 speed down an elevator shaft. However, she knew with certainty that this time she wasn't headed toward another century.

"Listen . . . ," she temporized, pulling her eyes away from their hands to glance up at him. "I-I think we should—"

"Should what?" he interjected with a challenging glint in his eye.

She gazed at him for another long moment and then laughed. "You tell me," she returned his challenge. "You started this."

He grinned at her like the conquistador he was descended from. Then he suddenly looked serious. "I think," he began judiciously, ". . . we should make love. Right here."

"You do?" she said, barely above a whisper.

"I don't think either of us can help it."

"You don't?" she repeated, sounding to herself like some woefully deranged parrot.

"Indeed, we cannot," he said gravely, pulling her against his chest. "You're right about those letters, though," he murmured against her hair. "They're positively . . ."

"Hypnotic?" she whispered against his cheek.

"Erotic . . ."

"Practically pornographic," she countered with a helpless laugh, feeling a shocking rush of warmth radiating throughout her abdomen.

You've been here . . . done this! a voice shouted in her head.

"Wrong, cowgirl," Luke whispered fiercely in her ear. "This is going to be much, much better. . . ."

He began to kiss her then, deeply, and with growing fervor. Aroused by the echo of her namesake's forbidden passion, Blythe leaned back on the brass daybed and held out her arms to him, inhaling a slight musty scent floating up from the antique feather mattress that only served to link her even more strongly to the past.

Luke stretched out next to her and began to nuzzle the sensitive spot beneath her ear.

"God, Blythe . . . ," he groaned as his lips moved lower to kiss the hollow at the base of her neck, and then the tops of her breasts through her cotton work shirt. She had no idea which Blythe he was thinking of.

"Blythe Barton Trevelyan really lived," she whispered against the dark shock of hair grazing his forehead. "She wrote those words we read today, all that time ago. She really felt like this . . . she felt like I do now. . . ."

And, behaving as wantonly as her ancestress, she began to place excited kisses on his ears, his eyelids, and finally his mouth.

Suddenly Luke pulled himself from her embrace and abruptly stood up.

Oh, no, she cried silently, he couldn't be having second thoughts! Not now. Not after this?

To her relief, he began to peel off his shirt in a few graceful motions. He swiftly unbuckled his belt and shed his Wellington boots and moleskin trousers. She caught an arresting view of the man, reflected in the antique pier glass, as he flung his underclothes to one side. Just as quickly, she became aware of another invasion of warmth and moisture, this time within the private world of her own, erotic self.

Without his clothes Luke looked as strong as a Wyoming bronc rider, tall and lean and tanned from working outdoors. And, unlike any Englishman she'd ever known, his chest—like his face—was bronzed. Conquistador, indeed.

By now the ghostly lovers who had once inhabited Barton Hall had faded into the stone stable's dark corners, and Lucas Teague was all that filled Blythe's thoughts. He remained standing, his heightened state of arousal piercing her dreamy state and bringing her abruptly to an excruciating awareness of his insistent presence.

"This is actually pretty terrifying for me," she ventured, pulling herself upright on the feather mattress and clutching a corner of the dust sheet in her fist. "It's . . . ah . . . it's been a long time—"

"It's the same for me, Blythe," he said. "I haven't been to bed with a woman for nearly three years now. Not since Lindsay became ill." Then he added, "I haven't wanted to."

"What about Chloe?" she couldn't refrain from asking.

He sat down beside her and slowly began to unfasten the top buttons on her cotton work shirt. "I am going to try frightfully hard to convince you of something," he announced with a ghost of a smile. "You . . . my Yankee cousin . . . are all I want."

Then Luke removed her denim shirt. Next, he swiftly skinned her jeans down the length of her legs and made fast work of the rest of her clothing.

At first only their hands were joined in a dance of light and tender touches. Luke brushed her cheeks with the back of his fingertips. In response she slowly smoothed her palms along the contours of his naked shoulders, his arms, his hands, until her thumbs gently chafed the inside of his wrists in a deliberate echo of his earlier success arousing her to her present heated state. Then, with a satisfied smile, she slid her hands in the reverse direction to gently explore the nape of his neck.

The curve of his elbow, the crease where her thigh met her torso—these once forbidden territories now defined the perimeters of their desire.

Soon, however, Luke was seized by an irresistible craving to engulf the woman who now clung to him fiercely, to melt into her body and stake his claim, like a Cornish miner certain of finding a rich vein of copper. A violent sexual yearning took hold of him suddenly, fueled by abstinence, and stoked with a hunger that had been driven for too long by dutiful denial. He pulled her down on the bed once again and smothered her body beneath his own before he rolled them both onto their sides. In his ear rang the litany of the first Blythe Barton's carnal yearnings.

Sinew and bone . . . flesh against flesh . . . the touch of my thigh . . . the taste of my lips . . .

Her thighs, her lips, her ravishing breasts—he couldn't seem to get his fill of the woman he held in his arms. On the contrary, he was experiencing a disturbing blend of pent-up desire mixed with an overwhelming urge to protect this Blythe Barton from her painful past. This potent brew resulted in his being forced to reckon with an urgent, unswerving compulsion to fuse himself to her—and soon.

As she had done when they'd kissed in the cave, Blythe offered him a sure sign that she had no intention of playing the coquette. With infinite grace she parted her long legs and whispered a seductive invitation that told him she was a woman who knew exactly what she wanted—and that she wanted it now.

When he reached for her, he wondered if he would embarrass himself with a feverish need to merge his body with her intoxicating warmth. An instant later, when he sheathed himself with wondrous ease, he raised his head and stared down at her flushed face, drinking in the sight of Botticelli hair spread like a fan upon the bed.

He was shocked when she opened her eyes, for he could see

in their depths that she, too, was mad with yearning, impatient, as was he, to surrender to the sheer, physical imperative of this mystical fusion. The force driving them both now was pure energy, pure light, something out of the past and part of the present as well, a reunion and a new beginning, a forgetting of old wounds and a remembering of this day, forevermore. He wanted her. He was her. She was him. They were one force heading toward oblivion.

He hovered above her lithe form like a soaring seabird lifted on the currents of a blaze so intense, its heat began to consume him, and he thought he might incinerate to ashes. As he rhythmically moved against her, he watched, transfixed, as she began to tremble and cry out his name. He closed his own eyes quickly to hide the moisture that rose behind his lids. Then he fell on top of her and buried his face in her hair, yielding to Blythe's body the essence of things he could not say, nor even dare to witness.

For several minutes Luke languished in a kind of daze, cushioned by the splendid softness of her breasts. With his eyes still closed and holding her against his chest, he offered a silent prayer of gratitude to Lindsay for having taught him to cherish a woman—as well as desire her.

Then, to his dismay, he sensed that Blythe was struggling to suppress a sob. His breath caught, a part of him enraged suddenly to think that the experience they had just shared had been anything but perfect for both of them. Instinctively he knew she was doing her level best to quell another wave of emotion. Even so, he was chagrined to think that, by this act, a deep well of sadness in Blythe had been tapped and was bubbling to the surface.

Then, despite the fact that she was crying softly, she burrowed the top of her head beneath his chin and tightened her arms around his waist. He was even more surprised when she kissed him tenderly beneath his ear.

"Darling . . . what is it?"

"Shh . . . ," she whispered, shifting her weight onto her side.

He wondered bleakly if she hadn't been too fragile to have taken this step. Could it be possible that what he had just been feeling had been a one-sided fantasy?

Before his customary remorse could take hold, however, he felt a poignant combination of kisses and tears brush against his chest, against his stomach, trailing lower and lower in an exquisitely slow and blatantly obvious attempt to arouse him once again.

"Whoa, Miss Wyoming," he protested softly. "What have we here?"

"What we have here," murmured a husky voice against his thigh, "is a wanton expression of my undying gratitude."

"For what just happened to both of us?"

"Yes. And for wanting me as much as you did, Luke."

"As much as I do," he corrected her.

"Do?" she repeated in a provocative whisper, looking up at him. Her solemn mood had shifted to one of deliberate teasing. "You mean, do this?"

Her hand cupped him intimately, and then she lowered her head once more in a gesture of erotic benediction.

"Oh . . . yes . . . ," he groaned, fresh waves of pleasure coursing through his entire body.

As Blythe cheerfully resumed her nethermost explorations, Luke could only marvel at the cloud of her auburn curls that felt like angel feathers grazing his skin. This time it would be completely different, he realized. This time would be full of fun and laughter and earthy familiarity—a celebration of the end to such a dark season of sadness.

And before long Luke was playfully entreating Blythe to sit astride his legs and provide them both with a firsthand demonstration of rodeo riding.

"I was wonderin' when you'd ask me to do that," she replied with a throaty chuckle, "and I'd be most happy to oblige."

Later that night, alone under the eaves of Painter's Cottage, Blythe fell into an exhausted sleep. She dreamed that she could hear Lucas's Land Rover honking its way through clusters of sheep in the cliffside field that plunged down to her private beach. However, when she ran downstairs to greet him, an impenetrable mist billowing up from the Channel made it impossible for her to spot the car's approach. Feeling utterly bereft, she stood shivering on the slate step, vainly peering through the fog for a glimpse of his headlights, but the world outside her door was damp and dark.

Oddly, someone was pounding a fist against that same door. How strange, she thought groggily, for wasn't she standing on the threshold? No . . . she was in her bed and the clock on her nightstand said two A.M.

The heavy oak door downstairs creaked open. Early in her stay she'd ceased bothering to lock it, day or night.

"Blythe?" a voice whispered hoarsely.

"Lucas?" she answered, her thudding heart recovering its normal rhythm.

"Yes . . . it's me."

She fumbled for her dressing gown, couldn't find it, and scrambled out of bed, embarrassed to be wearing only her pajama tops. A light had been turned on below. When she stared down the steep wooden staircase, Luke was standing in its golden pool in the middle of the room, looking exceedingly sheepish. He'd donned only a pair of trousers, Wellington boots, and his Barbour coat, as if he'd responded to a clanging fire bell. His tanned chest appeared even darker than usual against his forest-green jacket.

"I couldn't sleep," he announced. He glanced at her tousled hair. "I'm sorry . . . I see that you were."

"Having horrible dreams," she said with a rueful smile. "I had a nightmare that I heard the Land Rover honking, but I couldn't find you in the mist. It was awful. Is it foggy outside?"

"No . . . the sky's studded with stars. Come down and have a look."

"No," she answered with a grin any Cheshire cat would envy. "You come up here . . . and have a look."

He vaulted up the ladder, ducking his head to keep from bumping against the rafters, and enfolded her in his arms.

"I began to think that perhaps this afternoon was a dream," he murmured, kissing her neck. "After Richard went to sleep, I watched CNN till midnight and then lay in that bloody Barton Bed and wondered why Miss Barton wasn't in it."

"Because I'm here." She smiled, snuggling close. "Waiting for you in Painter's Cottage in my cozy double bed, designed for citizens of this century."

"May I stay with you tonight?" he asked humbly. "Make love to you again? Sleep with you? Really sleep until the sun wakes us up?"

"Yes!" she whispered, flinging her arms around his shoulders, "you most certainly may." Then she blurted, "That was one of the best parts of marriage, wasn't it? Waking up beside . . ."

She halted midsentence, wishing she could bite off her tongue.

"It's all right to say it, Blythe," Luke reassured her, drawing back to study her expression. "We'll both have quite a few ghosts to banish, I suspect."

There were some ghosts this local landowner wasn't aware were lurking around Barton Hall, she thought unhappily. She wouldn't think about that now, not when the evidence of Luke's rising ardor was pressing erotically against her thigh.

Yet the misty edges of the sensual haze that had begun to envelop her like the fog in her dream whispered somehow of . . . betrayal. In the stable loft she'd known what she wanted, and it was Luke. But here, among the shadows surrounding them, Ennis's paintings hanging on the walls downstairs, the easel standing like a sentinel in the corner, she was reminded of old wounds. Some were long buried, and others, still festering, rose and robbed her of the hot, single-minded desire she'd felt earlier.

Whom could I be betraying? she thought, bewildered. Lindsay's ghost, or her own set of specters, real and imagined?

She thought of Christopher, the only man with whom she'd had sexual relations for more than a decade. She had been a relentlessly faithful wife to an outrageously faithless husband. She couldn't possibly be betraying him! But somehow the memory of Chris and those first, intense months of their courtship, making love in student housing and on the beach at midnight in Malibu, crowded her thoughts. Today, in the stable loft, everything had been so perfect. Why must restless phantoms hover about at a time like this? she demanded silently, glancing uneasily around the cottage cloaked in shadows.

By this time Luke had shed his jacket and kicked off his boots. He turned and eased her gently on top of her rumpled bed, lowering his frame to recline beside her.

He had told her in so many words that he'd been a faithful husband. As he stared at her now, brimming with intense desire that was probably fueled by three years of celibacy, she was inclined to believe him.

"Prove to me this afternoon wasn't a dream," he challenged harshly, his fingers starting to undo the fastenings on her pajama top.

"Prove to me you're not a ghost in the mist," she returned the challenge, staring into blue eyes that had changed to the color of the midnight sky visible through their window.

"Couldn't be simpler," he replied, and seized her hand, drawing it toward his midsection.

"The time to dance is when the music's playin'," Blythe murmured, assisting Luke to divest himself of his trousers and briefs and tossing them onto the floor.

"Grandmother Barton?" he chuckled as he removed her pajama top and cast it on top of his own abandoned clothing. Then he lowered his gaze to her breasts.

"Grandma Barton had an endless store of wisdom and advice," she confirmed, feeling self-conscious under his intense scrutiny.

"God bless that woman," he groaned, covering Blythe's body with the length of his own.

And then, mercifully, there was only Luke, and the music, and the dance.

Chapter Nine

August 1, 1994

An early-morning hiker who had set out on the coastal path at dawn's light the next day would have seen the sun and moon winking at each other across the slate roof of Painter's Cottage. Inside, oblivious to everything but the woman lying next to him, Luke gazed through half-opened eyes at the dim light that filtered through the windows beneath the sleeping loft. Sighing contentedly, he aligned his longer frame, spoon-fashion, alongside Blythe's.

"Morning, cowgirl," Luke whispered in her ear. "The sun's up."

"Barely," she groaned, and turned over, facedown, burrowing into her pillow.

"Come back here," he growled, pulling her close. Her backside fit into the curve of his lap to perfection. "Mrs. Q will wonder where I've got to when she brings up morning tea."

"Ummm? Tell her you were out plowing the north forty."

"It's just before six. I feel like I'm back at university, about to sneak a girl out of my rooms before the proctor wakes up."

"You should sneak back in the house," she mumbled, "like a good daddy, so your son won't find out what a rake you've been."

Blythe rolled over again, nuzzling Luke's shoulder and inhaling the wonderful musky scent under his arm. You couldn't know a man unless you flat out smelled that part of him, she thought lazily, and felt sleep dulling her senses.

The palm of Luke's hand soon put an end to her attempt to return to her slumber as he began to stroke her upper leg from hip to knee. Then his fingers gently kneaded her thigh.

"You're so strong here," he murmured against her neck. "Will you go riding with me sometime soon? On a horse?" he amended, a finger gently beginning to trace the crease where the top of her leg met her torso. "There's a lot of the estate you haven't seen, but it's too risky to chance taking the poor old Land Rover over the downs."

"I never ask a man to show me the size of his spread," she giggled.

He laughed. "Look, Blythe, I want to show you the estate—all of it. Shall we have a go later this afternoon?"

"I don't ride anymore," she said, suddenly subdued.

"But you told me all about barrel racing . . . that you were 'Miss Rodeo Wyoming, 1976.' Last night you certainly proved it."

"Luke . . . ," she chastised him gently, embarrassed by his alluding to her brazen behavior.

"What's the matter?" he persisted playfully. "Think our Cornish ponies aren't good enough for a cowgirl like you, is that it?"

"No . . . that's not it at all."

She was wide-awake now. Lucas seemed to sense her distress as she stared off into space.

"Blythe . . . what is it? Why is this subject painful for you? I've asked you to go riding several times, and you've always refused . . . or changed the subject."

She looked at him, her happy, languid mood evaporating, and sat up in bed.

"A long time ago, in Wyoming . . . there was . . . an accident, and ever since I can't bear . . ."

She leaned her head back against the pile of pillows and shut her eyes.

"Who was hurt?" Luke asked quietly.

"My brother, Matt. He was killed bronc-riding. I was there."

"Oh, Blythe . . . ," he said, pulling her against his chest. "How awful to have seen something like that. But why won't you—"

"Ride? Because I'll never go near a horse again as long as I live!" she blurted, pulling away from his embrace.

"But why? It can't have been your fault that your brother was injured."

"Killed," she corrected him, staring down at the bedclothes. "No. It wasn't."

"Then what's this all about?" he probed in an uncharacteristically direct fashion. After their night of extreme intimacy she could tell this man wanted to know everything about her. Coming clean about what had happened when Matt had died, however, was asking a lot.

After the Barton family had buried her brother thirteen years earlier, Blythe had never again spoken of the day—or way—her brother Matt had died. Not to her parents, not to her grandmother, not to anyone, including Christopher. There was nothing to be gained from rehashing it all, and quite a bit to lose. And except for her former husband, they had all been witnesses anyway.

"I did a terrible thing . . . afterward," she said in a low voice.

"After your brother was killed? What could you possibly do that was so terrible?" he chided, kissing the top of her head. She clamped her lips shut and remained silent.

"Tell me what happened to Matt. How old was he?"

"Seventeen," she whispered.

"Weren't you still at university? How did you happen to be there?"

Blythe was suddenly awash in memories. As she began to tell the story of Matt's death, her words seemed almost to describe a disaster that had happened to someone else, some other family's tragedy.

"I had just graduated from UCLA that June, in 1981 . . . as

both my parents had. My Dad was incredibly proud. I didn't meet Christopher until afterward. That autumn."

"And?" he prompted after a few moments of silence while Blythe remained lost in thought.

"Dad wanted me to come home to Wyoming for the summer before I was to begin graduate school."

"In landscape design. In California, yes?"

She nodded. "Mr. Hill, the head of the Jackson Hole Rodeo Association, asked me to make an appearance that Saturday night after one of the saddle events. Matt being a contestant and all, and my grandmother Barton riding in the Grand Entry every week—it was kind of a Barton family reunion . . . a 'return of the local heroine,' I guess. I'd won the Miss Rodeo Wyoming title when I was in high school, and hardly any of the girls from there went on to college. I was flattered to be asked."

"And I'll bet while you were away in California, Mr. Hill had missed seeing you in your jeans," he ventured with a smile. Blythe didn't laugh.

"That night," she continued, "when Matt was climbing onto the horse in the chute, the animal went . . . wild . . . bucking and practically kicking down the stall. Matt jumped off while the other hands tried to settle it down. Matt knew that horse was really rank and—"

"Rank?" Luke repeated. "Translate, please."

"It means a horse that really bucks . . . acts ornery . . . gives a good show to the spectators. Matt knew that if he could hang on, he'd finish in the money."

"Are the horses they use for the rodeo . . . mental?" Luke asked. "What makes them buck like that?"

"Some horses just like to do it. The ones that hurt an amateur rider at some point, or can't be broken . . . well, the only place for them is the rodeo. Otherwise they'd end up as dog food."

"Pity," Luke said mildly.

"The harder a horse bucks, the more points the horse and

cowboy can earn. More points, more money. It's the rodeo way of life."

"But I thought the girth strap on the animal's testicles was the thing that made them so wild," said Luke. "Not true?"

"The bucking strap?" Blythe shrugged. "That strap doesn't touch their testicles. As a matter of fact, most rodeo horses don't even have their gonads anymore. Rodeo stock runs to geldings or mares. The strap just feels strange to them and they try to get it off. Basically these are horses that just like to buck—period—and they've never lost their taste for it."

"And Matt's horse?" Luke prompted.

"Sometimes a horse comes along that's more than rank . . . it's loco . . . crazy." Blythe was twisting the edge of the bed-sheet between her fingers. "The stock contractor's job is to supply all the animals for the rodeo each week—the bulls and bucking horses, the roping calves—everything. And he's trained to judge an animal's temperament and knows how to cull out the real lunatics." She stared up at the rafters and blinked hard. "The broncs are supposed to be rank, not crazy. Rodeos are supposed to test your skill, and they can be very dangerous . . . everybody involved knows that . . . but the cow-boys are supposed to have a chance."

"And because of that particular horse, you're saying that Matt didn't have a chance?"

Blythe merely nodded.

"Didn't the stock contractor notice that the horse your brother was going to ride was behaving strangely?"

"He did!" Blythe said, her voice catching in her throat. "Virgil Bailey's the best in the business. He spotted that son of a bitch as soon as he was unloaded from the stock truck that week. He told Oatsey—"

"Oatsey?" Luke inquired. "That's someone's name?"

"Nickname," Blythe said grimly. "Otis McCafferty was your typical ex-bull-rider rodeo hand who fancied himself the Marlboro Man. Full of himself and what he carried in his jeans."

"The man who taught you to play poker, yes?"

"And a few other things." Luke cocked an eyebrow at this but remained silent, waiting for Blythe to continue. "I say that, you see, because Oatsey and I had a very brief roll among the hay bales the summer after my second year at UCLA. He was a first-class jerk."

"And?"

"Virgil told Oatsey not to load the horse my brother drew, but Oatsey . . . he got distracted and forgot."

"And it threw your brother to the ground?"

"Right out of the chute—like a rag doll. There was no way Matt could have stayed on that horse, bucking like it did. When Matt fell off, his foot caught in the stirrup and he got dragged around the arena. That damned horse deliberately crashed into the chutes . . . whatever obstacle he could kick. The pickup men couldn't get to my brother in time."

"And . . . ?"

"Matt couldn't get free, you see," she said, her voice cracking. "He just hung there by one leg and the horse kept galloping in circles, dragging Matt like a sack of corn, slamming him into everything in its path. In about a minute my brother's neck was broken and his face was—"

Blythe closed her eyes and fought to regain her composure.

"How did they get him loose?" Luke asked gently.

"Virgil ran into the arena just as the pickup men finally got the bronc cornered and shut down. Virgil got to Matt first and got his foot free, but Matt wasn't breathing. It was too late . . . his neck had snapped like a dried stick. The emergency crew couldn't revive him. They did their best, but—"

"And where were you when this happened?" Luke asked quietly.

"I was on my horse, all decked out in my glitter-girl Miss Rodeo Wyoming outfit, waitin' to do my thing," she said sarcastically, her eyes rimmed with tears. "I even had my old sash on: 1976."

"And then . . . ?"

"I jumped off Ranger and ran into the arena with Virgil and everybody else. I screamed at him, 'Why was Matt riding a horse like that?' and he said he'd told Oatsey not to use him, but that Virgil hadn't checked to make sure, and that it was all his fault." She turned to face Luke and added fiercely, "But it wasn't. It was Oatsey and his girlfriend's fault! And then, after they got that horse away from my brother, I took my whip and started beating it on the head and neck as hard as I could!" Blythe had begun to pound her fist against the mattress. "I just beat it and beat it, and would have beat it to death if I could, but Virgil grabbed my arm and hauled me away."

The only sound beneath the rafters was Blythe's ragged breathing.

"It was unforgivable," she said, barely above a whisper. "The grandstand was full of kids. What I really wanted to do was beat Otis to death for killing Matt and maim that horse so it couldn't buck anyone! But beating a horse on the neck like that . . . making it bleed—I should never be allowed *near* a horse—"

"Your brother had just died. . . . You were in shock."

"That bronc was loco. . . . It never should have been loaded into the chute by that fucking rodeo hand who—" She buried her face in her hands. Luke put his arm around her shoulders as wrenching sobs nearly cut her breath off. "You'll think all I ever do is cry!"

"It was terrible to have done what you did to the horse," Luke said, rocking her in his arms, "but it *is* forgivable."

"No!" Blythe exclaimed, pulling her head off his shoulder and meeting his gaze. "It's not! I love animals. I loved horses until that night. Now I hate them!"

"I understand why you feel that way. . . ." He began to soothe her like a child as he stroked her hair. "But I don't think it's horses you hate . . . and I have no doubt that one day you'll even grow to like my Cornish ponies a wee bit. Perhaps even ride one. They're very low to the ground, you know," he teased gently. "And mine are quite sweet-tempered."

"You think so?" she murmured, drying her eyes with a corner of the bedsheet.

"They adore you," he teased.

"What do you mean, they 'adore' me?" she groused.

"They were lonely in that big stable. They find the piggery cozy and snug, and they give you all the credit for their improved housing conditions."

"How do you know that?" Blythe sniffed, reaching for a tissue from a box perched on the bedside table and noisily blowing her nose.

"They tell me these things," Luke said smugly, kissing the top of her head again. "And one day they'll tell you."

"Yeah, right."

"Will you at least think about riding with me one day?"

"I'll think about it."

"Well done," he praised her, giving her shoulders a squeeze. He took her hand in his, his thumb grazing the diamond band she still wore on her ring finger. "You said you met Christopher soon after your brother died."

"Yep," Blythe said, wondering what one did with a slightly used twenty-five-thousand-dollar anniversary ring. "I went back to UCLA that fall, agreed to help a dashing young Englishman with his student film, and signed up for a whole new life." She drew in a deep breath and turned toward him. "Oh, Luke," she sighed, putting her arms around his shoulders and pulling them both prone on the bed. "I've treated you like I was in some shrink session with your cousin Valerie. I'm sorry."

"There's nothing to forgive," he murmured, his lips grazing her forehead. "So I take it that you've met the gypsy in the family. At the village fete?"

"She's nice."

"A bit 'loco,' as you put it."

"No way!" Blythe protested. "She seems very knowledgeable about her field."

"Since she retired, I'm afraid dear Valerie's gone a little

over the top with all that paranormal claptrap. Or wasn't she wearing her red turban that day?"

"That was just for effect," Blythe laughed. "She's actually a pretty skilled therapist, I think. She hypnotized me in her gypsy tent."

"Ah . . . and did you spy anything in her crystal ball?" he teased.

"A baby."

"Goodness."

"Still attached to an umbilical cord."

"Oh."

Luke had ceased his bantering and looked uncomfortable.

"Which reminds me," she said self-consciously. "I think we need to talk about something. It's pretty personal. I'll probably blush."

"Ah . . . the subject of babies . . . ," he said, a muscle growing taut in his jaw. "Or is it about not producing babies?"

"Look, Luke . . . maybe this was just one mad night of passion—"

"Hardly," he interjected dryly.

"—and we need not trouble ourselves with the subject," she continued, forcing a light tone, "but if we're actually going to be foolhardy enough to continue riding down this trail . . ." She hesitated, wondering at the sudden shift in Luke's mood whenever the subject of children was raised. "The problem is . . . I didn't come to Cornwall exactly expecting to have . . . a relationship. I'm embarrassed to admit that I didn't travel with a diaphragm, I hate IUDs, and the pill doesn't agree with my body chemistry."

"I'm afraid I have to admit I haven't bought a box of condoms since my university days," Luke confessed.

"Is that where you met your wife? When you were in college?"

"Nooo . . . not at Cambridge," he chuckled. "I met Lindsay at Chloe's deb party."

"Don't tell me you were Chloe's date that evening?"

"I was indeed."

"Jesus!" Blythe laughed. "How did Lindsay manage to keep her as a friend, if I may ask?"

"The clever girl asked Chloe to be maid of honor at our wedding. Then she made her godmother to Richard."

Blythe liked the way Luke could speak affectionately of his late wife with perfect ease.

"It must have been so hard for you and Richard to lose her," she said quietly. "But at least a part of her lives on in your son. He's such a great kid. Did you never think about having a second child?"

She knew she was fishing in dangerous waters, and as she anticipated, Luke's answer was short.

"We considered it."

"But you had a vasectomy?" she blurted.

"No. A second child was out of the question because of Lindsay's illness."

"Oh . . . of course," Blythe responded, penitent. "It was a dumb question."

He smoothly changed the subject back to the practical matter Blythe had originally raised.

"Look, Blythe, I don't want you to worry about this contraception business. I'll purchase some condoms today when I go into the village."

"It'll cause talk," she teased, grateful that he had apparently forgiven her for her unseemly gaffe.

Luke leaned back and erupted with laughter. "How right you are," he said, grinning broadly, his good humor restored. "However, despite setting Gorran Haven on its ear, buying a box of condoms at the chemist's today fills me with delicious anticipation."

"My . . . my, aren't we the naughty boy," Blythe said, mimicking his plummy British accent.

He reached for one of her hands and slowly turned it over, planted a kiss on the palm, and then began to draw small, provocative circles with his tongue. With calculated deliberation he seized her forefinger and smoothed its pad from side to side across his lower lip. As an amazing current spread up her arm, he took the moistened finger into his mouth and sucked on it sensuously.

"Whoa," she breathed, "you are debauched." Nervously she glanced sideways and caught sight of the clock sitting on the nightstand. "Oh, my God! Look at the time!" she gasped. It was nearly eight o'clock, long past the delivery time for morning tea.

"When I get back to the Hall, I'll just tell Mrs. Q to expect you for breakfast," he replied calmly, releasing her hand.

"You wouldn't dare," Blythe declared, pulling the bedsheet protectively around her bosom.

"Watch me."

With that Luke bolted out of bed, pulled on his clothes, and within moments he was steering his Land Rover back to Barton Hall.

During the following weeks Luke and Blythe struggled to maintain a sense of decorum as they supervised the building of the temporary, plastic-covered Quonset huts and inventoried plant stock they had ordered from a large nursery in Devon. In reality there was a current of excitement buzzing between them like an ungrounded wire. It vibrated often enough to be disconcerting during the performance of the most mundane tasks.

Most nights Luke made his way to Painter's Cottage around midnight, where the two of them were plunged into a heated fog of sensuality, drenched with unreasoning desire for each other, like the unusually warm summer mists that boiled over the nearby cliffs. Shrouded from the outside world, they made love for hours inside Painter's Cottage. Yet each time Blythe couldn't escape from the demented notion that some vaguely disapproving presence was observing their consuming passion for each other.

I'm a free woman! she thought with exasperation. Lucas Teague is a free man! What in tarnation is wrong here? We're unmarried adults living in the feel-good twentieth century, for God's sake!

To underscore this fact to herself, Blythe dispatched a letter to her father at his new address in Jackson Hole. She announced that she had embarked upon the Barton Hall Nurseries project with the owner of the venerable estate where she was living in a stone cottage by the sea, and that she had decided to stay on in Cornwall for the foreseeable future. She hesitated as she reached the end of the page and then added:

It certainly appears that all
the remaining members of the
Barton family have embarked on
new chapters in their lives.

My warmest wishes to you and
Bertha for happy times together.
You deserve it.

Much love,
Blythe

Late one night Luke and Blythe lay sated on her bed with only a light sheet covering their bodies. She could hear the waves lapping quietly below the window and pondered how the water had been rolling ashore at that same spot since the coast had first been formed millennia before.

Propping herself on one elbow, she asked tentatively, "Luke . . . do you ever have a . . . sense of the chain of people who have lived before you at Barton Hall?"

"At times," Luke acknowledged, absently threading his fingers through her hair. "It's a kind of weight . . . the balance of all of them against just me, fighting to keep the place intact."

What Luke felt about the past was grounded in the present, she realized with disappointment. What he had described had no relation to the specters she had witnessed at the beginning of the summer. Nor did it allude to the sense she had that the triangle of Blythe, Ennis, and Kit still imbued the walls and corners of Barton Hall. And what about Luke's direct ancestor, Garrett Teague? Where did he fit in?

She turned over in bed and snuggled under Luke's chin. His ancestors were long gone, buried in the ancient soil in St. Goran's churchyard. Now there was practical business to take care of, she lectured herself. Luke was real. A flesh-and-blood lover of the highest caliber. Chris and Ellie were in Kenya. She should cut out the woo-woo stuff and concentrate on getting those seven temporary potting sheds constructed.

Despite these admonishments, however, by the end of the month following their discovery of the contents inside Ennis's trunk, Blythe continued to find herself shaken to her core by the avalanche of emotions she and Luke had shared in recent weeks.

As far as she was concerned, Lucas Teague was to love-making what Ennis Trevelyan had been to painting: talented, single-minded, and energetic. Much to her astonishment she had discovered that the gent in tweed clothing was at heart an unrepentant sensualist. Nearly every night he would seize her hairbrush and pull it through her unruly mass of curls until sparks crackled in the shadowy loft at Painter's Cottage. He delighted in their bathing together in the old-fashioned claw-and-ball tub that commanded a spectacular view of the Cornish coast.

And when Luke wasn't wooing her with bunches of wild violets he'd found growing on the banks of the River Luney, he was smuggling sweet Cornish cream out of Mrs. Q's larder, which he put to bewitching use in the middle of the night.

When it came to the sexual aspect of their relationship, a repressed Englishman, Lucas Teague definitely was not. However, as far as spoken communication was concerned, Blythe discovered that he tended to refrain from full disclosure. Chloe Acton-Scott did not return to Barton Hall, nor did Luke make mention of her. The August tourists departed. By early September the elegant blonde still hadn't made an appearance.

"Would you consider joining me in the Barton Bed one night soon?" Luke whispered with an evil grin late one afternoon while Richard was occupied with Mr. Quiller working in the walled garden. "I fear I've been spotted too many times by the local farmers driving home at dawn's light. I feel the need to mount a gallant attempt to salvage your reputation."

"Yours must be in tatters by now, too," she laughed. "Consorting with a Yank, no less."

"The Bawdy Bed of Barton could be fun," he said temptingly. "We can close the curtains on it and you can tie me to the headboard or something."

"How 'bout tonight? I'm great with a lariat."

"I take it that's some sort of rope?" he translated. "Excellent. Your cover story can be the early arrival tomorrow of all that polyurethane for the potting sheds. I'll just tell Mrs. Q you're staying to dinner and ask her to make up the blue room—that's five doors down from mine," he disclosed conspiratorially.

"And you really think she'll be fooled?"

"No. But Richard will."

"I don't know if I can even find the Bawdy Bed of Barton—or the blue room, for that matter—in that mausoleum of yours," she said, laughing. "I have some vague notion the master wing is down the corridor opposite the landing at the top of the grand staircase, but after that I'm lost."

"I'll draw you a map and put it under your plate at dinner."

"Are you serious?" she demanded, glad for a chance to escape the vaguely sinister musings that lurked at the back of her mind whenever they made love at the cottage.

"Absolutely serious," he said solemnly. "Look under the soup course."

That evening Blythe felt a frisson of anticipation when she surreptitiously lifted her soup plate and retrieved a hand-drawn map sketched on a small piece of stationery imprinted with the Barton Hall letterhead. She caught Luke gazing at her with a lecherous gleam in his eye from across the mahogany dining table as she tucked the provocative note into the pocket of her slacks. To hide her embarrassment, she quickly turned to Richard and asked him if he'd be willing to help her count rolls of polyurethane when they arrived in the morning.

"Oh, yes, please," he said happily. "What's poly— What is that, Blythe?"

"Sheets of very strong plastic . . . sort of temporary windows for the potting sheds."

After dinner Richard invited her to join him at a card table set up in the library where he had been working all summer long on a gigantic jigsaw puzzle depicting a wall of paintings that hung in the Louvre in Paris.

"This is a nightmare, Dicken," she groaned, fingering a puzzle piece colored an unrelieved shade of brown and signifying nothing, as far as she was concerned. "How do you have the patience?"

"Look!" the boy said excitedly. "You've got a bit of the *Mona Lisa*'s hair!" He took the piece from her fingers and snapped it into place.

"Brilliant!" Blythe said, admiringly.

She had purposely sat with her back to the Barton-Trevelyan-Teague genealogy chart. Luke stretched out on the brown leather sofa, cracked with long use, reading the newspaper. The two Labs were curled up in their wicker dog baskets flanking the fireplace and snored or scratched in blissful contentment.

The instant the clock on the mantel struck nine, Luke sat up, folded his newspaper, and announced, "Bedtime!"

"Oh, Dad," Richard protested, "can't we have fifteen more minutes? Blythe's just found the corner of the *Mona Lisa*'s mouth!"

"No. Sorry. Can't be done. Off with you, now."

"It's not fair!" Richard protested stubbornly. "Blythe and I were just—"

"Not another word!" Luke interrupted sternly.

"Will you come with me upstairs?" Richard asked Blythe in a small voice.

She darted a glance at Luke, wondering how far she should go in offering comfort and companionship to the ten-year-old who looked at her with a beseeching expression.

He's not your son!

Richard's father hesitated and then rose from the leather sofa. Instantly Derek and Beryl sprang from their baskets.

"I'll take you up," he replied quickly, and the awkward moment passed. "I'm a bit tired myself tonight," Luke added, winking at Blythe over his son's head. "Would you mind, Blythe, if I turned in too?"

"Not a bit," she answered, doing her best not to smile. "I'd like to read for a while. I spotted your copy of du Maurier's *The King's General* and thought I'd give it a try. Night, you two."

"Will you read me a story, Daddy?" Richard demanded.

"A very short one," Luke conceded.

"Good night, Blythe," Richard said, his good spirits completely restored.

"Good night, buckaroo." Blythe smiled and impulsively gave him a hug.

"Don't stay up too late," Luke warned, a ghost of a grin on his lips. "The chaps delivering the plastic rolls should be here around eight." He turned to the dogs. "Off to the kitchen with you lot . . . come!"

When they had shut the door, Blythe pulled Luke's hand-drawn map out of her pocket. At the bottom of the directions to his bedroom in the south wing Luke had scrawled, "I'll be waiting in the BBB. The curtains will be closed, but please don't let that stop you."

Blythe reached her hands over her head and stretched. She felt a fillip of excitement fluttering in her chest. The Bawdy Bed of Barton. How deliciously wicked that sounded! Luke had told her that generations of his family had lived, loved, given birth, and died in that four-poster.

"I try not to think about it too much," he had laughed.

She was consumed with curiosity to see what a piece of furniture with that much history attached to it looked like.

Despite Blythe's best intentions, she found her glance drawn to the wall over her shoulder where the enormous family tree looked down on her from its ornate gilt frame.

Taking a step closer, she couldn't resist staring at the long line of Teague ancestors that proceeded from Lucas's name directly back to Garrett's entry into the history of Barton Hall.

"Born . . . 1772. Died . . . 1848 . . . ," she murmured, carefully refraining from putting her hands near the glass. Well, at least poor Garrett had finally married someone in 1799 at age twenty-seven, she reflected, noting that Joan Vyvyan was ten years younger than the heir to Barton Hall. They had had a son to carry on the line and several other children as well.

She glanced over at the revolving bookcase, recalling the memory of seeing young Garrett urgently calling her namesake to escape with him into its depths. Had she slipped into some time warp that day, somehow catching a glimpse of the tumultuous events in the lives of Luke's ancestors? Or had she accessed a wayward notch on her own genes, as Valerie Kent described it?

She gazed once again at the chart, her eyes drifting from Garrett's name to her namesake's. Blythe recalled how she had pushed against the glass at that spot but had lost her nerve and had called a halt to the phenomenon.

Curiosity killed the cat, she reminded herself silently, just as the clock struck nine-thirty. Blythe then felt a delicious shiver run up her spine. The thought of Luke waiting for her in the Bawdy Bed of Barton was a powerful aphrodisiac, even more powerful than the undeniable magnetism that had previously drawn her to unearth the lives and loves of their eighteenth-century counterparts.

"Night, all," she whispered, switching off the light. The library was plunged into darkness, and Barton Hall seemed, for once, devoid of ghosts.

* * *

Later that night Blythe acquired a new understanding and appreciation of the lengths to which Lucas Teague would go to please her in bed.

Sure enough, when she finally found her way to the castle's master suite, the red velvet curtains of the enormous four-poster were shut tight. The drapery hung from the immense bed's oak canopy, which was ornately carved with cherubs clutching various family crests. The massive overhead structure was supported by spiraling Jacobean bedposts hewn from single tree trunks. Blythe closed the door gently and padded across a thick Persian carpet to the side of the bed.

"I feared you'd got lost," a deep voice rumbled from within.

"One wrong turn, but here I am," she laughed shakily.

"Are you removing your clothing, my darling?" the voice asked calmly.

"Y-Yes," Blythe replied, her fingers fumbling with the buttons on her silk blouse.

"What, exactly, are you removing?"

"My blouse."

"Excellent. And now what?"

"Luke!" she protested. "You're getting positively prurient."

"What?" he insisted.

"My slacks . . ."

"Standing in your knickers and bra, are you?" he inquired with sweet solicitude.

She remained silent for a moment.

"Panties only," she announced softly, feeling the muscles in her abdomen tighten excruciatingly.

"Please, dear heart . . . keep them on and come in here."

She drew the velvet curtain aside and gave a little gasp. Two brass sconces attached to the velvet hangings installed above the padded velvet headboard cast a golden glow over the scarlet enclosure. Luke's bronzed chest had turned to burnished amber in the shadowy light. He had thrown back the duvet and was lying on his side, looking to her like a capsized nude statue that sported a marvelous tan.

"Extremely hazardous, those," he announced, nodding to the candles burning above. "But it's worth the risk, don't you think?" Then, with elaborate ceremony, he placed two boxes on the feather duvet. One box contained a row of condoms wrapped in individual packets of foil; the other displayed an array of chocolate-covered cherries.

"One for you," he murmured, popping a chocolate into her mouth, "and one for me," he continued, placing a condom on the bedside table. Before she could seize a candy to present to him, Luke snatched the confections off the bed and chose one for himself. "I've saved the best for you," he said with a smug smile, and then placed it between his teeth.

Shaking her head, she responded, "Englishman . . . you never cease to amaze me." Then she crawled on her hands and knees across the wide expanse of the bed and faced him nose to nose. "Now, give me that!"

The candles had burned so low, they were nearly sputtering out. They cast an eerie glow inside the red velvet world that had served as their plush cocoon. The dancing liquid light played across Luke's immobile features and long, lean body as he lay faceup, eyes closed, like some effigy in a crypt, beautiful and timeless. Blythe recoiled from the image as soon as it wafted through her mind. She pulled herself to her knees and promptly blew out the tapers, careful not to splatter wax on the plush fabric. The interior of the Barton Bed was plunged into darkness, and instantly Blythe regretted not now being able to see Luke, to behold the man who had given her such pleasure and who had inspired her to return it in kind.

She sank down beside him, stretching out on her back, feeling uncomfortably like a companion effigy on a tomb, her left foot lying beside his right calf.

Now the curtained walls seemed close and confining, no longer the cozy refuge they had been from the moment she had slid into Luke's lair. It disconcerted her to think that some two hundred years earlier Blythe Barton and Kit Trevelyan had spent their wedding night in this very bed. What had her namesake done when all her attempts to escape her fate had failed and she was confronted with the reality of facing her new husband and physically surrendering to him? And where had Ennis and Garrett slept that night in 1789?

As she listened to Luke's even breathing, she thought about what it must have been like for women in earlier centuries, forced to marry against their will and to join their bodies with men they didn't want—or worse, couldn't physically abide. What would she have done in the same situation?

Blythe's thoughts drifted to the memory of her first glimpse of the slashed painting of Ennis she'd found in the stable loft. When had Blythe and Ennis first betrayed Kit? she wondered. Before or after Collis Trevelyan forced her to the altar in St. Goran's Church? And was it only Ennis whom Blythe took into her bed? From what little she had pieced together, Garrett Teague had somehow become entangled in the young woman's desperate need for love and affection.

Try as she might, Blythe couldn't refrain from mulling over the strange parallels between her sister Ellie's committing adultery with Christopher, and Blythe the First's betraying Kit with his brother, Ennis. Her sister had done to her what Ennis had done to Kit . . . coveted what didn't belong to them. They had seized what they wanted from their siblings, what they desired, and the devil take the hindmost.

But was that what had really happened? Blythe asked herself bleakly. Wasn't there more to it than simply that Ellie and Ennis were bad; or that Chris Stowe and her eighteenth-century namesake were highly sexed and faithless? Was she, Blythe Barton, utterly blameless in the Year of our Lord, 1994?

Blythe reflected on the impressions of the eighteenth-century world that she had glimpsed so mysteriously. When she had stepped outside the bare facts of her namesake's tangled affairs, she had been amazed to discover that she could empathize with everyone: the first Blythe Barton, Kit, Garrett, and even the roguish Ennis Trevelyan. None of them was perfect, but neither were they evil. Their flaws had been their undoing, and not some inborn rapaciousness engraved in their characters.

And if Blythe was scrupulously honest with herself, none of Luke's ancestors exhibited the all-consuming malevolence she had ascribed to Eleanor Barton. Even the essentially self-centered Ennis Trevelyan hadn't nurtured the degree of malice that Blythe had ascribed to her baby sister and that had brought her to the conclusion that there was such a thing as justifiable homicide.

She peered through the gloom at Luke, concerned that her insomnia might disturb his sleep. She could see by his even breathing that she was wrestling with the ghosts of Barton Hall completely on her own.

There was no excuse to be made for Ellie's behavior, Blythe considered moodily, but could there be a reason behind it that Blythe had never understood? Some notch on the "memory gene," which Valerie Kent claimed might exist, that made her sister Ellie feel that at the end of the twentieth century it was payback time?

And what if Luke was falling in love with her—Blythe Barton, late of Hollywood—merely as an unconscious echo of the secret love his forebear, Garrett Teague, had silently harbored for his cousin's wife? Or the original Blythe for him, for all anyone knew?

As the September dawn crept into the castle's master suite, Blythe could begin to distinguish her lover's silhouette in the gloom. How would Lucas Teague, the lord and master of Barton Hall, react to such a theory if she disclosed the ideas regarding ancestral memory his cousin Valerie had put forth that day at the village fete?

"Loco." That's what he'd say, in his cultured English accent.

But what if there was some kind of link between Blythe Barton, who cuckolded her husband with his brother, Ennis, in the eighteenth century, and Blythe Stowe, who had been betrayed by her husband and sister in the twentieth? If only, she wished silently, her partial understanding of the circumstances surrounding the complicated story of the Barton-Trevelyan-Teagues could translate into simple forgiveness in her own situation.

The haunting vision of her husband's naked back and buttocks smothering her sister's slender body flashed through Blythe's thoughts—and with it, a familiar and exhausting yearning for punishment and revenge.

There were some things—like beating a horse's neck to a bloody pulp, or boinking your sister's husband—that were simply unpardonable.

Blythe sat up abruptly, overwhelmed by a feeling of suffocation. The closeness of the atmosphere inside the confines of the bed curtains had suddenly become intolerable. Even in the afterglow of Luke's extraordinary lovemaking, she was forced to acknowledge the truth: that her weary heart could not yet forgive. And in her head there remained, undeniably, fantasies of retribution.

"The trouble with storing up resentment and wishin' ill on other folks is that it's like drinkin' poison," a familiar voice echoed in her memory. "You think it's gonna kill the person who hurt you. Usually it ends up killin' you."

Blythe simply had to stop drinking poison, she told herself. If there was a link between the Bartons, past and present, she had to discover what it might be. If she actually dared to look back at her family's history, perhaps she could avoid some of the kinds of mistakes her ancestors had made.

As Blythe's troubled gaze lingered on Luke's sleeping form, she wondered what their future was likely to be. Was her ultimate happiness to be found here at Barton Hall? Or were the repercussions of events that had transpired so long ago within these walls—within the curtains of this very bed, perhaps—still influencing the present?

Blythe carefully eased her frame toward the edge of the mattress, thrust her head between the velvet drapes. She took a deep breath of the colder air circulating in Luke's bedroom. Furtively, she quickly donned her beige slacks and silk blouse and tiptoed away from the Bawdy Bed of Barton.

When she reached the library, the early-morning light filtering through the casement windows made it possible for her to make her way to the genealogy chart without turning on the desk lamp. She could almost hear Valerie Kent's instructions to inhale and allow her mind to empty itself of extraneous thoughts. Meanwhile, she gazed intently at a single name, disregarding all others.

Then she extended her arm above her head, pressed her fingertips lightly against the glass-fronted family tree, and whispered, "Blythe Barton Trevelyan."

For one anxious moment she felt the now familiar sensation of a tremendous force rearranging her body's molecules. Suddenly she wondered—in the words of her cynical lawyer—whether she wasn't already in way too deep.

Chapter Ten

October 9, 1789

The sound of pebbles ricocheted off Blythe's window, but the seventeen-year-old was already awake, waiting. Fully clothed in a burgundy-colored wool traveling costume, she cast aside the bedcovers and ran, barefooted, to the window in her bedchamber that faced the rear garden. As her heart thudded wildly with excitement, she threw up the sash and leaned out into the cool dawn's light.

"You came!" she whispered hoarsely.

"Blythe—" Ennis began, looking up at her, handsome as a king's cavalier, dressed in a thick woolen cloak to ward off the chill air.

"Shh! I'll only be a moment," she hissed. "I'll just don my shoes and go through the secret door in the library."

Blythe ducked back inside, and with hands that shook with both fear and anticipation she slipped on her shoes and grabbed the handle of her portmanteau. Her arms ached from the weight of her baggage now laden with as much Barton silverware as could be quietly gathered the previous night when the servants were asleep.

Her wedding dress hung in the wardrobe, its billowing silk folds pressed in readiness for a bride who had no intention of ever wearing it.

By the time Blythe padded down the staircase and entered the library lugging her heavy burden, her back ached as well.

She must be careful not to strain herself, she thought suddenly—just in case she was, in fact, carrying Ennis's child.

She immediately set down her traveling bag and began to slide her fingers along the bookcase, searching for the secret catch.

For an instant she recalled the day, only six weeks earlier, when Garrett Teague had magically materialized from inside the hidey-hole to warn her that Collis Trevelyan was about to finalize the match between his eldest son and his ward to feather his own nest.

On that same day it had been Garrett who had kept Blythe from flinging herself off the cliff in desperation over her plight. What a dear, good friend he was, Blythe thought, feeling suddenly guilty that she had made no attempt even to send him a note of farewell. He had coddled her and soothed her that dreadful day, earnestly vowing that her fate was more promising than she thought and offering to spirit her away to America. How right he had been! Blythe thought triumphantly as her fingers found the hidden catch and the panel of bookshelves lurched inward. Ennis had been more than willing to sketch her in the nude and then seduce her in the wooded copse near Hemmick Beach, and now he was proving, to her unending gratitude, that he had far more honor in his soul than his bombastic sire ever gave him credit for.

When, a week earlier, her bloody courses miraculously failed to appear—just as she had prayed—she thought that the one flaw in her plan might, indeed, be her intended groom's unwillingness to marry her.

"Jesu, Blythe!" Ennis had exclaimed when she announced the news that she was with child. "How can you be certain so soon?"

"Because I am," she replied calmly. "Because I have only been with you, as you well know, and I have never before failed to have my courses appear—"

"Yes, yes," Ennis interrupted, with an ungallant grimace. "I realize that if you are . . . well . . . with child, I am, certainly, the cause of your distress."

" 'Tis not my distress," she had cried, flinging her arms about his shoulders, " 'tis my salvation . . . and my fondest wish that we should have this babe and wed in the bargain. You shall be a rich man," she said, affecting nonchalance, but watching him closely. "I want you to be able to paint . . . to create the works you wish to. . . . We can still go to Italy! Together!"

Ennis's expression had been unreadable, and he had heaved a small sigh.

"I wish the solution were that simple," he had said. "My father will slit my throat if I elope with you to Italy, not to mention what my brother would do."

"Kit holds no great fondness for me, nor for you, I'm sure," Blythe retorted. "He only does what your father orders him to."

"I think you misjudge my brother's essential decency," Ennis replied. "Likewise, you underestimate your own charm. Though, I vow, you've shown poor Kit not a shred of affection, so I can't imagine why he pines for your love."

"Pines for me?" she scoffed. "You must be joking!"

"Indeed, I'm not," Ennis replied. "But that is beside the point. My revered father doesn't just wish that our families be joined in holy matrimony. He wants his eldest son and legal heir to add the Barton estate to his own holdings so that the entire parcel can be handed down as an even larger legacy to future Trevelyan generations. If I bequeath Barton Hall to my heirs, it doesn't serve my dear *père*'s grandiose purposes, don't you see?"

"I don't give a farthing for Collis Trevelyan's lofty schemes . . . ," she retorted.

Blythe had outlined her plan for eloping to the Continent and coming back to Barton Hall after the baby was born. That way, she assured him, they would simply present everyone in both families with a fait accompli.

"Think of it. . . . If you marry me, you shall be master of Barton Hall, instead of being condemned to paint in some drafty garret," she cajoled.

And with that Ennis Trevelyan had agreed to her plan of escape.

Blythe gave a shove against the bookcase with her shoulder and was relieved when it slid open far enough to allow her to pass through the smuggler's storeroom with her portmanteau. She shivered in the chilly blackness and then gave a little gasp as she heard scurrying sounds on her right. Rats, no doubt.

When she emerged into the damp air outside, Ennis stood by as she struggled to pull the silver-laden baggage through the secret door.

"Good God, Blythe, did you pinch every last fork?"

"Well, help me, blast it all!"

"We're not eloping."

He said it calmly and with frightening finality.

"But you're here!" she cried. "You came at dawn, just as you promised."

"I'm not so much of a rogue that I wouldn't tell you in person that I've had a change of heart. Look, Blythie, darling . . ."

"Don't call me 'darling' and then have the insolence to tell me that you're not—"

"I can't do this, Blythe," Ennis said, running his hand nervously through his neatly coiffed blond hair. "Your wedding to Kit is to take place today! My father will—"

"Your father can do nothing if we leave immediately!" she shot back. "That's why they've finally let down their guard. Until today the grooms were told to watch the ponies, and the maids were told to watch me! Now they think they've won . . . they think it's too late for me to escape. That's the beauty of our plan—"

"*Your* plan!" Ennis exploded.

In the silence that loomed between them, Blythe could hear a cock crowing down by the henhouse. In a moment the sun would be swimming above the rim of the hills, and the estate workers would soon be bustling about their tasks on this, the mistress's wedding day.

"Ye gods, Blythe!" Ennis said hoarsely. "You know I care for you . . . that, if the truth be known, I'm quite mad for you. But this is folly—I can't go through with it."

"But 'tis your child! You can't deny it!"

"I don't deny it," he said quietly, "if you are, in fact, with child. You must admit, 'tis a bit early to be sure . . . and in any case, 'twill be better for all concerned if everyone else thinks 'tis Kit's child."

"Better for you!" she cried accusingly.

"Better for everyone . . . even you, perhaps," he asserted. "If this scheme did not involve an irretrievable break with my entire family, I would be sorely tempted, believe me. Don't think I've not imagined how delicious it could have been to travel through Italy with an impudent woman like you for company," he added, his voice tinged with a characteristic trace of teasing irony. He gazed at her with a look of mild regret. "But as it is . . ." He shook his head. "I know I must seem cruel and unfeeling. Perhaps, at bottom, I am."

"No!" was all Blythe could reply.

"If we marry without my father's consent," Ennis continued, "he will claim I defrauded him, and I fear, as your legal guardian, he will drag us to court. Meanwhile, he still controls the purse strings of your inheritance, and unless you can successfully petition to break your father's will, Collis Trevelyan could cut you off without a sou."

"How have you determined all this?" Blythe demanded suspiciously.

"I asked Garrett to see what the law books in his father's shop have to say on such subjects." Ennis shrugged. "He showed it to me in black and white."

"Your father will come to accept our marriage, after we elope," she insisted. "Just watch and see. After all, you are his son, too!"

"Blythe, how willful and naive you are," Ennis said wearily, "but I assure you, his lifelong goal has been to join his property with yours, and for the three thousand acres to be handed down in a grand gesture of patrimony to his eldest son. My being his second son, and thus dividing the goods, so to speak, will unleash the vengeance he is capable of. And make no mistake, that's precisely what will happen if we follow through with this solution to your predicament."

"I don't consider marrying you, or having your baby, a 'predicament,' " she said in a wounded tone.

"I remind you once again: You could easily pass the child off as Kit's, if you did your duty in the marriage bed," he replied coolly. "Except for the ravages of the pox, he and I look quite alike, wouldn't you say?"

"And if I tell Kit on my wedding night that 'tis your get in my belly," she said in a low voice, "then where will you be?"

"I expect I shall be in a great deal of hot water with everyone, regardless of which course I take," Ennis replied. He smiled faintly and took her by the hand. "Blythe, you should know that I intend to develop a sudden indisposition later today and will not be present at the nuptials. Though you may not believe it, 'twould be too painful for me to lose you to Kit in front of so many witnesses. Garrett and I sail Friday for France. I roused myself at this ungodly hour to bid you adieu."

And before Blythe could counter his determined refusal to carry out their planned escape, Ennis turned on his heel and strode through the walled garden toward the arched wooden gate.

Numbed by shock and disappointment, Blythe found herself staring at his retreating back. Ennis took the right turning and headed in the direction of their favorite wooded glen. Most likely he had tethered his horse beside a stream that meandered toward Hemmick Beach. She pictured him slowly riding down the shaded footpath toward Trevelyan House and, within the week, boarding a ship in Plymouth, perhaps never to return.

"Ennis!" she whispered. "Ennis . . . no! Wait!"

She was gasping for breath by the time she caught up with

him in the glen. He turned around at the sound of her approaching footsteps, his hands on his horse's reins.

"Go back, Blythe!" he commanded gruffly.

"Please . . . please," she sobbed. "Don't go like this. . . ."

She threw her arms around him, mortified that she should mewl like a lost kitten, but she couldn't seem to stifle the tears that were now streaming down her face.

"Oh, Blythie . . . Blythie . . . ," he said, comforting her as if she were more friend than lover. "Life has a habit of proceeding, day by day. You and Kit will find a way to—"

"Whatever you do, please don't speak of Kit," she cried brokenly. "Just hold me . . . please, Ennis . . . I—"

And then she kissed him and she knew, as a woman knows, that he would not resist her silent plea to make love to her one last time.

"The grass is damp with dew . . . ," Ennis murmured.

"Fortunately," Blythe breathed into his ear, "you've worn your cloak."

Then she sank to her knees and began to unfasten the buttons at his waist. A few moments later, when Ennis had reclined on his cape, she smiled at her lover with a look infused with passion and pride as she lowered herself, fully clothed, astride his naked thighs.

The small gold watch retrieved from the pocket of Ennis's crumpled breeches declared the time to be nearly nine o'clock. The sun was now slanting through the trees, casting a beam of light across the swath of grass where Ennis and Blythe lay beside the stream.

"Blythe, you are a witch, you know," Ennis groaned, replacing the timepiece in his trousers.

"Now do you see how much you mean to me?" Blythe whispered into his ear. "I'm to have your baby. Ennis . . . how can you leave me behind?"

Ennis gently disentangled himself and stood up.

"You are not only a witch, but a grand manipulator," he said wryly.

Reaching for an edge of his wool cloak, he draped it over her reclining figure to ward off the stiff breeze that had suddenly swept up the glen from the shore. Then he glanced down at his own midsection. Blythe, too, was staring in his direction with a stricken look on her face.

"Either I have pierced your maidenhead twice, dear heart," he said softly, "or your courses have come at last."

Blythe closed her eyes and shook her head. "Damn!" she whispered, unable to ignore the cause of the dull, cramping sensation she had felt in her abdomen since late yesterday.

Meanwhile, Ennis knelt beside the stream and washed. Then he swiftly donned his breeches and shirt.

"Well, at least you shall have a valid excuse to avoid the marriage bed this night," he said gently. She allowed him to pull her to her feet. Then he turned his back to permit his horse free rein to drink, thus offering Blythe a decent interval in which to restore her underclothes.

" 'Tis *my* inheritance!" Blythe said softly as she fumbled for the ties to her cotton drawers. "Pray tell me, why am I not allowed to share it with the man I love?" she demanded.

"Because . . ." Ennis shook his head in frustration, either with the tangled rein he was attempting to straighten, or due to the painful situation he faced.

"Because blood is thicker than water, is that it?" Blythe interrupted miserably. She smoothed the red skirt over her white petticoats and yanked on the waist of her matching jacket. Then she struggled to close the frog fastenings that cinched her tailored bodice.

"No . . . that's not it, exactly," Ennis replied moodily. Then he chucked her lightly beneath her chin. "Blythe, I'm sorry . . . truly, I am." He retrieved his cuffed coat. " 'Twas folly to have given in to lust just now. It doesn't alter what confronts us."

"And that is, that you're fond of me, as you say, but your greater passion is painting? That you can still go to Italy and study with the masters whether you marry me or not, isn't that right?" she said sharply, slipping on each buckled black shoe in turn. "Your father has promised you and Garrett the trip, just as soon as Kit and I are wed—isn't that so? A journey that might prove more amusing without the company of a wife?"

"Yes," Ennis replied frankly. He seized her hand in his. "Look, Blythie, darling . . . I'm not the romantic champion you would have me be. I long to see the world . . . to be free to explore sights I have never seen. 'Tis difficult to explain, but I am driven to experience things I cannot even imagine—"

"So am I!" Blythe protested, staring up at him as her eyes filled with tears.

"But you are a woman, and betrothed to Kit Trevelyan," he repeated impatiently.

"I've always said—as often as you—that I'd adore to go to Venice!" she exclaimed hotly. "I'd watch you paint. I could even be of help! And that portmanteau of Barton family silver would be useful, wouldn't it?" she added pointedly. "Surely you agree with that! Oh, Ennis, I'd risk your father's wrath! I'd risk anything to be with you! Why won't you do this—to be with me?"

"This was never part of my plan . . . ," Ennis began, and then halted, aware that he had revealed in that brief sentence the overriding reason he had decided that he couldn't go through with Blythe's scheme.

"But what about our plan?" she said with her jaw clenched as she struggled to maintain her composure. "What about those dreams we had as children, sitting on Dodman Point? Or was it always your intention to play the rakehell . . . the roguish debauchee on a young buck's trip abroad? You were pleased enough to sketch the contours of my form and take your pleasures in the wooded copse—"

"And you were more than willing to hazard your virginity, and you know it, Blythe!" Ennis retorted. "Please spare us any accusations of a maidenhood plundered against your will."

"I hazarded it all, and now I have to accept my losses like a man, is that it?"

"Yes, I suppose it is . . . ," Ennis replied softly. Then he smiled almost sadly. "One last thing. And 'tis important, so I hope you will listen carefully. I am not in the least fashioned to be the doting father. I am an artist!"

He said it proudly, almost arrogantly, she thought, as if such a declaration absolved him of life's more mundane obligations.

"That's all I've ever wanted you to be!" she cried with frustration.

"In view that you are not to be burdened with my child," Ennis continued while ignoring her protestations, "perhaps you should count your blessings. I'm sorry, Blythe. If I love anyone, I love you, but I think 'tis best all around the way that things have sorted themselves out—even for you, although I know you can't see that now."

Ennis slipped his booted foot into the stirrup and hoisted himself aboard his horse. And without a backward glance he cantered down the grassy path, now swathed in green shadows and the rustling noises of a new day.

"I heard and saw everything," said a voice as Blythe entered the walled garden through the wooden gate.

She gave a little gasp and whirled around to see Garrett looking pale beneath his bronzed countenance. For a long moment she stared at him in stony silence.

"Did you see everything?" she inquired icily. "Including the moment Ennis mounted his steed and rode away, or merely when I mounted him?"

"I . . . I heard him say you are not with child by him. Then I came here to wait for you."

"The sight of blood makes you faint, does it?" Blythe said bitterly, stalking toward the door to the servants' entrance.

"Blythe!" Garrett called after her, following in her wake.

She turned on her heel to face him, her cheeks scarlet with embarrassment and hurt. "I thought you were my friend,

Garrett Teague . . . not some prurient spy!" she cried. "If you saw me with Ennis just now, then you know how much I wanted him! And you know how much I hate that I'm to be married to his brother this day!"

"I know," Garrett said in a low voice, roughened by all the things she knew, now, he had witnessed. "I'm only here because I was ordered by my father and your guardian to meet at nine o'clock. Uncle Collis is determined that you arrive at St. Goran's on time. I feared that he would see you run to Ennis, so I followed you."

"And you remained for the bawdy spectacle, did you?"

"I—" Garrett began, and then shook his head and inhaled deeply, glancing at the clouds scudding overhead. "Why can't you see he's not worth—" Then he lowered his gaze and met Blythe's furious glare.

"I shall go inside now," Blythe said faintly, emphasizing each word, "and I haven't the slightest notion of what I shall do next, other than to order those snooping maids to haul hot water upstairs for a bath."

"And afterward, will you come with me?" Garrett proposed softly.

"With you?" she asked, startled. "Where?"

"I found your portmanteau where you'd abandoned it, near the secret entrance over there. I've hidden it in the stables. The silver's enough to buy us both passage to America."

"Are you serious?" Blythe said, incredulous. "You'd leave Cornwall?"

"With you? Yes, I would."

"After what you've just . . . ?" she continued uncertainly. "Why would you be willing to give up everything and leave—"

"Everything?" Garrett interrupted bitterly. "In England I have nothing but a dusty old bookshop and a bachelor's life ahead of me. I heard you tell Ennis you'd risk it all for him. Well, I'll risk what little I have as well. You, Blythe Barton, are all I want."

"Garrett, you know that I—"

Blythe suddenly felt utterly defeated and so exhausted, she thought she would drop where she stood. Her body ached. She was sore all over. And she needed to do something about her bloody courses.

She looked helplessly at her errant knight, wishing to find the words to thank him for his reckless kindness, when Collis Trevelyan suddenly stalked through the wooden gate.

"God's wounds! What is she doing out here?" her guardian thundered. He glared at Garrett accusingly. "One thing I asked of you, rapscallion!" he bellowed. "One thing, and in return, I told your father I would pay for you to accompany Ennis abroad: Make certain the mother of this baggage roused her daughter and dressed her in her wedding frippery before breakfast. And look at her!"

He peered nearsightedly at Blythe. Her dark-brown hair hung in clumps down her back, and her dress was soiled and damp.

"Inside, chit!" Collis commanded, and pointed toward the castle's kitchen door. "And be quick about it!"

Faint rays of morning sunshine slanted through the graceful windows and stone arches of St. Goran's as the door at the back of the church opened and the bride appeared. Blythe was flanked—indeed—by Collis Trevelyan and Donald Teague, who escorted her to the front of the nave where a handful of witnesses and the groom waited uneasily.

The walls and tower of the fifteenth-century church where the marriage of Christopher Trevelyan and Blythe Barton would take place this October day were made of Pentawan stone quarried north of the village three hundred years earlier.

The Reverend Randolph Kent peered anxiously down the aisle as the joyless procession approached the stone altar. Standing to the cleric's left was Kit Trevelyan, appearing as nervous as the vicar of St. Goran. Rivulets of sweat carved narrow channels in the thick mask of face powder he'd applied to his skin in an attempt to disguise the heavy scars that marred his countenance.

For years Blythe had heard it whispered that Reverend Kent had bowed to Collis Trevelyan's demands in allowing the church graveyard to serve as a haven for smuggled goods. Blythe assumed that the churchman rationalized this transgression of the law with the knowledge that "Free Trade" benefited a majority of the members of his village parish. This business, however . . . this forcing her to marry Trevelyan's son, obviously against her will, benefited only her guardian. A man of the cloth should have the moral rectitude to put a stop to it.

But Blythe knew that the Reverend Randolph Kent dared not protest. Collis Trevelyan could quietly see to it that the customs men learned of certain activities that had transpired on moonless nights in St. Goran's graveyard, and who could gainsay such a prosperous local landowner or make any counteraccusations stick?

She stared steadily into the troubled gray eyes of her confessor and saw him sigh. Then he raised his hand in benediction.

"Dearly beloved," he intoned, "we are gathered together here in the sight of God . . ."

Blythe heard the door to her late father's bedroom close with a thump. Then the key rattled and the lock clicked. Muffled male laughter could be heard receding down the hallway.

She turned to face her groom and said nothing. The enormous Barton Bed, regally hung with red velvet drapery, newly purchased in honor of their nuptials, loomed against the wall opposite.

"You must be greatly tired," Kit ventured, nervously patting the top of a wing-backed chair positioned near the matching velvet window curtains, closed snugly against the night air.

Flakes of face powder had fallen like snow on the shoulders of his handsome blue coat, purchased specifically for his wedding day. His neck linen had wilted, and his forehead was sheened with perspiration, as it had been during the entire day's festivities.

As if one could call the dirge that had substituted for a marriage celebration festive, Blythe thought darkly.

She and her groom of one day had sat stonily beside one another during their wedding lunch and then retired to separate wings of Barton Hall to "refresh themselves" before the marriage feast. Hollow toasts had been drunk to their health, after which they had been escorted to their bedchamber by a raucous gaggle of men organized by Blythe's guardian, doubling as the groom's father.

As promised, Ennis had been nowhere in sight. Nor had Garrett. Rosamund Barton had been composed and distant, as if she were preoccupied with some future plans of her own.

Now the two newlyweds had been locked like prisoners in a tower, expected to "do their duty," as Collis had leeringly informed her over his fifth glass of champagne.

"I am tired," Blythe agreed in a low voice. "Sick and tired. Tired and sick!" she repeated, trying to keep the edge of hysteria out of her voice. "Which leads me to some terribly disappointing news for you."

Kit stared at her, mute, as usual.

"I've started my courses this day," she declared.

He continued to gaze at her without reply.

"You do know what they are, don't you?" she demanded, pacing up and down in front of the fireplace. "The Red Flood? A time every month when a woman is unavailable to be put to stud," she said, tilting her chin and casting him a challenging glare.

"I do know, actually, what you're saying," Kit mumbled, blushing crimson beneath the remnants of his powder. "I work with farm animals, you know. . . ." He swallowed nervously. "It does not matter, as there will be blood in any case, and . . ."

His words drifted off as he continued to gaze at her, looking utterly miserable.

"Farm animals!" she spat. "That's about all I would expect

you to know about the marriage state!" She ceased her pacing and took a step toward Kit, her fists clenched. "I fear that I have another bit of disheartening information to impart to you." She smiled, perversely enjoying her announcement. "I come to you in no respect a virgin."

Her statement hung in the air between them, and she was pleased to see Kit's own hand ball into a fist.

"Who had you first?" he said in a low voice. "I have a right to know!"

"Are you absolutely sure you wish to know?" she mocked him.

"Such a transparent ruse cannot alter the path we tread tonight," he said abruptly, and crossed the room in a few swift strides. "You are now my wife!" he declared, seizing her hands in his own. "We are promised to each other, before God. And, by St. Goran, I am willing to do my best by it!"

Then he pulled her close and began to kiss her with frenzied passion, as if it were in his power to infuse her with his own feverish desire.

"Kit!" Blythe protested, shoving her hands against his chest.

"Please, Blythe . . . please . . . please," he murmured, strengthening his grip as his arms pressed against her sides and his hands became a stone wall at her back. "I shall be a good husband to you, I swear," he whispered hoarsely. Then he parted his lips and attempted to thrust his tongue against her clenched teeth.

"No!" Blythe cried, and turned her head away, a move that only provided him the means to kiss her throat and the hollow at the base of her neck. Suddenly she ceased to struggle against him.

Blythe knew perfectly well that she still possessed the physical strength to fight her groom's righteous, ardent advances even if she hadn't an ounce of mental energy remaining to her. She was utterly exhausted by the effort it had taken to keep from screaming her protests in front of the assembled guests and the Reverend Mr. Kent at the altar of St. Goran's Church. As she felt Kit's erection bloom against her thigh, she simply allowed her mind to go blank and her body limp.

She was done fighting them all, she thought absently. She would sleep and, on the morrow, confer with Garrett concerning their flight to Plymouth and an escape by ship to America.

Kit appeared to sense her shift in mood and her sudden acquiescence and scooped her into his arms. He placed her in the center of the magnificent Barton Bed. How many hapless Barton brides would be deflowered upon its goose-down mattress? Blythe wondered. She would not be among them, she contemplated proudly. A man *she* had chosen had pierced her maidenhead, and she would always be glad of it.

She watched with something akin to pity as Ennis's brother fumbled to divest himself of his coat, linen neckcloth, and shirt.

"Would you like to undress?" he inquired of her softly, blowing out the candle on the nightstand.

But Blythe didn't answer. She was determined to prevent any intrusion on her thoughts, which now floated in her mind like wispy clouds drifting lazily off Dodman Point. Illuminated only by the banked fire glowing on the hearth, Kit's silhouette, comparable in height to Ennis's, now cast a shadow against the far wall. The red velvet coverlet on which she lay felt as soft as the grassy verge near the stream where she had lain, this very day, with her husband's brother.

Blythe voiced no protest when Kit rolled her onto her stomach. He swiftly unfastened her silk wedding gown, her stays, and the various ties securing her muslin undergarments. Inside the majestic Barton Bed, curtains were drawn on three sides. Shadows cloaked her body, now naked, except for the small wad of rags wedged between her thighs. Resignedly she retrieved the stained cotton cloths and tossed them onto the floor as a rustling sound signaled that Kit was removing his breeches.

Blythe was aware that her groom of only a few hours had

slipped between the sheets. She wondered absently how an untried boy would do a man's job.

"I don't wish to hurt you," said a disembodied voice hovering above her.

"You won't," she sighed.

And then she felt him find her center without impediment.

Kit lay absolutely still, his body an oppressive weight against the length of her own. Silence reined in the bedchamber, and Blythe's detachment transported her from this plush velvet prison to a cool, imaginary glen where Ennis awaited her.

"Slut!"

The epithet reverberated inside the scarlet tomb of her ancestors.

Immediately Blythe felt cold air pimple her flesh as Kit bolted from their bed. Startled from her reverie, she announced in the direction of his retreating back, "I am not a slut. I am merely another man's lover. Surely you can't complain I didn't warn you."

"I thought you were merely being waspish," came Kit's shaken response.

She watched as he reached for a taper, ignited it in the glowing hearth, and lighted a candle that stood in a wall sconce next to the mantelpiece. Long, narrow shadows danced across the Persian carpet on the floor.

"I never took you for a common whore," he said, turning to stare at her across the bedchamber.

"How extraordinary," Blythe replied coldly, staring at his nakedness with a look of contempt, "for I took you for a fool, and lo, it appears my judgment was correct." She sat up in bed and pulled the coverlet under her arms. She was fully engaged now in the battle, and a latent fury boiled suddenly in her veins. "As a matter of fact, I was being waspish," she declared. "As waspish and cruel as I could be so that you could finally understand how deeply I resent what has happened here today!"

"And you think I'd choose a wife who abhorred the sight of me!" he retorted in a strangled voice.

" 'Twas up to you to confront your father—like a man!" she cried as her pent-up rage at the day's events burst forth unchecked. "Surely you must realize no pathetic woman could deter Collis Trevelyan from his course! But you, too, are beguiled by the thought of such a handsome estate being handed down to your heirs, aren't you?" she accused him. " 'Tis all about money and land, and the concerns of men!"

"I demand to know who bedded you first!" Kit bellowed across the room, mimicking his father's penchant for voluble denunciation.

"Ah . . . it always comes down to that, doesn't it, rooster?" she spat venomously. "The great question of the ages: Who reached the henhouse first?"

Kit strode across the chamber and loomed over her menacingly. "Well, who did?"

He appeared to have quite forgotten that he was bare as a babe, or that his erection had not been assuaged by their brief physical encounter.

Blythe narrowed her eyes and met his glance steadily. She would need time to marshal her resources, she thought as her heart thudded in her chest. There was no point burning every bridge that might eventually provide an escape. She would protect Ennis.

"A stable boy was my first," she lied airily, "last year. He ran away, after my father died."

"Slut," Kit repeated in a choked voice.

"And I must tell you, husband mine," Blythe retorted recklessly, "that the lad's lovemaking was vastly superior to what I've just sampled."

In response to this sally, Kit's deeply scarred features twisted into a grotesque mask of outrage and despair. Steadily meeting his furious visage, Blythe made a deliberate show of yawning like a bored cat and glancing disdainfully at her bridegroom's exposed manhood. The Trevelyan family flag had haplessly fallen to half-mast.

"Good night, Kit," she said with mock sweetness.

Then, pulling the bedcovers up to her neck, she turned her back on her mortified groom. She smiled to herself in the dark, wishing only that Collis Trevelyan had witnessed the consummation of this misbegotten marriage which the avaricious blackguard had masterminded.

Chapter Eleven

September 6, 1994

"Blythe? Blythe! A-Are you all right?"

Startled, she turned her head sharply toward the library door. "Dicken! What are you doing up?"

Lucas's ten-year-old son, clothed in flannel pajamas, stood at the threshold.

"I heard someone go down the stairs . . . and they didn't come back up."

Blythe rose from the spot on Luke's desk she'd been leaning against and collected herself. How long had she been staring at the genealogy chart? More to the point, what had Dicken witnessed of her "trance"?

"I'm fine, sweetie. I'm just sorry I woke you up," she apologized, flipping on the desk light. She studied Richard's face. The boy looked pale and somehow fragile. "Were you scared just now?"

"A little, when you didn't answer me," he admitted, walking farther into the book-lined room. "I woke up and couldn't go back to sleep."

"So you wanted some company?" She smiled, holding out her hand. He reached for it and then allowed her to give him a quick hug. They sat down at the card table where the half-completed puzzle was spread out on top of its leather surface.

"You're already dressed," he commented, looking at her slacks and blouse.

"I couldn't sleep either." She shrugged, smiling. "Does that happen to you very often?"

"Sometimes," he said in a small voice.

"Sometimes?" Blythe asked carefully.

"Since Mummy died."

He stared down at the top of the card table and then at a puzzle piece he had grasped between his fingers.

"I'll bet you miss your mom a lot," Blythe said gently.

"I do."

"I miss my mom a lot too."

Richard gave her a searching look.

"Did your mummy die too?"

"Yes . . . and, after that, my grandmother too, so I know how much you must wish your mom was still here."

"When did your mummy die?" he asked, and then quickly lowered his gaze to the tabletop again.

"It happened way before you were born, in 1970. I was just a year older than you are now."

"And your grandmother?" he asked earnestly.

"She died just last November. She was like a mother to me in a lot of ways. She was also my special friend and taught me about gardening and herbs. But she was very old and tired," Blythe said softly, "and one day last autumn she just closed her eyes and didn't wake up."

"Oh . . . ," Richard said in a low voice, "but at least she was really old."

"That's true . . . but it was still very sad," she agreed quietly. "In fact, I still feel sad sometimes. I think everybody does when they lose someone they care about. You probably still feel upset about your mom," she ventured.

"I do. Especially at school."

"I can understand why."

"I hate that school!" Richard blurted. "That's why I crammed everybody's knickers down the lavatories."

"You did?" Blythe asked solemnly, trying her best to keep a straight face. "What happened? Did you get in Dutch?"

"Dutch?" he asked with a quizzical look.

"In trouble with the school?"

"I was nearly sacked," he replied proudly.

"Expelled? Sent home, you mean?"

The ten-year-old nodded. "Aunt Chloe came and persuaded the headmaster to keep me. . . ."

"And your dad?" Blythe asked cautiously.

"Daddy said on the telephone that I had to stay."

"Why do you suppose he felt that way?" Blythe asked, wondering if she should be proceeding down this road.

"He said it was good for me."

"Perhaps it is."

"It's horrid!" Richard countered vehemently.

"That bad, huh?"

"I could learn just as much at the day school in Mevagissey!" he added quickly. "We're doing fractions at Shelby Hall, and my friend Amory Bice said they are too!"

"Really?" Blythe said. "Is that the boy who came to your birthday party? The one who invited you for a day at the beach with his family last month? He seemed like an awfully nice friend."

Richard nodded emphatically. Then he looked across at her inquiringly. "It's nice having you here this summer. Are you going to stay?"

It was Blythe's turn to stare at the partially completed puzzle. "Well, your dad and I have a lot of work to do to get Barton Hall Nurseries up and running," she said cautiously, looking up with a reassuring smile, "so I expect I'll be around for quite a bit longer."

"Good," Richard declared.

Blythe made a show of yawning and stretching her arms above her head.

"I don't know about you, but I think I'm sleepy."

"Me too," Richard agreed promptly. "Would you go back upstairs with me?"

"Sure," she said, wondering how she would eventually find

her way back to Luke's room without giving anything away. "Lead on, Macduff!"

Luke's son slipped his hand into hers and companionably walked beside her up the grand staircase, turning in to the same hallway she had traversed when exiting from the castle's master suite.

"I'm right across from mummy and daddy's room," Richard said, as Blythe flinched. She paused on the section of carpet that ran between the bedchamber with the red velvet canopy and the room opposite.

"No . . . farther down," Richard insisted, marching resolutely to the end of the hall.

"Your parents' room is down here too?" she said softly, so as not to wake anyone.

"Mummy didn't like the room with that big old Barton Bed back there," Richard explained in a conspiratorial whisper that matched her own. "She thought she and Daddy should have their own room, just the way they wanted it." He paused at a door on his right and turned the knob. "They made this room for me, even before I was born," he said proudly. Still clutching her hand tightly, he asked, "Will you tuck me in bed?"

"Of course."

Inside, Blythe could see that a loving hand had decorated the boy's bedroom. Despite the chamber's grand proportions, the walls had been painted a pale blue and stenciled with a variety of animals from Beatrix Potter's *Tales of Peter Rabbit.*

Richard could see that Blythe was glancing around the room. "I'm too big for Peter Rabbit, but I like him. I like all the animals," he acknowledged, casting Blythe a challenging look.

"We know about Peter Rabbit in America," she said reassuringly, "and I always loved him too, when I was a girl. I like Miss Moppet and Mrs. Ribby and all of the characters. Okay, pardner . . . into bed with you now."

Richard climbed dutifully under the covers. Next to his bed stood a photo of a woman with a soft, rounded face, light-colored hair, and a warm smile. Lindsay Teague. Richard's mother, she guessed.

"That's nice that you keep her right by your bed."

Richard gazed over at the picture and heaved a sigh. "She's never coming back."

"That's true. She won't ever come back," Blythe agreed gently. "I don't know about you . . . but when my mom died, I was a little bit angry at her. It was like she left me. I know she didn't die on purpose, but just the same, it made me mad that she went away from me."

Richard sat abruptly up in bed. "It did?" he asked, sounding relieved.

"Yes, it did," Blythe replied.

"Sometimes I'm angry at her, too . . . for leaving," he said in a strained voice.

Blythe lightly ruffled her fingers through his caramel-colored hair.

"She never would have left a wonderful boy like you if she could have helped it, Dicken," Blythe said urgently. "But you know, a part of her—a big part—lives on in you. Have you ever thought of that?" She pointed at the picture. "See her hair? It's a lot like yours . . . and look at the shape of her face. In a sense she'll always be with you. That's why it's important that you keep her picture with you, so you don't forget any of the nice things about her that you still remember." Blythe tucked the blanket into the side of the bed.

"I do still remember her," he whispered, gazing at the photograph.

"That's good," she praised. Then, with her thumb, she gently wiped the moisture that had slid silently down one of Richard's cheeks. "Listen, buckaroo," she murmured, "I think it's time we both get some shut-eye."

"Those poly—polyurethane delivery chaps will be here soon, won't they?" Richard noted, pointing to his Peter Rabbit alarm clock, whose hands in the shape of carrots announced it was nearly five A.M.

"When it's really morning, you start counting those plastic rolls if you get there first, okay?" Blythe grinned.

"Yesss, may-yam!" Richard drawled.

Blythe burst out laughing and quickly covered her mouth with her hand.

"'Night, Dicken," she said softly, backing out of his room. "Sleep well."

As she quietly shut the door to Richard's bedroom, she glanced across the hall at the room that Luke and his wife had apparently inhabited during their marriage. Blythe found that she was both relieved and rather pleased that Luke's orchestration of their romantic evening had not been a replay of one he'd already experienced with Lindsay. Gingerly she turned the knob on the door that led into the master suite where the magnificently carved and canopied Barton Bed dominated the room.

Blythe quickly shed her clothes and was relieved to realize she felt not one scintilla of jealousy toward Luke's first wife—and likewise had developed a very great deal of affection for Lindsay Teague's mischievous son. This night with Luke, in this extraordinary room, had been magical, and Blythe was profoundly touched that the owner of Barton Hall had wished to share it with her.

Smiling in the dark, she mounted the two small wooden steps beside the bed and eased her body under the mountain of covers.

"Blythe?" Lucas said sleepily, reaching for her with warm hands. "Did you find the loo all right?"

"Mm-hmmm . . . and much more to the point, baby," she said, nuzzling his ear and reflecting on the events she'd witnessed that had taken place in 1789, "I found my way back."

The next morning the sound of hammers rang in syncopated rhythm as the frames for the seven temporary hothouses began to take shape. Since Blythe was reassured to see that such visible progress in their overall scheme was being made, she gladly volunteered to drive Luke's Land Rover into Gorran Haven to run an afternoon's worth of errands.

In any event, she felt she needed some time "off the ranch." Leaving the gray towers and crenellated turrets of Barton Hall behind, she steered the car down the magnificent drive. When she reached the end of the tall column of larch trees towering overhead, she shifted gears under the arched stone entrance guarding the estate, turned left, and headed up the Gorran Haven road.

It was a Tuesday. Valerie Kent would be in her office. Because of the previous night's events, Blythe had decided it was time to have a discussion about her visions—or whatever they were—with someone who wouldn't treat her like some Hollywood lunatic. After all, Blythe reminded herself, the English psychologist was sworn to a strict code of patient confidentiality.

The shipwright's shop on Rattle Alley looked like a boat hospital. Sea kayaks and small sloops in various stages of repair perched on sawhorses in the stone-paved forecourt. Blythe mounted the wooden stairs attached to the side of the whitewashed building and climbed to the second story. On the wall next to a door were two weathered wooden signs that identified the location of Valerie's office and that of "Simon Vickery, M.D." She opened the door to a small foyer. On the left was a door identified as Dr. Kent's.

"Well, what a lovely surprise!" Valerie enthused, rising from her chair behind her scuffed, leather-topped desk the instant Blythe knocked and poked her head inside the small, cramped office. "Come in! Come in! I hear such wonderful things about the progress of Barton Hall Nurseries from nearly everyone in the village. Please sit down," she urged, pointing to an overstuffed armchair that looked a hundred years old.

"I hope I'm not interrupting—" Blythe began.

"Not a soul has stopped by today, though I seriously doubt that the mental health of our Gorran Haven residents is that tip-top!" Valerie laughed. The stocky psychologist sat down again and folded her hands on her desk. "What can I do for you?"

Blythe, confronted with such a direct question, suddenly wondered what possible rational explanation could be offered to describe what had been happening to her at Barton Hall—not to mention the overheated state of her love life.

"Well . . . ah . . . ," she faltered, at a loss as to how to begin this impromptu meeting.

"You've had time to think about what you saw in the crystal ball, I presume?" Valerie asked encouragingly.

"Well . . . that's not entirely the reason I came. . . ."

"No? How intriguing," Valerie replied, and then remained silent.

"It's . . . ah . . . a bit more complicated," Blythe said hesitantly.

"What is?" Valerie asked.

"Well . . . it probably sounds pretty crazy, but ever since I've arrived in Cornwall, I've seen . . . um . . . not visions like the one that appeared in your crystal ball, exactly . . ." She paused, trying to collect her thoughts. "More like movies . . . or scenes from movies . . . scenes that happened two hundred years ago. I wondered if you could help me try to figure out what they are."

"Scenes? Involving what?" Valerie asked quietly.

"The first Blythe Barton."

"Your namesake? And how have these scenes appeared to you?"

Blythe scanned the psychologist's face to see if she appeared to be about to call the little men in the white coats. To her relief the woman seemed genuinely interested to learn more of Blythe's bizarre experiences.

"Well . . . that's why I've come to see you," she continued. "I seem to be thrust into a kind of 'virtual reality' whenever I have more than a casual glance at Lucas Teague's genealogy chart. It's hanging in the library. Have you seen it?"

"Oh, yes, indeed." Valerie nodded.

"Well . . . ," Blythe continued. "It is a bit like that day I gazed into your crystal ball. The first time—in front of the chart, I mean—my eyes were drawn to stare at the name of Christopher Trevelyan, who lived in the late 1800s."

"The famous 'Kit' . . . first and only Trevelyan to own Barton Hall," Valerie replied.

"Yes, him." Blythe nodded. "I fixated on that name, I suppose, because of the coincidence that a person with the same first name as my former husband had married a woman named Blythe Barton."

"I can certainly understand why that might have caught your eye," Valerie deadpanned. "Well, what happened?"

"The instant my finger touched the glass covering the chart, and I inadvertently whispered aloud, 'Christopher'—whoosh! There I was in the eighteenth century, watching a kind of film about a traumatic moment in Kit and Blythe Barton's life!"

"How absolutely extraordinary!" Valerie replied. "Tell me more. Were you in the scene as well?"

"Well, that's the weird part," Blythe replied, her brow furrowed. "When this strange stuff was going on, I felt as if I was that Blythe. . . . I experienced everything that happened from her point of view!"

"And afterward?"

"When I came out of the trance, or whatever it was, I recalled everything I'd witnessed through my own perspective . . . as me, Blythe Barton, a woman of the twentieth century looking back on these people who lived two hundred years ago. I had empathy for all of them. I seemed to understand where each was 'coming from,' as we say in the States. It's just bizarre!"

Hesitantly, and as accurately as she could remember, she began to recount to the psychologist details of the encounters her namesake had had with the heartbroken, sword-wielding Kit, with Garrett, who had emerged from behind the secret bookcase, with Collis Trevelyan, when he announced Blythe's forced betrothal, and even with Ennis at the amorous rendezvous in the leafy glen near Hemmick Beach.

"And then, of course, there was the wedding night from hell!" said Blythe as Valerie listened sympathetically. Briefly she described the unhappy events in the room that contained the Bawdy Bed of Barton. "When it was over, I felt wretched for everyone involved! Isn't this too weird for words?"

"I think it's splendid!" Valerie declared.

"Well, I think it's pretty loony," Blythe responded fervently. "Do you think this is past-life stuff? Reincarnation? Am I having a nervous breakdown—or what?"

"Do you strongly identify with the first Blythe Barton?" Valerie asked.

"Sort of. Actually," Blythe amended, "I identify with all of them. . . . I even see why Collis Trevelyan wanted to join his property to the Barton lands. From his perspective it made perfect sense. Obviously he was no feminist. What did he care about such things as women's rights two hundred years ago, when, in his world, women were simply chattel, like cattle or silverware? Looking back, I find his behavior repulsive, but I understand his motivation. . . ."

"Without judging him as harshly as you would a man living in our era, correct?" Valerie inquired.

"Exactly!" Blythe agreed. "And it made me think a lot about my own relationships. It's made me want to understand what might be behind the . . . the things that have happened in my life that have been—painful."

"Wouldn't it be marvelous if one could learn what had transpired in the lives of one's ancestors," Valerie mused, "and discover how and why they responded to events and the consequences flowing from their actions and reactions in the past? If we could unravel their emotional history, perhaps we could avoid repeating their mistakes."

"I've thought that too . . . but what if we're driven by these forces . . . unconsciously driven to make decisions in our lives in some endless, predestined game of tit for tat?"

" 'Sins of the fathers' and all that?" Valerie replied. "I don't think that's it. . . . I think that if I knew—and gave serious consideration to—the mistakes and missteps of my forebears, I could learn from that, don't you think?"

"What I wondered, Valerie," Blythe proceeded earnestly, "is if you knew—or had heard—of anyone else having this kind of thing happen to them. I thought maybe in one of your past-life therapy journals you might have come across something."

"Nothing quite like this," Valerie admitted. "From what you've told me, it's a bit different—and very exciting! Rather than your being the reembodiment of someone who lived before, you appear to be a descendant who has the ability to peer into the past, as it was lived by specific ancestors whom you select by means of Luke's genealogy chart. What a wonderful gift!"

"My supposed ancestors," Blythe corrected her. "I've found no definite proof that any of the Bartons of Barton Hall ended up in Wyoming." Then Blythe shook her head. "I don't know, Valerie. Of all the places in the world, I decide to come here just because my grandmother filled my head since I was a child with a bunch of family lore that's probably half made up, anyway." Blythe shook her head ruefully and laughed. "Lucinda Barton was quite a character. She was known to spin some mighty 'tall tales,' as we say out west."

"Oral history!" Valerie nodded enthusiastically. "The story of a tribe handed down through the spoken word! Shamans and wandering storytellers can be found in every culture. . . . Certainly we've had our share here in Cornwall. It's simply fascinating!"

"But don't forget, Valerie," Blythe reminded her with a wry smile, "what's been happening to me comes in words and pictures. When this vision stuff starts, it's almost as if I'm watching TV, only I can empathize emotionally with all the people whose lives I'm seeing revealed each time I push against his or her name on the chart."

Valerie remained silent, deep in thought.

"Do you suppose," Blythe ventured, "that the glass on the chart provides a medium for that 'scrying' business you talked about that day at the fete?"

"Well . . . the glass inside the gilt frame is a reflective surface," Valerie mused, "and when you stared at it in such a concentrated fashion, as you've described to me, perhaps it created an atmosphere conducive to self-hypnosis." She made a note on a pad in front of her. "I'll check through the professional literature and see what I come up with." Then Valerie looked at her inquiringly and bit her lip. "Would you have any objection if I took down notes from our meeting?"

"I-I suppose that's all right," Blythe said warily, "if you agree it's just between the two of us and you won't have me committed—or sell your memos later to some tabloid."

"Heavens!" Valerie exclaimed. "I would never break my vows as a health practitioner!" Then she went on, "Here I am, totally fascinated by all this, and nothing unusual ever happens to me. I'm too rational, I'm afraid. You creative types are much more likely to experience this kind of thing. It's probably inscribed in your DNA!" she added jokingly.

"You said before that it's pretty well established that stress and trauma affect the chemistry of the body and brain," Blythe mused. "Now, I'll grant you that's possible. I've sure had more than my share of stress this year," she added ruefully. "But what I don't understand is, how could someone's altered body chemistry, in turn, alter their DNA? How do you account for what's been happening to me?"

"This is all highly theoretical, of course," Valerie replied, pulling an anatomy text from the shelf behind her chair. She turned to a page illustrating the body's various systems. "If you are confronted by a tiger in the jungle, your adrenal glands, here," she said, pointing, "secrete excess adrenaline to provide the energy you need to run away fast."

"Your body accelerates and kind of goes into overdrive?"

"Very much so. Your heart pumps faster. Body chemicals like serotonin, catecholamine, and dopamine increase—or decrease, as the case may be. Your electrolyte and T-cell levels change. And it's thought that these changes may cause new configurations in the cells themselves."

"In other words, being really scared by the tiger might change you on a 'cellular level,' so to speak?" Blythe queried.

"Perhaps." Valerie nodded. "And that could change the DNA. Some brain scientists theorize that a traumatic or significant event—let's say, confronting the tiger—could be scratched, so to speak, on a chip of DNA and passed on."

"Like a recording on a music CD or a file on a computer hard disk?"

"That's the theory. DNA is housed in the cells, after all. The question is, could these changes—or these 'records' of past events—somehow be encoded and passed down to the next generation in their DNA? The trick is in decoding what may be there."

"And you think that when a person's in a trance state, she can decode the information in her genes?"

"Possibly," Valerie said. "That might explain what's going on when you inadvertently put yourself into a hypnotic trance by staring at the chart so intensely and concentrating your thoughts."

Blythe recalled the image of the baby she'd seen in Valerie's crystal ball, and the fleeting visions that had appeared when she'd stared at Ennis's paintings above the fireplaces in Luke's sitting room and at her cottage.

"No one knows, exactly, what is the source of the information that's being accessed when one is in an altered state of consciousness," Valerie continued, closing the anatomy book. "Is it a forgotten memory from one's current life stored in the back of the brain somewhere? Or is it like a dream state . . . a clever parable or metaphor the mind invents to solve problems in daily life? Or, as these cutting-edge brain researchers postulate: Is it a record from an earlier time, imprinted on the DNA, just waiting to be fully recalled—but only in a hypnotic trance?"

"It's true . . . ," Blythe mused aloud, "each time I was totally focused on a particular name, it was as if I had pushed the right button to retrieve information about that part of the story. . . ." She sighed once again and cast Valerie a searching look. "But that sort of makes it forever yesterday inside a person's genetic code."

"That's rather a good way to phrase it." Valerie nodded thoughtfully.

"But why should I be the one suddenly experiencing this?" Blythe protested. "Why me? Why now?"

"Because, my dear Blythe," Valerie said gently, "your defenses are down. You've been exhausted by the recent upheavals in your life. The rational part of you has not been able to explain why such a tragedy should happen to you. I imagine you came to Cornwall seeking answers. Seeking a way to put your life back together after the traumatic events in Wyoming and California."

"I take it you watch CNN?" Blythe asked resignedly.

"That, plus some oblique remarks Luke has made over the summer when we've exchanged pleasantries in the village."

"Ah . . . yes . . . your cousin Luke," Blythe said softly. In the course of their conversation she had not disclosed to Valerie that she and Luke had become lovers. She was reasonably sure that the discreet Englishman would not reveal their relationship to anyone, even to his kinswoman.

"Has Lucas told you who originally drew that ornate Barton-Trevelyan-Teague family tree?" Valerie asked quietly.

"I had supposed it was done by some professional genealogist in this century," Blythe replied. "It's completely up-to-date. Even young Richard's name is inscribed."

Valerie rose and flipped the switch of her electric kettle, which was perched on a side table. Immediately it began to gurgle as the water inside heated up. As the psychologist placed two cups on their saucers, she explained, "Lindsay Teague had a friend who was a calligrapher. Within two days after the lad was born, he added Richard's entry, and he matched the script of the earlier ancestors' names as best he could. You should take a closer look at the chart. You'll see it has a consistency in ink and writing style up to about the year 1890."

Valerie deftly put three scoops of loose tea in a plain brown pot and poured boiling water into it. Then she looked over at Blythe and announced brightly, "My ancestor, the Reverend Randolph Kent, was the principal calligrapher on that family tree."

"Kent!" gasped Blythe. "The vicar who married Kit and Blythe in the church . . . St. Goran's! He's your direct ancestor?"

"Yes. He wrote it all down in one sitting . . . in 1795, I believe. But how did you know that he performed the marriage?" Valerie asked, amazed.

"I went to the wedding," Blythe laughed uneasily, realizing that she had neglected to tell Valerie about her brief glimpse of that joyless ceremony. "But how could he write out a genealogy chart in one sitting? That's impossible!"

"Well . . . the good reverend was also a scryer," Valerie revealed. "He foretold the fate of generations to come."

"You can't be serious!"

Lucinda Barton would certainly have enjoyed meeting the Reverend Randolph Kent, Blythe thought wryly.

"Indeed, I am most serious," Valerie assured her. "As the story goes, he used his powers as a scryer to predict the future of the Teague line. It got him in a terrible row with the Methodists back in those days. They called him a tool of the devil—and worse! He was a cousin by marriage to Garrett Teague's father, Donald Teague, and a reluctant ally of both Donald and Collis Trevelyan in the smuggling activities in the region."

"I know that. But how do you know he was a scryer?" Blythe asked sharply.

"I inherited Reverend Kent's diary," Valerie disclosed. "Apparently his scrying revealed visions that led him to believe he should not have married Kit Trevelyan to the Barton heiress."

"He didn't need a crystal ball to see that!" Blythe scoffed. "He felt guilty as hell when he was reading the words of the church service. He was just afraid Collis would turn him over to the authorities if he didn't do what Blythe's guardian wanted, which was to marry Trevelyan's son to James Barton's daughter and thereby join the two properties."

"I see," Valerie replied, pondering the realization that Blythe, in one of her trances, had learned information about her ancestors' past that could be verified, even today.

"Did Randolph Kent's diary say that he could forecast Kit and Blythe's future? Did he use his—what was it—a crystal ball?"

"He employed some sort of murky mirror to do his forecasting," Valerie explained. "You must read his diary sometime. He's not at all specific about what he saw happening in the future to Kit and the first Blythe Barton."

"He probably didn't want to chronicle bad news," Blythe noted dryly.

"He does say, though, that he felt terrible remorse for having wed them." The psychologist handed her visitor a cup of tea. "I don't suppose Luke told you about any of this business relating to the genealogy chart? In the diary the vicar lists the names of Teague-family descendants far beyond his and Garrett's own life spans, into the last quarter of the nineteenth century."

"Holy cow," Blythe breathed. "You mean he really, truly predicted Garrett's future descendants?"

"So it would appear. In his diary he says that his visions in the mirror foretold the identity of Garrett's succeeding heirs, right up to the year 1889, if memory serves me."

"Luke never mentioned this," Blythe responded slowly. "But, then, I don't think Luke gives much credence to the matters we've been discussing."

"I rather imagine you're right," Valerie chuckled. "Luke thinks the story that Reverend Kent forecast the future of Barton Hall is just so much family lore. He even suspects some great-great-uncle of mine faked the diary as part of a party prank."

"What do you think?" asked Blythe. "Is the diary genuine? Can you tell if it was written in the eighteenth century—and not in the late nineteenth or early twentieth?"

Valerie shrugged. "You must have a look at it yourself sometime. It appears genuine enough to me . . . the style of the leather binding . . . the type of paper . . . certainly the brown ink."

"Does the diary predict all the names of Garrett's future descendants correctly?"

"Name for name," Valerie confirmed. "The author claims in his diary that he simply copied everything he saw in the scrying mirror onto the genealogy chart. He apparently wanted to reassure the impecunious Garrett Teague that his line—and Barton Hall—would continue down the generations—or at least until the 1890s."

"I noticed on the chart that Garrett Teague ultimately married," Blythe said softly.

"About five years after he inherited the Barton-Trevelyan estate in 1794."

"Garrett inherited Barton Hall exactly two hundred years ago this year. . . ."

"Circles within circles," Valerie commented obliquely. Then she looked across the desk intently. "Blythe . . . the images you've seen thus far haven't involved a certain twentieth-century woman named Blythe Barton Stowe, have they?"

"No . . . just the past."

"Would you like to see what else we might learn if I hypnotized you today?"

Blythe put her cup of tea on Valerie's desktop. "You mean staring into your crystal ball again?" she asked apprehensively. "But haven't we agreed that all this probably hasn't anything to do with any past life of mine? I'm just eavesdropping, somehow, on the long-forgotten lives of others. How could past-life therapy be of any help?"

"Perhaps we could call this psychogenealogy therapy!" Valerie chuckled, and then she grew pensive. "It's possible that we've stumbled on a new type of treatment. One where we try to understand your present dilemmas through learning firsthand what happened to the ancestors in your bloodline. Perhaps certain events were set in motion during the first Blythe Barton's day that have echoed down through the generations to your branch of the family?"

"If it's really my branch," Blythe reminded the psychologist.

"We could see if putting you under again could tell us if your experiences here in Cornwall support or refute the theory of genetic memory. . . ."

"I don't know . . . ," Blythe murmured doubtfully. "I don't much like the feeling that I'm becoming some sort of paranormal guinea pig."

Eagerly Valerie opened a desk drawer and retrieved a dark blue velvet bag that appeared to contain something spherical. Then she placed a small brass stand decorated with a circle of three seahorses on the desktop. Their curved heads provided a cradle for the luminescent globe, which Dr. Kent carefully withdrew from the pouch and gently placed within the perimeter.

"There we are," Valerie said, unable to hide her enthusiasm. She smiled encouragingly. "Come, now, Blythe! Your people were adventurous enough to travel all the way out to the Wild West! Aren't you willing to give it another go?"

Blythe inhaled deeply, then blew the air from her lungs and shrugged. "Okay . . . but first let's finish our tea."

Chapter Twelve

May 8, 1792

A boy of about eleven years old burst into the smoky interior of the Pope's Head Inn.

"The *Mirador*'s been sighted, sir!" he said excitedly to Kit Trevelyan. "Just comin' into Sutton Pool. She's lowerin' her sails, and she should be tied up on the west quay in not more'n an hour."

Kit rewarded the young lookout with a few coins as Blythe pulled her cloak tightly around her shoulders and made a pretense of tying its neck ribbons more securely. She surveyed the other travelers lounging in the drafty, smoke-filled room overlooking a narrow street near the Plymouth wharves. It seemed impossible that she and Kit should finally be awaiting the arrival of her former lover to disembark from a Spanish ship after an absence of nearly three years.

My former lover.

Blythe felt a sudden sense of bitterness, a feeling she thought she had subdued long ago. She had discovered on the second day of her marriage to Kit that Ennis had been halfway to this very port, bound for France. Adding to her dismay was the news that by midmorning on her wedding day Garrett Teague had been commanded to hastily pack his small trunk and to assume the role of unpaid traveling companion to his cousin, the gentleman-artist. There had been no way for her to dispatch a message to her would-be rescuer with the urgent news that she had been willing, in the end, to flee with him from Cornwall to America. Garrett and Ennis had departed from Trevelyan House for Plymouth on horseback just as the halfhearted toasts to the bride and groom were being drunk at Barton Hall. By week's end the youthful travelers were en route to Italy on a grand tour of the Continent, and had been leisurely soaking up European culture on a journey that lasted thirty-six months.

"Shall I ring for more sherry?" Kit inquired of Blythe politely, startling her from her reverie. "I'll wager 'twill be of no good purpose to await Ennis and Garrett in this mizzle," he added, nodding toward a small grime-encrusted window that looked out from a private room reserved for entertaining ladies with an appropriate escort. The fine mist descending on bustling Looe Street outside looked as if it might soon turn into serious rain. "If we depart in twenty minutes' time, 'twill be soon enough to greet them as they come down the gangway."

Blythe nodded and responded in as normal a tone as she could muster. "Some more sherry would be lovely, thank you."

"Are you sure you're warm enough?" Kit asked Blythe anxiously. "You feel well enough to go down to the quay, do you, having made the journey thus far?"

She graced her husband with a faint smile, making a customary effort to match his considerate demeanor.

"I'm perfectly well, thank you," she assured him.

Much had changed, at least on the surface, since their misbegotten wedding night in 1789 and the death of their baby daughter just last autumn. Angela Trevelyan had been an infant conceived in holy wedlock, but bleak misery. The sickly child had greeted her new life without the will to survive and had expired three weeks following her birth.

Recalling her firstborn's fleeting existence, Blythe ventured to ask, "Had you written Ennis about little Angela? Does he know that she . . . ?"

"I believe Father informed him you were . . . uh . . .

expecting a child," he replied stiffly. "I wrote him of our shared grief at Da's passing so soon after we lost our little angel—"

"I see." Blythe nodded. "I expect we'll have many bits of news to catch up on."

Oddly, the death of their baby daughter had led to Kit's showing heartfelt concern for his wife's recovery and a genuine grief over the loss of the child. Blythe had found herself reconciled to the fact that, if she couldn't love her ill-favored husband, she could at least treat him more kindly. After all, the pockmarks disfiguring his face and body weren't of his doing, she reasoned. Therefore, she'd tried her utmost to accept their presence as one would a nasty gale or other force of nature. One merely strove to survive with fortitude and soldiered on.

The resulting change in Kit's attitude, however, had been astonishing. He did everything humanly possible to please Blythe. He showered her with thoughtful gifts: silk fabric from France, a stalwart Cornish pony, complete with a new side-saddle and well-oiled leather bridle. Blythe had responded with a valiant show of appreciation and soon discovered that if she behaved with a minimum of courtesy, Kit refrained from his nocturnal drinking and ceased demanding his conjugal rights as often. At length the couple appeared to have reached a polite accommodation.

There was no denying that life at Barton Hall had become infinitely more tolerable, even if it was deadly dull in the absence of Ennis and Garrett. Now, with the splenetic Collis Trevelyan banished to his grave in St. Goran's churchyard, Kit and Blythe had embarked on a small building project.

And the beauty of it all, Blythe thought, sipping her sherry as she gazed through the window in the direction of the Plymouth wharves, was that Kit thought Painter's Cottage was all his idea.

"Ennis has secured another painting commission," her husband had disclosed one afternoon in March following the delivery of a missive from his brother, posted from Naples.

" 'Tis to be a seascape of Capri and environs for Sir William Hamilton, the British envoy in Naples. Now that I've assured Ennis I will provide him with a yearly stipend, he says he's willing to come home as soon as 'tis finished. However," Kit had continued carefully, "he insists he'll be removing to London following his return. He says he doesn't want to complicate our lives by being underfoot."

"Ummm." Blythe nodded with apparent indifference. But her mind was racing.

Ennis would soon be home!

Kit, however wary of his brother's charm with the ladies in general and Blythe in particular, continued to be ignorant of the days of passion Blythe had spent with Ennis preceding her wedding. Since Ennis's departure she had managed to subdue her longing for him like a banked fire on the hearth in the library—quiet and unobtrusive, but dangerously capable of bursting into flame in the event dry tinder was to be tossed onto the coals.

Blythe thought of the small cache of Ennis's letters from Italy that she had hidden, for safety's sake, soon after her trusted housekeeper had delivered them to her hands. In her former lover's most recent correspondence he, too, had informed her he intended to live in London upon his return. " 'Twould be best to make my home in the capital, considering all that has passed between us."

The notion of being caged forever at Barton Hall while the only man she'd ever loved made his home permanently so far away from Cornwall was unthinkable!

" 'Tis a pity if Brother Ennis should abandon us for London," Blythe had responded casually to her husband. "Weren't you hoping he would assume some of the burden for supervising Trevelyan House?"

"That I was," he admitted glumly.

Mustering a look of concern for Kit's welfare, she added, "I suppose you're aware that your tenant there behaves like a pig, or so the maids tell me. Your father's study, I hear, has been used as a shooting gallery when that scoundrel's in his cups. Apparently he allowed a quarter of the hay to rot in the rain before he got around to mowing."

"Too true." Kit had nodded unhappily. "But what possible incentive could there be for Ennis to lend us a hand? His mind is set on continuing to paint. . . ."

"And there's certainly no chamber at Trevelyan House that would serve as a suitable working place for an artist," Blythe had quickly agreed. "None of the rooms large enough to accommodate his easel and canvases are positioned to allow for proper light."

"As you say . . . a pity," Kit had sighed worriedly, for the hay yield on the rest of the estate had been sparse, despite his best efforts to gather it in before the seasonal downpours.

Blythe realized full well that Kit might eventually be forced by tight financial circumstances to involve himself in smuggling—like his father before him. Such illicit endeavors were against Kit's basic inclinations, and, besides, they exposed the family to considerable risk, thanks to the increased activity of the customs men. A far preferable solution would be to have Trevelyan House run more profitably by a member of the family.

"When Ennis lives in London, he'll miss painting on that sweep of land above Hemmick Cove, I'll wager," Blythe had ventured. "The light's ideal there, didn't he always say?"

"Aye . . . ," Kit replied thoughtfully.

" 'Tis a shame that there's no watchtower on the cliff, or a sheep shed . . . something that you could convert to a painter's hut . . . to offer Ennis a place of his very own in exchange for looking after Trevelyan House and those surrounding fields. He wouldn't be intruding on our lives, certainly, if he lived at his father's former home and painted down there by Hemmick Cove, would he? And on the plus side, he'd be able to relieve you of some of the heavy burdens you've had to shoulder. After all," she added with a soft pat to his sleeve, "you've granted him a generous annual stipend. Ennis stands to profit handsomely from your hard work over the years."

An "essentially decent man," Ennis had once called Christopher Trevelyan, and although her husband's face and body did indeed repulse her, Blythe could count on the fact that Kit was at least that: a decent fellow.

Thus it had been child's play to persuade her husband that by doing his brother a good turn, he did himself one in the bargain. Following the conversation regarding Ennis's impending return to England, Kit soon dispatched workmen to the cliff overlooking the small cove situated to the west of Hemmick Beach. They swiftly measured the edge of the field and laid the foundation for a stone cottage especially designed as an artist's retreat. To Blythe's quiet delight the snug little building was speedily constructed, complete with an extravagant two-story window facing the Channel. It was ideal for a painter who specialized in seascapes. She had ordered a brass daybed installed and directed the local joiner to build a tall wooden easel, which she had positioned in the corner of the completed cottage the day before they'd departed for Plymouth.

"Blythe?" Kit's voice interrupted her musings. "The lad says the ship's been made fast at the wharf. Shall we go?"

She smiled, set down her glass of sherry, and took her husband's arm. Together they would persuade the prodigal brother to return to his home.

A fire on the hearth in Painter's Cottage crackled cheerfully, warming a cast-iron kettle full of savory stew.

Despite a wash of clear blue sky filling the floor-to-ceiling artist's window that faced the brass daybed, a brisk breeze blowing across Veryan Bay churned the waves below to a white froth. Rooks and gulls wheeled overhead in the chill September air, screeching greetings back and forth above the slate roof and granite walls of Ennis Trevelyan's new abode.

Blythe stretched her arms above her head and sighed contentedly. Then she rolled onto her side and planted a soft kiss on Ennis's naked upper arm. The painter's easel stood in the center of the room, abandoned by the artist for whom it had been built. Blythe gazed at the image of her face staring back at her from the canvas that Ennis had declared completed the previous afternoon. Then she laughed aloud.

"What?" Ennis said sleepily.

"You've rendered me as the proper wife of a proper Cornish landowner," she replied, laughing again. "And here we are. . . ."

She turned back to him, nuzzling her lips against his arm, and then playfully licking his smooth skin, tasting the saltiness of dried sweat.

"A proper wife? An impetuous feline, I'd say," he replied. "Look closely, and I think you'll see I've captured that quality around your eyes."

Blythe gently chafed her forefinger along his handsome profile and said softly, "Now that you've done my portrait, I'll have no more excuses to come here. I believe I shall have to sneak through the tunnel below us in the dead of night like some desperate smuggler and pop up through that door when you least expect me." She referred, of course, to the square opening carved into the cottage's slate floor. It was sealed by a hinged portal and disguised with removable stones and a large rag rug.

Directly beneath their bed a storage room had been incorporated into the cottage, which led to a passage that had been burrowed thirty feet into the cliff. The newly dug tunnel connected with a deep, naturally formed cave that opened onto the beach. The hidden chamber had yet to be used, but Kit had ordered it constructed when he'd built Painter's Cottage—just in case there might one day be a need to store additional contraband. As he'd reminded her often enough, honest money was scarce that year.

"Well, my wily saucebox," Ennis said languidly as he seized her wandering hand and brought it to his lips, "you'd best curb your lust, or at least disguise your visits here. However you may think you've bamboozled Kit into believing these sittings are purely innocent, I'm certain he disapproves of my having painted you."

"Well . . . you've done *his* portrait!" she argued.

"Ah . . . but he's lord of the manor. 'Tis only fitting in his eyes."

Blythe rose to lean on one elbow and stared searchingly into Ennis's face. In three years' time a web of fine lines had been etched around his enigmatic blue eyes, granting him a world-weary look. Was it the product of new maturity, or of an excess of dissipation?

"Please, let's not speak of Kit," she said in a low voice, warding off a vision of the joy that would light her husband's eyes when she told him she was with child once again.

"He's gone into Gorran Haven for the day. 'Twas the only reason I dared come again, now that the portrait's finished."

Then Blythe shifted her weight, hovering above Ennis. Slowly, seductively, she brushed the tips of her breasts against his chest. If only she could summon from this man an open admission of the same desperate longing that she felt for him. Surely he wanted more from her than mere lust. Surely. A kind of despairing desire seized her as she lowered her frame on top of his.

"However you may deny it, Ennis," she whispered, "you'd like me to steal into your bed in the dark, wouldn't you? You'd like me to touch you like this . . . wouldn't you . . . ?"

She closed her eyes and willed him to kiss her. Silently she prayed he would respond to her with a show of passion. She pressed her pelvis provocatively against his own.

"Blythe . . . you witch," Ennis murmured, amusement tingeing his voice. "You've such an appetite, minx. . . ." He seized her earlobe and nibbled it. "Well . . . so have I."

The bed linen slid to the floor as Ennis rolled her beneath him and kneed her legs apart. She was conscious only of a deep, empty place at her very core. A longing to be filled, to be surrounded and pierced, enveloped and invaded by him, to be—

The door to the cottage thudded heavily against the wall. A cold breeze, as sharp as a shard of glass, rushed in, and for one wretched moment, Blythe thought she had been tossed into the frigid bay.

"Get . . . off . . . my . . . wife!" a voice thundered. Reeling with shock, Blythe wondered fleetingly if Collis Trevelyan had risen from the dead. "You sod! You shameless, thieving cocksman! She is my wife! I am her husband! What kind of monsters are you?" shouted the same enraged voice.

Less than a minute later the two brothers were facing each other, toe to toe, on the edge of the cliff. Ennis had hastily donned a pair of breeches and a wool coat and stood motionless and silent as he accepted his brother's well-warranted denunciation. For her part, Blythe remained inside the cottage, the bed linen draped carelessly around her shoulders. Deaf and dumb, she stared at the drama unfolding in front of the window, unable to hear what they were saying—or, rather, what her husband was demanding with clenched fists.

Garrett Teague stood a little to one side of the pair, a rolled-up parchment clutched in one hand. Perhaps he and Kit had come down to the cottage to confer with Ennis about a plan to improve the bookshop in Gorran Haven in which Kit had taken an interest since his cousin's return from Italy.

A strange trembling in Blythe's limbs began to seize her, a force she couldn't seem to contain, regardless how many gulps of air she sucked into her lungs.

Oh, my God . . . oh, my God . . . oh, my God.

But she was certain that no God would take pity on her now—or ever. Only *she* could see to her own survival.

Ennis held up both hands in front of his chest in a gesture of defeat and supplication. Kit raised his right hand, only to have his wrist grabbed by Garrett. The Trevelyan brothers' cousin began to shout as well, his head swiveling back and forth as he addressed each of them in turn. The three men, who had been rivals and intimates since their births, continued to argue at the top of their lungs as the wind blew even more fiercely off the bay.

Suddenly Kit and Ennis both allowed their arms to fall to their sides, signaling an abrupt anticlimax to this emotional firestorm. Then Kit stalked off across the field in the direction of Barton Hall, while Ennis headed down the path that led to Hemmick Beach. Blythe watched in disbelief as Garrett strode toward the cottage's front door.

"You'll need to get dressed now," he said in a dull monotone as he came across the threshold, leaving the door ajar. "Kit wishes you to remain here, for the moment. He's asked you to sleep here tonight."

"And Ennis?" she whispered.

"Jesu, Blythe!" Garrett exploded, his controlled demeanor shattering. "Can you never get it through your head? The man simply considers you a tasty piece of flesh . . . a pleasing prick-pocket—"

"How dare you!" Blythe shouted, jumping to her feet beside the daybed and clutching the bedclothes to her chest.

Garrett stared stonily at her disheveled state.

"How dare *you*! How dare you betray in this tawdry fashion those who truly care for you!"

"And who is that?" Blythe inquired furiously. "I was merely handed over from one man to the next. From father to son. Caring had no part of the transaction."

"You are blind, and you are willful," Garrett pronounced wearily. "And I fear, now, it may very well be too late for you to make amends to your husband."

"Make amends!" Blythe protested shrilly. "Why can no one see 'tis I who have been wronged as well?"

"That is so," Garrett agreed quietly. "But you have deeply wounded Kit—and me. And for having wounded Kit, I fear you will pay a very high price."

"What?" she asked defiantly.

"Ennis leaves Trevelyan House tonight."

"For London?" Blythe asked fearfully.

"For Plymouth."

"Why Plymouth?" she asked with a look of foreboding. "Where will he go?"

"I don't know. If he's fortunate, perhaps he can join the Royal Navy and fight the damnable French, who threaten invasion, we hear. At any rate, Kit has cut him off without a farthing. Permanently."

"And what shall the king of Cornwall do to me?" she asked sarcastically.

"He shall ignore you, I should wager. At least for a while."

"Nay, he can't ignore me for long."

"And why is that?" Garrett asked with a look of surprise.

"I'm to have his child."

"You'll brazen this out to the finish, won't you?" Garrett sighed, slowly shaking his head. "What makes you think he'll believe the babe is his?"

"Never fear," she replied tersely. "Within the month he shall have good reason to think 'tis his own flesh and blood."

"But that would be impossible, my lady wife," a voice interrupted from the cottage's half-open door.

Blythe and Garrett, startled by the sudden intrusion, turned to stare at the master of the Barton-Trevelyan estate. Kit took a step farther into the room and shut the door behind him.

"As you well know," he addressed Blythe in a voice laced with bitter sarcasm, "you were loath, for some reason, to lie with me since my dear brother returned from abroad." He took another step closer to his wife and gazed at her with contempt. "I came back just now, idiot that I am, to try to make peace. To try, as Garrett earlier begged me to do, to find some way to live with you in harmony. If not as man and wife . . . then as companions."

His eyes narrowed, and he looked as if he might strangle her on the spot.

"But it appears that we are long past the point where you can woo me to your bed and then play me for a fool!" In a lightning move he slapped her cheek hard and with unforgiving zeal.

"You devious slut! You are filled to overflowing with my brother's seed," he continued, his tone laden with disgust, "and you would dare to try to convince me in a month's time—that it was my own? Have you no feelings for anyone but yourself?"

"And have you no care for anything but your precious lands and your possessions?" she jeered back, rubbing her smarting cheek with one hand.

Kit turned to address Garrett as if Blythe were no longer in the cottage.

"She shall live in this cursed place until the babe is born."

"And then?" Blythe shouted. "I am Blythe Barton! You know in your soul that Barton Hall belongs to me! The curse shall be forever on your head for what you and your damnable father have done!"

The Trevelyan House chimneys jutted above the burgundy-colored leaves of the copper beech that had guarded its entrance for two hundred years. But nary a wisp of smoke belched from the brick stacks, and the house looked utterly deserted.

Ennis's servants had deserted as well, Blythe discovered as she stealthily made her way up the back stairs leading from the butler's pantry. Kit had ordered the entire staff to vacate the premises until further notice. No one was to lift a hand to assist the younger brother's departure from the land of his birth.

"But he can't do this!" Blythe insisted, pacing before the cold hearth in the bedroom where Collis Trevelyan had once ruled supreme.

She had never seen the chamber's gloomy dark paneling before, nor the heavy, hulking furniture that surely dated back to the Jacobean era. She ceased her agitated tour of the thread-bare carpet and turned to confront Ennis, who was in the process of stuffing a saddlebag with a change of linen and a few other necessities for his impending journey. Suddenly she recalled his traveling trunk stored in the loft above the pony stables. Kit had even refused his brother access to his own property!

"I suppose he could have me hung on a nearby tree, if he wished," Ennis snapped. "Haven't you gotten it through your stubborn head, yet, Blythe? Kit Trevelyan is the master of our worlds! You are his property and I am now merely a cuckolding rogue, no longer entitled to my brother's largesse . . . an outlaw on my father's land. An outcast second son among what passes for society around here. What bloody fool nonsense it all is!" he said with disgust. "I'll be glad to see the last of all of you!"

"Ennis!" Blythe exclaimed, shaken to be included among those he appeared to despise most. "But what about . . . ?" She was too mortified by his tirade to finish her question.

"What about us, you were about to say?" He laughed mirthlessly. "What about our supposed summer idyll in Painter's Cottage? Pray, don't make me ill with protestations of love! I don't think I could stomach it!"

He slammed shut a drawer and began to rummage in the armoire that stood against a nearby wall.

"But I did love you!" she protested hotly. "I always did . . . you know that! I even wrote you of my . . . longings for you in the letters I dispatched to Italy—"

"You preferred me to my pockmarked brother," he interrupted curtly, not even deigning to look at her, "a judgment with which I certainly concur. However, shall we be brutally honest with each other at last, my dear? We have merely served as diversions for one another in this backwater, and that is about the extent of it."

"That's not true!" Blythe protested.

"Well, 'tis true for me," he said bluntly.

"But your letters to me swore—?"

"It amused me to describe my travels to you." He shrugged. "I assumed you'd save the letters, and I thought one day I might publish a book to enhance my lot as a painter. 'An English Artist Abroad,' " he added, sketching the outlines of the imagined volume in the air. "I suppose I expressed some mild endearments out of a twinge or two of guilt . . . and so you'd tuck those missives away safely, until I might have need of them."

Blythe stared at him, dumbfounded. He had asked to read the letters only a fortnight ago and then had failed to return them.

"So you never held any affection for me at all?" she concluded dully.

"Not true," he replied with a sardonic glance. "I very much liked your performance in the feathers."

"I suppose it 'amused' you," she said slowly. "Much like your writing to me about the sights in Italy."

"It stimulated me," he said, eyeing her critically. "And it kept me from abusing myself between visits to the trollops in the Via Veneto."

"Why are you being so wretched to me?" Blythe asked in a low voice.

"I? Being wretched to you, you ignorant chit!" he said between clenched teeth. "And what do you suppose my life will likely be from here on out?" he demanded, slamming the cupboard door. "I am to leave with only the money I have now in my pocket," he said, taking a threatening step toward her. "I may not have a horse on which to ride to Plymouth. My line of credit has been withdrawn. I may not even retrieve my brushes and paints from the cottage!" He stared at her coldly, adding, "And the worst of it is that I will be prevented from doing what I was born to do—which is paint, not to serve some pompous captain on a ship."

"Kit can't mean to be so cruel," she cried. "I shall bring your palette and brushes to you!"

"And you shall be apprehended by the guards he has posted in the field behind the stone hedges, you simpleton! Because of you," Ennis shouted, losing all semblance of control, "I am to have nothing of my patrimony! Get out of my sight!"

"But those are Kit's decrees, not mine!" she cried, stung by his invective. "Why not direct your venom at him?"

"Because if I do," Ennis said in a low, menacing voice, "he will have me shot . . . and then where shall I be? At least this way I have the satisfaction of venting my spleen, and I may yet remain breathing—and perhaps find some means to make my way for a while in the Royal Navy."

"And, pray, have you not a care what will happen to me?" Blythe asked brokenly, her hand on the latch. "I am with child. I carry your babe, Ennis!"

"If, in fact, you do, you scheming wench," he said in clipped tones that signified he considered this a shopworn ploy, "I assure you, it means absolutely nothing to me."

And in the very marrow of her bones, Blythe knew this to be true.

In the end, due to Garrett's persuasion, Kit sent one of the men from the estate to Plymouth with Ennis's brushes, paints, and wooden artist's palette wrapped in a length of canvas. Blythe learned from backstairs gossip delivered by the scullery maid who brought her food each day to the cottage that the master's brother had got himself a berth on a navy frigate whose duty it was to patrol the English Channel looking out for marauding French ships.

"Oh, those Frenchies are bad'uns, to be sure!" Mary Ann exclaimed as she poured a small pail of something resembling soup into the kettle that hung on an iron bar over Blythe's hearth. "I heard Master say their armies have invaded the Low Countries, now that they've chopped off the heads of their king and queen. They'll be on our coast next, 'tis what we all fear," she said, peering nervously out the window that faced the sea.

A sharp November wind, pregnant with rain and sleet, rattled all the windows and brought drafts whistling through the tiniest chinks in Painter's Cottage.

Kit had sent word that Blythe was not to light any candles at night to draw attention to the location of an estate ripe for attack. Occasionally, when hungry French seamen on patrol saw a chance to wade ashore in Cornwall, they stole whatever stores they could lay their hands on and retreated like streaks of lightning back to their ships.

By early February, eight months pregnant and perpetually chilled to the bone, Blythe had reached her limit. But when she ventured inside the library at Barton Hall, all she got for her troubles was a husband who slashed his brother's portrait to shreds and threatened her with the point of his sword.

"Go ahead," Blythe shouted back at Kit, whose disheveled appearance and wild eyes had driven her past caring that he might run her through with the weapon he was brandishing. "Have *murder* on your conscience as well!"

"And what pricks *your* conscience, you bloated wench?" Kit said derisively. He allowed his sword to fall to his side while he reached with his other hand for a half-empty bottle of contraband brandy, taking a pull. "Anything at all?"

Blythe inched around the desk in order to put the piece of furniture between her and her ranting spouse. Her fingers brushed against the handle of the top drawer. Perhaps Kit still kept his pistols there, she thought suddenly. Her husband took another drink, tilting his head back and allowing her enough time to slide out the drawer and curl her fingers around one of the guns. By the time Kit replaced the bottle on the table, she had leveled the unwieldy weapon and cocked the hammer. A matching pistol remained in the drawer. She seized it with her other hand, letting it dangle heavily by her side.

"I shall thank you not to call me disgusting names," she said grimly. "And furthermore, I no longer intend to freeze to death in that hovel by the sea. I shall have the baby . . . our baby, as far as the world knows . . . in Barton Hall in the bloody Barton Bed, like every other Barton that ever saw the light of day!"

"You shall not remain under my roof!" Kit shouted, lifting his sword and pointing it at her heart. "I forbid it, harlot!"

" 'Tis my roof, you thieving scoundrel!" Blythe shrieked, taking aim with the pistol.

"Stop it, you two!" demanded a voice from the opposite side of the library.

Garrett Teague, white-faced, stood framed in the doorway. Simultaneously Blythe and Kit turned to stare. "By all that's holy, you both sound as if you're eight years old and arguing over a turn at draughts!"

Kit lowered his arm and once again allowed the sword to thump against his thigh.

Meanwhile, the pistol in Blythe's hand began to tremble as a lightning bolt of pain, sharp as the point of her husband's weapon, slashed through her midsection.

"Ohhh!" she gasped, leaning heavily against the desk.

"Blythe!" Garrett said urgently. "What's wrong? You've gone white as a ghost."

The two pistol barrels fell with a thud upon the desktop, yet Blythe held on to the weapons for dear life.

"Oh . . . God! Ohhh . . ." She stared with terror-stricken eyes at the man who had served as her perpetual rescuer and friend, despite her transgressions. "Help me . . . ," she moaned as a gush of bloody water pooled at her feet. "Dear God, help me! The babe! 'Twill come on fast now!"

Garrett moved across the room in a few short strides. "Tell Mistress Tinney to fetch the midwife," he ordered Kit as if he, not his cousin, were the lord of the manor. He scooped Blythe's unwieldy form into his arms.

"The by-blow's not due till March or April," Kit rejoined in a hectoring tone. "I'll not have the chit—"

"Oh, bloody hell, Kit Trevelyan!" Garrett shouted. "All this shrying's brought on the babe early, you dolt! Do as I say!"

"I'm master here," Kit said stubbornly, his eyes riveted on the look of abject anguish contorting his wife's features. "Take her to the cottage. She'll have her bastard there!"

"Then at least tell someone to send for the midwife, blast

you!" Garrett said furiously, and shouldered his way out the door with Blythe moaning in his arms.

Blythe had few memories of being transported back to Painter's Cottage, except for a faint recollection that she continued to clutch the two pistols in a death grip against her chest as Garrett carried her down Hall Walk in the rain. Nor did she clearly recall the moment her baby was born. She was, however, acutely aware that she was buried in a cave of pain. It was a cavern whose walls were alive with flames that burned so fiercely, she thought at times that she had died in childbirth and had woken up in hell.

She dimly remembered Garrett sponging the sweat off her brow, and forcing her to drink sips of water from time to time. He seemed to disappear for long periods, and then he returned to the head of the bed, exhorting her in words she barely heard. She felt him tie her ankles to the bottom bedposts. Someone kept screaming, and then the searing knife of pain that was tearing at her belly suddenly abated. A strange silence fell inside the stone cottage. Then the screaming began anew, this time the high wails of a hungry child. And when Garrett held the babe next to her face to show it was alive, he was weeping with relief and triumph, and his arms were covered in blood. Her blood. Garrett Teague had served as midwife and sole witness to her private agony. No help had been summoned.

The next morning she awoke to see Garrett's face swimming before her eyes. Slowly her vision cleared and she smiled.

"You needn't play the bookseller any longer," she whispered, accepting a sip of water from a cup Garrett held to her parched lips. "I shall propose you for the post of village midwife . . . although I doubt Kit will allow it."

Amazingly enough, her estranged husband suddenly appeared at the cottage door the following day. Reluctantly Garrett had left her side to run all the way in a miserable downpour to Gorran Haven. There he hoped to hire a lass from the village to come look after her as she convalesced.

Blythe had been dozing when Kit shut the door against the howling storm outside. She opened her eyes to the sight of his pockmarked face staring down at her.

"So you both live, I see," he said, gazing with hostile curiosity at her matted hair and haggard face. He shifted his glance to the sleeping baby crooked in her arm.

"Pray, begone," she murmured listlessly.

"I waited behind the gate until I saw Garrett depart. I won't brook his interference with—"

"Begone, I said!" she demanded with an infusion of strength prompted by her fresh recollection that he had refused to send for the midwife. "Garrett saved my life, when you only wished me dead! What you've done is unforgivable!"

"And what of you!" he rejoined. "Few husbands could muster much forgiveness after seeing you, as I have all winter, ripe with my brother's child. 'Tis made me . . . not myself," he said thickly.

"I nearly died!" she exclaimed. "You know full well, 'twas murder you had in your heart, though what magistrate in these parts would have come to my aid, I wonder?"

"Can't you understand?" Kit mumbled, running an agitated hand through his unkempt hair. " 'Tis driven me quite mad, all this." He glanced down at the newborn, and his features hardened. "The fruit of your lust for my brother mocks me, even in its innocence."

"Oh, a pox on you, and I mean that most sincerely," she spat contemptuously, "for if you cannot bear the sight of this child . . . I assuredly cannot bear the sight of you!"

The last thing Blythe expected to see was Christopher Trevelyan's eyes suddenly fill with tears. He turned away and appeared to gaze at the forlorn seascape that hung over the rough stone fireplace. Slowly his eyes drifted around the dimly lit cottage, taking stock, she supposed, of the other paintings she had hung on the walls since Ennis had left. The pictures soothed her, somehow, and gave her hope, although perhaps they served as salt in Kit's wounds. If they did, it mattered not one whit anymore, she thought savagely.

"Well, then," he said coldly, turning toward the bed where she lay upon the straw-filled mattress. He appeared to have regained some measure of composure and now spoke in a dull monotone. "I suppose, therefore, I must inform you that I shall be leaving for London as soon as the storm abates."

"Excellent," she replied, glancing at the underweight baby wedged in the crook of her left arm. Would her milk be sufficient to boost this scrap of human flesh to a decent size? she wondered. Perhaps she should have urged Garrett to seek a wet nurse from the village, as well.

"I shall be petitioning the House of Lords for a divorce," Kit announced, jutting his unshaven chin in the air. "I shall charge you with adultery, of course. Thus this bastard child shall not inherit."

Despite her weakened condition, Blythe felt white-hot anger flood her veins. She struggled to sit up in bed, prompting the fragile infant to mew in protest at being jostled. Blythe slowly moved her right hand under the bedclothes and felt for the pistol she had begged Garrett to put under her pillow before he departed for Gorran Haven. Steeling herself, she grasped it and raised it to the level of Kit's forehead ten feet away.

"You shall do no such thing," she announced with all the courage she could muster. "For unless I have your promise that you will not hold me and the Barton-Trevelyans up to public ridicule, I shall simply pull this trigger," she added icily. "Whatever the authorities choose to do with me afterward . . . the fact remains that Ennis shall inherit if I shoot you this instant. And if I don't, you must guarantee that one day, either through you or through your unmarried brother—my flesh and blood shall be heir to Barton Hall."

Kit's gaze was riveted on the pistol aimed at his head.

Blythe leaned toward him and was gratified to see her estranged husband swallow nervously.

"And Trevelyan House?" he demanded harshly.

"What you do about Trevelyan House is no concern of mine. Live in it and prosper by its fields, if you so wish. Bequeath it to the village idiot, for all I care. Just give me your sacred word of honor as a gentleman that my son will inherit Barton Hall . . . or I shall shoot you in the heart," she added, lowering the pistol to the level of his chest.

Kit merely stared at her, a look of pure hatred expressing the thoughts he apparently could not articulate.

Meanwhile, Blythe released her hold on the baby and painfully eased her legs to the side of the mattress. She grasped the bedpost with her left hand and, in a single motion, pulled herself upright. The ivory-handled pistol weighed heavily in her right hand, and her arm ached. She must get closer to him, she thought in sudden panic, so she wouldn't miss her shot.

"What say you, then, to my proposal, husband mine?" she asked in a low voice. "I shall count to three, and then I must have your answer."

Kit remained mute. Blythe took several steps closer to her target.

"One . . . two . . ."

"Three!" announced Dr. Valerie Kent loudly. "I wish you to wake up now. There's a good girl. How do you feel, my dear?"

A telephone rang in the office next door as Blythe sat bolt upright in the lumpy upholstered chair. To regain her bearings, she glanced around the psychologist's tiny consulting room above Rattle Alley and laughed weakly.

"Why, Valerie Kent," she said accusingly, "for all your enthusiasm about 'searching for Past Truth,' you're a bit of a chicken!"

"Just call me a Cornish game hen," Valerie chuckled wryly. Then her face grew sober. "I thought it best to bring you back."

"But we didn't find out—" Blythe began to protest.

"I think we should be a bit careful, since what we're exploring is rather new to us both."

Rather new, indeed, Blythe thought ruefully. And rather old.

Chapter Thirteen

September 6, 1994

Blythe wheeled Luke's Land Rover down the shadowy corridor of tall larch trees and around the final curve of Barton Hall's stately drive.

Just ahead, parked in regal splendor under the granite porte cochere, was a cream-colored Rolls-Royce Corniche. The classic car's elegant curved fenders and pristine chrome bumpers were bathed in the golden glow of the afternoon sun.

"Shh-it!" she muttered. "Visitors!"

Blythe was in no mood to greet company. She was bone-tired from her foray into the bizarre world she had dared to reveal to Valerie Kent that afternoon. All she wanted was to sink quietly into a scalding-hot bath and absorb the scenery outside her cottage window.

Well, at least the unexpected caller wasn't Chloe Acton-Scott, she mused, savoring the pleasurable fact that the woman's blue Jaguar still had not made a return appearance at the estate.

Blythe pulled around to the rear of the castle and directed one of the workmen to begin unloading the back of the car. The first of seven temporary hothouses had been completely framed in her absence and now awaited its plastic shell. The foundations for the other six had been laid out and would be constructed over the next few days. Young Richard was working beside Mr. Quiller as the older man designated the appropriate number of polyurethane rolls for each of the structures that would soon take form in the field beyond the walled garden. The ten-year-old had on the pair of cowboy boots she'd had air-expressed from Corral West Ranchwear in Jackson as a belated birthday present. As soon as Blythe braked the Land Rover to a halt, the boy dashed up to the driver's side of the car.

"See how much was done today?" he cried enthusiastically.

"Fantastic!" she agreed with more energy than she felt. "Your father looks as if he's got company," she noted as she climbed out of the vehicle. "When you see him, Dicken, would you just say I've gone home to Painter's Cottage and I'll catch up with you all early tomorrow? All the items he ordered are stowed in the back of the car."

"He asked me to tell you as soon as you came back to please go up to the house, straightaway," Richard piped.

"But I look a mess!" she protested. "Just tell him I'm a wreck and in need of a bath."

"Mr. Teague said it was important," Mr. Quiller intervened, approaching the car.

"Really?" she said, wondering what it could be. "Well . . . all right," she agreed reluctantly, and headed for the castle's back entrance.

Perhaps the visitor with the Rolls-Royce was a relative whom Luke wished her to meet, although he'd told her recently that he had few close remaining relations. He had revealed late one night that, as was the case with Blythe's mother, Janet, his father had died of a heart condition when Luke had been in his last year at university. A few years afterward his mother had gone to live with her daughter and son-in-law in Canada. Perhaps the owner of the museum-quality wheels gracing the gravel drive belonged to one of his intriguing distant cousins just down for a brief sojourn from London.

Blythe entered through the back hall that led to the kitchen, reassuring herself that field representatives from the Inland Revenue didn't typically make their rounds in Rolls-Royces.

Mrs. Quiller was nowhere to be seen inside the large rectangular room bristling with hanging pots. However, the kettle was steaming quietly on the hob, and tins of cookies and cakes sat open on the long wooden table, indicating that the housekeeper was in the throes of putting together an impromptu but elegant tea party.

Blythe paused in the scullery to wash her hands and brush the hair back from her face. She dug in her purse for her lipstick and made a minimum of repairs to her face. Then she made her way to the sitting room, resisting the impulse to appear, suddenly, via the secret door that led from the pantry.

When she arrived at the threshold via the carpeted hallway, she halted abruptly, her feet rooted to the floor.

"There you are!" exclaimed an unwelcome ghost from her past. "Our host, who's been decent enough to ply me with tea and scones, promised you'd return eventually, but I began to think you'd given us the slip."

Christopher Stowe lounged gracefully on the chintz love seat, sipping from a gold-rimmed teacup and acting for all the world as if he took tea at Barton Hall every day at four o'clock. His tweed sport jacket and gabardine slacks were perfectly coordinated in subtle shades of brown and tan, and his open-collared shirt was of a rich cream color, similar in hue to the Rolls parked outside. His dark-blond hair—shorn of its ponytail—was neatly trimmed and blown dry in a careful style that effectively disguised the onslaught of irreversible male-pattern baldness. The taut, unblemished skin sheathing his regular features had softened since she had seen him last. Where she had remembered him sleek and dashing and incorrigibly exotic, he now appeared puffy around the eyes, giving him the aspect of a Golden Boy gone slightly to seed.

Even so, the man she had been married to for eleven years appeared every inch the well-heeled British film director who currently resided in Hollywood: Savile Row meets Rodeo Drive.

Mrs. Q handed the celebrated Mr. Stowe a plate laden with her finest delicacies, along with a linen napkin. For her part, Blythe was dumbfounded at discovering that the last man on earth she wished to see was cozily sipping tea in her lover's sitting room. She shifted her gaze to Luke, and back to her former husband, wondering if she'd wandered onto the wrong movie set.

"Why are you here?" she demanded bluntly. To hell with mincing, oh-so-English social niceties, she thought. Why should she cut Chris any slack?

Just rope 'im and run 'im outta here!

"Would you like to sit down first?" Chris inquired with elaborate politeness.

"No, I would not like to sit down," she retorted. "I would like to know what you are doing here!"

Chris's demeanor lost some of its laid-back polish, and he shifted in his seat. Mrs. Q backed swiftly out of the room and disappeared through the magic door, while Luke shot Blythe a look of concern.

Suddenly Blythe had an overwhelming urge to seize the fire poker standing to the right of the hearth and employ it to chase Christopher Stowe out of Barton Hall and to deliver a lethal thwack to the fender of his elegant Rolls-Royce in the process.

"I am here, my dear Blythe, because there is need for a business discussion between us."

"Call my lawyer," Blythe replied curtly.

"Oh, but I have. That's how I found you in this godforsaken outpost." He took another sip of tea, affecting a nonchalance Blythe speculated he didn't feel, although the son of a bitch was doing a much better job of acting cool than she was.

"Lisa Spector told you where I was?" she demanded indignantly.

"No, not exactly. She merely said you were out of the country and couldn't be reached. As you are no linguist, I knew that if you were going to leave America for any length of time, you'd probably come to England. I checked several of our old haunts, and then I thought, 'By Jove! I'll just bet she finally took the time to go down to Cornwall, ancestor-hunting'... and, wonder of wonders, here you are!"

"A woman rang up here, asking for you after you'd left for Gorran Haven," Luke intervened. "I'm sorry . . . I thought it might be—"

"You're in the phone book," Blythe sighed. "My travel agent couldn't believe it when she first called here." Then she turned to face Chris. "What woman called here to find me?"

"Look, Blythe . . . is there somewhere we can talk?"

Luke abruptly stood up. "Let me allow you two some privacy," he offered smoothly. "I'll just go have a word with the men out back."

And before Blythe could protest, he strode out of the room, closing the door behind him.

The English are goddamn unbelievable! Impeccable manners, even on the brink of World War III!

Blythe and her former spouse gazed warily at each other across the sitting room for a long moment.

"Why don't you sit down?" Christopher repeated quietly. Blythe complied, choosing the wing chair Luke had just vacated. It still radiated from his body's warmth. This comforted her somehow. "You're looking well, Blythe," her former husband offered for openers.

"Just tell me why you've come," Blythe demanded grimly. "Tell me why you've barged in here, unannounced—"

"The tabloids have no idea I'm here—" he began.

"Oh, Jesus! That's right!" she groaned. Then she glared at him. "If the Fleet Street ghouls have followed you down here and reveal where I am, I swear, Chris, I'll—"

"No one even knows I've left Kenya," he interrupted. "Ellie and I chartered a plane and flew out of there at three in the morning."

"Ellie is here?" Blythe said slowly. "In Cornwall?"

Suddenly she felt as if she were being assaulted in slow motion. Was there no place on the planet where her husband and her sister couldn't violate her life?

"Well, I couldn't exactly leave Ellie and the baby in the jungles of Africa, could I?" Chris said in an exasperated tone of voice.

"The baby?" Blythe echoed.

"Yes," Chris replied shortly. "A girl."

"Ellie delivered her baby in Africa?" Blythe asked, astonished.

"There is a perfectly adequate hospital in Nairobi, founded by the British," he retorted tersely. Then he added, "We named her Janet. After your mother."

Blythe wilted against the back of the chair as the reality of Christopher's unwanted presence in her life hit her full force.

The baby. Chris and Ellie's baby. Named Janet.

A new member of the Wyoming Bartons had entered the world. It dawned on her that she, Blythe, would be linked to this new family forever. However far away she tried to remain, ties of blood and a shared history would keep her in bondage to all of them. She wondered suddenly what surprises this child's DNA held encoded in her infant cells.

Blythe stared blindly out the nearest window. A golden afternoon haze had transformed the rolling fields into a rich emerald hue as they angled toward the blue depths of the English Channel. The shaggy Highland cattle grazed in pastoral contentment on the September grass. How could her surroundings look so peaceful and bucolic when there was such a storm of emotion churning inside these castle walls?

"Look, Blythe . . . ," Christopher said with a hint of penitence, "I can imagine that my arriving today so unexpectedly has been a shock, but there was no other way. I had to find you."

"For heaven's sake, why?" Blythe asked faintly.

"Because . . . I need your help," he disclosed. "Because you are, in actual point of fact, the only person in the world who *can* help me."

Blythe roused herself from her paralyzed mental state to look at him in amazement. "I? How could I help you? And why *would* I?"

"I don't know if you would—or if you will," he amended. "That's why I came all this way," he added with a crooked grin that she suspected he was employing to try to charm her. "I do know you could help me. Save me, in fact."

"Chris," she said with manufactured coolness as she rose from her chair, "you and I have nothing to do with each other any longer. Our marriage is over. The settlement papers are signed. You've got a new wife . . . a new baby . . . a new picture to direct. It's finished between us—business and pleasure—so if you don't mind—"

"I understand you have a new business partner," Chris interrupted pleasantly. "I asked about all the activity going on around this antique pile, and your landlord's son told me all about the . . . what is it? Some sort of plant palace you hope to create here?" He laughed. "You do have a weakness for us Brits, don't you, Blythe?"

"My current venture with Lucas Teague is not at issue here," Blythe said, furious at detecting an all-too-familiar, demeaning attitude on her ex-husband's part. This was a stance, she recalled with mounting irritation, that he had often maintained when it came to anything having to do with her interest in horticulture. Although Christopher Stowe had never deigned to hold a trowel in his uncallused hands, he assumed that only the English could be experts at serious gardening. "What is at issue," she said icily, "is that I'd like you to leave. Now."

"But you haven't asked why I've come to see you."

"I don't care why you've come."

"Actually . . . I-I realize that," he said, and suddenly, from the way he drummed his fingers on the arm of the love seat, Blythe knew instinctively that a great deal of turmoil was lurking below Christopher Stowe's suave exterior.

"Cut the ruffles and flourishes, then, and just tell me," she demanded. "I'm tired, and I want to get back to my cottage."

"You mean you don't live here?" Chris asked quickly. "With Lucas What's-his-name?"

"Either tell me what you came here to tell me, or get out," she retorted angrily.

Chris inhaled deeply and then said, "I need you to sign over the deed to the Scottish forest property."

"The what?"

"The land I bought as a tax shelter . . . years ago," he disclosed testily. "Putting your name on the documents back then was just a formality. A tax dodge. Since it was property held in the UK, it wasn't included in our divorce settlement."

"How much is it worth?" Blythe asked, arching an eyebrow and thinking of the bills piling up on the desk in Luke's library. Half of the net value of a large stand of trees in the Highlands might be handy in paying for some of their capital outlays—without disturbing any more of her capital.

"That's beside the point," Christopher retorted. "That land was bought with money from *Sally's Girls*."

"May I remind you: I was the production designer on *Sally's Girls*," Blythe said sweetly.

"Yes, but—"

"And now that I'm living in the UK for the foreseeable future," she added, beginning to enjoy this conversation, "why wouldn't I be entitled to half of the profits from any sale of such jointly held property?"

"Because—may I remind you, dearest—England, thank God—unlike California—has no automatic community-property provisions!"

"But you need me to sign off on the sale," she noted demurely. "Why is that?"

"Some bloody stupid ruling of your Internal Revenue Service," he fumed. "Since both our names are on the purchase papers, the IRS requires us both to sign the documents of sale for me to transfer the funds."

"Why is it so important that the forest be sold?" she asked, walking over to the tea trolley and pouring herself a cup of the bracing brew.

"I need the money."

She turned, teacup in hand, to stare at him. "You? Why?"

"*In Kenya* is . . . disastrously overbudget," he revealed reluctantly.

"What happened?" she asked. She was interested, in spite of herself, in the fate of the film she had worked on briefly during preproduction in Hollywood.

"We've had hideous weather on location . . . mud, floods . . . the whole bloody lot! The blasted actors have got dysentery because they didn't follow the health officer's warnings. There was even an attempted political coup! And"—he shook his head with disgust—"the production designer I replaced you with is a freaking idiot! His mistakes have cost me hundreds of thousands of dollars."

"How difficult for you," she deadpanned.

"I know you're pleased to hear all this," he said grimly, "but if I don't post a seven-million-dollar personal bond in ten days' time to cover the excess costs, this picture—which I consider, Blythe, to be the culmination of everything I've tried to achieve as a film director—will be shut down. *Finito.*"

"But why should you have to provide funds personally?" she asked skeptically.

"Because I signed a contract saying I would, to persuade the studio at the last minute to allow us to shoot on location in Africa—instead of faking it in Simi Valley, California!" he said agitatedly. "I never thought it would come to this, believe me! I figured the production schedule was padded enough to finish the film on time. But that's what I signed to get the picture done right. In the last week I've put up everything I own that the banks would lend on, but I'm a million short. Fortunately, I quickly found a buyer for the property in Scotland. I just need you to sign."

"Hot damn!" Blythe chortled. "Who'd ever think a tract of

trees in Scotland could appreciate so much in value in eight years?"

"If I don't come up with the last million, the picture—which, mind you, is two weeks from being finished—will be shut down," he added with increasing impatience. "My colleagues will literally be stranded in Kenya, and Ellie, the baby, and I will be virtually penniless."

"Goodness . . . is that all?" she commented dryly.

"Not to mention that my reputation as a director who can deliver the goods on a high-budget production will be down the plug hole!"

"And why do you think I'd lift a finger to rescue you?" Blythe asked, taking another sip of tea.

Christopher smiled obliquely. "Because you know this could be a great film. And because you're an essentially decent person."

Blythe froze, her teacup halfway to her lips. "Don't be so sure."

"And I'll repay you half the proceeds you apparently think you've got coming," he added grudgingly. "That is, if I ever dig myself out of this financial snake pit."

"And you don't think I earned my half of those goddamn Scottish trees?" she demanded, feeling her temples begin to throb.

"Technically? According to British divorce law? No, if I can prove to the government that I bought it—while in the UK—with my earnings from *Sally's Girls*. My problem is, I don't have the time to prove anything. I just need the money. Now."

"Not a very politic thing to say, if your intention is to get me to sign," she noted curtly. "*We* bought it—while in the UK—after *we* finished *Sally's Girls*."

"All right! You earned half of that forest. In fact, I know it firsthand, now that I've worked with that sot Patrick Corrigan."

"Who's Patrick Corrigan?"

"The useless Irish boozehound who's my production designer."

"Not good, huh?" she inquired innocently.

"Will you sign?"

"I'll have to speak to my lawyer about this first," Blythe replied solemnly, now enjoying herself.

"Christ, Blythe!" Christopher exploded. "If we get the lawyers involved in this, my picture will go to bloody hell!"

"Your picture! *Your* picture!" she said, setting down her teacup so hard, she feared she might have broken it. "You waltz in here, pleading poverty while driving a Rolls-Royce! Who knows how many reptiles from the tabloids are lurking in the hedges, trying to blow my cover and give you a little publicity blast for your precious movie! And you have the unmitigated gall to ask *me* to do you a favor? A very expensive favor?" she cried, pacing in circles in front of the low-burning fire. "You insult me, you're rude to my host, and you disparage my attempts to get on with my life after you and Ellie trashed it—then you ask me for a million dollars?" She was shouting now. "You are certifiable, Christopher Stowe! Don't you ever think of anything but *yourself* and what *you* want?"

She hated herself for the tears that were clogging her throat.

"Blythe . . . Blythe . . . *please* . . . I *am* sorry," Christopher said in a rush. His face had turned ashen up to the roots of his dark-blond hair. "I've gone about this all wrong. I-I didn't mean to insult you. I've had plenty of time to see what a cad I've been, and to regret so much of what happened. It's just—"

She looked at her former husband closely. Unbelievably, he, too, seemed near tears. Blythe blinked hard several times herself and struggled to regain her composure. Meanwhile, it was Christopher's turn to rise from his seat and pace up and down on the carpet. To avoid closer physical contact, Blythe retreated to her upholstered chair and concentrated on staring at her fingers, which were resting in her lap.

"It's all been too much," he said in a voice choked with emotion. "I thought I could handle all the changes in my life by merely plunging into work. But my judgment has been skewed for months, and nothing seemed to go as planned. Ever since you moved from Bristol Drive, it's been an unmitigated mess. It's too much," he repeated hoarsely, and turned away from her to rest his arm on the mantel. Then his head sank onto his forearm.

Blythe was so astonished by Christopher's abrupt change of mood and apparently heartfelt words of regret that she couldn't utter a word. Instead, she continued to stare at his back. As the silence between them deepened, her eyes drifted above his head to gaze at the seascape painted so long ago by Ennis Trevelyan.

Ennis had been an extraordinary talent—like Chris. He had always done exactly as he'd pleased in the pursuit of art and pleasure. How similar these two men were, she thought. Briefly she recalled her hypnotic session with Valerie Kent. Had it been only that morning? Ennis Trevelyan had gone off to sea when his brother had cut off his funds. Did he ever paint again? she wondered. Would Christopher's career truly be washed up if she didn't sign the documents she assumed were in the briefcase that rested near the chintz-covered love seat?

"Look, Chris . . . ," she said haltingly, "I'm not going to sign anything without reading it and having a talk with my lawyer. Why don't you leave the papers and let me have a look at them?"

Chris turned around and peered at her hopefully. "I promise I'll pay you your half someday, if I possibly can."

"Yes, you've said that already."

"I'll put it in writing, if your lawyer insists," he added, making an effort to bestow on her one of his familiar jaunty smiles.

"I'll tell her that."

"If I can just get this picture finished," he blurted in a pleading tone that unwittingly revealed the extent of the pressure he was under. Then he let out a nervous laugh and attempted to lighten the atmosphere. "I swear, Blythe, the dailies are bloody marvelous. I might get a second Academy Award for this!"

"I'm sure you could," she replied wearily.

"Look," he volunteered, retrieving a batch of documents from his briefcase and handing them to her, "I'm staying at some appalling little inn in Gorran Haven. I'll call you from there."

"The Smugglers' Hotel? On Rattle Alley?" She must have driven by Ellie and Chris's lodgings on her way to see Valerie Kent.

"That's it! Appalling."

"It's quite nice, in fact . . . just rather small."

"The baby's been whining constantly and—"

"Please, let's not go into any of that," Blythe said quickly. "I probably won't be able to get back to you until late tomorrow—or the day after—depending on my finding a way to fax the documents to Lisa Spector, and receiving her call."

Christopher appeared about to protest her timetable and then shrugged his shoulders. "Well, do the best you can. It's important."

"I'm sure it is. To you."

"Let's have dinner together tomorrow night, Blythie . . . or . . . or the day after, so you can tell me your decision. Just the two of us, of course," he added hastily, "although your sister is really anxious to see you while she's here."

"Well, I'm not interested in seeing her," Blythe snapped, "so tell her to forget it! I'll show you the way out."

"I'll ring you about dinner," he enthused as they passed through the front door and under the porte cochere.

"You can't. . . . My cottage doesn't have a phone."

"It doesn't?" he asked, appearing amazed that the high-powered woman he had worked with so intensely for more than eleven years had completely cut herself off from the world. "Where are you living? In a tree house?"

"No. On a cliff. It's wonderful," she added for good measure. "I'll leave a message for you at the inn when I come up to the house tomorrow . . . if I've been able to get in touch with my attorney—and if I've reached a decision."

Christopher opened the door of the Rolls-Royce a few inches and cast a glance at his pastoral surroundings.

"Well . . . so far no lowlifes from the press lurking about," he laughed with another stab at his old rakish charm.

"Not yet," she replied grimly. "However, don't be surprised if somebody from the *Gorran Gossip* asks about the dude driving the rented Rolls."

"Have to keep up appearances, darling." Chris grinned.

Without replying Blythe turned on her heel, reentered the castle, and restrained herself from slamming the front door.

"He still calls you 'darling,' " said a voice from the shadows.

"Luke!" Blythe gasped. "You startled me." She tilted her head to one side and smiled at the figure standing directly beneath a portrait of Garrett Teague painted by an artist far less skillful than Ennis Trevelyan. The plaque on the piece stated the work had been rendered in 1794, the year the bookseller assumed the stewardship of Barton Hall. "You were eavesdropping, weren't you?"

"I just happened to walk by the open front door, wondering if the bastard had left yet."

"Well, the bastard has—finally. I need a drink," she announced, and headed down the hallway toward the library, with Luke following along in her wake.

"Brandy or sherry?" he asked when they had arrived in the book-lined chamber.

"Brandy. A double."

"What did he want?" Luke asked, his gaze glued to the crystal decanter as he poured their drinks.

"Money. From an investment we made in Scotland years ago that I'd completely forgotten about," she replied, gratefully accepting the brandy snifter. "He wants me to sign it over to him so he can bail his picture out of bankruptcy." She gave a shaky laugh. "Can you believe it? A bunch of trees we bought in some reforestry scam is now worth about a million bucks!"

"Are you going to do it?" Luke asked quietly.

"I don't know. . . . ," Blythe sighed. "I want to read the documents and show them to my lawyer."

"It's *your* decision . . . not your lawyer's."

"I know it's my decision," she said testily, "but I always run this kind of stuff by her."

Or almost always, she thought, remembering the dressing-down she'd received from Lisa Spector for not consulting her when she and Luke signed their agreement creating Barton Hall Nurseries.

"Why should you lift a finger to help a man who's treated you so shamefully!" Luke exclaimed, setting his glass of brandy down abruptly. "Tell him to go to bloody hell!"

"I appreciate your sentiments," Blythe said evenly, "but it's really my decision to make."

A muscle in Luke's jaw tightened, but he remained silent. Blythe took a sip of her brandy and played for time. Time to think. Time to sort out feelings stirred by Chris's unexpected appearance. From the moment she had set eyes on him, lounging like some pasha in Luke's sitting room, she had felt as if an unseen hand had turned up the heat on a bubbling cauldron of emotions.

Meanwhile, Luke was gazing in moody silence out the window at the setting sun. Blythe glanced up at the Barton-Trevelyan-Teague family tree and searched for a safer topic of conversation.

"Oh . . . guess who I saw today in Gorran Haven. Your cousin Valerie."

"How was she?" Luke asked, and Blythe realized he was also seeking to find common ground.

"Cheery as ever. She told me about the saga of Reverend Kent's predicting the names of the future generations of Teagues," she said casually, pointing to the center of the chart.

"Ah . . . yes . . . the Genealogy Genie," Luke replied with

barely veiled sarcasm. "All the ancients of the village will swear that their dear old grannies vowed on the Bible that this"—he gestured in the direction of the gilt-framed parchment—"was made in the late eighteenth century by the old vicar, who was imbued with extraordinary powers. They love to tell the legend of how Reverend Kent spelled out Garrett Teague's descendants for generations to come."

"And you don't believe it?" Blythe affirmed.

Luke shrugged and sipped his drink. "My grandmother says her grandmother insisted that the vicar of St. Goran's accurately foretold the names of those who came after Garrett, but it's preposterous, of course."

Blythe walked closer to the chart. "But look!" she pointed out. "The calligraphy does change after the year 1890. See? It's right here!"

"Come, now, Blythe," Luke chided. "Someone in the family—perhaps late last century—probably had the chart recopied to that point in time. You know how these tales get embellished by family members as they're handed down."

"But Valerie said—"

"Valerie is very amusing," Luke interrupted, "and I'm extremely fond of her, but she is a bit of an eccentric, wouldn't you say? Charming, but eccentric. I tend not to rely totally on her view of things."

Blythe didn't attempt to counter Luke's gentle ridicule of his older cousin. Instead, she carefully set her glass on the silver tray and announced, "Well . . . as they say in Wyoming after a monthlong cattle drive, 'I feel like I've been rode hard and put away wet.' I'm completely bushed. What I need is a long, hot bath and a good night's rest."

"And time to think?" Luke said coolly. "Alone in your own bed?"

She raised her chin an inch and met his steady glance. "Yes . . . time to think."

* * *

Blythe's face and body flushed pink and her bare skin radiated warmth as she stepped out of her bath and wrapped herself in her newly purchased terry-cloth robe. She poked around at the back of her small refrigerator and found a container of lentil soup, which she warmed in the microwave oven for dinner.

After pouring the steaming liquid into a mug, she sat in a chair near the window, her legs curled up beneath her, and stared out over the darkened English Channel. Despite her soothing soak in the tub and the aroma of Mrs. Q's delicious soup, her stomach still was in a knot and she felt slightly nauseated—sensations she had always associated with nerve-racking spells in Hollywood, not in Cornwall. Christopher Stowe suddenly turns up, and the stress and pressures she'd labored so hard to put behind her were confronting her again, full blast.

And then there was Luke. Luke was hurt and probably a bit jealous, she mused. As a consequence, he was angry with her as well. Like any sane observer, he wondered why in the world she would even consider helping her ex-husband out of a jam, especially since the man had, in Luke's words, treated her so shamefully.

Why would she consider it? she wondered. Was it a debt owed, two hundred years overdue? And due whom?

Her stomach gave an alarming lurch, and she wondered for a moment if all this conflict suddenly boiling up was actually making her sick. She pulled out her traveling makeup kit from the closet, rummaged around to find some Di-Gel, and popped two into her mouth.

Yuk! She felt as if she'd suddenly been transported back to a bad day on the Paramount lot!

Despite her firm resolve not to explore the Barton-Trevelyan-Teague triangle any further without the professional guidance of Valerie Kent, her glance drifted over to the painting by Ennis Trevelyan that hung over the mantel. The bleak seascape had a kind of desolate perfection, its stark beauty saying a great deal, perhaps, about the artist's inability to people his world with warmth and human commitment.

Blythe set her empty mug of soup on a side table and approached Ennis's work of art. Responding to some inexplicable impulse, she placed a footstool in front of the fireplace and gingerly climbed up on it.

The painting was difficult to detach from the hook on which it rested, but eventually Blythe managed to remove it from the stone wall and lean it against the length of a standing lamp in order to have a closer look. The nearer she drew to its thick swirls of dried oil paint, the blander the colors became. Grays and creams and sage-greens blended together indistinguishably. The granite cliff Ennis had depicted jutting above Hemmick Beach could barely be differentiated from the pewter-hued water lapping at its base. She couldn't find his signature on the front, so she turned the painting around to examine the back. Then her heart skipped a beat. Scrawled in charcoal on the back of the canvas were the words "For William."

William?

It was a name she'd never heard Luke mention, nor, from what she remembered of the genealogy chart, was it listed among any of the forenames of the Barton-Trevelyan-Teague clans.

Intrigued, she approached a smaller seascape hanging on a wall near the wooden easel that stood beneath the sleeping loft Luke had installed when he'd decided to rent the cottage to summer visitors. Like the painting she'd just examined—along with the larger work hanging in Luke's sitting room—this picture also depicted a lonely view of the English Channel outside her window: a study in light and dark tones on a blustering, rainy day.

Blythe eased it down from the wall. Also scrawled on the back: "For William."

Her eyes darted quickly about the stone chamber. On the reverse side of the painting that hung near the closet, as well as on the back of the artwork next to the entrance to the bathroom, someone's large, generous hand had also penned, "For William."

Puzzled, Blythe restored the seascapes, one by one, to their respective places on the cottage walls. She pulled her terry-cloth robe more tightly about her shoulders to ward off a sudden chill and wondered who the person was to whom this collection of paintings had been dedicated.

Who in the world was William? And what was he: a Barton . . . Trevelyan . . . or Teague?

Blythe awoke the next morning wondering if her good ol' Di-Gel had lost its punch. Her stomach was still in a knot, and tea was the only possible refreshment that had any appeal. As she read through the documents concerning the sale of the Scottish forest property outside the Highland ski resort of Aviemore, she wondered worriedly if she was developing an ulcer as a result of merely setting eyes on her ex-husband again.

As she waited for the electric kettle to boil, she heard the Land Rover honking its way across the field to her door. Young Richard Teague bounded out of the passenger side of the car, carrying a basket that Blythe suspected contained a silent peace offering from his father.

"We've brought you some fresh scones!" Richard shouted excitedly, running toward her open front door. "They've just come out of the Aga!"

"Did you and your dad make them?" she teased, casting a friendly wave in Luke's direction. He responded with a look of immense relief and waved back.

"No," Richard replied seriously, "they're Mrs. Q's, but Daddy and I wrapped them up and brought them to you, didn't we, Daddy?"

"Well, you're both very sweet." She smiled and gave his slender shoulders an affectionate hug. "I've just put the kettle on. . . . C'mon in."

As Blythe busied herself organizing their morning tea, Luke

showed his son some of the additional drawings Blythe had made for the newly expanded herb garden. She had propped various versions of the proposed layout against Ennis Trevelyan's two-hundred-year-old easel.

"Oh . . . this one's my favorite, Blythe," Richard complimented her, pointing to a particular rendering. "Will you dry some of the herbs, or just sell them fresh?"

"Both," she told him promptly, smiling over his head to let Luke know that she was glad to see him as well.

"Would you teach me how to dry them?" Richard inquired, his eyes alight.

Before Blythe could answer, Luke said, "You'll be away at school, I'm afraid, when the herbs come up in the spring."

A stricken look invaded the ten-year-old's eyes, and he turned to his father pleadingly.

"Please . . . Daddy . . . couldn't I go to Mevagissey Day Sch—"

"The matter's been settled, son," he said firmly. "Please don't go on about it. You'll ruin Blythe's breakfast."

Blythe retreated toward the kitchen area and asked over her shoulder as she arranged their tea things on the tray, "When do you go back to school, Dicken?"

"This Friday," he said miserably. Then he blurted out, "I hate it!"

"Richard!" Luke said sternly.

Blythe's heart went out to the boy, but she remained silent. After they'd finished their tea and Blythe had nibbled on a scone for politeness' sake, she asked Luke to drive her to the village so she could attempt to fax Lisa Spector from the stationer's shop next to the post office.

"So you still haven't made up your mind," Luke asked as the three of them headed down the Gorran Haven road.

"Made your mind up about what?" Richard asked, sounding apprehensive.

"Richard, don't be rude!" Luke said sharply. "This concerns adults, so you must refrain from being a pest."

Richard leaned back and began rhythmically jamming the toe of his cowboy boot into the driver's seat in front of him.

"Stop that!" Luke called over his shoulder irritably.

Silence reigned, except for the hum of the car.

In an attempt to lessen the tension crackling inside the Land Rover, Blythe said carefully, "I'm thinking of selling some property I own, Dicken." She declined to look at Luke when she added, "I've decided to ask for some advice from my lawyer . . . solicitor, I mean."

"Oh," the boy said, sounding both relieved and chastened.

In the tiny stationer's shop Blythe paid nearly ten pounds to fax the documents that Christopher had given her. The last page transmitted electronically was a draft letter that detailed Christopher Stowe's promise to repay to Blythe half of the profits of the sale "at a date to be determined," guaranteed by some form of Chris's collateral, "the nature of which to be determined, since Herr Stowe has apparently pledged practically everything he owns to get his picture finished." In a PS she requested that Lisa Spector call her to discuss the matter at the Barton Hall number at four or five o'clock that afternoon, Cornwall time, or at the latest, the following morning after eight.

Luke and Richard both appeared to be in a subdued mood when Blythe rejoined them near the car.

"I meant to ask you earlier," Blythe said with a nod in the direction of the tower of St. Goran's Church, silhouetted against an overcast sky. "Do you recall any member of your family named William?"

"William who?" Luke asked, perplexed.

"Well, that's just it," Blythe replied. She explained how she had found the words "For William" scrawled on the back of four of Ennis's seascapes.

"I've never noticed that name on the chart," Luke said thoughtfully. "And I doubt those paintings have been taken down off the walls for a hundred years."

"Since St. Goran's is just down the road, do you suppose I could have a tour of the Reverend Randolph Kent's former domain? And while we're at it," she added, "maybe we could also have a look to see if there's some William Barton-Trevelyan-Teague in the family plot? Perhaps on one of the gravestones?" she suggested.

"Well . . . all right," Luke said reluctantly, prompting Blythe to assume he wasn't pleased to encourage her in the realm he felt best left to his cousin Valerie.

Luke, with Richard following closely by Blythe's side, first conducted her on a tour of the stone church. She felt her pulse begin to quicken as she surveyed the chapel's chilly interior, which had remained, over two hundred years, nearly identical to the St. Goran's she recalled from her observation of Kit and her namesake's marriage ceremony.

As the trio emerged into the crisp September sunshine, Luke pointed to a row of weathered headstones in the burial ground. However, hard as they searched among the older grave markers, there was no sign of any eighteenth-century William having been buried in the family plot in St. Goran's churchyard.

However, an enormous headstone whose carvings were encrusted with moss-green lichen attracted Blythe's attention.

"Collis Trevelyan . . . ," she murmured. "Right where he belongs, the old skunk!" Luke looked at her strangely. "Valerie told me some wonderful tales about his smuggling activities," she added quickly. "Is it true that he stored contraband that couldn't be hidden at Barton Hall or Trevelyan House right here in this graveyard?"

Luke nodded but didn't elaborate on the story.

"Daddy?" Richard said in a small voice. "Can we show Blythe where Mummy's buried?"

"I don't think that's how we should entertain our guests," Luke said, his voice suddenly sounding tight. "Come, son . . . I think we all should go home."

"If you'd like to show it to me," Blythe said softly, "I'd very much like to see your mother's grave, Dicken."

The boy slipped his small hand into hers. He led her to a section of newer headstones, where he gazed at a marker made of pink marble. Freshly carved dates chronicling his mother's birth and death were etched deeply into the stone.

Sensing the child's pent-up grief, Blythe knelt beside him and put her arms around his small frame. His slender shoulders began to quake, and then he turned to her shoulder, no longer able to hold back sobs that wrenched her own heart.

"I know, Dicken," she whispered into his hair. "You miss her so much. . . . It's all right, sweetheart . . . it's all right to cry."

At the sound of his son's weeping, Luke abruptly turned and stalked out of the churchyard. Fortunately, Richard wasn't aware of his father's angry departure. He continued to cry the deep, cleansing tears of a child long denied his own sadness.

Luke was sitting stonily behind the wheel when Blythe and Richard climbed back into the Land Rover. For his part, Richard looked a bit pale, but he immediately began to chatter about his plan to help Mr. Quiller and the workmen measure the lengths of plastic that would soon enclose the remaining hothouses.

"But, first, how about some lunch?" Blythe suggested, displaying a cheerfulness she certainly didn't feel. Luke had not uttered a word to either of them since he strode out of St. Goran's churchyard.

Within minutes the car rolled to a stop behind the old pony stable. Also parked next to its high stone wall was Chloe Acton-Scott's dark-blue Jaguar.

"Hello, darlings!" she called, slamming the door to the driver's side. Richard's godmother was clad in a subversively simple suit and silk blouse the color of ripe peaches. A waist-length double strand of pearls nestled provocatively between her fulsome breasts. Considering that the rest of them were all wearing trousers, one might say the woman was a tad overdressed for the country. Or one might say she looked absolutely stunning.

"Chloe . . . what a surprise . . . ," Luke said with less than his usual grace.

"You haven't looked in your diary," she chided him with a frosty smile in Blythe's direction. "I'm to take Richard for his final fitting of his school uniform today, so he'll have it ready before he leaves for Shelby Hall on Friday."

Blythe darted a glance at Luke's son and was dismayed to see fresh tears rimming the lad's eyes.

"Oh . . . right you are," Luke acknowledged sheepishly. "I had forgot about the bloody uniform. Won't you join us for lunch?"

"No time, I'm afraid," she replied crisply. "Can you have Mrs. Q pack you a quick sandwich, Richard, and come back here straightaway?" Without waiting for her godson to respond, she graced Luke with a coquettish smile and added, "We should be back around teatime. My parents are longing to see us both. Would you be free for dinner tonight in St. Austell?"

There was a momentary pause, and then Luke replied, "How very kind. That would be lovely."

He really *was* angry at her! Blythe realized with some surprise. She suspected that his irritation centered on her lack of resolve regarding the presumptuous demands of her ex-husband. Or was he upset by what had just transpired in the St. Goran's churchyard with his son? Either way, it appeared that he would seize Chloe's invitation as a means of punishing her for her sins.

Typical Englishman! she seethed. Don't say what's bothering you! Just behave like a bloody jerk!

By now Blythe's stomach was definitely in turmoil. She wondered vaguely if she was actually coming down with the flu.

"If you all will excuse me," she said in a tight voice, "I'm actually not feeling up to par. I think, if you don't mind, Luke, I'll take the afternoon off."

"I'll drive you home," he offered quickly. He turned to his

son. "You run along with your godmother, Richard, and I'll catch up with you before Aunt Chloe and I leave for dinner."

A sullen, stubborn look had replaced Richard's tears as he turned and headed for the back door of Barton Hall.

"Actually," Blythe said, feeling both angrier and increasingly ill by the minute, "I'd rather walk."

And before either Luke or Chloe could respond, she strode toward the public pathway where the sign's arrow pointed toward Painter's Cottage.

Bugger all! she seethed, mentally adopting Christopher Stowe's most vulgar epithet, reserved for occasions of unbearable frustration. Luke was hopeless when it came to understanding children! What was it with these Brits? she fumed. Some sort of cultural barrier to the simple act of giving their kids a hug when they were unhappy?

Ten minutes later Blythe emerged from the shaded path. She had just caught sight of the slate roof of her rented abode when she heard Luke's car grinding its way around a curve in the road that separated the estate from the coastal properties.

He rolled to a stop just as she secured the gate to her own field.

"Blythe! Wait!" he called through the car window. "Are you sure you're all right?"

"No! I'm not!" she retorted angrily, and kept walking.

Luke jumped out of the Land Rover and caught up with her by the time she reached her front door. The tide was out, and now dark cumulus clouds had gathered on the horizon like a big black cat, ready to pounce.

"Blythe, please!" Luke began tersely, grabbing hold of her arm to force her to look at him. She stared at him without expression. "Believe me, I don't look forward to dinner with Chloe and her parents. It's just that I didn't appreciate you stirring up unpleasant memories where Richard is concerned, and I stupidly—"

"Unpleasant! We're not talking 'memories' here," she said, with biting sarcasm. "We're talking *wounds*, for God's sake!

You can't expect him to deal with his grief as you have! You can't ask him to stifle such unpleasant little emotions like losing his *mother*!" Blythe felt tears filling her eyes. "He's only a small boy . . . and after two years coping with this gigantic loss—utterly on his own, Luke—he's still bleeding from every pore! As far as I can see," she cried in a ragged voice, "you and Chloe are a pair of matched bookends!"

And with that she ran into the cottage and slammed the door. Blindly she made her way to the bathroom in the nick of time and was profoundly sick to her stomach.

Chapter Fourteen

September 7, 1994

Blythe wandered out of the bathroom in a daze. She stumbled across the cottage floor and sank into the chair that faced the window overlooking the Channel. Mercifully, her nausea had ceased. In fact, she now felt perfectly well, except for a slight sensation of light-headedness.

With stunning clarity she knew that her health problem had nothing to do with an incipient ulcer. Nor did she have the flu. Not even the unexpected appearance of her ex-husband had caused this stomach distress.

Luke's scrupulous attention to modern birth-control methods the previous six weeks could not mitigate the consequences of twenty-four hours of abandoned lovemaking the day they discovered the letters in Ennis Trevelyan's trunk.

Blythe's hands trembled as she flipped through the pages of her daybook. Her period was thirteen days past due.

Gawd Almighty, Blythe, you're up to your hips in it now!

Her grandmother had always said, "About half your troubles come from wantin' your own way, young lady. The other half come from gettin' it."

Blythe rested her hands on her belly as tears suddenly filled her eyes for the second time that day. This was Luke's baby as well as hers. In St. Goran's churchyard an hour earlier she had witnessed a graphic demonstration of the man's aversion to the emotional needs of his own flesh and blood. She couldn't bear it if he welcomed this baby—if, indeed, there was a baby—with the same lack of enthusiasm that he had exhibited toward Dicken most of the summer.

Despite this, she knew that she had never longed for anything as much as she ached to bear a child created by the overwhelming passion she had shared with a man she loved. It was time for some straight talk.

She had fallen in love with Lucas Teague.

It was classic. Just as her lawyer had feared, she'd taken a mad fancy to the tall, dark, handsome guy with a leaky roof!

From the first she'd been attracted by Luke's humor . . . his innate courtesy . . . his core understanding of who he was and where and how he'd chosen to live his life. She respected his sense of history and commitment to continuity, as well as his steady, unflappable attitude about shouldering the burden of an eight-hundred-year family legacy. She appreciated his kindness toward the people who worked for him, and his regard for her own organizational and artistic talents. She even admired his taste in tweed jackets and his passion for tea at four o'clock.

And she flat-out adored him in bed: the brass daybed in the stable loft . . . her double bed in Painter's Cottage . . . and most certainly the memorable, mad, bad Bawdy Bed of Barton!

She crossed into her small kitchen area and turned on the tap. Her hand was trembling as she filled a glass with water and drank it down. Then she turned around and leaned against the copper sink. Suddenly she was assaulted by a sharp stab of regret that their intense love affair, this wildly romantic idyll, would end so soon. Was she actually prepared to face the reality of remarriage—especially to another Brit—with all that implied? More to the point, would the Brit want a pregnant Yankee wife? Having the baby she always longed for was one thing . . . but, to put it bluntly, was she willing to swallow the whole enchilada?

The thought of being some man's wife again—in tradition-bound Britain, no less—gave her pause.

Not "some" man's wife, she told herself sternly as she stared out over the English Channel. Luke's wife. Considering the gravity of the issues that could divide them, how strong would her love be for a man who couldn't welcome fatherhood with the same sense of blinding joy she was beginning to feel?

Even so, Blythe couldn't deny the depth of her emotional connection to this Englishman. It had sneaked up on her, like the stealthy wave that had caught them unawares that day at the beach.

The problem, she realized with a combination of awe and dread, was that she had fallen in love with someone who was extraordinarily warm and affectionate toward her, but who kept himself emotionally remote from his son—as well as from anyone who dared to take him to task for his cool behavior. The alarm bells that had dimly rung each time she had observed the way in which Luke distanced himself from Dicken now clanged with a deafening warning. The kindest "California psychobabble" interpretation she could put on the situation was that Luke had avoided dealing with the grief related to the loss of his wife, and that attitude had cruelly injured an innocent child.

However, his aloof manner toward ten-year-old Richard could easily boil down to the uncomplicated fact that Lucas Teague simply didn't enjoy being a father.

And so the question became: Would he want another child in his life? Specifically, would he want *her* child? *Really* want it, and not merely accept it as part of a Blythe Barton–and–Her–Millions package deal?

The miserable irony was, in every other aspect Luke had proved to be the loving man of her fantasies. Unlike Chris, he was not an egomaniac, not a narcissist. He wrapped her in the circle of his warmth. Yet something was drastically wrong. Why did he behave in such a detached way toward his own offspring?

Blythe inhaled deeply and rested her hands on her abdomen. Lost in thought, she let her gaze follow a flock of gulls flying in the face of a freshening wind. If she were, in fact, pregnant, she would have this baby—even if it meant having it on her own. Any child of hers would be surrounded by love as it grew up, and not merely tolerated on school holidays. Under no circumstances would she permit her son or daughter to be ignored or made to feel a burden.

Lucas Teague, however much I care for you, I will do what I must to protect this baby from a life like that!

Blythe continued to stare moodily out the window at the surf crashing on the rocks below. In nine months' time would she still be living in heavenly, mysterious, forget-the-7-Eleven Cornwall with a man who would likely be unhappy at hearing he might be a father for the second time?

Blythe closed her eyes. Perhaps all this speculation was distinctly premature, she lectured herself. Like Scarlett O'Hara in *Gone with the Wind*, she wouldn't think about it now. She'd think about it tomorrow, after she'd been to see Dr. Vickery above Rattle Alley.

As she drifted off to sleep sitting in her chair, she wondered if she was simply one of those women destined to have disastrous taste in men.

The sound of a car's engine woke Blythe with a start. Huge thunderheads had gathered over Dodman Point. Late-afternoon sunshine bled through the gloom and slanted off the water in front of the cottage, turning it into a sheet of tarnished silver.

Groggily Blythe rose from her chair, relieved to discover that, for the moment, calm continued to reign within her stomach's inner sanctum. If fact, she was ravenously hungry.

En route to the front door to see who the visitor might be, she snatched an apple from the bowl perched on her small dining table. She reached for the iron latch and immediately found herself staring at a cream-colored Rolls-Royce parked just outside the gate on the other side of the field.

Eleanor Barton closed the driver's side of the vehicle and then opened its rear passenger door. Her head and shoulders disappeared inside. A few moments later the young woman straightened up, cradling a child's molded plastic infant seat in her arms.

Oh, Jesus . . . this is perfect! She's brought the baby along!

Probably as a shield, Blythe added silently. Her sister was shrewd enough to know that she'd slam the door in her face otherwise.

Blythe watched as a younger version of herself picked her way across the moist grass, avoiding sheep dung as she slowly walked toward Painter's Cottage. Ellie's curly hair was the same shade of auburn as Blythe's own, cut inches shorter now. Her long legs were clad in faded blue jeans, and she wore a big navy-blue sweater. Its weight failed to disguise the new mother's full bosom, swelled to bovine proportions from breast-feeding her infant, Blythe speculated.

If you've got it, flaunt it—in your sister's face.

When Eleanor finally arrived at Blythe's front door, she halted and inclined her head toward the sleeping child.

"The minute we drive in the car, she conks out," Ellie announced brightly, as if popping by with her baby for tea were an everyday occurrence.

Wordlessly Blythe gazed at the sleeping infant tucked under a luxurious pink blanket. She saw that the child had no particularly distinguishing features. She was plump—bordering on pudgy—with a fuzz of blond hair the color of Chris's capping her head.

They call her Janet, Blythe thought suddenly. Named for the baby's grandmother. That made this child her niece, and Grandma Barton, if she'd been alive, a great-grandmother.

Just then a biting wind swept across the field, and a few splashes of rain splattered on the stone step that separated the two sisters. The baby stirred in its sleep and appeared about to wake.

"You'd better come in."

"Thanks," Ellie said, and followed Blythe inside the cottage. "I've just fed her, so she should sleep for at least an hour or two."

"I asked Chris to tell you I didn't want to see you while you're here," Blythe said quietly, pointing to a shadowed corner where Ellie could settle the infant seat on top of a square table. "Why did you come anyway?"

"Because Dad told me to," Ellie said with a trace of her old truculence. She glanced curiously around the stone chamber. "And because I thought you should see the baby . . . see that she's real . . . see that we both have to accept what's happened, including Dad's marrying that real-estate lady and selling the ranch."

"And why are you suddenly doing what Dad tells you to?" Blythe countered, ignoring Ellie's remarks. "You never have in the past."

"I knew this was how you'd be," Ellie snapped. "Always playing the Good Sister to the max."

"Well, I certainly don't qualify as the Bad Sister, since you've perfected that role your whole life."

"Look, Blythe," Ellie said in a tight voice. "I didn't come here to hear this."

"And what, exactly, did you come to hear?" Blythe replied evenly. She was doing her level best—and failing—to mask her outrage at this deliberate invasion. "That all is forgiven? That I've gotten over walking in on you—twice—while you fucked your brains out with the men in my life!"

"You couldn't stand Otis McCafferty by the time he got his hands in my pants," Ellie declared, "so don't play the Tragedy Queen on that one!"

"There was quite another tragedy involved—on *that* one!" Blythe said bitterly.

"Well, glory be," Ellie retorted, her voice dripping with sarcasm, "I figured that when it suited you, you'd break your precious code of silence!"

"And have you ever had the guts to come clean?" Blythe asked, trying her best to regain control of her temper.

"Yes, I have."

Taken aback by Ellie's unexpected answer, Blythe merely

stared while her sister added flippantly, "All that shrinkage you paid for must have done me some good." Then she shrugged. "Last spring I thought it was time for some truth telling at the old Double Bar B."

Blythe turned and gazed out the window as the sea moved in massive swells toward the shore. A steady rain had begun to pelt the windows.

Truth telling.

Blythe had simply buried the truth about her brother's death, just as she had helped her family bury a seventeen-year-old in the hard Wyoming soil. And then, for more than a decade, she had refused to speak to anyone of the events that had followed the life-changing moment when Matt Barton was dragged to his death by the bronc that had been mistakenly loaded into the bucking chute.

Today, however, as Blythe turned her back toward her younger sister, she suddenly saw herself at the age of twenty-one, sitting astride Ranger just inside the rodeo arena on that cool July evening in 1981. The majestic Grand Tetons were rising in the distance, still dusted with patches of snow at their highest elevations. Blythe and her horse waited in the shadow of the grandstand as the final glow of sunset descended on Jackson Hole. That night she had worn her turquoise jeans and a matching shirt that Grandma Barton had embellished with a five-inch row of fringe dripping with silver sequins. Suddenly Matt was lying in the dirt. She could see at a glance that his broken neck was attached to his shoulders merely by the blood-streaked flesh that covered his bones. As if she were watching a home movie, Blythe pictured the young woman she had been then, scrambling off her horse to confront the stock contractor. Virgil Bailey's anguished cry had galvanized Blythe into action.

I told Oatsey not to buck him out tonight!

She had stared at the grizzled veteran for a long moment, and then had raised her whip over her head and began to lash Matt's panting horse so hard, its neck soon looked like a piece of bloody lace. Amazingly, the pickup men who'd finally got the animal shut down merely stood by, holding the reins, and watched. Then Blythe whirled on the heels of her turquoise cowboy boots and rushed past the distraught officials. She had headed directly for the corrals that were adjacent to the bucking chutes.

She had found Otis McCafferty inside the shed behind the rodeo arena. Her rejected boyfriend, a twenty-six-year-old former bull rider with a bum knee, stood with his back to her, his jeans draped around his ankles and his bare buttocks shunting back and forth at a frantic clip.

Blythe closed her eyes against the memory of her startled sister gaping at her over Oatsey's shoulder. The youngster—for that was what Ellie had been at fifteen—also was half-naked, her jeans pushed down below her knees. She'd been awkwardly reclining on a horse blanket tossed on top of three hay bales stacked against the wall.

Blythe had only been able to utter a shriek of rage before she ran over, fists raised, and began to pummel Oatsey's back. His exposed buttocks glistened obscenely beneath his filthy cowboy shirt. The sweat-stained fabric had been red, she remembered—like her brother's blood.

To escape Blythe's attack, Otis fell forward onto the hay bale where he'd been penetrating Ellie with carnal concentration. Somehow he gracefully twisted his body sideways and regained his footing with the agility of the bull rider he'd once been.

All three had stared at one another for an eternity, gasping for breath.

"My brother is dead!" Blythe screamed. "He's dead because of *you*! Virgil told you to get rid of that horse, but you were too *busy*!" Otis continued to gaze blankly at her as if they were separated by soundproof glass. She had turned toward Ellie and shouted, "Pull up your pants, you slut!" As her younger sister fumbled to zip her jeans, Blythe confronted the rodeo hand, her fists still clenched like a prizefighter's. "If you ever mention to a soul you were in here fucking my sister, I swear I'll get the men in this town to cut off your balls!"

Then she grabbed Ellie's wrist, hauled her out of the shed, and shoved her against a two-horse trailer.

"You were buying a Pepsi when it happened," Blythe commanded hoarsely. "You didn't even see the accident—got that?" Then she swiveled in place and retched her guts out into the horses' water trough.

After that night the Barton sisters had kept the secret between them—and Blythe never climbed on the back of a horse again.

Otis McCafferty kept the bargain, as well, she remembered bitterly. He had immediately moved on to Bozeman, Montana, or so she'd heard. Ellie had graduated from high school in 1982 and enrolled in Cal Arts near Los Angeles. When Blythe had saved enough money, she arranged for her sister to receive counseling from a psychiatrist. That same year Blythe finished her master's program in landscape design at UCLA, and Christopher Stowe graduated with honors from the university's film school.

Foolishly Blythe had thought that Ellie's subsequent accomplishments as a children's book illustrator were a sign that her sister was getting some direction in her life. Her latest series of juvenile books were proving to be steady sellers and, lately, dependable moneymakers. Yet despite both sisters' career successes, Blythe and Ellie had never found common ground, nor mentioned what had happened behind the rodeo arena that summer night thirteen years ago. Until today.

At length Blythe turned around and met Ellie's challenging stare.

"You had the affair with Chris to pay me back for finding you that night with Otis—isn't that right?"

"It may surprise you to learn that Christopher and I had fallen in love!" Ellie retorted.

"Oh, give me a break!" Blythe said, rolling her eyes. "I called you a slut that night. I forced you to carry the burden of knowing that you were the reason Otis forgot to pull that bronc from the rodeo. I was trying to protect Dad and Grandma and you—though you never saw it that way."

"Don't pretend to be so noble," Ellie replied, rancor lacing each word. "You were just ticked off that Otis thought I was pretty hot stuff. And you can't believe that Chris loves *me* instead of *you*, can you?" She smiled spitefully. "Not Miss Rodeo Wyoming! Not Miss National Merit Scholar! Not the person in the Barton household who could do no wrong!"

"I made plenty of mistakes along the way!" Blythe shot back. "The trouble with you is that you refused to acknowledge or value the hard work that went into it all! You only saw the rewards and wondered why I got more than you did!" If it hadn't been for the baby sleeping peacefully in the corner of her cottage, she would have begun to shout a litany of harsh invective at her sister. Instead, she added hoarsely, "The reason you never got as many rewards yourself for so long was that you deliberately screwed up every time you got close to something worthwhile—and that wasn't my fault."

"Well, it wasn't my fault that the family thought you were the bee's knees and I was a dope," her sister said in a tight voice.

"For God's sake, Ellie, you were five when Mom died. How do you know what she felt about anything?" Blythe demanded.

"She didn't want another daughter," Ellie cried bitterly. "She already had you and Matt. I was a mistake."

"Oh, don't give me that 'I was an unwanted child' crap!" Blythe countered. "You're twenty-nine years old! Mom was three years younger than you are now when she had you!"

"Exactly!" Ellie retorted venomously. "I hardly remember her."

"She got really sick after you were born," Blythe replied with mounting exasperation. "She didn't do it on purpose! Why do you always cast yourself as the victim?"

"Well, Grandma Barton certainly didn't need another kid to raise at that point in her life. She already had you! You were the star . . . and you pretended to like whatever the old crank liked."

"I didn't pretend—"

"You loved those goddamned flowers of hers," Ellie cut in mockingly, "so she paid attention to you."

"That's not the only reason we got along," Blythe said wearily. "When you hit your teens, she was getting to be an old lady, and she just didn't have a high tolerance for brats anymore."

"Matt was Dad's favorite," Ellie continued, unleashing the rest of her detailed accounting of long-held grievances. "Even you couldn't get his attention. And let's face it. Grandma Barton was an ornery old bat—and a show-off. All she ever did was get on my case."

"That's because all you ever did was behave like a dink."

"No one gave a shit about me!"

"I did," Blythe said quietly. "Despite your consuming envy from the time you could talk, I cared about what happened to you."

"Not that I noticed," she snapped.

"I know you didn't. And you didn't notice how much alike you and Dad were. You were his clone."

"The main thing I remember was that he went away for weeks at a time, taking tourists on those pack trips. When he was home, all he did was moan about the collapse of the cattle industry."

"He was a rancher and an outfitter," Blythe protested. "Grandma Barton worked her ass off with her flower business. That's how we were fed and clothed, in case you didn't notice."

Tragically, many ranching families like theirs that had been on Wyoming land for a hundred years had discovered during the 1960s that it was nigh impossible to earn a decent living by raising cattle. By the nineties, tourists and "dudes," not cows and roundups, became the mainstay at spreads like the Double Bar B.

After Janet Barton had dropped dead beside her clothesline, Blythe had watched her father work harder than ever. During his few hours off he withdrew behind his copy of *Feedlot News*. Meanwhile, her grandmother worked days, nights, and weekends to make a go of her mail-order flower business so that they wouldn't lose the land.

Considering all those years of struggle, who could blame their father for his decision to sell the place for top dollar? He'd earned it.

The problem for Ellie in her formative years was that neither parent nor grandparent had the time or energy to focus enough attention on this "afterthought," as Will Barton had affectionately dubbed his youngest child. And no one knew what to do with a moody kid who could sketch and paint but was bored with reading and hopeless at math.

Grandma Barton, of course, had tried to take her granddaughter in hand when she was young, but by the time Ellie became a teenager, the old woman was growing increasingly frail and, it was true, cantankerous.

They all did the best they could.

Wasn't that the truth that Blythe had eventually accepted about Will, Janet, and Lucinda Barton? Why couldn't Ellie come to the same conclusion?

"Why did you name the baby after Mom?" Blythe asked after a long pause.

"I had a perfect right, if I wanted to," Ellie answered belligerently. "You didn't think I'd honor the sacred Barton tradition and name her Blythe, did you?"

"I just wondered why you named her Janet, since you just said you hardly remember her."

"Dad said the baby kinda offered a clean slate," Ellie said in a low voice. "A new start. I went to see him in Wyoming after . . . after you and Chris had filed for divorce and right before we flew to Mexico to get married. He introduced me to Bertha Pyle when I was there, and I figured they had a thing going. That was when he asked me to call the baby Janet if she was a girl . . . so I did . . . to please him," she finished, a note of triumph edging her voice.

Blythe recalled the conversation she'd had with her father early in her stay in Cornwall. Will Barton had always been a man of few words, and the family debacle in far-off Hollywood had rendered him more taciturn than ever.

"I'm sorry for the fix you're in," she recalled his saying. "But remember one thing. You're a lot stronger'n Ellie. You gotta take that into account."

Gazing at her sister now, thousands of miles from the Wyoming ranch where they grew up, she wondered if the weak didn't prevail in the end.

"And what else did Dad tell you when you visited him?" Blythe wondered aloud.

"That I was the result of the best night of sex they'd ever had," Ellie laughed smugly. "Up in Yellowstone . . . on a camping trip, when they'd left you and Matt with Grandma Barton."

Blythe suddenly felt like an orphan . . . a fatherless child.

"He told you that?" she marveled.

Her parents had seemed to spin in such separate orbits on the ranch that she had often wondered, once she'd grown up, if they had ever shared the kind of physical and emotional intensity she'd experienced in her early days with Chris—and now with Luke.

"I had to know why they'd even bothered to have me!" Ellie said in a rush. "Did you know," she added as a faintly malicious smile began to tug at her lips, "that Mom was pregnant with you when they got married?"

"Thanks to the second-best night of sex they ever had, I suppose," Blythe responded dryly. Long ago she had subtracted her birth date from the date of her parents' wedding anniversary and come up two months shy of a full-term baby.

"They were engaged and jumped the gun." Ellie nodded charitably. "But they were in love, Dad said. I asked him what happened to their marriage after I was born, and he just grunted,

'Life.' And then he told me that he hoped I'd do a better job raising my daughter than he and Grandma did with me."

"I hope you do," Blythe replied, meaning it kindly. She glanced at the baby slumbering peacefully in her carry cot. "May I see her?"

Ellie glanced warily in Blythe's direction and then nodded. Blythe tiptoed across the slate floor and stared down at her month-old niece. Ellie stood next to her as they both gazed at the child.

Another Janet Barton, Blythe mused. Perhaps, inside her own womb, another version of Blythe was heading for the planet. Or another rendition of Matt.

Silently she compared her own family drama to that of Luke's hot-blooded ancestors who had inhabited Barton Hall. Would the cycle of blame and jealousy, angry silences and retributions, reverberating down the lines of the Barton-Trevelyan-Teagues never end?

Blythe studied the cherubic face of Ellie's month-old child.

"She's really very dear," she said on a long breath. "And now I think it's time for you to go. Please tell Chris I haven't heard from California yet."

"Will you sign the forest over to us?"

Us.

Sometimes, Blythe thought with a surge of anger, Eleanor Barton Stowe had the sensitivity of a rhinoceros.

"I haven't decided."

Her sister glanced around the room. Her gaze came to rest on Ennis Trevelyan's wooden easel standing in the corner.

"Painter's Cottage is a perfect name for this place," she commented. "I'd feel so at home working here. . . ."

"Your home is on Bristol Drive in Brentwood, California, remember?"

Ellie pursed her lips but didn't respond. She carefully picked up the infant seat and cradled it in her arms with considerable ceremony.

"We really do need you to sign those papers Chris gave you."

"So that's why you came here today," Blythe snapped. "No making amends or anything like that. Just business."

"Well . . . ," Ellie replied uncertainly. "Chris and I both thought that if you saw . . . that you'd . . . ah . . . at least like to see the baby," she finished, increasingly flustered.

"And thus realize how dreadful it would be to deprive my own flesh and blood of life's necessities, once you and Chris returned your rented Rolls-Royce?" Blythe asked sarcastically.

Ellie lifted her chin with an air of injured innocence.

"You wouldn't refuse to sign the papers just for spite, would you?" she said in a faintly hectoring tone.

"I honestly don't know," Blythe confessed. She gestured toward the cottage door. "Good-bye, Ellie," she added pointedly.

"For God's sake, Blythe!" Ellie lashed back, a petulant glare kindling in her brown eyes. "Dad gave you the best piece of land—not to mention that you ended up with a couple of million bucks out of the divorce! Don't you think you're being a little greedy?"

Greedy?

Blythe's last vestige of good manners and civility—the remaining thread of emotional restraint that she had been clinging to for dear life—suddenly snapped. She gazed at her younger sister through a haze of white-hot fury and worried that her blood pressure had zoomed into the stratosphere in the length of time it took Ellie to utter those two syllables.

"Greedy?" Blythe echoed, feeling her temples begin to throb. "Believe me, Mrs. Stowe, I earned every cent of that divorce settlement, you little—"

Blythe was barely able to stop herself from uttering the most insulting epithet against women in the English vocabulary—a vulgarity that, under normal circumstances, she truly abhorred.

"That's not what all your friends in California are saying behind your back." Ellie smiled malevolently.

Blythe stared at her sister for a long moment and then began to speak in a tone of voice she hardly recognized.

"You've been a whining, covetous pain in the ass your entire goddamned life," she said as a rush of blood stained her cheeks. She narrowed the distance between Ellie and herself, her fists clenched at her sides. "And despite everything that your family tried to do to help you, the older you got, the more lethal you became." Ellie glanced uneasily around the cottage and took a step toward the front door. Blythe began to wonder vacantly if she would, in the end, be able to refrain from scratching Ellie's eyes out. "All you ever wanted was to try to steal my life! You didn't give a flying fig that Chris was *my* lover . . . *my* husband . . . *my* partner in a company we'd built together. Well, now you're married to him, and I'm here to tell you that no matter how devious and manipulative you may be, you will *never* get what you want from Christopher Stowe! You're too much alike! And furthermore—you disgusting little sneak—I hope he makes you as miserable as he did me!" Blythe shouted, having finally lost all semblance of emotional control. "Get out of here right now! Get *out*!"

During the balance of Blythe's tirade Ellie had remained rooted to the flagstone floor. Now she inhaled deeply, as if she were about to dive into deep water.

"*You're* the one who's terminally jealous!" Ellie yelled at the top of her lungs. "And it's not just about Chris preferring me over you!" The manic gleam in Ellie's eye bore witness to her delight at having successfully provoked her even-tempered older sister into such a state of fury. "You're green with envy about the baby, aren't you?" she taunted. "And I'll just bet now you wish you hadn't always been such a Goody Two-shoes, and had chucked out the ol' diaphragm when you had the chance!"

"Ellie, I'm warning you . . . ," Blythe began. She was grateful they weren't standing near the cliff outside her front door, for she knew that she was fully capable of shoving her own flesh and blood over the steep precipice. "I'll give you exactly ten seconds to get the hell out of here! *Now!*"

In response to this earsplitting exchange, little Janet awoke with a start in her pink infant seat and commenced a series of shrill wails. Galvanized by this convenient excuse to beat a hasty retreat, Ellie glared accusingly at Blythe, turned on her heel, and grabbed for the door latch.

"If you don't sign over that forest property right now, you'll really regret it!" she threatened over her shoulder.

"I don't think so," Blythe replied between gritted teeth. Her fists remained so tightly clenched by her sides that her knuckles ached. Fortunately, some small shred of good sense prevented her from indulging in a burning desire to sock her sister between the shoulder blades. "But, then, I'm sure Chris and I will have a chance to discuss this matter thoroughly when he takes me to dinner tomorrow night."

"Well, then, I hope he tells you what he *really* thinks of you!" Ellie screeched, whirling to face Blythe. Meanwhile, Blythe clamped her jaws shut and returned her sister's glare as the baby's cries raised the decibel level to an excruciating pitch. "I hope he tells you what he's often admitted to me," Ellie continued, measuring her words in nasty little parcels, "that the last thing Chris ever wanted was to have a kid by *you*!" After several seconds, during which the infant's wails bounced painfully off the cottage's stone walls, Ellie shifted the infant seat to one hip and fumbled to lift the iron latch on the heavy oak door. Finally it swung open on its metal hinges. Then, clutching the plastic infant seat to her breast, the younger woman charged past the threshold and stalked along the path that led across the field.

For a few moments Blythe gazed numbly at the retreating back of her sole surviving sibling. Janet's cries grew fainter and fainter. Blythe then closed the door. She wondered how things could get any worse.

After ten minutes of wandering aimlessly around the cottage and mulling over each nuance of the disastrous confrontation with her sister, Blythe determined that the only remedy to calm her unsettled state was to embark on a challenging walk before the sun set on the south coastal path that skirted Hemmick Cove. By the time she had made her way up the steep incline to Long Rock, she was out of breath.

The rain had lessened to a fine, blowing mist. Gell Point marked the midway spot on the four-hundred-foot assault up to The Dodman, as the locals called it. Blythe paused to rest and take in the awe-inspiring view of a landscape that jutted for miles of rocky coastline stretching in both directions. The surf crashing below sent out "mare's tails" blowing off the waves. The Cornish swore such plumes of white sea spray predicted a gale in the offing. She wondered if perhaps she should turn back when she reached the deserted stone watch house, an octagonal hut that served in the late eighteenth century as one of a chain of Admiralty signal stations.

However, she couldn't face returning to the confines of the cottage where she had finally come face-to-face with the primal force of her sister's envy—and her own pent-up rage.

Instead, Blythe set her sights on Dodman Point and kept walking. The demanding hike gave her time to consider the only reasonable explanation for Eleanor Barton's wanton betrayal and utter lack of remorse.

Resentment, obviously. Jealousy, obviously. The loss of a mother at such a tender age? Unresolved guilt about a brother's tragic death? Wasn't this the poisonous brew that had prompted Ellie to look for love in all the wrong places, and to sneak around gathering crumbs from her big sister's table—even if they were rancid?

When it came to Otis McCafferty . . . he had been a bull-riding lothario with charm like July snow on the Tetons—it evaporated quickly in the harsh light of day. And as for Christopher Stowe, Blythe could see now that Ellie had set out to beguile the man in some twisted and continuing rivalry of one-upmanship. Over the years her behavior had increasingly taken on an aspect of "settling past scores." But what scores? And how old were they? Blythe wondered.

The biting wind lashed at her face, forcing Blythe to concentrate on traversing the narrowing path that led to the headlands. After about twenty minutes of hard climbing, she reached the Iron Age fort on the promontory of Dodman Point. A two-thousand-foot-long ditch was all that remained of the surviving earthworks. The icy gusts whipped her auburn hair into a tangle of curls as she gazed at the large, stark stone cross on the summit. Luke had told her on one of their expeditions that it had been erected in 1896 as a navigational aid to mariners. It had been built at the direction of the rector of St. Michael Caerhays, a quaint Norman-style church that was adjacent to the castle of the same name.

Gazing through the mist at the imposing religious symbol that had endured countless gales for nearly a century, Blythe had difficulty gauging whether she felt better or worse for having finally confronted Ellie over their lifelong series of clashes. Today's debacle had been their first brawl since that wretched day on the Paramount back lot. Given the horrendous circumstances, their meeting at Painter's Cottage certainly could never have turned into a forgive-and-forget fest. But why was it *so* bitter? Why had both of them said such egregious things to each other?

It occurred to Blythe that in real life, unlike some cleverly contrived final scene in the movies, deep-seated emotional problems could not always be resolved by the last reel. Predictably, Ellie's ingrained covetousness had asserted itself in spades again this afternoon, despite the fact that the younger Barton was now the sister with the glamorous director-husband, the new baby, and the elegant house in Brentwood. And, just as predictably, Blythe had allowed herself once again to get hooked into trying to defend against her sister's perverse view of the world.

As Blythe more calmly considered Ellie's parting shot—that Chris had not wanted to have a baby with his first wife—

she wagered that this vicious crack probably reflected Ellie's own secret fear that the prodigiously self-centered director had not wanted to have a child with any woman.

But why was Ellie so vituperative when she appeared, now, to have everything she'd formerly begrudged her older sister?

DNA or no DNA, Blythe realized suddenly that her sister's long-standing feelings of inadequacy, coupled with her conviction that she had somehow been shortchanged by her entire family, had transformed her into a kind of unguided missile. When it plowed into the earth, anyone who happened to be in the vicinity could get wounded by shrapnel. The trick, Blythe supposed, was to try her damnedest not to take Ellie's behavior too personally—and to stay out of the line of fire.

She turned her gaze from the stone cross standing sentry on the headlands to face the churning English Channel. Cornwall was about as far away from Hollywood as you could get, she thought, her spirits lifting. If you can't fight 'em . . . put six thousand miles between you and such lethal weapons!

She began the return journey to Hemmick Beach and felt relieved that the blustering wind was now at her back, making the trip considerably easier. As she resolutely put one foot in front of the other, it occurred to her that she could never have controlled Ellie's or Christopher's actions. She could, however, do her best to understand the forces that had brought about their gut-wrenching collision today, and on that unforgettable November afternoon in California last year.

Despite the emotional blows Blythe had been dealt by her nearest and dearest, she wondered now if the only way to go forward was to systematically recover the bits and pieces of herself that had been stolen from her, or that she had given away to the likes of Chris and Ellie—people who had demanded chunks of her time, talent, and nurturing, and hadn't given much in return.

I must gather the scattered bits of my soul. . . .

It was a daunting task—this process of putting a life back together—but somehow she knew that she was well on her way. It was time, now, that she made some decisions concerning exactly how she wanted to live in the future.

And that brought her full circle to Luke—and the baby they might have created together. She must tell him. And she must be certain of what she truly wanted when she heard his response.

"I'll sleep on it," she said aloud to a gannet dive-bombing for fish in the turbulent waters at the base of the cliff. In the gathering dusk, Painter's Cottage now seemed a welcoming refuge from the stiff wind that had been pushing her along the entire walk home. She fixed herself a light supper that, fortunately, settled nicely at the bottom of her fragile stomach. Then she tucked herself into bed even before a sliver of moon winked between the billowing dark clouds overhead. She was grateful for the sheer physical exhaustion that had invaded every atom of her body—and prayed it would ensure a dreamless slumber.

Luke poked his head into Mrs. Q's kitchen and called, "Good night, son," as Richard surveyed his supper in silence.

"Night," he mumbled.

"Good night, sir," the housekeeper added quickly. "Tonight Dicken and I are going to give that puzzle another go, aren't we, lad?"

"I wish Blythe were here to help," was Richard's only reply.

"She's not feeling well," Luke said evenly. "Perhaps we can pay her a visit in the morning and see how she is."

"She's ill?" Richard said with a worried glance toward Mrs. Q.

"Nothing serious," Luke assured him. "A touch of the flu, I expect," he added, recalling her hasty retreat into Painter's Cottage earlier that afternoon.

"Luke!" Chloe's voice called plaintively from the hallway. "We're going to be late, darling. My parents are waiting for us!"

"Is she staying here tonight?" Richard asked.

"Aunt Chloe's our guest. . . . Yes, of course," Luke replied as Richard's godmother approached the entrance to the kitchen.

"Do you like her better than Blythe?" Richard demanded.

"Richard!" Luke said with exasperation. "You're being extremely tiresome. No pudding for you, my lad, until you remember your manners, isn't that right, Mrs. Q?"

"Will you be late, sir?" the housekeeper inquired, nodding her apparent willingness to carry out Luke's edict. "Shall I lock up before I go to bed?"

"We shall never get there at this rate," Chloe said in high dudgeon.

"No . . . just close up the kitchen," Luke directed wearily. "I'll do the rest."

Richard stared down at his plate. If his father and Aunt Chloe didn't care about how Blythe was feeling, *he* certainly did!

He glanced outside, reassured to see there was at least an hour of daylight remaining. Fortunately, the rain had stopped, although large, black clouds still hovered overhead. If he took his father's torch with him, Richard thought, there would still be time to explore the cave below Painter's Cottage. He prayed the tide would be low, as he'd been longing to see how far back it cut into the cliff. Then he'd visit Blythe and surprise her with some of Mrs. Q's lemon cake! If she offered him a piece to eat while he was paying a visit, that wouldn't be naughty, would it? he wondered.

"We'll just be off, then," Luke said, and when his son made no further response, he retreated down the hallway toward the front of the house where Chloe and her Jaguar waited under the porte cochere.

While Mrs. Q was doing the washing up, Richard located his father's big black torch, which he then hid in the cloakroom.

"Come back straightaway, now, Dicken," the housekeeper warned. "Just feed the ponies those scraps and then I'll fix you some drinkin' chocolate when you come back. I think the rain'll be bedeviling us before long."

"Yes, ma'am," Richard replied, heading for the cloakroom.

He darted across the stable yard and set off down the leafy tunnel that led to the narrow beach and the pirates' cave Mr. Q swore had once been connected to Painter's Cottage.

He'd surprise Blythe for sure!

Luke and Chloe arrived back at Barton Hall a little before ten-thirty. Luke was relieved they'd made it an early night.

"I'll just close up everything down here," he announced, hoping that his houseguest would take her cue to retire to her room in the guest wing.

During an extremely tedious evening spent with Colonel and Mrs. Acton-Scott at their club outside St. Austell, Chloe had more than her share of the two bottles of Bordeaux the colonel had ordered with uncharacteristic expansiveness. Now his daughter seemed poised to do or say something that might prove highly embarrassing.

"Can I pour you a little nightcap, Luke, darling?" she asked, following him unsteadily into the library.

"I've had quite enough to drink tonight, thank you," he said pointedly. "Of course, if you'd like one . . ."

"Oh, all right, spoilsport," she pouted. "I'll be a good girl." She took a step closer and began to fiddle with his tie. "That is, I'll be good if you'll be good. . . ."

A beam of light outside the library window caught his attention. Then he noticed there was a second flash.

"What the devil?" he exclaimed.

"What the devil what?" Chloe asked, sounding irritated.

He cracked open the window and felt a rush of chill, moist air.

"Hallo . . . hallo out there!"

"Oh, Mr. Teague . . . thank the Lord you've come back! We can't find Dicken!"

"Mrs. Q? Quiller? Stay where you are. . . . I'll be right out."

"What's happened?" Chloe asked, raising her hand to her temple as if she were dizzy.

"Are you all right?" Luke asked hurriedly. "Can you make it

upstairs on your own? There's some sort of problem. . . . I must go see what it is."

"I'll just go up to my room now," Chloe announced faintly.

"Are you sure I can't help you—"

"No," Chloe said firmly, and made directly for the grand staircase. Surprised, he watched her scurry up the steps and disappear into the shadows of the guest wing, as if she were on some urgent errand.

Luke nearly collided with the Quillers at the kitchen door.

"I've looked everywhere!" cried Mrs. Q. "He only just went out back to feed the ponies some carrots left from supper."

"But it's nearly quarter to eleven!" Luke noted sharply. "How long has he been gone?"

"Since sundown, Mr. Teague," Quiller said apologetically. "He promised the wife he'd come right back. We kept waitin' and waitin', thinkin' he'd be back any minute. Then we started to search, thinkin' maybe he be havin' a bit of fun off us."

"We called and called," Mrs. Q said, wringing her chapped hands. "It's not like the lad to play such tricks. We tried to think what restaurant you and Miss Chloe might be gone to. We made some calls, but—"

The poor woman seemed close to tears.

"Now, let's everybody stay calm," Luke said, forcing himself to inhale deeply. "Have you checked with Mrs. Stowe down at Painter's Cottage?"

"That was to be our next—"

"I'll take the car down there and have a look."

"Shall we call the constable?" Mrs. Q asked worriedly. "Oh, where could that little scamp have got to?"

"Quiller, do be so kind as to call Mr. Seaton and put him on alert," Luke said firmly. "Inform him that if Richard's not to be found at Painter's Cottage, I'll come directly to the Gorran Haven police station. Mrs. Q—perhaps you should search the rooms and the cupboards, one by one. I'll ring you from the village within the hour."

"Here, sir, you'd better take my torch," Quiller said, handing it over. "I looked for your larger one, but it's gone missing."

"But I always keep it—oh, never mind. Thank you."

Painter's Cottage sat perched on the cliff in utter blackness. A crescent moon offered only faint illumination as ominous black clouds scudded across the night sky. Blythe's front door was locked, a fact Luke found keenly distressing. He wondered if she'd thrown the bolt as soon as she'd slammed it shut after their argument earlier.

A sudden crack of lightning, followed by a loud thunderclap, heralded the beginning of a downpour as Luke curled his fist and pounded on the oak planks. Eventually a light went on downstairs and Blythe peered through the window.

"Richard's disappeared!" he shouted.

She quickly padded to the door and opened it. "He's missing?" she asked, her voice full of concern as she pulled on the collar of her bathrobe to ward off the chill air and spitting rain that slanted through the door. The downpour had begun in earnest. "Come in! Come in!"

"I take it, then, you haven't seen him?"

"Not since . . . after we came back from St. Goran's."

"Oh, Christ!" Luke exploded, stalking into the cottage. "Now, why would he do something like this, the little bugger!"

"Maybe he wants to get your attention," Blythe said quietly.

"What's that supposed to mean?"

Another crack of lightning lit up the cottage's dim interior.

"I don't think he wants to go back to that school," Blythe said, staring at the natural fireworks on display outside the tall artist's window.

"It's by far the best place for him," Luke declared. He paused, waiting for the accompanying thunder to subside, and then added, "It'll give the boy a bit of backbone. And from what I witnessed today, he needs it."

"Don't be idiotic," Blythe said wearily, and folded her arms across her chest with a look of frustration.

"And I suppose you understand my son's needs better than I do?"

"I can't imagine how you think you understand anything at all about Dicken," Blythe retorted. "After all, you've hardly spent an entire hour alone with the boy since he returned from Shelby Hall!"

"I've been damned busy this summer, as you well know!" Luke said defensively. "He seemed perfectly happy to me."

"He cried his heart out at his mother's grave today, for God's sake, Luke, and you just stalked off to the car. I wouldn't call that the picture of a happy child! And now you're banishing him to that prison you call a school for another year. No wonder he ran off!"

Luke began to pace in front of the fireplace. "Excuse me, Blythe, but I am well aware that my son has suffered since his mother's death. You do not have to lecture me in that department, thank you!"

"Well, then, perhaps you should lecture your dear friend Chloe!" Blythe rejoined, stung. "You two have shamelessly left Dicken to grieve alone for two goddamned years! Lord knows if you've permitted yourself to shed a tear. Stiff upper lip at all costs, I suppose!"

"Taking pop-psychology lessons from my dear cousin Valerie?" he replied cuttingly. "Or has she got you gazing into her crystal ball to ferret out all my flaws?"

"Don't be a jackass!" Blythe yelled. "Just tell me what I can do to help find your son!"

Chapter Fifteen

September 8, 1994

Luke and Blythe made their rain-drenched trip into Gorran Haven in silence, except for the sound of the windshield wipers clicking back and forth like a metronome. As the Land Rover came to a halt in front of the police station, Blythe bolted and slammed the door. However, she waited under the eaves at the entrance to the stone building to allow Luke to enter first.

"Ah . . . Mr. Teague . . . ," said a wiry man of about fifty sitting behind a desk. "Your housekeeper rang from Barton Hall to say that so far they've had no luck locating the boy."

"Constable Seaton, this is Mrs. Stowe, who's been leasing Painter's Cottage. I went round on my way here to see if perhaps Richard had gone there."

"And he hadn't?" the constable inquired of Blythe.

"No," she said quietly. "As I told his father, I last saw him today about lunchtime outside Barton Hall."

The door opened and several people entered quietly. All of them wore bright-orange anoraks with "West Country Search and Rescue" emblazoned on the back.

"Hello, Henry . . . Jeremy . . . Jack. Thanks for coming," the constable greeted the volunteers quickly. "I thought it wise to alert our local team to scour the area adjacent to Barton Hall," he added. "Now, as I understand it from the Quillers, you'd gone out to dinner, Mr. Teague, leaving your son with the housekeeper. Is that correct?" Seaton inquired.

"Yes."

"And can you think of any reason the lad might have gone off? Did he seem upset about anything? Had you had words before you left?"

"He seemed perfectly normal," Luke said, a muscle tightening in his jaw. He clearly was discomforted speaking of his relationship with his son in front of strangers. He paused, then added reluctantly, "He'd been a bit cheeky to his godmother, who is staying down from London for a few days . . . and I told him he couldn't have pudding."

"Anything else?" Seaton asked pleasantly.

"Well, he's due to return to school soon. Perhaps . . . ," Luke declined to finish his sentence.

"The lad is . . . how old again?"

"Ten."

"Ten," Seaton repeated. "First year at the school?"

"Beginning his third," Luke answered.

"I see. . . . And, therefore, he's been attending there since . . . let's see . . . around the age of seven or eight, is that right?"

"Since my wife died. Two years ago."

"Of course. Tragic, really," Constable Seaton reassured him kindly.

The door to the office opened again, and several other volunteers walked in, including Valerie Kent, fitted out in an oversize orange anorak.

"Oh, Luke . . . you poor dear!" Valerie declared in a rush. Then she saw Blythe. "It's good of you to join the search. I'm sure he won't have come to harm. . . . He's such a keen little lad."

"Well, everyone," the constable addressed the group, "I think perhaps it's best to start in the area between Barton Hall and Painter's Cottage. Henry," he said to his colleague seated behind a desk, "do check to see if the lifeboat brigade has launched yet. They'll be patrolling along the coast and checking the beaches." To the others he said, "Let's start out in our usual teams. Valerie, why don't you ride with Mr. Teague and Mrs. Stowe and follow along with us? Everyone got their mobile phones? Call in every half hour to report your positions. Henry will coordinate from this end. Let's be off."

Wordlessly Blythe and Luke climbed back into the Land Rover, joined by Valerie Kent in the backseat. The older woman leaned forward and rested a hand on Luke's shoulder as the heavy downpour continued to pelt the metal roof over their heads.

"We'll find him, Lucas. He's not the silly sort."

But Luke didn't answer. Instead, he gripped the steering wheel and then slowly leaned forward, resting his forehead against his gloved hand.

"You're absolutely right, Blythe," he said in a low, ragged voice. "Every single, blasted thing you accused me of earlier is true."

"Luke . . . please! I realize how hard the last two years have been for you both," Blythe replied softly, aching for him.

"Valerie knows, don't you?" he said, his voice muffled by his sleeve. "I have kept my son at arm's length for two years. Oh, my God!" he added hoarsely. He raised his head and stared at Blythe with a haunted look. "If something's happened to Richard, I'll never—"

"We shall find him, Luke!" Valerie said crisply. "But we can't accomplish that if we're sitting in this contraption. The constable's just turned left. Follow along, now."

After nearly an hour of tramping in the pouring rain along the cliffs and shouting Richard's name into the biting night wind, they arrived back at Barton Hall a little past two A.M. Mrs. Quiller had set up a tea bar in her expansive kitchen, and it soon became the headquarters for the search effort. In groups of two and three, the teams, refreshed, set off once again, fanning out in a systematic scheme to cover the nearby territory.

Constable Seaton chatted briefly with Mrs. Quiller as she refilled his mug of tea. Then he sat down at the kitchen table where Blythe, Luke, Valerie, and Mr. Quiller were preparing to depart for another sweep along Hall Walk.

"The housekeeper mentioned just now that the lad's a great admirer of yours, Mrs. Stowe," he noted.

"He's a lovely boy," Blythe replied, and as she said the words, she felt as if she might burst into tears from the strain. "It makes me feel awful that I might have been asleep when he came by Painter's Cottage. Maybe I didn't hear him knock."

"It's certainly possible he might have headed down there," Luke interjected quickly. "He knew Mrs. Stowe hadn't been feeling well yesterday and expressed concern."

"He did?" Blythe said, touched. "But that entire area around the cottage has already been searched by one of your teams. Why haven't we found any sign of—?"

She couldn't finish her sentence.

"Y'know, Constable," Mr. Quiller mused, "the lad was always talkin' about that cave down there."

"What cave?" Seaton asked sharply.

"It's small and narrow. Hard to find unless you know right where it be . . . and impossible, this time of year, if the tide's a-coming in. I showed it to Dicken and Mrs. Stowe here earlier this summer."

Luke and Blythe exchanged glances. They both knew exactly where the cavern was located.

"It's a natural cave near that snippet of beach right below Painter's Cottage," Luke volunteered soberly.

"Some say 'twas connected—away back when—to a tunnel that went all the way to Mrs. Stowe's place," Quiller explained for the constable's benefit. "In the time of the Free Traders, don'cha know."

"That smuggler's tunnel collapsed a hundred years ago," Luke protested. "You know that."

"But does Dicken know that?" Valerie asked quietly.

"I think so. . . ."

"Did you ever go down there with him?" Valerie probed. "Show him where the cavern ended?"

"We've been so busy," Luke explained. "He asked me to go a few times, but we just never got around to it."

"But, sir," Quiller said with alarm, "Dicken was always pesterin' me to take 'im way to the back to explore—like he be a pirate, he'd say. But each time we went down there, either the tide be in, or we'd not the proper torch with us. . . ."

"Didn't you say tonight that my large torch's gone missing?" Luke asked sharply.

"That it did, sir. . . . It were nowhere t'be found tonight, and that's a fact."

Just then the constable's mobile phone emitted a peremptory series of pips.

"Right . . . right . . . all right, Henry. Any word from the lifeboat brigade? Right you are. What's the weather forecast? Damn! Call me if anyone reports in with something we can go on." He pressed the off button on the portable phone and then announced quietly, "The lifeboat brigade's concentrated on Hemmick Beach and Dodman Point. Perhaps the team missed the cave on that little stretch of sand below Painter's Cottage. Shall we have another look?"

Blythe and Luke watched in silence as several teams of orange-jacketed search-and-rescue workers led the way along the treacherous path that corkscrewed down to the narrow beach. Then, one by one, Constable Seaton, Luke, Valerie, and Blythe gingerly followed in their muddy footsteps. A stiff, icy wind lashed their faces and tore at their clothing while the beams from their flashlights performed a danse macabre on the side of the cliff.

Blythe's rain-slicked stone cottage loomed above their heads as they slowly descended to the bottom of the one-hundred-foot perpendicular drop. The solitary lamp that glowed in the window on the first floor winked at them through the continuing downpour. Blythe saw it as a beacon of hope they would find Richard before sunup.

"Oh, Christ!" Luke exclaimed over his shoulder. "The tide's been in."

He pointed at the stretch of sand that had been recently

saturated with seawater up to the base of the cliffs. Strands of seaweed the color of dark amber lay marooned on the glistening rocks. Their coils, severed by the boulders' jagged edges, released a pungent, vaguely fetid, odor into the damp air. Fortunately, the rain suddenly began to let up as the eastern horizon lightened with the promise of dawn. As soon as the entire search party reached the beach, they instinctively formed a huddle.

"I'd like to go in first, if you don't mind, Constable," Luke requested, his eyes riveted on the shadowed entrance to the cave.

"Of course, sir," Seaton replied.

Blythe seized Luke's gloved hand in hers and said, "Please . . . let me go in with you."

Luke pulled his gaze away from the drenched escarpment and gave her his attention. For a moment she thought he would refuse her request. Then he gave a brief nod and headed for the cave, with Blythe following single file.

The temperature inside the narrow cavern was a few degrees warmer than the rain-washed night air outside. The beam from Luke's flashlight cavorted eerily on the gray stone ceiling and bounced off the damp walls. They trudged through a few yards of seawater up to their ankles. Then, for some fifteen feet beyond the entrance, wet sand made a squishing sound under the soles of their rubber boots. As they proceeded deeper into the cave, Blythe sensed that the surface beneath her feet had become drier and more uneven. Within a few more yards she found it increasingly difficult to tramp through the mounds of sand. To regain her balance, she reached out and steadied herself by bracing her right palm against the dank wall.

Suddenly a rustling noise caught Blythe by surprise, and she involuntarily uttered a yelp as a creature zoomed overhead.

"Bats," Luke announced, his voice echoing against the dome of the cave. "You don't have to come any farther, if you'd rather not."

"Don't be ridiculous," she laughed shakily. "Bats are practically Wyoming's state bird. It startled me, that's all."

Luke had halted abruptly, causing Blythe to bump against the back of his oilskin Barbour coat.

"Oh, God," she heard him say. Her view, however, was completely blocked by his broad shoulders.

"What?" she demanded. When he didn't respond, fear began to ball in her stomach like a curled wave poised to break thunderously on the shore. She suddenly thought of how quickly one's life can turn on a dime. One day her brother, Matt, was a vibrant seventeen-year-old, sassing everyone in sight—the next, he was lying prone in a rodeo arena, his neck broken in two places and his skull crushed.

She ducked down and butted her head underneath Luke's right arm to see what had prompted his exclamation. The beam from his flashlight illuminated the cave where an ancient rock slide marked the crevice's termination. There, on a flat boulder five or six feet above the floor of the cavern and three feet below its rocky ceiling, lay Richard Teague resting on his right side, his eyes closed.

The ten-year-old was holding Luke's giant-sized flashlight under his chin as if he were clutching a teddy bear. The electric torch had either been turned off, or its batteries were now dead. The child's clothes were soaked, but Blythe saw that his hair appeared to be only damp, not drenched in seawater. Suddenly, like an angel rising from a stone sarcophagus, Richard fluttered his eyelids and sat up.

"Blythe!" he said joyfully, looking past his father. "You're feeling better!"

"I'm fine, Dicken!" she quickly assured him. She was deeply touched that her well-being was the first concern of this lost child who obviously had been stranded by the incoming tide. "But are *you* all right?"

"I think so," he said slowly. "I dreamed, just now, you'd find me!" he added. "And there you were!" Then he blinked slowly and stared at Luke, his gaze growing apprehensive. The boy's stricken expression made it appear as if he were about to cry. "Daddy . . . I-I'm sorry," he faltered. "I was playing pirate. I knew I oughtn't, but I thought I could find the hidden tunnel and surprise Blythe by coming up under the cottage floor."

"Come here, son." Luke spoke in a choked voice so unlike his own, Blythe hardly recognized it.

However, Richard remained where he was, adding in a rush, "I didn't realize the time passing. I looked and looked for the smugglers' passageway, but then the tide came in. I-I was frightened, and so I climbed up here and—"

"Go back and tell them we've found him!" Luke commanded Blythe hoarsely. Then he spoke to his son. "Dicken, please give me your hand. I'll help you get down from there."

Blythe swiftly made her way out of the cave, using her gloved hand against the damp walls as a guide.

"He's there!" she shouted to the huddled group. "He's alive! Bring some blankets! He's wet and cold but seems okay, as far as I can tell."

"Well done!" Valerie exclaimed as a cheer went up from the others.

And then Blythe turned toward Luke's cousin and was enveloped in a hearty embrace. Valerie pressed Blythe's head against the pillow of her ample shoulder. Then, like a harp string stretched to the breaking point, Blythe felt her own shoulders begin to vibrate.

"We've had quite a scare, haven't we?" the older woman soothed, patting Blythe's back as if she were the child who had just been rescued.

"Thank God, Dicken's all right," Blythe moaned. Dr. Kent's empathy suddenly unleashed a floodgate of emotions. Blythe wept for the boy who had survived this ordeal and for her brother who hadn't. She sobbed aloud her own terror at the thought of the terrible tragedy that might have befallen young Richard Teague and his father—and cried silently for the sorrow that might lie ahead for herself and her own child.

"Thank God . . . ," she repeated between gulps. "I don't think I could have stood it if one more person—"

"Thank God, indeed," Valerie sniffed, pulling out a handkerchief and wiping her eyes, then offering a clean corner to Blythe.

Just at that moment Luke appeared at the mouth of the cave carrying Richard in his arms. His face was half-obscured by the folds of the psychedelic-orange blanket that enveloped his son.

"Put him on the stretcher, sir," advised one of the volunteers. "John here and I will carry the lad up the cliff in a tick."

"Shall we take him to hospital?" Constable Seaton inquired of Luke. "Or back to Painter's Cottage up there and call the doctor?"

Luke glanced at Blythe. "What do you think?"

"What do *you* think, Dicken?" she asked the boy with a watery smile. "Do you feel well enough to go straight home and pop right into a hot bath?"

"Yes, ma'am." He nodded, his eyes very round. Then he added with a pleading look, "Will you come?"

Blythe groaned inwardly. She was fatigued to her very marrow and desired nothing more than to fall into her bed in the cottage above them.

"Oh, Dicken . . . I'm sure your dad will—"

"Perhaps you'd drive the car," Luke suggested in a clipped tone, as if he were dealing with an intractable servant. Whatever emotion he had displayed upon rescuing his son was now strictly under control. However, it was obvious that Richard's preference for her company had disturbed his father. "I'll stay with Richard in the backseat, if you don't mind," he added firmly.

Now Blythe felt genuine irritation. For three months the man had virtually ignored his son. Now he appeared determined to ward off any unwanted interlopers—and that most definitely included her. Before she could answer, Luke turned to address the Search and Rescue Team.

"My deepest thanks to you all. I will never be able to express my gratitude—ever. Especially to you, Constable, for asking the right questions . . . and you, Quiller, for knowing the mind of this rapscallion as well as you do. He was playing pirates, everyone," he announced to the assembled crowd with an air of apology, "and was trapped by the incoming tide while he looked for the old smugglers' tunnel that used to lead to Painter's Cottage."

"None too worse for wear, are ya, lad?" said John, one of two stretcher bearers. "But you'll not be tryin' this again, will you, now?" he added with a wink as he tucked the blanket more tightly around his charge.

"No, sir," Richard said in a small voice.

"Right Cornish, though, isn't he?" the other stretcher bearer chortled. "Came through it all like an old Free Trader, hidin' from the customs men! Got a bit of the ol' smuggler's spirit in you, my lad, and that's a fact!"

Within minutes Blythe sat at the wheel of the Land Rover and prepared to put the vehicle in gear. Luke was in the back, with young Richard stretched out along the seat. The boy remained bundled head to foot in the borrowed blanket.

"I'll ring you tomorrow to see how you've all settled yourselves," Valerie announced through the car window. "Constable Seaton'll give me a lift to the village. Get some sleep, now, will all of you?"

Within the hour Richard had been bathed and tucked into his bed, not by the conscientious Mrs. Quiller, but by his father. Meanwhile, Blythe had raided the pantry of saltines to quiet her queasy stomach, and hoped for the best as she mounted the grand staircase to bid Richard good night, as promised. Her attempts to stave off the now familiar twinges of discomfort she was feeling in her midsection had not been entirely successful. She was so tired, she felt like lying down on the nearest rug.

"Sleep well, buckaroo," she called softly from the door to Richard's bedroom. "Take your time about showing up for work tomorrow. As a matter of fact, I think we should all take the day off."

"Are you going?" Richard cried, sitting up in his bed with alarm. "Couldn't you stay with me until I fall asleep?"

Blythe was embarrassed by his request and looked to Luke for guidance. His careful lack of expression revealed that his son's preference for Blythe's ministrations had cut him to the quick. However, he merely stepped aside, allowing Blythe to sit on the side of the boy's bed. She gently stroked the lad's brown hair, so similar in shade to that of the woman whose picture stood on Richard's bedside table.

"I'm very sorry I caused everyone so much trouble," the youngster said sleepily.

"I'm very sorry you've had such a scary time," she answered. "And I'm very glad you came through it all right. Do you promise never to be quite such a daredevil again?" she whispered in his ear, then brushed her lips lightly against his cheek.

"I promise . . . ," he whispered in return and, in an instant, was fast asleep.

"Blythe . . . ?" Luke murmured. "We need to talk."

"Luke, I can't," she replied as an alarming jolt of nausea suddenly invaded her stomach. "I can't keep my eyes open."

"I-I feel I must explain why I sent Dicken away to school . . . why I decided two years ago that—"

"Look, I am about to drop in my tracks," Blythe interrupted in a tight voice. "And I'm afraid I'm just not up to debating child-rearing philosophies at the moment."

"Please! Hear me out!" Luke said urgently. "Let's just have a brandy downstairs."

To Blythe the thought of such libations was suddenly revolting. Before Luke's astonished glance she dashed past him into Richard's bathroom and abruptly shut the door.

A few minutes later, nearly blind with fatigue and white as a sheet, she emerged. She avoided meeting Luke's eyes.

"Blythe . . . were you ill just now?" he demanded.

"I think the last twenty-four hours would make anyone ill,"

she said weakly. "I'll be all right. Just let me get out of these wet clothes and go to sleep," she whispered urgently over her shoulder as she exited Richard's bedroom. "I think this scare with Dicken tonight brought back a lot of bad memories about my brother, Matt," she temporized when they had reached the hallway.

"I'm utterly exhausted myself," Luke agreed with a defeated shrug. They walked along in silence down the carpeted corridor in the opposite direction from Richard's room. At the end of the hallway Luke offered, "I suppose we'd best try to get some sleep during what's left of the night."

For an awkward moment they hesitated outside Luke's room.

"Look," Blythe said as a mantle of misery closed in around her, "I'll sleep in one of the guest rooms."

Luke gave her a strange look and shook his head. "Don't be idiotic. My room's just here."

"I'd go back to the cottage," she added stubbornly, her pride wounded, "but I honestly don't think, at this point, I can walk or drive."

"Blythe, you're being silly," he snapped, his own strain and fatigue overtaking his customary courtesy.

Nearly catatonic by now, Blythe allowed him to lead her into his bedchamber with its enormous four-poster looming against the rose-colored wall. She barely remembered his stripping her of her wet clothing, or his joining her inside his white-tiled shower. As if she were dreaming, she felt the soothing hot water cascade down her body. A few minutes later she kept her eyes closed as he toweled her dry with a large terry bath sheet and slipped her arms into his cashmere dressing gown.

"In with you," he said, pulling back the red velvet coverlet on the gigantic Barton Bed. The next thing she knew, the bed linen was pulled under her chin. An instant later she was fast asleep.

Two hours afterward Blythe was insensible to the sound of the door to the master suite opening. Nor did she hear a female voice saying coquettishly from the threshold, "Darling . . . it's seven-thirty. I practically had to wrestle Mrs. Q to the kitchen floor so I could bring you your morning tea—and an apology," the woman purred as she closed the door behind her. "I was such a bad girl last night, wasn't I? I don't even remember finding my way to my room—can you imagine? I fear I had just a teensy bit too much to drink at the club," she admitted, making her way across the Persian carpet toward the gigantic four-poster. "So I thought, before you and that ambitious Mrs. Stowe were up to your ears in potting soil or something, I'd come here to tell you in person how sorry I was that I—"

Oblivious to the foregoing, Blythe was roused by the sound of a tea tray being set down on the bedside table with a loud thump, on top of which followed the nerve-jangling clattering of stacked chinaware. Chloe Acton-Scott's final comment—before the young Englishwoman angrily slammed the bedroom door—received Blythe's full attention.

"Bloody hell!" Chloe screeched. "Damn you, Lucas Teague! I can't believe you've allowed that wretched American woman in your bed!"

Blythe pulled herself up to a sitting position and stared at the reverberating expanse of the oak-paneled door. Luke rolled over in his sleep—roused by the disturbance, but not fully awakened by it—and then buried his head, facedown, into his pillow.

Blythe had utterly forgotten Richard's godmother had been visiting Barton Hall! The woman must have been drunk as a coot not to have been awakened by the commotion engendered by the search-and rescue squad invading the castle's kitchen in the middle of the night. Imagine the effect on Chloe's hangover having discovered someone else occupying the Bawdy Bed of Barton! Blythe thought sourly.

She swung her legs over the side of the bed and poured herself a much-needed cup of tea.

The second time the cups and saucers rattled on their tray

roused Luke more thoroughly than even the outraged exclamations of Chloe Acton-Scott.

"Blythe?" Luke said in a voice that sounded as if it came from the depths of a gravel pit.

"Yes," she replied evenly.

"What was that Mrs. Q said just now?"

"Nothing."

He rolled over and declared to her cashmere-clad back, "She said something. I heard her. . . . I just couldn't make it out," he added sleepily.

"Your tea was delivered by Richard's godmother this morning," she replied quietly.

"What!" Luke exclaimed, sitting bolt upright in bed. "You must be joking."

"And she brought two cups . . . see?" Blythe said sweetly, handing him the one she'd poured for herself and immediately serving herself another. "She appeared to know Mrs. Q's morning routine to perfection."

"Blythe . . . you're being silly."

"That's the second time in twenty-four hours you've called me that," Blythe said in a calm voice that did not match the tumult of emotion churning inside her. "I don't much like it."

Luke remained silent as Blythe took her first sip of tea. She continued to stare across the velvet-clad chamber at the carved fireplace and its cold hearth. Luke's implied denial of intimacy with Chloe Acton-Scott was reminiscent of all-too-familiar conversations she'd had in the past. So much for her romantic notions about Luke's celibacy since his wife died—or his fidelity, for that matter. Suddenly she felt like an utter fool.

Long before she had discovered her husband making love to her sister in his director's trailer, Blythe had occasionally suspected Christopher of cheating on her. Whenever she summoned the courage to confront him with various pieces of blatant evidence, he had more than once looked her boldly in the eye and denied the facts with an air of injured innocence.

She took another sip from her china cup and then set it on the bedside tray.

"I think I'll have a nice hot bath, if you don't mind," she said pleasantly. "I don't think I've got the chill out of my bones yet."

And without giving Luke a backward glance, she slipped into the bathroom, locked the door, and ran the tap. Meanwhile, she dressed in the clothes she'd worn the previous night, which she found draped over the radiator to dry. Her jeans were stiff as boards, and her sweater was a bit clammy. However, as soon as she had made herself presentable, she shut off the water without bathing, unplugged the drain, and escaped out a side door that led to Luke's dressing room, and another that led to the hallway.

She reached Mrs. Q's kitchen just in time to catch sight of Chloe stalking toward her Jaguar.

"She's certainly getting an early start," Blythe commented, nodding through the steam-streaked kitchen window. Then she poured herself a second cup of tea from the pot nesting under the quilted cotton cozy. "Off to London?"

"Not that she had the courtesy to tell me," Mrs. Q retorted with uncharacteristic pique. The previous night's strain had taken its toll on the indomitable Margery Quiller.

The housekeeper scrutinized the departing guest through the window. "She hasn't got her overnight bag with her," she added glumly. "She'll be back."

"Arm-wrestled you to get Luke's tea tray, did she?" Blythe sympathized.

"Oh, Lord!" the housekeeper groaned, and sat down on the nearest chair. "You saw her?"

"Sure did." Blythe smiled grimly. "She nearly brained me in bed with the cups and saucers."

"Oh, Lord!" Mrs. Q repeated, as the older woman obviously envisioned the scene that must have recently transpired in her employer's bedchamber. She shook her gray head. "I did m'very best to dissuade her from—oh, Lord!"

"Don't feel bad. I watched every episode of *Upstairs Downstairs*," Blythe said with a stab at humor, "so I understand your dilemma completely."

"I've known all along that woman would like nothing better than to be the next Mrs. Teague," Mrs. Q declared ruefully, "but she be never up to that sort of thing afore."

"Perhaps she never had to . . . before I arrived on the scene," Blythe said carefully.

"Oh . . . no, believe me—"

"Oh, Jesus!" Blythe interrupted, pointing out the kitchen window at the sight of a Rolls-Royce emerging from the column of larch trees and heading toward the porte cochere. "I'm surprised Chloe and The Great One didn't have a head-on crash halfway up the drive!"

Mrs. Quiller and Blythe were mesmerized by the sight of Christopher Stowe bringing his imposing chariot to a halt. Within seconds he unfolded his tall, nattily attired frame from his car and strode toward the large oak front door. The housekeeper shook her head in bewilderment as the British director picked up the heavy door knocker and began to pound it authoritatively against its brass plate.

"St. Goran preserve us!" the housekeeper pleaded, and turned to gaze at Blythe questioningly. "What will you be wantin' me to say to him?"

"I'll deal with this," Blythe responded wearily, and headed down the dark corridor toward the castellated front entrance.

"Well, good morning!" Chris declared with forced cheer as Blythe opened the door a few inches. "First off, I stopped by at your cottage this morning—rather early, I might add. Since you were nowhere to be seen and your unmade bed proved to be empty, I used my brilliant powers of deduction and came over here."

"You went inside my cottage and had yourself a thorough look-see, did you?" Blythe demanded.

"The door was unlocked and a light was on downstairs," he

said with a shrug. Then he glanced over his shoulder. "Not disturbing the lord of the manor, I trust? Quite a slugabed, is he?"

"We've had a rather eventful twenty-four hours."

"You, I know, are always up at the crack of dawn," he said, ignoring her last remark, "so I assume I shan't have upset your routine too much by just popping by." When she didn't immediately reply, he added with impatience, "I need to have your answer about the forest, Blythe. Time is running out."

Behind them footsteps were descending the grand staircase.

"If you'd like to discuss anything in the language of the agreement," Christopher continued, "why not let's have dinner tonight, as I have proposed, and sort it all out?"

Blythe felt Luke's presence directly behind her.

"Good morning," said the owner of Barton Hall to Christopher Stowe, who remained standing on the flagstone step. "Would you two like to discuss this matter in the sitting room so we might close the front door? It's rather chilly, and we appear to be heating the great outdoors."

"Hold on a sec," Blythe said emphatically over her shoulder. "Let's get this over with. I'll meet you tonight. What time?" she added, hoping to be rid of Christopher as quickly as possible.

"I'll pick you up at seven-thirty, shall I?" Chris replied enthusiastically.

"At the cottage. And it's just the two of us, understood? No more surprises?" she added cryptically.

Chris nodded. "Absolutely."

Did he know about Ellie's visit to her cottage? Had her sister's frontal assault been part of Chris's overall strategy to wear her down?

"Where shall we have this little get-together?" she asked coolly.

"Do you know Boscundle Manor near St. Austell?" Chris inquired. "Lovely food, I'm told. I've made a reservation for eight o'clock. Is that all right?"

"Fine," Blythe replied grimly. "I'll try to reach my attorney today."

"I must know either way, Blythe," he insisted.

"Good-bye, Chris," Blythe cut in pointedly. "You'll have your answer tonight."

Christopher smiled with genuine warmth. "Good girl! I've checked on the wine list at the inn and am delighted to inform you that they stock our Lafite Rothschild eighty-nine. I've also learned that they are masters of your favorite dessert, my darling, so I've ordered us a chocolate soufflé to finish."

"Fine," Blythe said shortly, and closed the front door.

"Why in heaven's name did you allow him to bully you—" Luke began.

"He didn't," Blythe interrupted tersely. "I want to get all this behind me. I want to get everything that doesn't make me happy behind me."

She turned and marched through the foyer, past the portraits of Kit Trevelyan and the first Blythe Barton. Luke followed closely in her wake. When they passed the sitting-room door, he grabbed hold of her arm.

"Please, Blythe . . . come in here for a moment. I must talk to you."

She carefully pulled her arm from his grasp. Before she had any more discussions with Lucas Teague about the state of their relationship, or the future of the business they were supposedly engaged in, she needed to know all the facts.

"Look . . . I feel like a thousand head of steer have just stampeded over my body," she announced. "The only thing I'm good for right now is a morning nap. See ya," she added with as much flippancy as she could muster.

However, instead of heading down Hall Walk toward the cottage, she set out on the mile-long road to Gorran Haven. When she arrived at the doctors' offices on Rattle Alley, Valerie Kent's door was closed, with an "In Session" sign hung over the latch.

"Dr. Vickery is on a domiciliary," explained a woman of

about forty who apparently served both as nurse and receptionist for the general practitioner.

"A house call?" Blythe queried, her heart sinking.

"That's right," the nurse replied. Then she peered more closely at Blythe. "Aren't you Lucas Teague's summer let?" She smiled. "Valerie's mentioned how lovely for young Richard it's been with your leasing Painter's Cottage and starting a big nursery business and all. The lad's a keen gardener, just like his father." She laughed. "That's where Doctor is right now! At Barton Hall, checking on that young scamp after his high adventure last night. Must have given you all a bit of a turn, didn't it?"

"Yes," Blythe agreed weakly. The only car that had passed her on the Gorran Haven road must have been Vickery's.

"What can I do for you . . . Mrs. Stowe, isn't it?" The nurse smiled cheerfully.

"What I'm here about is highly confidential," she said, feeling flushed and embarrassed to be speaking of such an intimate matter with an utter stranger.

"Of course," the nurse replied, sobering immediately. "I am a nurse practitioner. Perhaps there's something I can help you with until the doctor returns?"

"Can you administer a pregnancy test?" Blythe asked in a subdued tone.

"The easy part, yes," the nurse replied with a searching look. "Could you roll up your sleeve? We'll need a blood sample."

Blythe remained silent as the nurse competently went about the business of drawing blood. Then Dr. Vickery's assistant handed her a paper cup and pointed to a door marked WC.

"Step right in there," she said kindly. "Please fill this at least a quarter full."

As Blythe headed for the rest room, she considered how foolish she probably was not to dash up to London for a gynecological exam and avoid the risk of her private life becoming a subject of tittle-tattle in this small, gossip-ridden village.

However, the simple truth was she couldn't stand to wait another minute to find out if she was pregnant. Within minutes she had emerged from the bathroom holding her urine sample in her hand just as Valerie's door opened and the psychologist bade farewell to a pimple-faced teenager.

"Why, Blythe!" she exclaimed as her client trod heavily down the wooden stairs outside. "Are you ill after last night, you poor dear?" Then the older woman's glance fell on the paper cup Blythe had been in the process of handing Dr. Vickery's nurse. She arched an eyebrow. "Just a routine checkup, I hope?"

Blythe stood in the middle of the doctors' reception room and stared wordlessly at Dr. Kent. Her vision was suddenly blurred by the tears that had welled up despite her best efforts to maintain her composure.

"I'll just take that," the nurse said quietly, relieving Blythe of the paper cup. "Just pop around tomorrow, after nine o'clock, and we'll have the test results. You can see the doctor for a complete examination then."

Valerie put a gentle arm around Blythe's shoulder and drew her into her office.

"Sit down, dear," she said. "You've had quite a time, haven't you?"

And then Blythe proceeded to tell Valerie everything.

"I feel like some reckless teenager!" she finished. "I picked the most unlikely guy in the world to be the father of the child I've desperately wanted."

"Why do you say that?" Valerie asked quietly.

Blythe stared at her in amazement. For a psychologist, and Luke's cousin to boot, the woman would have to be blind not to have observed Luke's cool, distant treatment of his son.

"He sent a grieving eight-year-old away to boarding school!" she exclaimed. "Doesn't that tell a lot about his attitude toward children?"

"Have you ever asked him why?" Valerie inquired.

Blythe paused and then she said, "Isn't it obvious? The man

is uncomfortable around kids. He's preoccupied with keeping Barton Hall out of the hands of the Inland Revenue. I don't know, Valerie!" she said with exasperation. Then she studied the woman who sat across the desk from her more closely. "Do you know?"

"Perhaps you should talk to Luke about these matters—and soon," was all she would say.

"Well . . . there's another problem," Blythe mumbled.

"What?" Valerie asked.

"Chloe Acton-Scott."

Valerie erupted in laughter.

"She's only a problem if Luke can't run fast enough! That woman has tried for twenty years to persuade my cousin to marry her."

"Well, apparently she's approaching the finish line," Blythe retorted. "She brought us morning tea today . . . only I wasn't supposed to be at the tea party."

"You'd better ask Luke about that as well," Valerie replied, sobering.

"Oh, God . . . it's too stupid for words. And another thing," Blythe said as a sense of futility took hold. "I could never come clean with Luke about the visions—or whatever they are—that I've been having," she continued moodily. "Yet I can't keep such a thing from him forever. And if I told him, he'd either mock me or have me committed to the nearest loony bin. Would he believe you, do you suppose?" she asked expectantly.

"I think it best if you tell him about it yourself, when the time is right," Valerie declared gently. "I'm afraid I'm not a wizard. I can't wave a magic wand. . . ."

Blythe gazed at Luke's cousin thoughtfully. "You are, too, a kind of wizard, and you know it! Look what happened when you pulled out your crystal ball!"

"You're the one with the visions, not I," she said mildly.

"But the baby!" Blythe exclaimed. "I saw that baby in your glass before Luke and I—" She halted midsentence and flushed with embarrassment. "And here I am," she continued weakly, "probably pregnant as a sow in early spring."

"Who knows what that baby signifies?" Valerie cautioned. "You never explored the vision, remember? You got frightened and brought yourself out of the trance on your own."

The image of that baby, floating in the infinity of Valerie's crystal ball, had continued to haunt Blythe. Had it foretold her own child? Was it a vision of Ellie's? She supposed it could even be a conjuring of the two children that the first Blythe Barton had borne in such pain and misery.

She thought, suddenly, of the dedication that had been scratched in charcoal on the back of Ennis's paintings hanging in the cottage. Now, there was another enigma!

Who was William?

If only she could discover the identity of the person behind that name, she might at least be able to see where he fit into the eighteenth-century family puzzle. For reasons she couldn't explain, even to Valerie, she felt compelled to get to the bottom of the role that the mysterious William had played in the tortuous saga of the Barton-Trevelyan-Teagues. There was no way to predict the future between Luke and her. However, she could at least attempt to determine whether the unrelenting anger and resentment she harbored toward Christopher and Ellie—and they toward her—were somehow rooted in the past.

She had searched Luke's genealogy chart top to bottom seeking William's name—but an entry for him was nowhere to be found. Perhaps Valerie's crystal ball could help her solve that part of the conundrum?

"Okay, Valerie," she said at length. "I'm willing to explore what I saw that day at the village fete."

"You're a courageous woman, Blythe," Valerie replied. "And I'll be right here, whatever happens." She smiled reassuringly.

After securing the office door, Valerie lit a candle, placed it ceremoniously on top of her desk, and dimmed the lights. With infinite care she brought the crystal sphere out of its velvet pouch and set it gently in the brass holder that was decorated with curved metal seahorses.

"Now, breathe deeply, and focus your eyes on the depths of the crystal . . . breathe in and out . . . in and out . . . that's a good girl," Valerie said soothingly. "I want you to relax . . . just let your mind float free . . . free as the baby you saw drifting in space. Breathe in . . . exhale. . . . That's good!" she whispered. "Now I am going to count from one to three and snap my fingers. When I do, I want you to create a spiral staircase in your thoughts that is completely translucent. One . . . two . . . three." Valerie snapped her fingers and then scrutinized Blythe. "Do you see it?"

Blythe nodded. Valerie continued to speak in a low, rhythmic voice.

"You are standing at the top step of that staircase. It is constructed of a clear material that radiates soft, crystalline light. You shall now descend the steps, one by one, as I begin to count . . . and when you reach the bottom, you'll see . . ."

At this point Blythe heard nothing but the sound of her own rhythmic breathing as she concentrated her thoughts on one name.

"William . . . ," she murmured. "Who is William . . . ?"

Chapter Sixteen

February 6, 1793

Loud piercing wails rent the air in Painter's Cottage. Kit shifted his attention from the dueling pistol Blythe held pointed at his heart to the newborn infant squalling on the bed.

The baby, swaddled in a length of cloth that Garrett Teague had found among Ennis's cleanest paint rags, was pathetically small but made up for his size in lung power.

Blythe's arm ached from the weight of the heavy gun as she held it steady, fully prepared to shoot her husband in the chest. As the child's outraged shrieks intensified, Kit slowly began to shake his head from side to side in defeat. Then he turned his back on the weapon's threatening barrel and slumped into the settle near the hearth. Oddly, the baby ceased its protests immediately and began sucking on an edge of the cloth with its rosebud mouth.

"Oh . . . so you accept my proposal," Blythe said softly, allowing the ivory-handled pistol to fall to her side. "You shall not proclaim me harlot to the world. And William here shall be adopted as your heir, is that agreed?"

"If I do this, you must understand one thing," Kit replied dully. "I shall have nothing more to do with him . . . or with you."

"Are you, or are you not, accepting my proposal?" Blythe demanded with renewed irritation.

"I shall see to the legalities," he mumbled, his expression

glazed with bitterness. Kit's gaze returned to the infant lying on the bed. "And, pray, why have you not called him Ennis and made my shame complete? I've not heard the name William among the Bartons or Trevelyans."

" 'Tis in honor of William Shakespeare," Blythe announced without further explanation. She very much doubted that Kit could tolerate the additional affront of learning that she had read every one of the Bard's love sonnets during Ennis's long painting sojourn in Italy. She'd often included some of her favorite lines in her illicit letters to him. She scanned her husband's furrowed, discontented brow and demanded crisply, "Is it also agreed between us, then, that I shall reside in Barton Hall and determine its policies? Half the gain of it shall be yours, if you wish," she added as an afterthought, hoping to mollify his pride so that they might forge some sort of truce.

"Trevelyan House remains solely mine," Kit insisted with the first show of resolve he had mustered since the moment his wife had threatened him with her pistol.

"Agreed. However," Blythe intervened swiftly, "everything of Ennis's shall be put in my charge. His paintings, his books, his personal effects. You shall not be troubled with a single possession that belonged to your brother. I shall keep everything safe until his return."

"You are a hard, willful woman, Blythe Barton," Kit said in a low voice. "You leave a man hardly a shred of dignity."

"I grant you no honor because you have not a manly mien," she replied coldly, regretting that she had yielded him anything of Barton Hall. "You would leave a woman to die. Not to put too fine a point on it, you are no gentleman."

"I told you before," he said, staring into the glowing coals near his feet, "this . . . this tangled coil has made me not myself. You and Ennis have driven me to it."

" 'Tis at your father's door all this is to be laid."

"He is dead. I am alive . . . and I must live each day without a wife or heir."

"We shall be happily ensconced next door," she said sardonically. "And if you are very kind, we might eventually reach a companionable accommodation."

"And when Ennis returns?" Kit demanded. He turned his head to meet her gaze, his eyes alight with accusation.

"Ennis is an artist," Blythe said curtly. "I have learned, to my sorrow, that one cannot expect such men to observe society's strictures." She glanced at her portrait, which still stood on the wooden easel in a shadowy corner under the eaves. "Whatever you or I may wish of him, he invariably does as he pleases." She glanced down at the baby, who now stared at her from the bed with a look of wide-eyed innocence. "But both Trevelyan brothers shall know this," she declared with sudden vehemence. "My son shall inherit my lands and whatever painted legacy his father creates."

And with that she replaced the pistol, along with its twin, in a drawer in the bedside table. Then she slowly and painfully made her way to the easel, every muscle and sinew in her body still aching from the ordeal of childbirth. She seized a piece of charcoal from the easel's wooden lip and scrawled "For William" on the back of an unframed seascape that leaned against the base of the stone wall.

"Whether Ennis intends to or not," she said with a gleam of triumph in her eye, "he, too, shall leave William a patrimony."

Blythe took a step backward in the entry hall and squinted an eye in the direction of the portrait Ennis had painted of her.

"There!" she said, admiring the newly framed work that Garrett had mounted on the wall beneath that of her father, James.

"How regal," her mother, Rosamund, pronounced with a hint of her former sarcasm. However, the thirty-eight-year-old woman had a death's-head quality to her appearance these days, a persistent wasting away of her flesh that foretold an early demise.

Rosamund Barton had returned to reside in Barton Hall immediately upon receiving word at her sister's in London that

Blythe had, amazingly enough, regained control of the family's estate.

As for her bastard grandson who played quietly on the carpet in the reception hall, the widow Barton was more than willing to participate in the fiction of his legitimate birth. Kit had not yet kept his word and completed the documentation necessary to adopt young William as his legal heir. However, he insisted that it was only a matter of time until he would receive the proper papers from the Court of Chancery in London, and then return them with the necessary signatures—including that of Ennis Trevelyan.

Meanwhile, Kit had moved into Trevelyan House, as he had reluctantly agreed to do. The owner of the property adjacent to Barton Hall appeared increasingly silent and withdrawn each time Blythe encountered him. Christopher Trevelyan had continued to lose his hair and gain in girth. His pockmarked cheeks were now as depressed as his spirits, giving his face a gaunt, discontented look, while his body grew as plump as a well-fed partridge.

Occasionally Blythe's estranged husband would exhibit a flash of temper, reminiscent of his late father's thunderous fulminations, but his anger would usually erupt when dealing with a hapless groom or misbehaving horse. Kit appeared careful not to antagonize his wife. At the same time, he made no effort to please her. He sometimes gave the impression of being a man caught in a hellish limbo, dead to feeling, frozen in action, waiting, watching, scanning the Channel as if some sign relating to his future would one day appear on the horizon.

Blythe had become accustomed to Kit's dark moods and silences. She refrained from goading him during his infrequent visits and pledged to herself to behave pleasantly, so long as he maintained a courteous manner toward her.

Blythe turned to Garrett, who had been standing quietly in the reception hall, hammer in hand.

"What say you?" Blythe teased as young William pulled himself to his feet by grasping her voluminous skirts. "Has

Ennis succeeded in making me look like a devoted Cornish wife—or a fishwife?"

"He has rendered you a sly puss, with slanted eyes and a calculating gaze," he pronounced candidly. "I believe you could pass for Cleopatra in a Shakespeare play."

"Excellent!" Blythe laughed. "Now, if I only knew the complete works of the Bard as well as you, my friendly bookseller, I might take that as a compliment."

Garrett Teague had proved a friend, indeed. His dark good looks had intensified in the last year, and at times Blythe even considered taking the man as a lover. However, she was loath to abandon their easy companionship, or complicate his life by serving him up as fodder for the village gossip mill. Lord knew, those crones in Gorran Haven and Mevagissey had tittle-tattle enough to chew on, considering the odd residential arrangements that the two branches of the Barton-Trevelyan clan had designed for themselves.

Thus far Garrett had never married, nor seemed inclined to tie the knot with any of the local wenches who pursued Blythe's handsome cousin by marriage. And there were moments when she even wondered what joys her life might have held if she had taken him up on his first proposal that they run away to America. Once she was forced into her marriage to Kit, Garrett had never again spoken of his obvious devotion to her. Instead, he seemed to unleash his pent-up affections on her son—the child he had ushered into the world with his own bare hands.

Shaking herself from her reverie, she announced to Garrett, "You have earned yourself a brandy. In fact, we all have."

Just then they heard sounds of horse's hooves pounding the turf along the winding drive that led to the entrance of the Hall.

"Good heavens!" Rosamund exclaimed, peering out one of the narrow windows that flanked the front door. " 'Tis Kit! His steed is lathered to its neck! That man never did have it in him to treat horseflesh decently."

Garrett and Blythe exchanged glances. Something momentous must have happened for the dour, phlegmatic landowner to expend such energy racing to the door of Barton Hall at breakneck speed. Had the marauding French invaded their shores, as so many feared they would?

Blythe bid the liveried footman open the door. Kit stomped in, breathless. He stood in the foyer and gazed at each of them in turn, his eyes resting, at length, on his wife.

" 'Tis over," he panted, with an odd gleam of triumph in his eyes. " 'Tis finally finished." He extracted a piece of parchment from his coat pocket and waved it in his estranged wife's direction. Then he inhaled deeply, as if to steady himself, and announced, "Ennis has died at sea. Shot by a French musket in a close exchange off the coast of Calais."

Kit's gaze sought each of them in turn, as if he were relishing their shocked reactions, one by one. His roving glance ultimately rested on Blythe, whose lips were parted slightly in an expression more of shock than of dismay. Kit turned to address Garrett.

"His captain says in this missive that the body may be claimed at Plymouth in May when the ship puts into port," he disclosed, pointing a plump forefinger at the official notice of his brother's demise. "It says here they've managed to seal him in a lead-lined coffin of the type they keep in reserve aboard ship for fatally wounded officers. Fortunately, he won't stink too badly." Kit laughed mirthlessly.

"Kit . . . don't!" Garrett protested.

"Don't what?" he asked belligerently. "Don't sound pleased? Grateful? Relieved? Overjoyed?" He shot an indignant glance at his wife. "Well, I am! I am overjoyed! For now, my dear, you shall get the treatment from me you've deserved all along!"

"Kit . . . why not sit down?" Rosamund offered soothingly, perhaps hoping that a glass of brandy might assuage her son-in-law's unseemly display.

Christopher, however, was not to be diverted.

"As long as Ennis was alive," he said for his wife's benefit, "you and that bastard babe had me caught in your damnable web . . . but now I shall alter my will as I please," he proclaimed with a maniacal gleam in his eye. "If you wanted to kill me, now that your lover is dead, 'twould be of no use to you or your by-blow here," he added harshly, gesturing toward the wide-eyed toddler who clung to Blythe's skirts. "There's no younger brother on this earth to claim what is, and always has been, mine!" His gaze narrowed as he crudely pinched Blythe's left breast with his fingertips. "What court would not deem you an adulteress now, my dear?" he hissed between clenched teeth. "Everyone in Cornwall knows our sorry story," he continued, shouting now, "that I have not tasted these fruits since the day Ennis returned to Barton Hall!"

Blythe angrily swatted away Kit's marauding hand and merely stared at her husband. She was astonished to see the change that had come over him. His eyes were alight with determination. His shoulders were thrust back, and he had an air of demonic purpose.

Ennis is dead.

She hardly knew how she felt. Ennis's parting words had been so cruel that they had severed her from all her girlish fantasies. To Blythe's chagrin she had learned the truth about the self-centered artist who she naively thought might save her from the fate that her father and guardian had designed for her.

She glanced at her portrait and the painting Ennis had also done of Kit. Gazing at her ranting husband, she realized that he looked nothing like the artist's flattering rendering of a young landlord in 1792, newly married and the owner of all he surveyed.

"Kit . . . ," she murmured, hoping to calm his fevered raging by a show of gentle supplication. "There is no need for either of us to try to wound each other anymore. Ennis is gone forever," she added quietly. "I'm sorry he won't paint again . . . but my heart is dead to his—"

"*Your* heart! What of *my* heart?" Kit demanded. "What of my *life*, which you and my brother destroyed!" He turned and faced Garrett. "I refuse to claim the carcass of a brother who betrayed me! I refuse to keep a wife in silver and silk who never has been wife to me!" He turned back to Blythe, and she suddenly saw the ultimate damage wrought by Collis Trevelyan. Kit now looked and sounded exactly like his long-dead sire.

"I shall ride this night for London!" he announced with a bitterness that was palpable. "My brother's bastard shall not inherit either Trevelyan House or Barton Hall. Ennis is *dead*!" he repeated shrilly. "And I *live*, if only to divorce you and marry again! At last I need not be chained henceforth to him, nor to you, you wicked slut! I will plow my fields and make them fertile. I will find a wench and make her my legal wife and give her my seed for nights on end until I have a *son*!"

Kit was gasping for breath, unable to shout any more threats. Garrett took a step forward and rested a restraining hand lightly on his cousin's arm.

"Kit . . . Kit, listen to me, my man. . . ."

"Leave me be!" he whispered hoarsely. "I will not bury that sod. If you wish to, you can claim the body from the *Neptune* when it puts into port. As for me," he said, casting a haggard glance in Blythe's direction, "I shall be off this night to plead my cause before the courts. You are an adulteress!" he shouted, his voice rising to the rafters once again. He pointed at William, who had begun to cry and cling anxiously to Blythe's skirts. "That bastard child is all the proof I need to succeed in my petition. When you receive the bill of divorcement, you shall quit these premises forthwith!"

"You're mad!" Blythe cried. "William and I shall never leave this place! 'Tis my home!"

"Oh, yes, you *shall*!"

Everyone stood frozen in a horrified tableau as Kit's words rang out in the Hall. Then stunned silence followed in Kit's wake as he stormed out the front door and rode off toward Trevelyan House.

Before long the inhabitants of Barton Hall learned to their

dismay that Kit Trevelyan remained true to his word. At first, during the long winter of 1793 and into the spring, Blythe heard nothing from, or about, Kit's machinations in London.

Then, in early May 1794, a stranger appeared at the door with official notices of a judgment of adultery from the House of Lords—endorsed by the ecclesiastical court—and an order to remove Blythe, her mother, and her bastard son from Barton Hall by the end of the week.

Why hadn't she shot Christopher Trevelyan when she'd had the gun aimed at his heart! Blythe thought with mounting panic.

She gazed toward the Channel, smooth as a baby's skin this bright spring afternoon. Barton Hall had never looked so lovely. The gardens were at the height of their bloom, and the sun overhead cast a quality of golden light that made the lush green fields seem to glow like polished emeralds.

She would be destitute, she thought with a swift intake of breath. She reread the parchments embellished on their lower left corners with official red wax seals. She would be a subject of gossip and derision . . . a scarlet woman, forced to earn her bread with her unskilled hands, or worse, with her body on the narrow, filthy streets of Gorran Haven.

Even Garrett Teague could do little to help her, living, as he did, in cramped quarters above his bookshop while looking after an ailing mother.

A feeling of desperation seized her as she realized that William's guardian wasn't even here to offer counsel. Garrett had gone to Plymouth to retrieve the lead casket from the deck of the Royal Navy ship *Neptune*—as Kit knew he would.

Blythe glanced around the long dining-room table where she was studying the parchments that had been delivered by Kit's new man of affairs. Silver platters lined the shelves of the Welsh dresser. On the wall opposite, several pieces of silver engraved with the Barton coat of arms stood on the mahogany sideboard. The polished metal gleamed in the shafts of sun that poured through the casement windows. She thought of the day five years earlier when she had stashed the family silver in her portmanteau, foolishly believing that Ennis Trevelyan would step forward as her savior and elope with her to Italy.

It had been Garrett Teague, all along, who had loved her and had been willing to risk everything to escape with her to America.

She picked up a silver water jug and thought back to her hellish wedding night when she lay limp in Kit's arms and allowed him to think he could possess her. Grazing her thumb along the crest engraved with sheaves of wheat on its escutcheon, she concluded she couldn't fight the Trevelyans then, and she couldn't fight them now. She could merely plot an escape for herself and Garrett from this damnable country where only the eldest son succeeded, regardless of talent or wit. And she would make certain the cursed Trevelyans would never track her down.

And, suddenly, Blythe Barton Trevelyan knew precisely what she must do.

"Mary Ann, you silly chit . . . calm yourself at once!" Blythe commanded the tearful maid who stood near bales and boxes of goods being loaded and unloaded from ships tied up at Plymouth's western quay. The *Argus* lay at berth next to the Royal Navy vessel *Neptune*. The passenger ship was being made ready to depart on the following Friday for Annapolis, Maryland, in the former Colonies. Blythe fully intended that she, Garrett, her lady's maid, and the baby would sail with her.

There was good reason for the three-master to be berthed near the *Neptune*. Blythe had learned this morning that the eighty-four-gun frigate would escort the smaller ship beyond the French-infested Channel to the open sea. The madmen in France had declared war against England in February of 1793. Now, over a year later, word had reached Cornish shores in May that the leftist Danton had been executed in April and that the butcher, Robespierre, was all-powerful in Paris.

" 'Twas an awful mistake to come down here, mum," Mary

Ann pronounced, gazing apprehensively at a swarm of rough stevedores bustling about the quay. " 'Tis no place for decent women here on the wharves!"

"We can't very well find Mr. Teague if we don't look for him, can we?" Blythe demanded curtly. "Meanwhile, see that you attend properly to Master William, and leave me to worry how we shall manage."

Mary Ann had stubbornly refused to be left alone at the inn, and thus Blythe had been forced to stash the heavy portmanteau, filled with Barton family silver, under her bed. A few of the smaller items emblazoned with the family crests, along with six small but exquisite silver platters, were hidden under a pile of the baby's dirty rags, which Blythe had heaped in the corner of their bug-infested quarters. She kept the dueling pistol tucked beneath her cloak for protection, even though it was cumbersome to transport in this fashion. So cumbersome, in fact, that she had been forced to leave its twin in the drawer beside her bed at Barton Hall.

Fifteen-month-old William sat perched on the housemaid's hip, sucking on his middle finger while he surveyed the bustling quay like a contented pasha. William had his mother's dark hair and vivid coloring, along with Ennis's way of viewing the world calmly, as if he were surveying what in it might be of use or of pleasure to him.

Blythe had unhappily discovered when she'd arrived in Plymouth that Garrett was no longer in residence at the Pope's Head Inn. However, she had learned from the surly innkeeper that the *Neptune* remained in port to be refitted for its next voyage. She had scratched a note to the captain and now was waiting at the bottom of the gangway for a reply. Within the hour a young man resplendent in a red lieutenant's uniform made his way over to them.

"Mrs. Trevelyan?" he inquired. From the way he glanced at Mary Ann, Blythe knew that he was puzzled that a woman of such obvious means had no male servant attending her in such boisterous, disreputable environs.

"Yes," she said eagerly. "Is Mr. Teague aboard? Seeing to arrangements concerning my deceased brother-in-law, I trust?"

"No," the young officer said briskly, taking her measure. "He's already departed Plymouth."

"When?" Blythe asked, her heart sinking.

"Yesterday. He hired a small sloop to sail close to the shore and is transporting his cousin's heavy casket by sea. I believe he said the family plot is in Gorran Haven. Isn't that where your people are from? I fear you have come all this way to no purpose. However," he offered, casting a suggestive leer, "perhaps I could be of some assistance while my ship is in port?"

Blythe was instantly aware that the officer suspected that she was merely some abandoned doxy of Garrett's, or a local tart he'd picked up while taking care of this sorry business in Plymouth. For her part, she was too distressed at hearing the news of Garrett's departure to bristle with indignation at his insulting behavior.

"He's returning to Gorran Haven by boat?" Blythe echoed faintly. No wonder she and Garrett hadn't passed each other on the road to Plymouth—as she was sure they would have, if he'd already completed his task and had been heading home. It never occurred to her he wouldn't bring Ennis's body back by wagon.

The bravado that had carried her this far suddenly evaporated. By the time she returned to the inn, Mary Ann added to Blythe's misery by loudly voicing her reproach.

"We've come all this way on a goose chase!" she said. "Mr. Ennis couldna have a care whether he's buried at St. Goran's or Neptune's grave!"

Wordlessly they mounted the stairs to their dingy room at the back of the hostelry. Their quarters were in the least desirable location imaginable, and Blythe suspected that such rooms were routinely assigned to women who were unaccompanied by male protectors.

The instant the two women entered their dismal chamber,

Blythe realized that someone had rifled its contents. Her portmanteau sat on the bed, devoid of its valuable contents. The only item within the four walls that had been left undisturbed was the pile of William's dirty swaddling. The rags reeked malodorously, even from the threshold.

"Jesu!" Blythe cried, hurrying inside. "Damn! Damn! Damn!"

From the truculent attitude of the innkeeper, Blythe suspected that he or his minions had numbered among the thieves.

"Pray, mum, let us return home straightaway!" Mary Ann wailed. "Plymouth is a horrid, foul place."

Blythe surveyed the paltry few pieces of engraved silverware that she had retrieved from under William's filthy rags. They were all that remained of the booty she had taken in the dead of night from Barton Hall. Distraught, she wondered if such diminished treasure would provide enough capital to purchase passage for two adults and an infant to Annapolis and leave enough to launch Blythe and her son in a modest new life, far from Cornwall—and without the company of Garrett Teague.

"We can't go home," she said dully.

"W-what?" stammered Mary Ann.

"They think I'm dead."

"But, mum!" protested the maid. "What cause have they to think such a thing?"

"There will be signs enough to give them reason to suppose you ran away and I took my own life," she said slowly. "If we return to Barton Hall, I truly believe that my husband . . . my *former* husband," she corrected herself carefully, "will kill me—or have us both hanged from a tree as thieves."

Ennis Trevelyan was laid to rest beside his father in a prominent location in St. Goran's churchyard on a gloomy May morning that could have passed for November.

Garrett had heard the news about the disappearance of the

mistress of Barton Hall as soon as he'd dropped anchor in Gorran Haven.

"Vanished into thin air, she did," the harbormaster said wonderingly. "There's not a trace of her or the babe, though I heard that the best of the Barton silver's been pinched. Some folks think they were murrr-dered, along with the housemaid," he said in a low voice, "and the bodies thrown into the sea. Some say as Trevelyan himself did it—or had it done!"

"He's back, then, from London?" Garrett asked, reeling from the shocking tale.

"Just returned," the harbormaster revealed. "I heard he's a-ranting and a-raving! Wants to evict her in person, they say, and wants to know where the Barton silver's got to. A right crackbrain, he is these days, from all accounts. Touched in the 'ead. But, then," he added sagely, "that vixen of a wife drove him to it."

Garrett had Ennis's casket transported directly to St. Goran's churchyard and buried without ceremony. The Reverend Randolph Kent stood soberly by as the gravediggers heaped the moist soil onto the lid of the coffin with dispatch.

"Has anyone heard word of or seen Mrs. Trevelyan yet?" Garrett asked the cleric, not convinced that the harbormaster wasn't spinning a fanciful tale.

"Not a trace," the vicar said softly. "I knew that marriage was against God's law. I blame myself for not standing up to that tyrant." He gestured at the massive Trevelyan family headstone. "There lies Collis Trevelyan, in his grave years now, and still the man's greed does the work of the devil!" He stared at Ennis's lead-lined coffin now mounded with fresh, moist soil. "There'll be more graves in this cursed plot of ground before this story ends," he pronounced.

Garrett looked sharply at Reverend Kent. He'd heard talk that this man of the cloth was wont to employ some sort of murky mirror to look into the future. A "shewing stone," some gossip at the bookshop had told him in hushed tones.

"Let's hope not," Garrett replied, anxious to make his way to Barton Hall and investigate these matters for himself.

Blythe Barton had a will of iron and a constitution stronger than the rocky cliffs on Dodman Point, he thought. Who knew better than he did what strong stuff she was made of? He'd pulled little William from her bloody loins and watched her fight for her life with nothing but his hand to hold on to. It would take a force of nature to slay her, he told himself.

Or a crackbrain.

Trevelyan House was deserted as if a plague had swept through it in Garrett's absence. At Barton Hall he encountered a few servants huddled together in the large kitchen. A spring storm had risen up suddenly, and rain hissed on the logs as it pelted down the large chimney where meals were cooked for the castle's inhabitants.

"Where is Mrs. Trevelyan's mother . . . Mrs. Barton?" he demanded.

"She'un left for London town," one scullery maid ventured timidly. "Says she'll not stand for the master's loony tricks. Gone to her sister's, I wager. Real sickly, she looked, but I packed for her, and Charles took her trunks t'the fly over t'Bodmin Moor this mornin'."

"And Mr. Trevelyan?" Garrett inquired uneasily.

"Came to Trevelyan House yesterday, and here by suppertime, wavin' his decrees and such," the cook revealed. "Right mad with disappointment he couldna throw her out! Searched high and low . . . every chamber and cupboard. Even climbed the four towers, he did, addlepated that he be. We told 'im she and Master William disappeared a week since, but he'd not believe us."

"Accused us of pinching the silver, he did!" the scullery maid announced, red-faced with indignation. "Said he'd send whoever did it to the gallows—or for transportation," she added, shuddering.

"Where is he now?" Garrett asked, filled with foreboding.

"Painter's Cottage," grunted the cook. "Went down there an

hour ago and h'ain't been seen since. And if I had m'wish, he'd fall off the cliff!"

The cottage stood forlornly at the edge of the waterlogged field. Its windows were dark, and its front door stood open to the beating wind and swirling mist. Kit was slumped in a chair in the shadowy stone chamber. His expanding paunch provided a resting place for a small piece of parchment that he clutched in his pudgy right hand. Several official-looking decrees, resplendent with their red wax seals affixed at the bottom, littered the stone floor.

Kit's stringy, unkempt hair fell about his shoulders. The front of his linen shirt was stained, as if he had not changed it upon arriving home from London. The deep pits puncturing the skin on his face stood out in sharp relief, like some woeful lunar landscape. He looked up with bloodshot eyes, a brandy bottle dangling from the other hand.

"May I see?" Garrett asked softly. A growing sense of dread sent shock waves down his arm so that he could hardly hold the foolscap that displayed Blythe's distinctive hand.

> *I cannot fight you anymore. Take*
> *Barton Hall, and may all the misery*
> *it has caused me be on your head*
> *and haunt you the rest of your days.*
> *And if your seed should see the light*
> *of day . . . I swear by St. Goran I shall*
> *curse your heirs from the watery grave*
> *I now seek.*
> *May you hear my cries in the wind and*
> *the rain. May you hear my babe's*
> *moans when the sheep miscarry and*
> *the cattle waste away. By all that's*
> *holy, Kit Trevelyan, you are rid of me and*
> *my line . . . but may yours never prosper.*
>
> *Blythe Barton of Barton Hall*

Kit remained motionless, staring through the open door to the English Channel. Garrett followed his line of vision and was startled by the sight of an overturned dinghy, floating in the choppy waters at the mouth of the cove.

"What in damnation—?" Garrett said hoarsely.

He grabbed his staghorn walking stick, bolted out of the cottage, and raced to the cliff. He was forced to squint through needles of rain that soon turned into a heavy downpour.

The small skiff bobbed in place, an indication that Blythe had taken the boat into deep water and anchored it with a rock tied to a length of hemp that was fastened to the bow. As he gazed at the churning waters of Veryan Bay, he felt a part of himself break away and drift out to sea.

After a while he became aware of Kit's presence, standing to his right side.

"When 'tis calm," Kit said in a strangled voice, "I shall drag the bottom of the cove and recover the silver."

Garrett turned to face his cousin, who stood unsteadily at the edge of the cliff. The bookseller knew, suddenly, that he was capable of committing murder.

"You swine!" he cursed, barely above a whisper.

Kit cocked his head and shifted uneasily on his feet.

"What say you . . . ?" he mumbled with a befuddled expression clouding his haggard eyes.

"I, of the cursed three of us, loved her best, you Trevelyan sod!" Garrett shouted to the rising wind. He turned suddenly and pushed against Kit's shoulders with the length of his walking stick clutched in both hands. The force of the blow sent his corpulent cousin reeling to the soggy ground. "I loved her . . . I *loved* her. . . ." Garrett's words were carried on the stiff breeze for a mere instant and then came back to him full force. "I loved her," he cried brokenly. "And I loved her babe. I shall never forgive you and Ennis for what you have done!"

Slowly Kit struggled to his feet as the rain and wind howling off Dodman Point lashed at their clothes.

"And I shall never forgive *her* for what she has done," Kit answered heavily, "for my wedded wife never . . . loved me . . . at all."

Then the owner of the Barton-Trevelyan estate heaved a shrug and wove a meandering path toward Painter's Cottage, disappearing within the maw of its open door. Within minutes the wind and rain suddenly quieted, and an eerie calm descended on the cliff where Garrett stood, leaning against his staghorn staff.

He flinched when he heard the report of a pistol from inside the cottage. However, his boots remained planted in the dewy grass as he continued to gaze out to sea. Once again his despondent glance drifted to the overturned dinghy as it swayed in the surging tide. Long after he was dead and buried in St. Goran's churchyard, the Channel's watery rhythms would ebb and flow.

Eventually the tall, dark-haired figure turned his back to the sea and made for the gate at the far side of the field. He strode past the stone abode without even glancing through the tall artist's window. In ten minutes' time he had retraced his steps along Hall Walk.

Until Garrett Teague came within view of the castle's four towers rising above a thousand shades of green, it did not occur to the proprietor of the modest bookshop nestled in Rattle Alley that he—the last remaining male of his generation—was now the unchallenged master of Barton Hall.

Chapter Seventeen

September 8, 1994

"So," Blythe exclaimed with an amazed expression, "William was Blythe Barton and Ennis Trevelyan's out-of-wedlock son!"

Valerie pointed to a pad she had used to scribble notes while Blythe had been under hypnosis.

"Apparently William and his mother sailed for America in May of 1794," the psychologist added.

"Exactly two hundred years ago last spring," Blythe interjected. "In the same month I arrived at Barton Hall. Holy cow, Valerie! This is actually getting creepy."

"Perhaps you've found the link to your branch of the Bartons, after all," Valerie ventured as she carefully eased the crystal ball back into its velvet pouch and replaced it in the bottom drawer of her desk.

"My *father's* name is Will!" Blythe suddenly blurted. "All this time I've been searching for a William who lived and died in Cornwall! The Will-William connection never occurred to me because my dad's always been called just plain Will." Then her face fell. "Of course, both the names William and Barton are fairly common in America. If Blythe and her son survived the voyage to Annapolis, they could have remained in the southern states. We still have no proof this is the branch that eventually migrated to Wyoming."

"But your name is Blythe," Valerie insisted, "and that is

rather unusual, especially coupled with 'Barton.' It seems to me that it's a reasonably good indication there's a connection here, somewhere. Plus, didn't you tell me your grandmother insisted that your parents carry on the tradition of naming the eldest daughter in the family after a famous ancestress from Cornwall? Perhaps it was also a tradition in your branch to name the eldest son William after the original Blythe's natural son?"

"But wouldn't the eighteenth-century William's last name be Trevelyan, not Barton? After all, he was Ennis Trevelyan's son, too."

"Back then . . . and even in this century as well," Valerie said thoughtfully, "children born out of wedlock usually took their mother's maiden name. It's perfectly possible Blythe's son went by the surname of Barton—especially if your namesake had washed her hands of the Trevelyans, as her supposed suicide note indicated."

"So our branch might definitely have originated on the wrong side of the blanket." Blythe grinned lamely. "This is all pretty amazing, isn't it?"

"The specific information you've retrieved under hypnosis is what I find amazing."

"Maybe I should have been a screenwriter instead of a production designer. I could hypnotize myself whenever I want to cook up some fabulous film plots!"

"But is it mere invention?" Valerie mused. "So many of the details of what you say you saw in your trance match up to actual facts I've gleaned from Reverend Kent's diary. Too many for it just to be coincidence, you might say."

"Let's just call it a 'Capital *C*' coincidence and leave it at that," Blythe answered uncomfortably. "I'm beginning to feel like I've become some paranormal tuning fork. You know: Got a message from the past? Twang it to Blythe!"

"So . . . ," Valerie inquired of the younger woman who sat across the desk from her, "has our session been of any real use in trying to resolve some of the personal problems you're grappling with?"

"I'm certain about one thing," Blythe declared, rising to prepare for her departure. "Back in 1794 each of the family members blamed someone else for the tragedies that occurred. Not one of them forgave each other for the hurt he or she had inflicted. Blythe . . . Kit . . . Ennis . . . even Garrett—they all held on to those resentments and jealousies throughout their lives. And as for Kit Trevelyan," she added soberly, "jealousy and resentment drove him to suicide."

"Now, suppose the traumas that happened so long ago at Barton Hall caused some sort of genetic alteration in the survivors," Valerie postulated. "There are some theorists who believe the body stores both physical and emotional toxins for a long time . . . perhaps for decades. These are what might alter the cells and change the DNA of succeeding generations."

"So if the Wyoming Bartons are, in fact, descendants of the Cornwall Barton-Trevelyans," Blythe mused, "then you're saying that Luke, Ellie, and I are supposedly carrying around a bunch of eighteenth-century emotional poisons? What a troubling idea!" she exclaimed. She glanced at her watch and grimaced. "Speaking of traumas . . . I've got to go back to the cottage and get ready for a dinner date—with my ex-husband."

Late that afternoon Blythe rounded the curve on the coastal path and spotted Luke's Land Rover whizzing down the road toward Painter's Cottage. Her heart gave a lurch as she watched its owner get out of the vehicle and unlatch the gate in the field. He had obviously come to pay her a call.

When she walked through the door five minutes later, he was waiting for her inside.

"You did a very clever vanishing act from my bedroom this morning," he said tersely. He slapped his leather driving gloves against one palm, a sure sign he was either incensed or genuinely worried about her absence.

Guess!

"Look, Luke, I . . . ah . . ."

"Then you refused to speak with me in the sitting room and disappeared for hours," he continued, punctuating his words with a toss of his gloves onto her dining table. "I drove by here several times to see if you'd come back, but you hadn't."

"I-I took a long walk," she replied, doffing her Barbour coat and hanging it on a peg. She hadn't told too bold a fib. She had walked at least two miles to and from Drs. Vickery and Kent's office in the village. En route she had stopped for a bit of lunch to ward off any incipient stomach upset and then had purchased three boxes of saltine crackers, which she'd crammed into her backpack for the trip back to the cottage.

"A six-hour walk?"

"Luke," she intervened hastily, "I'm sorry you were running around looking for me. I suppose one day you'll have to put a phone and an answering machine in here . . . or at least an intercom system or something."

Luke ignored her suggestion and said, "Your lawyer, Miss Spector, called the Hall this morning. It seems she is most anxious to speak with you." He studied his watch. "It was midnight in California when she called. It's the next morning there now. She's probably just getting to her office."

"Thanks for coming all the way down here to deliver the message."

Luke gazed at her quizzically. "I'll drive you to the house to ring her back, if you like."

"Thanks," Blythe repeated, "but I don't want to call her just now."

"But your dinner with your—with Christopher Stowe?" Luke amended carefully. "Didn't you promise him this morning you'd give him your answer about the Scottish property?"

"As you said yourself," she reminded him with a faint smile, "it's my decision to make, not my lawyer's."

"And?" Luke demanded.

"And I'm afraid I'll be late if I don't move my tail and start getting dressed. Chris is due here any minute," she added pointedly.

"You're going to sign over the forest property to him, aren't you?" Luke said dully.

"I haven't decided."

"Oh, Christ, Blythe! Can't you see he still has the ability to manipulate you? He flashes his so-called artistic genius to get you to do what is good for him, regardless of what's in your interest."

"That's probably true," she agreed calmly.

"Then why do you allow him to do it?" Luke demanded. "Why are you going to give him what he wants?"

"I haven't done that yet," she gently pointed out.

Luke searched her face for some sign of exactly what she meant by her enigmatic statement. She walked over to the electric kettle and started water boiling for a cup of tea. It was close to dusk, and she needed a pick-me-up, considering her lack of sleep the last twenty-four hours. And besides, tea and saltine crackers seemed to help in staving off her persistent twenty-four-hour brand of morning sickness.

"I'd like to talk to you about Chloe," Luke said in a low voice, abruptly changing the tenor of their conversation.

Blythe turned around to look him squarely in the eye. She held up both hands as if to ward off his words and replied, "Whatever all that was . . . or is . . . there's no need for explanation."

"But it wasn't and isn't anything!" Luke protested. "I told you . . . there's been no other serious relationship in my life since Lindsay! Chloe has always wanted things to get more serious, but—"

"There's no need to justify what went on before we met, Luke," Blythe tried to reassure him.

"But that's the point!" he exclaimed with frustration. "Nothing . . . significant . . . had gone on! Chloe's always . . . she just pops down and—"

"So I've noticed," Blythe said wryly.

Luke continued, oblivious to her attempt to make his explanation easier for him. "Before you arrived last spring, I was thinking that perhaps . . . that is, well . . . Chloe was Richard's godmother, and I thought—for a time—that perhaps we might try . . . but then you—"

Luke suddenly halted, midsentence, as if he were becoming increasingly unable to choose his words properly.

"Luke! I *understand*! But I've got to get ready!"

"Oh, bloody hell! I can't talk to you anymore!"

"Yes, you can," she said more quietly. "And I can talk to you—and I want to—but *not now*, Luke! I've got to get dressed for dinner."

"Of course," he replied, rising as if to depart. "The Great One has snapped his fingers—"

Blythe suddenly burst out laughing.

"What's so blooming funny?" he demanded.

"That's what I always called Chris behind his back. 'The Great One.' " She was convulsed in giggles. "He'd rant and rave about something that wasn't getting done to his impossibly high standard, and then he'd literally snap his fingers at his underlings and walk off, satisfied that he'd made everyone cower."

"You couldn't have been pleased to be put in such a difficult position. There you were, his wife and his employee."

"It could be very tough," Blythe agreed soberly. "That's why I called him 'The Great One' to the film crew . . . so they'd see I understood their plight."

"But you were at his mercy, as well," he countered. "And it would appear that you still are."

"Oh, Luke . . . ," she began gently, reaching for his hand. "Remember that first day when we made love . . . and you said that both our hearts were sore? It's still true. I think we both have a certain amount of personal baggage left from the time before we met. I know I do."

"I suppose you mean to say that everything that has happened between us was just an interlude?" he demanded. "That now you're going to return to your real life?"

"No . . . that's not it at all," she protested. "What I'm saying is that your relationship with Chloe and with your son, and the tidying up I still need to do with Chris . . . these are *separate* issues. And I know, as far as I'm concerned—however it turns out between you and me—I can't go forward until I've cleaned up the debris left over from before."

"And I'm supposed to do the same?"

"That's up to you."

"Well, there's nothing to 'clean up,' as you put it, between Chloe and me," he replied curtly, "regardless of the fact she barged in on us this morning. And I don't exactly see how my losing my wife to cancer and your divorcing Christopher Stowe equate. As for Richard—"

Blythe held both hands up once again.

"Okay! Okay! I'm the one with the baggage."

And oh, brother . . . was it ever heavy, she thought with a sinking heart.

Surprisingly, Luke suddenly reached out and drew her to him in a fierce embrace.

"Oh, Blythe . . . I don't want to lose you to him."

"Luke," she sighed. "It's not a contest."

"It feels like one," he said, resting his chin on the top of her head.

"That's such a guy thing," she laughed unsteadily.

"Don't go tonight," he said in a low, urgent voice. "I'll tell him when he comes here that he has to leave . . . that you don't want anything to do with him or his demands any longer."

She closed her eyes and luxuriated in the feeling of his body pressed against her. It would be so easy to let this strong, protective man tell Christopher Stowe to go to hell.

Nothin's for free in this life, m'girl.

Blythe suddenly felt as if she were in dire danger of bartering away yet another piece of her soul in exchange for Luke's affection.

"Luke," she said softly against his chest, "I'm the one who has to talk to Chris." She leaned back in his arms to study his lean face and troubled blue eyes. "But you are dear to offer to fight my battles for me."

"It appears you rather enjoy fighting them yourself," he replied, letting go of her abruptly. "As my dear cousin Valerie would probably say . . . perhaps you're addicted to his kind of treatment."

"That's a cheap shot," Blythe retorted.

"Or perhaps you realize, seeing him again in that ridiculously gaudy car, that you miss the glamour of your former life?" he said, his eyes suddenly glinting with anger.

"We're divorced!" she snapped, her ration of patience reaching its limit. "He's married to my sister now, for God's sake. They have a child!"

"I expect that Cornwall's isolation and our simple life are no longer quaint novelties for your racy Hollywood soul," he continued with veiled sarcasm. "Perhaps you don't even intend to see the nursery project through?"

Blythe suddenly recalled the Barton Family Graduated System of meting out punishment to misbehaving children.

Strike one! she warned Luke silently.

"Is that what's at the bottom of these insults?" Blythe asked, her temper beginning to flare. "You're not as concerned about my well-being as whether you can save your precious estate—is *that* the problem?"

"Well, are you going to see it through?" Luke demanded. "Or are you going to leave at the crucial moment?"

Blythe felt tears of anger and frustration clog her throat. It was almost as if Luke *expected* her to leave him . . . as if he had been accustomed to the women in his life abandoning him "at the crucial moment," as he put it. He had never talked intimately about the period leading up to Lindsay's death . . . nor what it was like for him in the aftermath. She suddenly thought of Luke's ancestor, Garrett Teague. Had he felt the same way about the Blythe Barton he had loved? As far as Garrett had known, Blythe had taken her own life without a word of farewell to the one person who had remained unfailingly loyal. Was Luke's attitude the result of some sort of lingering byte of genetic memory, as Valerie had postulated? Or was it simply a matter of a man who had shut down his emotions following the death of his wife?

Blythe silently despaired as she gazed at the immobile mask that was Luke's face. If the man made a practice of steadfastly denying the facts of his emotional life, she realized sadly, she certainly couldn't do his feeling for him. In these cases, as Grandma Barton used to say, it was best to "stick to her own knitting."

"I, of course, will support Barton Hall Nurseries, as I have agreed to do in our contract," Blythe assured him with as much calm as she could muster.

"Just with money?" he asked in a clipped tone.

"Read the contract," she retorted.

It was the old, brittle Blythe speaking, and she hated the bitchiness in her own voice.

Just then they both became aware of the purr of a car pulling up to the cottage. Chris's Rolls appeared starkly out of place parked beside Luke's battle-scarred Land Rover.

"Well . . . I'll just be off," Luke said brusquely, adding, "I find myself with a dinner date tonight as well."

"You do? Where?" Blythe demanded, thinking of Richard, who was probably still recovering from the previous night's trauma and needed his father's reassuring company.

"At Barton Hall, funnily enough," he disclosed with studied nonchalance. "Chloe's apparently asked Mrs. Q to whip up a cozy supper in front of the fire."

"That's *two*!" Blythe shot back, waggling her fingers at him. "Where I come from, three strikes and you're out!" Chloe had returned, just as Mrs. Q predicted. "Do give my love to Richard—if you see him," she added with mannered sweetness.

"I've locked him in one of the towers for the night," Luke snapped. She stared at him openmouthed. "For Christ's sake,

Blythe," Luke said, really angry now, "I'm not Bluebeard where my son is concerned, I assure you! I'll give Richard your regards. Good night."

And with that he stalked out of the cottage and practically collided with Blythe's incoming visitor.

"Not interrupting anything, I trust?" Chris inquired in a solicitous tone of voice.

"Just business," Luke muttered darkly, striding toward his car. He climbed in, slammed shut the driver's-side door, and started the engine. Then he thrust the vehicle in gear and sped noisily across the field. Midway to the gate he laid a heavy hand on the horn to warn any hapless sheep in his path.

"I came round a bit early," Chris announced, waving a bottle of Cuvée Dom Pérignon champagne at Blythe, who stood at the door, silently watching Luke's car disappear around the curve in the road. She glanced overhead at a flock of herring gulls who cawed raucously above the cliff in the golden light of sunset. How, she wondered, could life have suddenly become so complicated in such a remote and pastoral setting? "The weather's turned so fine," Chris continued, "I thought we could enjoy your view with a bit of the bubbly in hand." He paused, taking in the sight of her jeans and sweater. "Darling Minnie Rag Bag . . . I fear that a bit more formal attire is in order at Boscundle Manor in the evenings."

"Open the champagne," she directed testily, "and I'll just get dressed."

During their evening meal in the candlelit dining room at the charming country hotel set in the outskirts of the town of St. Austell, Blythe felt as if she were in two places at once.

In her mind's eye she pictured Luke and Chloe sitting at a small linen-draped table in front of a crackling fire in the library. No doubt Richard had been exiled to the kitchen, eating his supper with the Quillers, while Derek and Beryl were curled up in their posh wicker dog baskets near the hearth.

She vowed that if Mrs. Quiller served them her chocolate cake during their romantic little tête-à-tête, Blythe might actually slip poison in Chloe's morning coffee.

Meanwhile, Christopher had arranged for a sumptuous repast at Boscundle Manor. There was a flurry of bowing and scraping on the part of staff members as Blythe and the celebrated director were relieved of their coats and ushered into the dining room. As promised, Mrs. Stowe the Younger was nowhere in evidence.

"Even if you'd agreed to dine with us both, Ellie was forced to remain at the Smugglers' Hotel in Gorran Haven tonight," Chris said, pouring himself another glass of champagne as soon as they'd taken their seats. "Her Nibs has contracted a cold, and so has Baby Nibs."

Blythe glanced over at her former husband, wondering what sort of description her sister had given Chris of their confrontation at Painter's Cottage the previous day.

"Is the baby all right?" Blythe inquired carefully. "There's a GP just down the street from you in Rattle Alley. A Dr. Vickery."

Chris waited to reply while their waiter snatched Blythe's snowy linen napkin from beside her plate and snapped it out of its exotic folds in an exceedingly startling fashion. Then he placed it in her lap with exaggerated flourish.

"I'm sure they'll both be fine," Christopher said, utterly ignoring the ardent attendant when his own napkin was unfurled with a similar dramatic effect. He studied her face closely over the rim of his wine goblet. "Dear, dear Blythe . . . always so adept at coping with an emergency. I miss that admirable trait of yours, I can assure you . . . both on and off the set."

Blythe listened carefully for any hint of mockery in his voice and found none.

In fact, it seemed to her that his smile kindled with a warmth that had been missing between them for a couple of years. He laughed softly and said, "Jeff Raymos said just ten days ago—

you remember him, don't you?" Chris interrupted himself parenthetically. "The production coordinator? Well, Jeff was telling someone on the set about the time you climbed into that big-rig truck—when the number-two stunt driver got hurt, remember? 'That amazing woman coolly wheeled that ten-ton monster down the San Diego Freeway during the chase scene in *Good Chemistry* so we wouldn't go into Golden-Golden Overtime!' Now, *that* was something your admiring colleagues won't soon forget, I assure you . . . nor will I." Chris's handsome features grew somber as he added, "That was a fifty-thousand-dollar shoot that day. It was a pivotal scene, and it would have all gone down the plug hole if it hadn't been for you."

"I expect the union would have supplied a replacement by midday," Blythe replied mildly, lowering her eyes as she sipped from her water glass.

"But the Paramount suits would have had my hide for the overtime," he countered.

"*Our* hide," she reminded him. "*Good Chemistry* was a Stowe and Stowe Production, remember?"

"I certainly do." Chris's pale-blue eyes surveyed her black silk evening suit with approval. "My darling Blythe, you may have amazing capabilities both as a production designer and a lorry driver," he said fondly, "but damned if you don't also look like a bloody film star tonight."

To her astonishment her sister's new husband was gazing at her now with undisguised affection, apparently unleashed by a second bottle of champagne. She began to feel uncomfortable under the heat of his ardent gaze.

"Look, Christopher . . . ," she ventured, and then cast her eyes about Boscundle Manor's elegant dining room in an attempt to catch their crestfallen waiter's eye so they could proceed with ordering their meal. "I'm famished," she lied. "Flag that fellow again, will you?"

The manor house–cum–country hotel had been constructed in 1650 of blushing pink granite chiseled from a local quarry.

It had been built for an Admiral Truebody, Chris had explained breezily on the ride over. As soon as the Rolls-Royce had pulled into the gravel courtyard, they had been effusively welcomed by the proprietors, Andrew and Mary Flynt.

The Flynts had transformed the small, low-ceilinged dining room into a charming, intimate space where a mere eight tables in various sizes and shapes served a select clientele. Their dapper maître d' had ushered them to a table for two set like a throne and positioned against one wall, where all the other diners were sure to recognize them. Blythe felt as if she were suddenly thrust back to the days when Chris's Hollywood publicist engineered center stage for his boss whenever they went to Spago's or Bernard's.

At their seats a crystal vase with yellow water iris welcomed them, along with a second bottle of champagne cooling in a silver ice bucket. On the dining-room walls, their waiter had earnestly explained, were the works of celebrated local artists. The paintings depicted Cornish scenes on sunny days—in stark contrast to Ennis Trevelyan's moody views of the windswept coastline.

"I'm not too proud to admit that I've sorely missed your professional contributions," Chris interrupted her reverie. He reached for her hand across the crisp white damask tablecloth. Out of the corner of her eye Blythe saw that one woman was staring at them with avid curiosity, poised over her potted shrimp. "And that's certainly not all I've missed, Blythe, darling."

She gently withdrew from his grasp and took a sip of her mineral water. Chris had looked at her with puzzlement when she had refused all repeated offers of spirits.

"Ellie came to the cottage yesterday," Blythe disclosed conversationally, although her pulse rate felt as if it were speeding up at the mere mention of their previous encounter. "Did she tell you?"

Chris nodded. "She did, indeed." He took another draft of champagne and then gazed at her steadily over the rim of his glass. "I hope you'll believe me when I say that I didn't ask her to do that. In fact, I told her to stay away, as you requested."

"It felt just like old times," Blythe replied sardonically.

"Pretty poisonous, I gather."

"She demanded that I sign over the Scottish property, of course."

Christopher began to toy with his fork. Then he cast a glance across the dining room at their waiter, who leaped to attention as if galvanized by an electric cattle prod. The attendant uncorked the Lafite Rothschild '89—a spectacular claret—and, before Blythe could decline, poured them each a glass. Then the waiter took their orders and discreetly retreated to an alcove, awaiting, she supposed, the next wave of Chris's hand.

He just makes movies! she wanted to yell at everybody in the room. *He's not the Dalai Lama!*

After a moment Blythe's former husband looked up from the silverware and declared quietly, "Surely you must also feel—as I do—that Ellie is sometimes driven by demons even she doesn't understand." When Blythe offered no further comment, he ventured, "Was your sister always such a . . . solitary soul?"

"Are you asking me, 'Is she moody?' or 'Does she prefer spending time on her own?' " Blythe inquired warily.

"Both," Chris replied. "I've discovered, to my shock, that she hates to travel. She cannot stand living on location, she says . . . and she utterly detests the industry functions one must attend constantly."

"I could have told you that, if only you'd asked earlier," Blythe commented evenly.

Letting the remark pass, Chris set his fork back down beside his plate. "Everything seems such a drama to her," he added glumly, "especially since the baby arrived. She's sure I'm having it on with every bit of fluff who looks at me cross-eyed."

"Are you?" Blythe inquired, taking another sip of her Perrier. She certainly didn't want to play Mother Confessor to her ex-husband about her sister, for God's sake!

"No!" Chris replied, draining his wineglass. Just then the waiter appeared without being summoned and refilled it. "One major disaster in my life will suffice, believe me."

Blythe ignored his leading statement as another white-coated waiter accompanied by a grinning assistant arrived to serve their dinner with elaborate ceremony. She and Chris began to tuck into their roasted rack of lamb encrusted with mustard and rosemary-mint sauce while he guided their conversation in a safer, more amusing direction. He recounted witty tales about the shooting of *In Kenya*, including astonishing anecdotes starring her replacement, Patrick Corrigan, and the havoc the Irish production designer had wreaked on the film's budget.

As soon as the waiter had served their chocolate soufflé with appropriate ceremony, Blythe's former husband emptied another wineglass and stared somberly across the table.

"You've been a model of restraint through all of this, you know," he declared abruptly. "Any other female would have tried to ruin me . . . to punish me for the dreadful things inflicted on you this past year." Then he added morosely, "And before."

Blythe nearly choked on her Perrier. Was this a full-fledged apology she was hearing? From Christopher Stowe?

"Thank you for acknowledging that," she responded quietly.

Chris reached across the table and clasped Blythe's hand for a second time, his thumb fingering the spot where she'd once worn her diamond anniversary band.

"We were a good match, you and I," he continued in a regretful tone, "and then I went and blew it all to hell!"

"Christopher, this isn't going to solve the problem you came all the way to Cornwall to talk about," she reminded him, deliberately lowering her voice almost to a whisper.

Then he made an admission that startled her into utter speechlessness.

"I was a proper bastard to have denied you a child and then allowed Ellie to get pregnant," he confessed. He lowered his eyes to the wilting scoop of soufflé that lay on his plate awash in vanilla custard sauce. "However, in actual fact, I may have done you a favor. I don't think I'm much cut out for fatherhood. At least, that's what Ellie tells me."

So! she thought with a flash of satisfaction. Her sister's vicious parting shot at her cottage door had merely been a projection of her own desperation that Christopher was not enthusiastic about becoming a parent.

Then Blythe's reflections drifted to poor Kit Trevelyan, who had grieved for little Angela and would have so loved to welcome Blythe's second child—if it had not been conceived in an act of betrayal. There were some men who wanted to be fathers, she reminded herself firmly. Not the ones she fell in love with, though.

"I don't know what it was, really," Chris mused almost to himself. "A kind of midlife madness came over me last year . . . a feeling of my own mortality, I suppose . . . that stupidly drove me to seek the flattering attentions of a younger woman. It was insane!"

"But why my *sister*?" Blythe whispered harshly, her rigid control starting to slip.

"Because she was nearly as pretty as you are," he answered with unconscious candor. "And she didn't give a farthing about my shortcomings on the set," he added. "I have a lot of people constantly pecking at me, as you know. In the mood I was in last year, you seemed to be just another pesky duck. I was being idiotic, of course."

"But there was so much at stake!" she blurted, and then glanced worriedly around the room to see if she'd been overheard. "Our marriage . . . our business . . . even the well-being of your film—and you just chucked it all!" she added, sotto voce. "You knew I'd eventually find out. I think now you *wanted* me to find out . . . to punish me for something I still don't completely understand!"

Chris now had a faraway look in his eyes. "I resented you. . . . It was a feeling I just can't explain. I suppose I did want to punish you in some way for being right so much of the time." His gaze held hers and his grip tightened. "What I did was unforgivable. I acted like an adolescent fool and I know I've hurt you terribly. I am very sorry for it all, Blythe . . . believe me." Christopher looked at her for a long moment and then confessed with sudden vehemence, "I wish that baby were ours, Blythe! If she were . . . and I still had you in my life, perhaps I could . . . learn to be a decent father. I didn't have much of an example set for me, as you know."

"Oh, Christopher . . . don't!" she cried softly. She despised the fact they were in such a public place conducting the most intimate conversation of their lives. Chris's father, a widower still living in the Midlands and retired from chinaware manufacturing, had been an undemonstrative, mostly silent presence during her former husband's youth. "It's far too late for this discussion to be taking place."

"Why?" Chris declared fervently. "Seeing you tonight has only underscored how much I *need* you in my life! You and I could even have a child together, if it's what you really want!"

"It's too late!" she repeated, more loudly than she intended. Upset and embarrassed, again she darted her eyes around the dining room to see if they were becoming an object of attention.

"Come work with me on the picture," he urged, ignoring her protest. "My God, Blythe," he added with near demonic intensity, "what more can I say than that I realize now I made the biggest mistake of my life last year!"

She stared across the candlelight, stunned by his totally unexpected expression of remorse and his unmistakable plea for her to come back to him. Was it possible that this man who had caused her such excruciating mental anguish could have finally come to value her as a wife . . . as a partner, and as a talent on her own?

The candle's golden glow cast a flattering light on the world-renowned film director. The fine web of lines around his eyes and the thinning of his blond hair were hardly noticeable—as if his living portrait had been airbrushed by some studio still photographer. As she stared at him now, he appeared almost to be the exciting young man of her youth. He seemed to be admitting that he'd made a colossal wrong turn in his life and now deeply regretted it. He seemed to be asking her forgiveness and her permission to retrace his steps.

She suddenly became aware of how closely Christopher was watching her. She had the uncomfortable sense that he was scrutinizing her every response to gauge her reaction to his startling revelations.

How could he have been so reckless? some voice said in her head.

Why had this man exercised absolutely no restraint in the way he had behaved toward her—and, at this very moment, was behaving toward Ellie, for that matter?

Could she, Blythe, ever really trust a person who conducted his life in this fashion? She needed little convincing that Christopher's innate, absurd recklessness had, indeed, made him the brilliant, bloody-minded director he had become—a man who would risk all . . . who would do virtually *anything* to realize his cinematic vision, or satisfy his personal needs. Oddly, since their agonizing divorce and his difficulties on location in Kenya, he apparently had come to recognize that she had always been a good match for him in many key respects. Even so, it appalled her that he would behave toward her sister tonight with the same brutal lack of regard he had demonstrated toward herself in the past.

Meanwhile, Chris had begun to insert and retract his thumb seductively between Blythe's fingers. It had been a signal, in their lust-filled days of yore, that he was in the mood for sex. Considering the fact that he had evidenced only sporadic interest in making love with her when he'd been secretly conducting his affair with her sister, she considered this gesture manipulative as hell.

Then it suddenly hit her.

Damage Control.

This entire evening—the intimate country hotel . . . the anecdotes about their shared past . . . the champagne . . . the candlelight . . . Chris's expression of heartfelt remorse . . . and especially his flattery and praise for her accomplishments as his business partner, along with his bid to reconcile their marriage—it had all been nothing more than Damage Control.

Instead of relying solely on his familiar brand of lethal charm to get her to sign the sales documents and come back to work for him, Chris had appealed to the aspects of their former relationship he knew she most admired: *his* talent as a filmmaker, *her* talent in production design, and their remarkable ability to work as a creative team. He had even tried to seduce her back into his employ by offering her the one thing he knew she'd wanted most of all: a baby.

God, the man was clever! she thought, suddenly feeling short of breath. Diabolically clever.

Christopher Stowe wanted her back in his life because of the way her talent could enhance his own. Everything that had transpired since he had set foot on British soil had been about *him*, not about her. And certainly not about them as husband and wife . . . or as parents of a child they might have created together.

Blythe was reeling from the enormity of tonight's subterfuge while other thoughts careened around her brain.

Chris wanted her money and her production skills so that she could help make his film as good as it could possibly be. He didn't particularly care about her—or Ellie—or anyone but himself. He was an artist. Like Ennis. The thing he truly cared about was a two-hour strip of celluloid that might win him another Oscar.

Blythe felt dizzy from this unfiltered glimpse of Christopher Stowe's character. Suddenly an ingenious plan of reprisal popped into her head. For a moment, she admitted to herself, she was sorely tempted to give back as good as she got. Resentment, retaliation, and self-righteousness could be a potent force in her hands this night.

All she had to do was make love to her amorous, inebriated former spouse this night upstairs in the sumptuous suite he had undoubtedly reserved for them, and then the next morning refuse to sign the sales agreement designed to generate funds to save his picture. Ellie would pitch a tremendous fit when she learned of Chris's infidelity and perhaps even leave him. As an added bonus the studio would pull the plug when Chris didn't deliver the promised funds. Everything he'd worked for would evaporate—while she remained the well-heeled ex-wife.

As she gazed across the table at the man looking at her expectantly, she was struck by how difficult it was to break such a cycle of long-held bitterness and desire for revenge. Forgiveness could be an excruciating and exacting choice. So could standing up to a force of nature like Christopher Stowe.

Suddenly it didn't matter to Blythe anymore what her ex-husband's agenda might be.

"You know, Chris," she remarked, smiling faintly as she reached for her evening bag, "you remind me of someone I know . . . a painter of magnificent seascapes."

"Really?" Chris said absently. "As I was saying, Blythe . . . I—"

"Yes," she interrupted. "As it happens, you could practically be his twin." Then she snapped open the clasp of her bag and withdrew the documents he had given her and a handwritten addendum. "If you'll just hand me a pen, I'll sign them," she announced, certain now of the course she wished to take.

"You will?" he replied, startled. "Well . . . that's wonderful! Stupendous, in fact!" He flashed his eighteen-carat smile and waited for the waiter to remove their dessert plates and pour black coffee into gold-rimmed demitasse cups. Chris's hands trembled slightly as he handed her the legal papers. "This calls for a celebration, don't you think? Oh, Blythie, darling," he chortled. "Everyone will be thrilled to hear you're taking over for Corrigan. Me most of all." He was gazing across the table at her with the same expression of passionate intensity that she had observed him coaxing from his actors preparing to film a love scene. "We'll sort all this hash out with Ellie somehow! Just let me see to booking a suite for us upstairs, will you, angel? I long to show you how wonderful it could be for us again. . . ."

At the conclusion of Chris's lengthy monologue, the silence between them was interrupted only by the murmurs of the other diners quietly enjoying their meals. Blythe shook her head.

"No."

The word hung in the air as Chris looked at her blankly. Blythe reckoned that few people of the director's acquaintance had ever uttered the word in his presence.

"I have handwritten a statement you'll have to sign before I sign those papers," she announced quietly, handing him a sheet of stationery engraved with the Barton Hall letterhead. "It simply says that you will reimburse my half of the forest's profits within five years' time, guaranteed by your share of future profits from the films we made together that are now owned by the newly constituted Stowe Productions."

Chris hesitated and then replied in an injured tone, "Well . . . if you feel you need such a written guarantee—"

"I do feel that," she said calmly. She continued to gaze at him steadily until he reluctantly took pen in hand and signed the addendum guaranteeing her reimbursement. Then she reached for the paper and inspected his signature. "I'd like to tell you why I'm signing the forest over to you," she continued softly. "I'm buying my freedom. Once we both have agreed to these arrangements, we have nothing that links us any longer. It's *over,* Chris."

Her dinner companion's lips parted slightly, as if he were about to say something. However, he remained silent. An odd expression of confusion invaded his eyes.

Blythe realized, suddenly, that Chris's attempt to manipulate her in such devious fashion had not been aimed at her personally. There had been no lack in *her* that had prompted his elaborate machinations. There had never been any great lack in her. It was simply the way he operated in his life in order to get his films made.

All along the lack had been Chris's.

Like Ennis Trevelyan, the extraordinarily accomplished film director sitting opposite her in the candlelit dining room lacked compassion and empathy toward people. And like Ennis, he had been driven by an overweening desire for success to invest his emotions only in his art. Both men had simply channeled those feelings into their work, declining to "waste" such passion and sentiment on family or colleagues.

"It's over?" Chris repeated with a caustic edge to his voice. "Blythe, my darling," he said, the familiar, mocking tone reasserting itself during the time it took him to push the sales documents across the table for her to sign, "there's really no need for you to make such dramatic pronouncements. I expect you'll be pleased enough to hear from me when I pay you back the money, as I've just agreed to do."

"When that day comes, please call my lawyer, not me," she instructed him pleasantly. She tucked Chris's IOU into her purse. Then she added with warmth that surprised even herself, "You are a wonderfully talented director." She seized the pen he proffered her and briefly surveyed the deed to the Scottish forest. "I did criticize you often in front of the crew, and sometimes even behind your back," she acknowledged apologetically, scratching her signature beside the first of several red *X*'s. "It would have been more helpful to both of us if I'd discussed my views in private and offered you my suggestions away from the set." She looked up and spoke from her heart. "I wanted people to treat me as their colleague . . . not as your wife. My behavior stemmed from my own insecurities," she added as she glanced down once more and signed the last page. "I'm truly sorry that I acted like a pesky duck."

"Oh . . . Blythe . . . ," Chris sighed, slipping the legal papers into his briefcase. He was looking at her now with an expression closely akin to regret. "Couldn't we somehow just rewind this film . . . ?"

"We can't," she concluded quietly. As she uttered these words, a heavy weight seemed to lift off her shoulders. "One last thing," she said, reaching across the table to lay her hand lightly on his sleeve. "I ask your forgiveness, Christopher, for anything else I might have done . . . along the way . . . that hurt you."

Gratitude—mixed with puzzled remorse—invaded the bemused countenance of the man she had once loved very deeply. And in that instant the months of crushing anger dissolved, as if by magic.

Blythe stood in preparation for her departure, inhaling deeply, just to be sure the wonderful sensation of lightness hadn't been in her imagination. It wasn't.

"Blythe!" Christopher exclaimed. "Please don't go! Can't we—"

"No, we can't," she said, smiling wistfully. "I'm sure you'll save your picture. The best of luck with it, Chris."

"But, Blythie, darling—" he protested, springing unsteadily from his chair.

She bent forward and brushed a kiss against his cheek. "I'm glad you and Ellie came to Cornwall." And with that she rested a hand on his shoulder. "Truly, Christopher . . . I wish you well."

"But I'll drive you—"

"Please finish your wine," she directed firmly. "Mary Flynt will ring for a cab from St. Austell."

Blythe's glowing sense of peace and well-being lasted until the clattering black taxi deposited her beside the gate at the entrance to her field. The solitary lamp burning in the cottage window offered little welcome, for her thoughts were plagued by visions of Luke and Chloe under the same roof at Barton Hall. By the time she had crossed the pasture, she had managed to step into sheep dung with each of her velvet pumps.

It was nearly midnight, and she found that she was both exhausted from her emotional encounter with Chris and, likewise, unable to sleep.

She soon found herself pacing around the small confines of Painter's Cottage while she nibbled on saltines from a box she held clutched to her chest.

On one hand, she reasoned, she wanted nothing more than to don a pair of jeans and her Wellington boots and to tread along Hall Walk in the crisp, star-filled night. She pictured herself slipping into the castle and climbing into the Bawdy Bed of Barton with Luke. Unfortunately, she couldn't banish from her memory the sight of another female who had attempted that very thing within the last twenty-four hours—with highly embarrassing results.

Blythe sank into a chair and bleakly surveyed through the window the silvery rays of moonlight dancing on the water. In her mind's eye she saw Chloe lying beside Luke in his red-velvet-draped enclosure. Then she pictured Luke alone, reclining on his back like a beautiful stone effigy in a church crypt. A pangy kind of ache had begun to gnaw at her insides.

Is this what it feels like to pine for someone? she wondered ruefully.

For the second time that evening her thoughts drifted to Kit Trevelyan. How many nights had he lain awake in the Barton Bed, longing for Blythe to come to him of her own free will? And what of poor Garrett Teague, sleeping on his bachelor's pallet above the bookshop on Rattle Alley?

She recalled, suddenly, that she had twice deflected Luke's requests earlier that day to tell her something of the agonizing period following his wife's death and his decision to send Richard to boarding school. Now, despite the late hour, she wished she could sit beside him in front of the hearth and simply listen to what he'd had to say.

However, to Blythe's chagrin, she could not manage to

swallow her pride and make her way through the shadowed woods to Barton Hall. And thus, alone in her cottage by the sea, she spent a long, sleepless night attempting to divert herself with du Maurier's 1943 novel, *Hungry Hill*.

Chapter Eighteen

September 9, 1994

When Blythe arrived at Barton Hall the next morning, she was relieved to see that an army of workers, hired from the village, was swarming over the half-constructed hothouses. The brick foundations of all but one of the buildings had risen on their concrete pads, while the wooden frames of three sheds had already been completed. One team of hired hands was stretching rolls of plastic sheeting on two of the structures that had been sited in the flat area on the far side of the field nearest the pony stalls. Eventually all seven hothouses would offer shelter to tender plants in their earliest stages of growth.

Blythe glanced around, looking for young Richard, whom she expected to see assisting the workers.

"Good morning, Mr. Quiller," she greeted the gardener. "Have you see Dicken?"

"I believe he's inside, mum," he replied, his features growing grave. "The wife is puttin' his belongings in order. Leaves for that school over t'Devon after lunch, I'm sorry t'say."

"Not *today*!"

Blythe had been so preoccupied with her own concerns that she had forgotten he was scheduled to depart so soon.

"We'll all miss him, and that's for certain," he said, shaking his grizzled head. "At least, most of us will."

Blythe looked up and glared at the highest tower of Barton

Hall. Luke might as well have locked his son in the turret at home as send him to Shelby Hall, she fumed. The poor kid obviously hated the place!

Stick to your knitting!

Blythe longed to sit down in the kitchen for a nice cup of tea and one of Mrs. Q's freshly baked scones, but she supposed the housekeeper was still upstairs, helping Dicken pack his clothes.

Her stomach gave an ominous growl, which she ignored. Instead, she skirted past the kitchen and dining-room windows, carefully avoiding looking inside. She certainly didn't feel like running into Luke and Chloe having breakfast together. She continued across the stable yard and ducked inside the refurbished stable, determined to tackle the invoices that awaited her on her desk.

She and Luke had decided to maintain the essential character of the stone structure despite its being converted into offices, a small "schoolroom" for eager gardeners, and the point-of-sale department. Consequently the wooden horse stalls served as office dividers for Lucas, Blythe, and the small staff they intended to hire. A slate floor and lighting grid overhead, plus electric outlets and heating units installed along the base of the walls, were the principal alterations to the 250-year-old building. Valerie Kent had been kind enough to alert Luke to a gaggle of used filing cabinets that were being auctioned off in Mevagissey. Blythe herself had negotiated from the bank in Gorran Haven the purchase of several scarred but serviceable desks put up for sale during the branch's modernization. All in all, she and Luke had turned the Cornish ponies' former home into an attractive space that accommodated both the public and private uses required by the operation.

Blythe began to tap into her calculator the prices of the supplies they had ordered and received in the last two weeks. Soon she became oblivious to the sound of hammers ringing outside.

"Oh . . . there you are," said a well-modulated voice from the shadows.

Blythe looked up, startled, and then silently groaned. Chloe Acton-Scott was standing at the threshold of Blythe's new office, looking as if she were about to depart for a tea date at Fortnum & Mason's. She had donned a royal Stuart red-tartan pleated skirt and a black cashmere turtleneck sweater with matching cardigan. Every hair in her blond chignon was in place, and even from where Blythe sat, she would bet a prize bull that the woman's lacquered nails didn't have a single chip on their bloodred surfaces.

"Well . . . good morning," Blythe replied, wondering exactly to what she owed this unpleasant interruption.

She glanced down at her jeans and suddenly wished she'd worn her nice pair of gray flannel slacks for office work. Why in God's name did this woman's mere presence make her feel like a Wyoming edition of Minnie Rag Bag? Chloe's fine-boned features and sleek, patrician good looks put Richard's godmother in the category of a genuine English Rose. Staring now at her visitor's blond chignon, Blythe felt like Wilma the Wildflower.

I know, I know, Grandma! Cowboy up.

"So sorry to disturb you," Chloe said, venturing farther into the office, "but I wonder if I could just ask you to do us a very small favor."

"And what's that?" Blythe asked warily.

"Luke and I thought it best if I just depart quietly with Richard directly after lunch and avoid any tearful good-byes with staff."

"Staff," Blythe repeated. "By that do you mean the Quillers, the men hammering out there—or me?"

"Well . . . everyone, in fact," Chloe said pleasantly. "I would be grateful, indeed, if you would cooperate with us on this."

"Luke asked you to speak to me?" Blythe asked coolly.

Chloe flicked an invisible piece of lint off her black cashmere sleeve.

"It's what we'd prefer."

"Really?" Blythe replied, recalling suddenly some of the

battles royal she'd fought with presumptuous associate producers and ambitious secretaries in Hollywood. "Perhaps I should ask him, just to make sure you understood him correctly," she added, rising from her chair and heading for the door. She swore silently that she would deck the woman with a right to the chin if she refused to allow her to pass.

"Mrs. Stowe!" Chloe said, holding up a hand as if she were a school crossing guard.

"Yes, Chloe," Blythe replied, deliberately using her Christian name.

"Perhaps I'd better cease prevaricating. . . ."

"Perhaps you had."

"Lindsay Teague was my best friend," Chloe said, "I'm godmother to her son, and Luke and I are extremely fond of each other."

"I'm aware of the accuracy of your first two statements."

"Well . . . ," Chloe continued uncertainly, "until you came . . . there was no doubt in anyone's mind that Lucas and I would eventually . . . ah . . ."

"Have an affair?" Blythe asked sweetly.

"Why, marry, of course! Only you Hollywood people, with your vulgar money and your—"

"Careful, now," Blythe said, wagging a warning finger back and forth in front of the flawless skin of her visitor's face.

"Lucas may think he's infatuated with you," Chloe retorted, her china-blue eyes narrowing, "but I guarantee you that he's convinced himself of that because he's so terribly desperate to save Barton Hall from the Inland Revenue!" She stared at Blythe with an air of triumph. A smug little smile had begun to tug at her lips.

"Likes me for my money, you say?" Blythe replied as if she were merely inquiring about the weather. Meanwhile, she wondered if they might both be telling the truth.

"Well, surely you don't think your type would fit in with the people he and Lindsay and I associate with, do you? There's not a film star among us!" She laughed, as if she'd made a terribly witty remark.

"Not even one rodeo queen?" Blythe queried in dulcet tones.

"The point is," Chloe continued somewhat breathlessly, "that it's only a matter of time before Lucas realizes how unsuitable you are for his kind of life. . . ."

"And what kind of life is that, Chloe?" Blythe demanded abruptly. "Look at this place!" she exclaimed, gesturing through the open door. "I might point out the obvious fact that when I got here, this outfit was falling apart. Luke wants to put it back together again, and he's willing to dirty his hands to do it. Are *you*?"

"Well . . . I—"

"And until I came here, his *life* was falling apart, and so was Richard's!"

"I fail to see how you could possibly know a thing about it!" Chloe retorted. "Lindsay passed away more than two years ago and—"

"Died," Blythe snapped. "The poor woman died . . . a long, slow, agonizing battle with cancer! She left a husband and son who didn't know how to cry for her. Luke still doesn't." She glared at the intruder. "And why are you so certain you can get your hooks into him now? You never succeeded before, did you?"

"*I* get my hooks into him!" Chloe said with righteous indignation. "How dare you say that! Look at you! Climbing into a stranger's bed when you've barely put six months between you and that dreadful divorce of yours!"

"And I suppose you and your ex-husband ended your marriage over crumpets and tea?" Blythe asserted.

"Well, I didn't immediately throw myself at the first man who—"

"That's not what I heard," Blythe drawled.

"Well, the *entire world* heard every sordid detail about that disgusting husband of yours—"

"Former husband," Blythe corrected, doing her damnedest to keep her temper in check.

Sometimes you just need to take the bridle off, throw the skillet away, and let the she-wolf scream.

Stay out of this, Grandma! Blythe thought grimly.

"Well . . . practically everyone on the planet knows that Christopher Stowe was caught, in flagrante delicto, with your own *sister*!" Chloe declared, ignoring Blythe's interruption. "He certainly didn't have to look far for a paramour to replace you."

" 'Paramour'?" Blythe repeated, incredulous. "Now, that's really quaint." She took a step closer toward the unwelcome visitor. "Look, Chloe, darling," she purred in an approximation of the woman's own plummy accent, "this is getting dangerously close to a catfight." She fixed the intruder with a hard stare and assumed her best cowboy twang. "May I suggest you just skedaddle right outta here and let me go back to work?"

"I don't want you upsetting my godson!" Chloe shouted, her icy control melting completely.

"What you don't want is to have your apple cart upset!" Blythe yelled back, her patience finally having been exhausted. "You know as well as I do that as far as kids are concerned, you consider them a major nuisance—and Richard merely a means to an end, so don't dish out that fairy-godmother malarkey to me!"

"Malar—what?" Chloe responded with an outraged screech. "You don't even speak the language!"

"Just cool your jets, gal," Blythe continued. "And as for Luke, you and I will have to take our chances, won't we? Now, clear out!"

"You're telling me to—?" she shouted.

"This conversation is *over,*" Blythe announced, pointing toward the door while keeping her eyes glued to her adversary.

"How dare you order me to leave!"

"That's just what I'm doin'," Blythe replied, smiling grimly and ratcheting her Wyoming drawl up a notch. Then she made an elaborate show of pounding her fist on her desk. "This here is Barton Hall Nurseries—and I own *half!*"

"Mind if I interrupt?" cut in a deep male voice.

A moment of dead silence echoed beneath the stable's hand-hewn rafters. Then both women turned to stare at Luke, who was standing in the doorway. His handsome features were composed in an unreadable mask.

"Jesus, Mary, and Josephina—how long have you been standing there?" Blythe demanded.

"Quite a while," he said with a shrug, and settled his six-foot frame against the doorjamb.

"Oh, brother!"

"Lucas . . . I am extremely upset by this woman's presumptuous attitude toward you and your son—and toward Barton Hall, I may add!" Chloe declared loftily. "And if you had your wits about you, you would be too!"

"It would be a tremendous help, Chloe, if you would go inside and check on Mrs. Q's progress with the packing," he requested calmly, advancing into the room.

"I'd be delighted," Chloe said with a brittle smile, and flounced out of the chamber.

"Have you a moment?" Luke inquired politely.

Blythe sank into her desk chair. "Shoot," she answered with an air of resignation. Then she glanced up at him standing a few feet away. "Exactly when did you arrive at that door?"

"About the time you were saying that Barton Hall and I were both falling apart."

"Oh, God," Blythe groaned, sinking her head into her hands.

"Did you and Christopher Stowe survive your get-together last night? No broken crockery, I presume?"

Blythe looked up and searched his face for some hint to Luke's state of mind. His expression revealed very little except a look of tremendous fatigue etched around his eyes.

"It actually went much better than I expected."

"I thought you might come by the Hall last night and tell me what you'd finally decided to do about the forest."

"I didn't want to interrupt your little fireside supper."

"Look, Blythe," Luke confessed, "I just said that nonsense about Chloe's ordering up dinner in front of the fire to even things a bit. I can assure you that as far as she and I are concerned—"

"Chloe Acton-Scott is the least of my troubles right now," she declared.

"Well, then . . . let's *do* talk about your decision last night. Did you sign the documents, as he asked?"

"Yes."

"You gave in."

"I wouldn't describe it that way."

"But why in the world would you turn yourself into a rescuing angel for that faithless sot after the way he behaved toward you?" Luke demanded.

"He's a brilliant director," Blythe replied wearily. "I don't expect you to understand—but I did it partly to save his picture. The rest of my reasons are a little complicated."

"And because you're still a little in love with the bastard?"

"No," she replied, concluding that the concept of buying one's freedom from an ex-husband with the proceeds from a Scottish forest could not be satisfactorily explained to one's jealous lover. "I am not in love with Chris anymore, but I have discovered, much to my surprise, that I still admire his talent." She noted the look of puzzlement and distress that had invaded Luke's eyes. "Believe me, I was astonished myself to discover I felt that way. What I also realized is that it was about more than just the money."

"It should have been about *you,*" Luke retorted. "It should have been about putting your life back together without your being chained to the past."

"And I suppose *you're* free from the burdens of the past?" she shot back.

Somehow, she realized, Luke had fathomed on some intuitive level that the current dilemma in her life was very likely connected to the past. If only he could guess how very far in the past, she thought grimly.

"Christ, Blythe!" Luke swore in a voice that reflected a lack of sleep. "Why couldn't you have just allowed the man to sort out his own troubles? I'd hoped that you wouldn't do this to yourself!"

"You'd hoped *what*?" she asked sharply. "What does it matter to *you* what decision I made about the damned forest?"

"You just handed your ex-husband a million dollars—and I seriously doubt you'll ever see your half again."

"And I suppose you had other plans for that money?"

"That's not at all what I meant," he declared vehemently.

"But you *do* want to dictate what I do about it," she goaded him.

"I want you to do what's in your *interest*!" he said with exasperation. "Sometimes I wonder if you have any idea what that is . . . or if you even feel you're entitled to it."

"And I suppose you know exactly what my interests are," she demanded, considering Chloe's insinuation that Luke's determination to save Barton Hall from the tax collector might, indeed, be an unspoken factor in their relationship.

"On some levels . . . yes, I think I do," he countered.

"In my experience," Blythe replied tersely, thinking of Chloe's recent "request," "people who say that they know what I should be doing usually have something they want me to do for *them*!" She jumped up from the desk chair, hands on hips, and announced, "I intend to continue to make up my own mind about the important things in my life! And by the way—I'll spare you a scene in front of your son today, but I intend us to have our good-byes, and that's the end of it!"

She turned to exit the stables and came face-to-face with Richard, who stood at the threshold of the office door. The little boy's mouth was opened slightly, and his eyes were filled with apprehension. As with his father, Blythe hadn't the slightest notion how long he'd been standing there. Without warning the ten-year-old ran to her side and lashed out at Luke.

"You've hurt her feelings, and now she's leaving!" he cried. "She cares much more about me than *you* do," he added accusingly. Luke stared at his offspring, dumbfounded as his son declared tearfully, "She wants me to stay at home, and you want me to go to Shelby Hall so I won't be a bother to you. That's why you're being horrid and driving her away! I hate you—and I hate Aunt Chloe!"

Luke's look of bewilderment soon turned to one of anger as his mouth set in a straight line. "You're being a very rude young man," he replied in a clipped tone of voice. "I assure you, my lad . . . Blythe and I are merely having a disagreement. Everything is perfectly all right. And, besides, I would thank you not to eavesdrop on your elders."

"She's going away!" Richard sobbed, throwing his arms around Blythe's waist.

"Oh, Dicken, sweetie," Blythe began, "your dad was just—"

"You're making her go away!" he repeated.

"Blythe is *not* leaving us, are you, Blythe?" Luke declared, a tone of desperation edging his voice. "To begin with, we're business partners now in the nursery project. It'll be all right, I tell you! You've utterly misunderstood our conversation!"

His son raised his head and glared at his father. "You *always* say everything is all right . . . but you're just pretending! You said Mummy was going to be all right, and she *died*!"

"But, Richard, I—"

"And you said Shelby Hall would be all right, and it was horrid! The other boys made fun of me because I cried at night and—" His small face crumpled and fresh tears began to course down his cheeks. "You never even came once to see me at school," he said, his voice cracking, "even when I—" Richard halted midsentence. Then he shouted in a tone laden with misery and accusation, "Even when you know things are horrible, you always pretend it will be all right . . . and it *never is*!"

And with that, he whirled around and dashed out of the office.

"Luke!" Blythe said urgently. "Oh, Luke, you must go to him!"

Richard's father, however, slowly turned his back to her. He walked over to a small window and wordlessly stared into the stable yard. Then, to Blythe's utter astonishment, his shoulders began to heave.

"Christ!" he said, his voice choked with emotion. "Why in the name of heaven can't I ever get the words right?" Blythe remained motionless near her desk. "I couldn't think what to say. I couldn't think how to tell an eight-year-old child that his mother was dying."

"Oh, baby . . . ," Blythe said, instantly sympathetic despite her rush of anger a few minutes previously. "Sit here . . . ," she urged, gesturing toward her chair.

However, Luke remained standing and gazed silently out the window. At length he said slowly, "I know full well that at times this summer, when it came to Richard, you've thought me a callous, unfeeling sod. So often I wanted to tell you what it was like when—"

Luke's voice broke, and he covered his eyes with his right hand.

"Tell me now," Blythe said softly.

"Words . . . ," he murmured, "it's so bloody hard to find the words."

"We both speak English," she replied. "At least I sort of do . . . ," she jested halfheartedly. "Just tell me what happened between you and Richard."

"It's very little to do with Richard, really," he began, turning to face her. "Lindsay and I discovered that she was pregnant with our second child at the same time she received the diagnosis of breast cancer."

"Oh, my God . . . ," Blythe whispered.

"She had to make a choice. . . . *We* had to make a choice," he corrected himself carefully. "Lindsay could have an abortion . . . take the cancer drugs . . . and try to save her own life. Or not take them . . . hope the mastectomy would stop the disease, and try to save the life of our unborn child." His gaze assumed a faraway look, as if the debate over the agonizing decision were being made as he spoke. Then he closed his eyes for a moment and said in a low voice laced with sorrow, "We both wanted that child so much. . . . We didn't care if it was a boy or girl . . . just that our baby would be born whole . . . that Richard would have a brother or a sister . . . and that Lindsay would live to see Richard and the baby grow up."

Luke walked over to the open door and stared out at the granite wall that enclosed the kitchen garden, awash in chilly September sunshine.

"And so both of you had to decide, didn't you?" Blythe murmured. "Who should be granted the best chance to live?"

"The cancer turned up again three months later. Then the doctor gave us *new* odds," Luke continued dully, closing the door left open by his departing son. "There was a reasonable chance that the drugs might put Lindsay in remission. However, if she took them, then she could not—or should not—have the baby. Without the chemotherapy there was almost no chance that she would live long enough for the baby to survive to term."

"Oh, Luke . . . ," Blythe said, tears clogging her voice, "I'm so sorry. . . ."

"After I saw how the cancer started to take over, I begged her to have an abortion and seize the chance that she might get well with chemotherapy. I told her that perhaps by some miracle—we could have another child together," he said, meeting Blythe's stricken gaze, "or at least we could still hold out the hope for adoption of a second child after she went into remission."

"Did Lindsay agree?" Blythe asked.

"Yes . . . but in the end we lost all the bets," Luke disclosed in a monotone. "She had a five-month abortion, chemotherapy, and died anyway." He gazed at Blythe with a haunted expression. "The baby was a girl," he said finally. "For weeks after Lindsay's funeral I had a series of ghastly recurrent dreams in which a newborn infant was left abandoned in a desert . . . or dying alone in the woods . . . or falling off a cliff into the sea."

Blythe's pulse quickened as she tried to suppress a sharp intake of breath.

The baby floating in Valerie's crystal ball!

She had thought after her last session in Valerie's office that perhaps the unborn child represented the mysterious William to whom the eighteenth-century Blythe had dedicated Ennis Trevelyan's lonely seascapes. Now she wondered if that baby, lost in space, was a glimpse of the doomed infant in Lindsay's womb.

"Each time the dream recurred," Luke continued, "I'd wake with a start. I'd sit bolt upright in bed with my heart pounding, trying to catch my breath in that bedroom across from Richard's. Then I'd start to blubber like a baby. After a few weeks of this I moved into the room with the Barton Bed. Even so, I was afraid I'd frighten Richard when those tides of sadness overwhelmed me." In Luke's glance she now saw undisguised despair. "Every time I laid eyes on my son," he disclosed, his voice hoarse with emotion, "I thought I'd fall apart. All I could think of was that we'd killed his sister and then lost Lindsay in the bargain! So despite everything my wife and I believed in, Blythe, I sent my eight-year-old son away to school."

"Didn't you try to talk to someone about . . . the dreams? Your doctor? Even Valerie?" Blythe asked gently. "Wouldn't they have understood the terrible grief you were going through?"

"I told no one about the dreams . . . or my reactions to them. I might well have, but I just kept lecturing myself, 'Get a grip, man!' After that I avoided all thoughts of babies and the sight of children—my child, to be specific. I suppose I thought it would keep my devils at bay if I kept clear of . . . reminders. And the plan worked. I haven't had the dream since."

But I have, Blythe mused. Or some strange version of it.

"Oh, God, Luke," she sighed, sympathetic and exasperated

in equal measure. "The way you deal with some things is so . . . English!"

"Of course," he acknowledged with a bitter smile. "One year became two, and I simply became accustomed to the relief that resulted by my remaining aloof from Dicken." He cast Blythe a beleaguered gaze. "I asked Chloe to take care of everything regarding Shelby Hall."

"Even when Dicken stuffed his roommates' underpants down the johns in an obvious bid to get your attention?" Blythe asked evenly.

"He told you about that?" Luke asked, and then shook his head in self-disgust.

"Just the other day, in fact," she answered quietly.

"Well, bastard that I am," Luke continued, "I have told myself for two solid years that I was sending Richard away and keeping my distance from him for his own good . . . so he wouldn't see what a weak, pathetic man his father had become."

"Grieving for the loss of your wife and baby was not pathetic!" Blythe insisted fiercely, thinking of the raw waves of anguish that overwhelmed her without warning in the months following Grandma Barton's death.

"Last May you walked into my life," Luke continued as if she hadn't spoken, "and then Dicken ran away . . . and I was forced to see that—" Luke pulled up short. Then he said in a voice laden with shame and regret, "The appalling truth was, for the last two years I was simply making it easier on *myself*!"

This soul-searching admission once again rendered Luke unable to speak. He turned to gaze out the window for the second time.

Meanwhile Blythe's thoughts were galloping ahead of any words she could form to comfort him. Her stomach was in increasing turmoil, and she was sorely tempted to blurt out her strong suspicion of her own pregnancy—if only to offer him something tangible in the way of solace. Just then, however, there was a knock on the door.

"Excuse me, sir," Luke's housekeeper announced, poking her head into the room. "It's Master Richard. . . . He's terribly upset, sir. Mrs. Acton-Scott is very angry with him, and he's locked himself in his bedroom and won't come out."

Luke kept his back to his housekeeper and continued to stare out the window, so Blythe intervened quickly.

"Could you be a dear, Mrs. Q, and tell Richard that Mr. Teague will come up in just a few minutes?"

Blythe's stomach gave a lurch, either from the unpleasant sound of Chloe's name—or from another impending bout of morning sickness.

"Of course, mum," she said, nodding. "Right away."

Mrs. Quiller's puzzled gaze had fixed upon the broad expanse of her silent employer's back. Then she looked at Blythe, who tried to disguise her concern for Luke, as well as conceal the chaos currently reigning in her abdomen. Blythe cast her a pleading look—which Mrs. Q acknowledged with an understanding nod.

"I'll just pass on the message," she added softly. "Sorry to disturb."

Moments after the housekeeper's retreat Blythe could no longer deny the unwelcome sensation of a fresh attack of nausea.

"Luke . . . could you excuse me for a bit?" she asked in a tight voice. "I really want to continue our talk, but I'm afraid I'm feeling kind of rotten after not getting much sleep for the second night in a row. I'll see you later."

And without further explanation she made her way as quickly as possible across the stable yard, into the castle's rear entry, and down the hall to the bathroom adjoining the library.

Luke returned his gaze to the kitchen garden and the adjacent fields, whose contours gently rolled toward the sea. He wondered gloomily if Blythe's hurried exit merely demonstrated an understandable distaste for his recent show of emotion. After spending several minutes indulging in such negative speculation, he exited the silent office and walked past the flock of workmen without uttering a word to any of them. Entering the castle through the kitchen door, he found Chloe pouting over a cup of coffee.

"She just dashed through here, if that's who you're looking for," she said sullenly. "I know she'll upset the boy just as we're about to leave!"

"As I understand it, he's already upset," he said wearily. "Has Blythe gone up to see Richard?"

"I haven't a clue," Chloe retorted, and turned to glare reproachfully at Mrs. Quiller, who was whipping a creamy mixture in a copper bowl with her back to them both.

As Luke prepared to mount the grand staircase in search of his son, he paused for several moments on the landing next to the door to the bathroom that adjoined the library. A look of concern furrowed his brow. Then, with a thoughtful expression, he slowly climbed the stairs. When he reached Richard's room, he knocked softly.

"May I come in?"

"Yes, sir, it's open now," his son said, abruptly sitting upright on the bed, where he had obviously been crying, face-down into his pillow.

Luke closed the door behind him. He and Richard stared at each other in silence for a long, awkward moment.

"I've . . . ah . . . come to apologize about several things, Dicken," he began tentatively, "and to tell you how grateful I am that you were all right the other night when the tide came into the cave."

"I'm sorry, too, Daddy," Richard said in a small voice, "for what I said in the pony stable."

"You were upset," Luke said slowly, "and I'm sure you didn't mean to be hurtful."

The look of relief and wonder that flooded Richard's eyes was an open invitation to Luke to sit down on the side of the bed. Wordlessly he pulled his small son against his chest and rested his chin on top of the boy's head. Suddenly he was overwhelmed by the bittersweet memory of Lindsay's silken brown hair, identical in texture and color to Richard's own.

"Oh, Dicken . . . ," he breathed, feeling as if the tremendous pressure in his throat would strangle him. "We've had a very hard time of it these last two years, haven't we?"

The boy then threw his arms about Luke's neck and began to cry deep, wrenching sobs, as he had earlier beside his mother's grave. Luke stared over Richard's head at the photograph of Lindsay perched on the nightstand next to the bed. As moisture filled his own eyes, his wife's face began to blur, and he found himself holding on to the ten-year-old for dear life as wave after wave of emotion assaulted him.

After a few minutes Richard hiccuped, "I m-miss her so much, Daddy, d-don't you?"

"I miss her, and I despise how much she had to suffer," he replied softly. Then he added in a tone both serious and amused, "And believe me, Dicken, she would have been very upset with me if she knew I'd sent Aunt Chloe to Shelby Hall in my place to talk to your headmaster when you almost got sacked."

Dicken nodded solemnly but remained silent. Luke reached for a tissue from the box sitting next to Lindsay's photograph and gently wiped his son's cheeks. He urged him to blow his nose. Then he seized a tissue for himself.

"I'm sorry I let you down that time, son," he said finally, pulling the child against his chest once more and feeling comforted beyond measure by the sensation of the boy's arms around his waist. "I was feeling so sad myself back then, I became rather paralyzed. I knew what a dreadful period it had been for you, but I didn't want you to be frightened by what a difficult time I was having, coping with everything that had happened."

"I wouldn't have been frightened seeing how sad you were, Daddy," Richard assured him, patting his father's sleeve. "I was really sad too," he disclosed gravely. "We could have kept each other company."

This time Luke didn't attempt to disguise the feelings that swept through him.

"You are such a wonderful young man," he said, his voice choked with emotion. "I'm so proud . . . and fortunate . . . to be your father."

And as Luke and his son continued to talk, the eldest member of the Teague family was suddenly filled with confidence that he would, at last, find the right words to express to his and Lindsay's child the many other things that had needed to be said for so long.

Blythe slowly opened the door adorned with the wooden sign that announced "Dr. Valerie Kent, Psychologist." In her arms she held a long rectangular package.

"The nurse told me you'd come in today to catch up on your bookkeeping," she said.

"My dear!" Valerie replied with immediate concern when she saw that Blythe's cheeks were damp with tears. "Please come in. Here, let me take that," she urged, relieving Blythe of her burden. "Good heavens!" she exclaimed as she set the box down on her desk. "How extraordinarily heavy."

"They're a pair of old, beat-up silver candlesticks," Blythe announced ruefully, pointing to the customs declaration pasted to the package, "and a few pieces of flatware that my grandmother wanted me to have." Blythe reached across Valerie's desk for a tissue from a box reserved for her emotion-prone clients and dabbed her eyes. Meanwhile Valerie stared, mesmerized by the battered box that was smothered with two long rows of colorful U.S. postage stamps. "When my father sold the ranch at the beginning of the summer, I guess he just packed up the stuff and sent it over. Thrifty gent that he is, Dad obviously shipped the package from Wyoming the slow, inexpensive way—by land and sea. The postmistress hailed me on my way to see Dr. Vickery."

Valerie pointed to the ancient upholstered chair reserved for her clients and urged Blythe, "Please . . . please, dear. Sit down. Now, won't you tell me what's happened?"

"I'm pregnant," Blythe noted in a voice filled with awe. "Dr. Vickery just confirmed it . . . the blood test, the exam—everything. He said this baby is locked on the uterine wall like a barnacle at low tide."

"That sounds like Vickery," Valerie noted dryly. "Well . . . how do you feel about it?"

"Even though I was already pretty sure . . . I-I can't quite believe it's true," she said with a fragile smile. "I'm delirious . . . terrified . . . and I can't even begin to imagine what the future will hold." She laughed softly. "I'm quite undone by it all, as you Brits say."

"Please . . . sit down," Valerie urged again, gesturing to the chair opposite her desk. "Have you revealed to Luke yet that you suspected as much?"

"No . . . not yet," Blythe answered slowly. Then she met Dr. Kent's steady gaze. "He told me just this morning about the horrible dilemma he and Lindsay faced when she got sick."

"Ah . . . yes." Valerie nodded gravely. "Then you understand now, do you, a bit about his complicated relationship with Dicken?"

Blythe nodded and then asked, "How did you know about it? He said he didn't tell anyone."

"He didn't . . . at least not to me," Valerie agreed. "However, Lindsay had disclosed to me early on that she thought she might be pregnant again. After the family was told of her diagnosis, I could easily imagine what dreadful choices they faced. When Luke's behavior toward Dicken changed so dramatically . . . it wasn't difficult to deduce that 'survivor's guilt' probably played a role." Valerie shook her head and heaved a sigh. "I had hoped he'd come talk to me about the difficulties that he was having . . . but he never did."

"Then he didn't tell you about the disturbing dreams he had for months that Lindsay's baby was lost, or stranded and in terrible jeopardy? It was almost an identical vision to the one I had in your crystal ball."

"Why, no . . . ," Valerie said, a look of amazement spreading across her rounded features.

"Did you try talking to Luke about his change of behavior toward Dicken after Lindsay died?" Blythe asked pointedly.

"A few times," Valerie said. "He kept insisting that he was coping as well as could be expected and gave me that *look*."

"Oh . . . I know *that* one." Blythe nodded glumly. "I-I can't imagine how he'll respond to my news."

"You will tell him, though, won't you?"

"After Dicken leaves for school," Blythe replied. "What will happen after that is up for grabs," she added, her tone hardening.

"Lucas was dealt some very heavy blows these last years," Valerie reminded her gently, "but after you arrived at Barton Hall, and after he thought he might have lost his son the other night—I think he's beginning to view his life in an entirely new light."

"I hope so," Blythe said sadly, "but what about our outlook on parenthood and our views as to what's appropriate as far as the education of children is concerned—not to mention the issue of discipline?" She heaved a heavy sigh. "Maybe we're just too different in our attitudes to be able to . . ."

She allowed her sentence to trail off into the ether.

"You'll just have to talk it through, though, won't you?" Valerie said encouragingly.

"*Yes,* Valerie," Blythe responded, rolling her eyes with mock exasperation. Then she sobered. "But even if we can come to some accommodation on what we both think it means to be parents . . . what about the . . . well, you know . . . the visions? He'll think I'm a nutcase if I ever come clean with all the stuff we've been doing."

"It's true . . . Lucas has always been a skeptic when it comes to the paranormal," Valerie agreed with a wry smile. " 'Hocus-pocus claptrap,' I believe he calls my trade. I could never even persuade him to try the Ouija board when he was a lad."

"Well, I really think I've got to tell him *something* about what I've experienced at Barton Hall, don't you?" she asked anxiously. "After all, these are more his ancestors than mine. How could I remain mum about a thing like that . . . and still have a life with him? Worse yet, what if these folks keep popping up all the time?" she demanded.

Valerie remained silent, apparently deep in thought. Then she started drumming her fingers on her desk.

"Do you love this man?" she asked suddenly. "Can you accept him as he is, quirks and all?"

"But what about my 'quirks'?" Blythe insisted. "I mean, it's not every man who'd want a wife who sees a bunch of—"

"Do you *love* this man?" Valerie repeated stubbornly.

Silence filled Dr. Kent's small office.

"Yes," Blythe answered finally. "I love him. And I accept his quirks, as you call them—except for two."

"You can list them?" Valerie asked with gentle sarcasm.

Blythe nodded. "I cannot live with someone who would not trust me to be telling the truth about what I've experienced here in Cornwall. But if I tell him, he'll never believe me . . . he'll think I've merely had a nervous breakdown, or—"

"And second?" the psychologist prodded.

"I will not turn my child over to other people to raise."

"So?"

"So . . . I'm going home to Painter's Cottage, have a few saltines for lunch—and think."

Chapter Nineteen

September 9, 1994

Chloe stalked into the sitting room where Luke had just replaced the telephone receiver on the long-necked antique instrument that perched on his desk.

"The camp trunk simply will not fit in the back of my car, Lucas!" she announced irritably. "Two suitcases were plenty for that child last term. I can't understand why he's being allowed to take those cowboy boots and—"

"Dicken is extremely fond of those boots," Luke said mildly, tapping his silver-plated pen against the desktop. Then he added with a glint of amusement brightening his fatigued countenance, "He insisted that he needs them at school to show the other boys—"

"What that boy needs is to be taken in hand," Chloe countered sharply. "And if you aren't of a mind to, then Mr. Hewitt at Shelby Hall is perfectly capable of—"

"I don't think you understood what I said," Luke said with elaborate politeness. "The gift of those boots means a great deal to the lad."

"It's that American creature, isn't it?" Chloe pronounced bluntly just as the phone on Luke's desk gave a shrill ring. "Or Valerie Kent, that lunatic cousin of yours," she added acidly. The telephone immediately ceased ringing, a signal that Mrs. Q must have answered it in the kitchen. "Both of them coddle my godson as if he were a broken doll. You've said yourself that Valerie should be locked up for all that hocus-pocus she prattles on about while claiming to practice psychology!"

"Well, I'm certainly not one for ghosts and family legends and all that nonsense," Luke acknowledged evenly, "but I'm actually quite fond of my eccentric cousin."

"And as for that common parvenue," Chloe declared, ignoring Luke's aside, "she's just trying to play up to you with all her vulgar millions, but you're too blind to see it!" Chloe glanced around the sitting room. "She'd like nothing better than to be mistress of this house."

"Well, I know *one* of you would," Luke said dryly, "but from what I've seen lately, I'm not at all sure it's Blythe Barton."

"Just because her maiden name is Barton, I suppose she's got some romantic notion that she could become—" Chloe glanced at Luke sharply. "What did you just say?"

"I said that I'm not at all sure Blythe Barton could be persuaded to be mistress of Barton Hall—unless there are a few more changes around here."

"Such as?" Chloe demanded.

Luke hesitated and then said quietly, "As Richard's godmother, Chloe, you'll always be a welcome guest at Barton Hall, but do promise me you won't inconvenience yourself in future by bringing me my morning tea—in bed."

Chloe flushed the same shade of red as her royal Stuart tartan skirt. She opened her mouth as if she were about to unleash another torrent of invective against the particular object of her wrath. Then she glared at Luke and snapped, "If that's how you feel, then drive your *own* bloody son to school!"

Next, she turned on her heel and exited the sitting room without uttering another word. A few minutes later Luke heard the sound of the Jaguar purring by. He glanced out of the bowed window at the base of the tower alcove that housed his desk and watched the petroleum-blue car disappear into the ancient column of trees that flanked the winding drive.

In the next instant the door hidden in the bookcase swung open without warning.

"Daddy!" Richard chimed happily. "Mrs. Q said to tell you that lunch will be fifteen minutes late. She's set it in the dining room because Cousin Valerie called just now."

"She did?" Luke replied, puzzled.

"I answered the phone," Richard said proudly. "Since she was coming over anyway, I invited her to lunch and she said yes." He gazed warily at his father's furrowed brow. "I hope that was all right?"

"That showed very good manners on your part," Luke assured him, wondering why his cousin didn't ask to speak to him on the phone, if she was inquiring about the aftermath of Richard's late-night adventure in the cave. "Did she give the reason she'd like to see me today?" he inquired of his son.

"No . . ."

"Will Blythe be joining us for lunch?" he asked casually.

"Mrs. Q said no," Richard reported. "No one's seen her since this morning." Richard gazed at him anxiously. "You really are going to be friends again, aren't you, Daddy?"

Luke nodded affirmatively and hoped that he was telling his only child the truth. Then he went into the kitchen to inform Mrs. Q that Mrs. Acton-Scott would not be having the noonday meal with them.

As soon as Valerie Kent's pint-sized Morris pulled to the back of the castle, Richard went running out to greet her.

After the trio had consumed their lunch, topped off with Mrs. Q's velvety cream custard smothered in raspberry sauce, Valerie smiled and folded her napkin. "I wouldn't say no to a small brandy if you offered me one, Lucas," she announced cheerfully, placing by her empty plate the damask cloth monogrammed with the Barton crest, with its distinctive embroidered sheaves of wheat.

"You? Brandy?" Luke reacted with surprise. "In the middle of the day? What would your patients say?"

"I'm off duty," she retorted primly, pushing back her dining-room chair. "And, besides, with Dicken safe at home, I doubt I'll be called out on a search-and-rescue mission anytime soon," she added with a touch of irony. "Now, be a good host and escort me to the library." The gray-haired sixty-six-year-old turned to look affectionately at her youngest cousin. "I would very much like to have a private chat with your father, if you don't mind, dear."

"All right," Dicken replied, casting the adults a curious look.

As Luke poured each of them a splash of brandy into two crystal snifters, he inquired, "Now, to what do I owe this pleasant, but rather mysterious, visit?" He noticed that Valerie had quietly closed the library door.

She accepted her glass of spirits and remained standing.

"Cheers," she said with an enigmatic smile, "and congratulations."

"Congratulations?" he echoed. "For what?"

"So many things." Valerie smiled benignly.

"Like what, for instance?" Luke asked suspiciously. Valerie's smile merely grew broader.

"Valerie!" he said with exasperation. "Will you tell me what this riddle is all about?"

"I can't tell you," she said judiciously. "But I can show you."

"Then please do so," he urged with a hint of genuine impatience. "I've got legions of workmen out back whom I should be supervising. I've no time to waste."

"I'm afraid this will take a half hour or so," she announced.

"What will?" he demanded.

"Please be so kind as to move that leather chair over here, next to the genealogy chart," she directed, "and sit down."

"See here, Valerie," he said brusquely, "Dicken and I have to leave for—"

"Odd that you should mention the word 'time.' " His elderly

cousin smiled, sphinxlike. "Because, in actual fact, time has a great deal to do with what I hope to discuss with you. Will you sit down, please?" she repeated forcefully.

Luke reluctantly surrendered to his kinswoman's iron will and took his seat. Valerie then brought a straight-backed chair from the other side of the desk and placed it opposite him. She settled her ample proportions on its wooden surface and smoothed her woolen skirt.

"Is this a game of psychological kneesies?" Luke asked, deadpan, as he gazed across the short space that separated them.

"Now, quiet, please!" Valerie ordered, a satisfied smile tugging at the corners of her mouth. Then her expression grew serious. "If you will merely trust me, Luke, and believe that I care very deeply about you and Dicken—and if you will allow yourself to keep an open mind—I am certain that what I am about to try to convince you of could be very important to your future."

For his part, Luke was completely mystified by her cryptic words. However, he was struck by her heartfelt sincerity.

"You've always been a great friend, Valerie," he allowed soberly, "but I must confess, I feel a bit foolish sitting across from you like this."

"I can understand why you would," she replied calmly. "If you'll only make an honest effort to listen to what I have to say, Luke, and to consider what I am about to show you . . . I think I might be of some assistance to you—and to those dearest to you."

"Are we also speaking of Blythe?" he asked in a low voice.

"Yes, indeed we are," she said with a nod.

"Well, as I learned this morning . . . Blythe has her own demons from the past that she continues to wrestle with. I can certainly understand why she is not up to coping with mine."

"I happen to be aware of all that," Valerie disclosed crisply.

"She's spoken with you about . . . us?" he asked slowly.

"You know perfectly well that the details of what Blythe and

I have discussed within my office walls must remain completely confidential," the psychologist replied tartly.

"She's been seeing you professionally?" Luke asked incredulously.

"Let's just say we've had a variety of interactions over the summer," Valerie replied cautiously. "She has asked me to describe to you some unusual experiences she's had here at Barton Hall, hoping, perhaps, that you would be more prone to believe her if I could corroborate some of the—"

"What exactly do you mean by 'unusual experiences'?" Luke interrupted. "She mentioned something to me about seeing some sort of infant floating around in your crystal ball, but I—"

"I told Blythe, however," Valerie continued breezily, ignoring the thrust of Luke's question, "that you were likely to be skeptical of anything I said as well . . . and that it would be better if she described these phenomena to you herself at . . . ah . . . some point," she amended.

"What sort of other 'phenomena' are we talking about here, dear cuz?" Luke pressed sternly.

"Oh . . . things like genetic memory . . . past lives . . . long-term post-traumatic stress syndrome," Valerie replied, affecting nonchalance. "You know, Lucas . . . all that hocus-pocus claptrap I find so utterly fascinating!"

Luke's cousin began digging inside the voluminous handbag she'd retrieved from the reception hall en route to the library after lunch. Eventually she located a tattered brown leather volume and placed it in her lap.

"Not Reverend Kent's diary again!" he groaned, and sank back against his chair.

"Now, hear me out!" Valerie said emphatically. "You've made it abundantly clear what you think of my investigations into certain paranormal aspects of the Barton-Trevelyan-Teagues and the links to my branch of the Kents . . . but I'm warning you, my dear Lucas: This is serious business! For your own happiness, you must put aside your perpetual role as a

Doubting Thomas for a moment and allow me to read you a few passages from this journal."

"But, Valerie," Luke protested good-naturedly, "even you say that the good reverend's supposed forecasting of future Teague heirs left off at the end of the last century. Surely you can't make a claim that he predicted a way out of my own current emotional entanglements!"

"Oh . . . but he did!" Valerie said delightedly. "In a roundabout fashion." She dug into her handbag a second time and popped a pair of reading glasses onto the end of her nose. "Look here," she declared, pointing to the diary. "In one passage written in 1794, he made an extremely interesting notation at the end of the list of names he said he saw in the shewing stone—"

"Ah, yes . . . the old murky mirror where Reverend Kent claimed to see his visions of the future," Luke interrupted with veiled sarcasm.

"Exactly!" Valerie said, beaming. "Now, just look at this!" she continued excitedly, pointing to a paragraph in the yellowed diary and handing it over for him to inspect. " 'And the Children of the House of Barton shall ne'er be lost,' " she recited aloud, " 'nor will they wander alone. . . . Their path will be lit by Silver Candlesticks into a land of misty waters and fertile ground.' "

Luke looked at Valerie and pronounced, "I'm afraid you've lost me."

"Did you know that Kit Trevelyan died a suicide?" Valerie queried. Luke arched an eyebrow in surprise but remained silent. "Reverend Kent writes in his diary that he was castigated by his fellow churchmen for allowing Kit to be buried in St. Goran's churchyard. See?" she said, pointing to a paragraph at the bottom of the page. " 'Despite all, I must grant poor Kit a refuge in hallowed ground, for certainly the Lord God would find me culpable in that poor soul's death. And if I am smote by my brethren, 'tis but the penance I deserve.' "

"What does any of this have to do with silver candlesticks,

or more to the point, with Blythe and me?" Luke demanded impatiently.

"Are you aware that Blythe received a pair of silver candlesticks just today, sent from her family in Wyoming!" Valerie announced, her voice laden with her customary heightened sense of drama. "Her late grandmother Barton wanted her to have them."

"Candlesticks!" Luke exclaimed, his patience apparently nearly exhausted. "That hardly constitutes proof of anything out of the ordinary, my dear Val. There must be millions of pairs of silver candlesticks on both sides of the Atlantic—"

" 'The Children of Barton Hall shall ne'er be lost'!" Valerie repeated excitedly, pointing again to Kent's diary. "The first Blythe Barton and Christopher Trevelyan had no legal surviving heirs! Yet look what Reverend Kent's predictions say: 'Their path shall be lit by Silver Candlesticks into a land of misty waters'! Blythe *must* be a direct descendant! The candlesticks, along with the unusual experiences she's been having since she arrived here, establish that fact!"

"I grant you that she may be distantly related to the Cornwall Bartons, but as for 'misty waters,' may I remind you that Wyoming is about as far away from the sea as one can get in America?" Luke said wearily. "And, besides, what does any of it matter—"

"I haven't a clue about the 'misty waters' bit," Valerie admitted reluctantly. "However, doesn't it strike you as significant that the candlesticks from the Barton family in America just happened to arrive *today,* to 'light the way' for the two of you!" she concluded, as if dispensing a piece of airtight logic. "The Bartons of America have come home after all these years! You two are meant to—"

"Have you seen these candlesticks yourself?" Luke intervened quietly.

"No . . . ah . . . they were still in their wrappings, but—"

"I have something to show *you,*" he said, walking over to one of the bookshelves where the yearly ledgers chronicling life at Barton Hall were kept. He withdrew the volume stamped 1794. "This is one of the few old ledgers I've ever perused. . . . It's from the year my ancestor Garrett Teague inherited the place, and I was curious to see the resources the poor chap had been bequeathed." He flipped through several pages, looking for a specific entry. "Ah . . . here we are." He returned to his chair and sat down. Then he pointed to a line written in brown ink halfway down the page. "I only remember reading this because it was part of an inventory that detailed the contents of the house at the time of Kit Trevelyan's death. Look . . . it says 'Silver Candlesticks with scroll motif and Barton crest—lost or stolen.' "

"Do you recognize the hand that wrote that inventory?" Valerie demanded.

"It's Garrett's," Luke replied. "I'm certain of it, because I've read some of his other correspondence. There weren't any Barton candlesticks in 1794 when Kit died and Blythe Barton disappeared, or died, or whatever happened to her. Garrett obviously felt he couldn't afford to replace such luxuries. The silver ones we use in the dining room are very modest, as you know."

"Your Teague ancestor may not have known the entire story of what eventually happened to the first Blythe Barton, or to the candlesticks!" Valerie countered quickly. The psychologist appeared to be about to enlighten him further but then pursed her lips and remained silent.

"But, see . . . ," Luke insisted, "the inventory lists a number of other items of family silver that had gone missing over the years." He looked over at Valerie and concluded soberly, "I do not doubt you in the least, Valerie, when you say Blythe's father sent her some family silver by post. But I'm afraid your candlestick theory is not going to be able to prove whatever you and Blythe think you saw in your crystal ball."

"You are a stubborn man," Valerie replied, looking crestfallen, "but I must respect my vow of confidentiality, so I cannot say anything further on the subject . . . other than this—

which Blythe has given me permission to do. Since she's been in Cornwall, she has gained some unusual information concerning our mutual ancestors. Only she can decide whether to risk telling you about it, or about the way in which she acquired her insights. And if she does tell you about her experiences, only you can decide whether or not to believe her."

Luke's cousin slipped Reverend Kent's diary into her voluminous handbag and stood up, obviously ready to make her departure.

"Look, Valerie," Luke said quickly, escorting his cousin toward the closed library door, "I do appreciate your providing Blythe a sounding board, in light of all she's been through . . . and thank you for taking an interest in Dicken's and my welfare. It was very kind of you to have dropped by."

"Thank you for lunch," she replied crisply. "I'm glad to see that Dicken looks fit, despite his recent ordeal." She paused, her hand on the doorknob. "All I'm urging you to do is to keep an open mind, Lucas. There are aspects of the mind and memory—which some people know intuitively—that will one day be proved by science!"

"Yes, Valerie," Luke said patiently.

"Think about the mystery of what happened to the first Blythe Barton," she urged, ignoring his slightly patronizing smile, "and keep in mind the strange circumstances surrounding the way in which the Teagues inherited this castle. 'The Children of the House of Barton shall ne'er be lost . . . ,' " she quoted Reverend Kent once again, pointing to her handbag. " 'The Silver Candlesticks shall light the way.' " Then she drew herself up and pronounced with a dramatic flourish, "Just consider how all the pieces fit!"

However, Luke merely heaved a sigh of amused exasperation. "You Kents have always been a meddlesome lot," he said affectionately. "Safe trip home, Valerie, my love."

The bathwater had grown tepid during the forty-five minutes Blythe had been luxuriating in the antique porcelain tub. She silently blessed the unknown sybaritic soul who had installed it on its claw-and-ball legs behind a tapestry screen in the corner of her living room. Moist tendrils of hair clung to her neck as she leaned back and gazed dreamily through the window at the surging waters of the English Channel.

A Bathtub with a View.

What a lot had happened in her life, she thought, since the first time she had taken her landlord's advice and slipped into the tub's relaxing depths. She reveled in the pleasure of doing absolutely nothing but soaking up the spectacular scenery as the fragrant water soothed her skin.

Her eyes drifted to the dining table positioned in the middle of the cottage. On it still stood the pair of tarnished silver candlesticks so prized by Grandma Barton. Surrounding them were a few other small pieces of family silver and the shredded remnants of the packaging her father had improvised, studded with a panoply of postage stamps and labeled "Antique—Older than 100 Years—NO DUTY!"

As she gazed at the odd assortment collected on the nearby table, a flood of memories from her childhood at the Double Bar B engulfed her. The candlesticks had witnessed unnumbered dinners and occasions where toasts had been raised in times of family celebration. Blythe had lit long white tapers to illuminate the log bedroom where Lucinda Barton had lain in peace at last. Later she'd transferred the scratched and scarred beauties to the chimney mantel in the living room during the reception that followed her grandmother's funeral when the mourners had returned to the ranch for refreshments.

Galvanized by such morbid thoughts, as well as the bathwater's chilly temperature, Blythe climbed out of the oval tub and toweled herself dry. She marveled that her stomach was flat as ever. In fact, its ordinary appearance seemed in direct contradiction to the secret life that she had confirmed today was taking hold inside.

Next, she donned a clean pair of blue jeans and slipped on a bra, conscious that her breasts, at least, were beginning to show signs of her pregnancy. They felt tender to the touch and had acquired a strange voluptuousness. As the air stippled her skin, her nipples also became hard, and she felt a velvety rush of warmth radiating through her pelvis. Her thoughts drifted to images of Luke, and she wished that he were with her at this moment, holding her against his body and kissing her senseless.

Luke.

She suddenly felt a sense of urgency grip her as she searched for the rest of her clothes. With shaking fingers she swiftly pulled her ivory cable-knit sweater over her head, zipped up her jeans, and donned her Wellingtons. She made a grab for her jacket and dashed out the door.

Blythe strode purposefully across the field with her back to the sea, reminded of the first day she had taken Hall Walk up to the castle commanding the hill. That afternoon had been in mid-May, and her surroundings, as she had set out from Painter's Cottage, had been glowing in a thousand shades of green: undulating emerald fields, viridescent foliage that clung to the English oaks and larches, and the dense black-green underbrush that flanked the leafy tunnel leading through the woods toward Barton Hall itself.

As on that day when her heart had been so sore, the sun this September afternoon had begun to sink toward the western horizon. Its magical rays cast sage-gray shafts of light sparkling with motes of dust that filtered down through the ancient trees and lacy ferns lining her path.

She approached the now familiar giant oak whose gnarled roots pushed up fat tentacles from the moist ground to form a natural cave some three feet in diameter. She suddenly envisioned the child she was carrying in her womb sitting in that vaulted space playing "tea party" or "pirates" beneath its moss-clad roots. She allowed herself to indulge in the momentary fantasy that a son or daughter of hers might one day embrace these twisting vines and this ivy-cloaked wood as its enchanted playground—and birthright.

Suddenly Blythe began to walk faster, not slowing down even when the path slanted steeply upward toward the summit on whose crest perched the turreted castle. Her breathing became labored and her heart pounded with exertion, but still she didn't slacken her pace. As she broke into a run, she formed sentences in her mind and saw herself hurtling into Luke's arms, babbling incoherently the wonderful, astonishing, incredible news that they had made a baby together.

She was gasping with relief when she finally emerged from the wood and scrambled over the wooden stile. However, as soon as she came within view of the stone wall that led to the former pony stable, she halted in her tracks, dismayed as she surveyed the scene.

The stable yard, as well as the field next to it, was deserted. The seven hothouses in their various stages of construction were devoid of workers, as was the stable itself. Both the Land Rover and the Quillers' Ford Fiesta were nowhere in evidence. Neither was Chloe's blue Jaguar.

She glanced at her watch. It was half past four. Obviously the construction crew had gone home, as the days were much shorter now, and by six o'clock an inky darkness descended over the coast. But where was everyone else?

Blythe concluded with a sinking heart that young Richard had been banished to Shelby Hall for another year and the rest of Barton Hall's inhabitants had gone on about their business.

In a daze she entered the deserted castle through the kitchen door and sank onto a chair near Mrs. Quiller's long worktable. A dull weight of misery settled in her chest as the silence of the Hall became increasingly oppressive. It felt to Blythe as if all the unhappiness endured by its former inhabitants had penetrated the very walls and reverberated on some level, like a high-pitched whistle only dogs could hear.

Earlier in the day, after she had recovered from her latest bout of morning sickness, she had climbed the grand staircase to seek out Richard in order to say her good-byes. The door had been closed, and behind it she had heard the muffled sounds of

Luke's deep voice and Dicken's youthful chatter. She had tiptoed back down the hall and had then set out for the village to keep her appointment with Dr. Vickery. Fool that she was, she had been convinced that after Luke's emotional catharsis, he would never exile the boy for another year.

Apparently he had.

Blythe suddenly experienced a rush of protectiveness toward the fate of the baby she carried, so primal in its fierceness that she found herself holding on to the edge of the kitchen table with an iron grip. After several long minutes she rose from her chair and wandered down the carpeted hallway past the sitting room where she had first joined Luke for that memorable tea four months earlier. She stood in the high-ceilinged reception hall gazing up at the portrait of Kit Trevelyan, along with that of the first Blythe Barton. She searched their expressions but could find in their opaque eyes no answers to her own dilemma.

Did she want her child enmeshed forever in the legacy of Barton Hall? she wondered. She glanced around at the other portraits of male Bartons, Trevelyans, and Teagues whose life stories she didn't know as intimately as she'd come to understand those of Kit, Ennis, and Garrett. The women who had either loved or hated these men over the centuries had been—by virtue of their gender—at their husbands' mercy.

As Blythe had learned to her regret, marriage, even in the waning years of the twentieth century, was still a legal contract, with binding obligations and responsibilities weighted, more often than not, in favor of the man of the house.

Suddenly Blythe thought of William Barton, the natural son of her courageous, reckless, often misguided namesake. She shifted her gaze back to the portrait of his mother, captured in oil by her lover, Ennis, who had depicted her with faintly feline eyes and abundant dark tresses. If Blythe Barton—ex-Stowe—didn't ultimately marry Lucas Teague, then her baby, like the offspring of the original Blythe Barton, would be called bastard—with the suffering for a child that label might entail.

Blythe suddenly felt an urgent need to know what had

happened to her namesake's out-of-wedlock son—and what the future might hold for this tiny human, created by Luke and her, whom she already dearly loved.

Had Blythe Barton Trevelyan's infant survived the torturous journey across the Atlantic? she wondered. Did he and his mother make Annapolis, Maryland, their home? And most important, had his illegitimacy scarred and twisted his life?

What had been the fate of William Barton?

The library was full of shadows when Blythe paused at the threshold in the growing dusk. However, she didn't bother to flip on the desk lamp as she entered the chamber flanked with floor-to-ceiling bookshelves. The lingering light filtering through the tall casement windows illuminated the genealogy chart amply enough for Blythe to locate a particular date. It was the record of her namesake's death.

"One . . . last . . . time," she murmured in a whispered promise to herself.

As she placed her fingertips lightly against the glass and began to inhale slow, even breaths, she wondered if the notation "d." on Reverend Randolph Kent's parchment, followed by the year "1794"—plus an enigmatic question mark written beside it—could tell her anything about the destiny of Blythe Barton's only son.

Chapter Twenty

June 24, 1822

With each gulp of air Blythe found the act of breathing increasingly difficult. For hours now she had labored to inhale the humid summer's air into her lungs and longed for the oblivion of a dreamless sleep. The stifling temperatures mantling the Tidewater region of Maryland this sultry June day had relentlessly invaded her sickroom. The heat had grown more intense by several suffocating degrees as it rose to the top of Antrim Hall, transforming the narrow space allocated to her into an oven nearly as sweltering as the plantation's cookhouse. Yet Blythe was shivering with cold.

"Mama," her twenty-nine-year-old son said softly, "you're likely to die of asphyxiation with all those blankets piled on top of you like that."

She felt a cool compress touch her forehead, and then each cheek as William gently applied a cotton rag dipped in a diluted solution of witch hazel.

Then, with great effort, she fluttered open her eyes and tried to smile.

"I reckon I'll die, regardless," she whispered hoarsely, "and I'd like to depart this world without my teeth chattering."

"Shh . . . don't try to talk," he chided her gently as he raised a tumbler of tepid water to her lips, "just sip this. You've a touch of ague, is all. I only wish you weren't exiled to this devil's hellhole in the attic!"

She attempted to focus her gaze on her lanky, handsome son, who had to stoop in order to enter the spare quarters allotted to Antrim Hall's longtime housekeeper. At length she summoned a reassuring smile to her lips but could only maintain it for a few seconds as she patted William's ministering hand.

Blythe's son was a Barton, through and through, which gave her immeasurable satisfaction. Tall, with dark hair like her own, he was lean of limb, hot-tempered when provoked, yet born with a generous heart. William had been her constant blessing, a child who had compensated for the many disappointments that had plagued her life.

And, as he sat carefully on the edge of her narrow bedstead, she knew the time had come to tell him the truth.

"And where is that scalawag brother of yours?" she rasped, her throat raw and painful due to the infection that had taken hold of her body three days earlier.

She never referred to Maxwell Fraser as William's stepbrother. From the time they were small lads, they had been raised together, and when William was six, they had become siblings following the marriage of their parents in 1799.

"Max has gone into Annapolis," William revealed. "He's to meet with an agent of General Ashley's about the expedition."

"Ah . . . your great adventure," Blythe murmured. "I'm sorry to be the reason you stayed home from the appointment."

The boys had excitedly shown her the advertisement for "enterprising young men" placed by W. H. Ashley, a fur trader and politician from St. Louis, Missouri, and his partner, Andrew Henry. Both men had manufactured gunpowder and made fortunes during the War of 1812, the conflict with Britain in which Max's father, Thomas Fraser—who was also Blythe's second husband—had been severely wounded.

The Missouri bigwigs, Ashley and Henry, hoped to undertake a fur-trading expedition to the upper Missouri River. They also intended to forge a trail deep into the new American West along the paths first discovered by the explorers Lewis and

Clark. "Max will tell us whether Ashley's man is a trickster or not," William said reassuringly, "and then we'll decide whether St. Louis shall be our next destination."

Blythe knew with a strange certainty that, however Maxwell's interview went with General Ashley's man this day, she would never see America's "jump off" metropolis, as St. Louis was coming to be known.

She succumbed to a fit of coughing, as if her body were confirming what her heart already knew . . . that she was, indeed, dying.

"William," she said with difficulty when she was able to speak again, "please open the bottom drawer of the cupboard and fetch the large velvet pouch you'll find there."

Casting her an indulgent look, her son promptly did as he was bid.

"There's no need to tell me about the candlesticks again," he teased. "I know you wish them to be mine—and they will be one day . . . but not for many years."

"Give them to me!" she commanded sharply, and then struggled with a second paroxysm of coughing.

"Take care, Mama," William cautioned, "they're heavy." He gingerly set the pouch next to her on the bed and took a seat near her knees.

Blythe inched her hand into the soft confines of the velvet bag, feeling for the dueling pistol she kept there, along with the Barton silver candlesticks.

"This shall go with you wherever your life's journey should lead," she said, straining for breath.

"Don't turn morbid now, Mama, just because you've reached your fiftieth year," he cautioned, and then smiled in an obvious attempt to lighten the atmosphere.

Ignoring his jest, she placed the ivory-handled weapon in her son's large, callused palm. "This pistol saved my life many a time before Thomas and I met—and a few times since."

A sudden, intense memory overcame her—of a kindhearted man with silvery-red hair who had occasionally frequented

Reynold's Tavern on West Street in Annapolis so long ago. Thomas Fraser had long treated her with courtesy before they had struck up a conversation about young William. Thomas, twenty-five years her senior, had often indulged in chats with the little boy, who passed the time playing quietly in the sawdust beneath one of the tavern's tables while his mother tended customers.

On that fortunate day the large, well-built Scotsman, then in his early fifties and a widower, disclosed that he was serving as estate factor for his brother-in-law, Beven O'Brien, at Antrim Hall, a few miles northwest of the city.

Thomas's son, Maxwell Fraser, had been a motherless child for eight years by the time Blythe encountered his father and was offered the position of housekeeper on the wheat plantation. Fortunately, Max and William had become fast friends after climbing the willow tree by the stream that ran beside poor Arabella O'Brien Fraser's grave. The two boys and their parents soon recognized that they had been lonely for too long.

Blythe's meandering reminiscences were interrupted by a soft knock on her door. The black housemaid carrying a cup of broth looked startled as she caught sight of the pistol cradled in William's hand.

"Mistuh O'Brien's still sleepin'," she whispered, "and Miss Mercy's wid the babies. Cook says she'll send up supper in a bit." She eyed the white man she'd always assumed was a peaceable sort. "You fixin' to use that?" she demanded, arching an ebony eyebrow in the direction of William and his weapon.

"No," he assured her in a hushed tone as the housemaid tiptoed out of the room. "Thank you for bringing the soup, Sally."

O'Brien's still sleepin'.

Sleeping off his latest drinking binge, presumably, Blythe thought sourly.

She would have considered her life supremely blessed as Thomas Fraser's second wife and titular chatelaine of the plantation—if it hadn't been for Beven O'Brien.

The owner of Antrim Hall was forever shouting for her to bring him another bottle of port, or trying to break the lock on the bedroom door of every beleaguered housemaid in his employ. For years Blythe and Thomas had held out hope that he would simply drink himself to death, and that his nephew, Maxwell Fraser, would inherit the prosperous wheat plantation that Thomas had run so conscientiously in his first wife's interest all these years.

However, it was certain now that Maxwell would not inherit Antrim Hall, after all, nor would his stepbrother, William Barton, serve as factor.

The ague that crept into the Tidewater this spring had raged through poor Thomas's weakened seventy-four-year-old body. Blythe had buried him beside Arabella, gauging that there would be just enough room for her own casket on his other side when the time came.

And now, she knew, it wouldn't be long before both their sons, bearing her coffin on their shoulders, would make that short journey from Antrim Hall's stately white portico to the plot beneath the willow tree.

"Here, Mama, let me help you," William said as Blythe struggled to retrieve one of the ornate silver candlesticks from the pouch.

Her son stood it on its broad base upon the lumpy mattress. Blythe's fingers curled around the scrolls that wound up the stem and found herself reflecting on how the best-laid plans so often go astray.

Beven O'Brien had already hired Thomas's replacement, she reflected bitterly, a disreputable drinking companion named Obadiah Layton, whose sister, Mercy Layton, had been clever enough to produce a strapping set of twin sons at Easter, a scant five months after her wedding day. Beven had never sobered up after the christening. He had simply given his disenfranchised nephew and his extended family a month to find other employment and living quarters.

Just as they were about to vacate the premises, Blythe, too, had been felled by a wicked fever and banished to this attic hellhole, so as not to endanger the newborn sons and heirs of Antrim Hall.

Recalling the unfortunate series of events that had led to her family's perilous situation, Blythe struggled to raise her head from the pillow.

"You must put the candlesticks in a vault in St. Louis as soon as you arrive," she whispered fiercely. "I want you to promise me you will never sell them, whether fortune blesses or curses you. Promise me, William!"

"I promise," he said slowly, and she realized she was wise to have extracted this pledge.

"Do not use them to fund your journey," she warned, "or for any such purpose. They came from Barton Hall . . . where you came from."

"I know, Mama," William said patiently.

"But there is something important that you *don't* know," she countered with as much strength as she could muster. She momentarily closed her eyes and contemplated how difficult it would be to shed an enduring family fiction. "Your father did, indeed, die at sea, but not on the voyage to America," she said, focusing her gaze on her beloved son. "*My* name was Barton, not his. The man who gave you life was Ennis Trevelyan. He was killed fighting in the Royal Navy against the French off the coast of Calais—and I was not married to him," she added matter-of-factly.

William stared at her, dumbfounded. She was well aware that the story of his mother's tragic widowhood had been the foundation of his young life. Her son and Max had long marveled at how many common struggles they and their parents had endured. William thought his birth father had also been named William Barton, a man of means from Cornwall who had been swindled out of his inheritance by a neighboring family named Trevelyan and had boldly chosen to make his way to the land of opportunity. At least that was what Blythe had always told him. Now she had no time for face-saving invention.

"I am in my right mind, if that's what you're wondering," Blythe said, swallowing with great difficulty.

William stared at her, and Blythe knew that she had read his startled expression correctly. He needed to be convinced that the fever had not made her daft.

"Well, then, why did you lie?" William asked in a low, reproachful voice.

"Because I would rather have been a tavern maid than a whore," she replied. "Those were the only two occupations open to a woman in my situation."

"And this other man . . . What did you say my father's name was?" William demanded gruffly. "Who was he? A seaman who drifted into your life? Was Barton Hall your fantasy as well?"

"No!" she declared hoarsely. "You may choose to call me strumpet, but I was the mistress of Barton Hall! My family had owned those three thousand acres in Cornwall since the Conqueror! I was in love with your father at the time you were—"

"Then why didn't you marry him?" William asked accusingly.

"I was already married," she said, barely above a whisper.

"To whom?"

"Your father's brother," she disclosed. "Christopher Trevelyan of Trevelyan House . . . the property next to Barton Hall."

"Jesu . . . ," was all William said.

"Ennis Trevelyan was an artist . . . and a fine one," Blythe said. "I'll wager that his works still hang in the Hall and at Painter's Cottage. I couldn't transport the pictures, but the paintings belong to you. I inscribed your name on all of them . . . ," she added, wondering if her words were making any sense to her bewildered son. "I had always wanted to marry Ennis, but my wretched guardian forced me to marry the eldest son."

"And then you fled, disgraced by my birth," William said dully.

"I chose to leave in ninety-four," she replied, "because there was no other future for me after your father died at sea."

There was nothing to be gained by telling him about her feelings for Garrett Teague. She herself had come to fathom their depth when it was far too late. And now Garrett was married and a father as well.

Several years after Blythe's voyage to Maryland aboard the *Argus,* a Cornish friend of her maid's, Mary Ann, later emigrated to Annapolis with word that the overbearing master of Barton Hall and Trevelyan House had taken his own life with a dueling pistol. Much to the delight and astonishment of the villagers in Mevagissey and Gorran Haven, the bookseller Garrett Teague had inherited Barton Hall, lock, stock, and smuggler's hidey-holes.

Garrett, she'd learned, had finally married a village lass named Joan Vyvyan and had produced an "heir and a spare," as the former fisherman had put it. Blythe knew then that she would never reclaim her home. Fortunately, she had already invented the mythical William Barton, Senior, to retain some semblance of respectability.

"Why are you telling me this now?" William asked tensely, interrupting her reverie.

"Because I think enough of you to tell you the truth," she sighed, "and because I feel certain you and Max must seize the opportunity to follow fortune and head west." With great effort she lifted the candlestick and placed it on her abdomen. "Do you see the Barton crest?"

"Many a time, Mother," William replied testily.

"It has an escutcheon engraved with two sheaves of wheat, signifying the fertility of the earth." She gazed at her son with burning intensity. "Find land! Take possession of as many acres as you can that will be fruitful enough to sustain the family you establish in the West. Raise cattle and sheep . . . and a few flowers, as well," she added with a weak smile. A peculiar sinking sensation had begun to take possession of her. She struggled to raise herself upon her elbows. "Land is always the source of wealth," she exhorted her son. "Trapping and selling fur can bring you short-term riches, but use what you earn to purchase property!" She closed her eyes for a moment to gather her strength and then opened them, declaring in a hoarse whisper, "You are descended from English landed gentry. Don't ever forget that!"

This time there was blood when her coughing fit had subsided. William eased her back against her pillows and placed the heavy candlesticks on the table beside the bed.

"Mama . . . stop talking, will you?" he begged, his innately affectionate disposition reasserting itself.

"One more thing," she whispered. "You are a fine Cornish lad. Remember that, always. . . . Be proud of it."

"I will, Mama," William replied softly.

"And remember, too, my darling . . . you were the only child of my heart."

"I will," he repeated, and Blythe could see that moisture rimmed his eyes.

"I've so often told you about the soft, sweet air along Hall Walk, and your homeland's thousand shades of green," she said urgently. "Promise me, William, that you will tell your children of it . . . and your children's children," she pleaded. "The candlesticks tell the story. . . . Pass them on to the eldest child. . . ."

"I'll remember all the stories, Mama," William said in a choked voice.

"Tell your children!" she repeated urgently.

"I promise."

"Perhaps one day you—or those who follow you—will return home . . . and be proud that their ancestors came from Barton Hall."

Her breathing became shallower, and she began to envision the lovely green willow that her boys had scaled near the plantation's private graveyard. That tree was such an exquisite shade, she thought dreamily. Its leaves were like lace . . . emerald lace . . . and the shafts of light that filtered through its branches were sage-colored, like the golden-green light she had so loved when she had taken Hall Walk to the sea.

"Remember . . . a thousand shades of green," she murmured.

And then in her mind's eye she saw a dark forest loom up before her eyes. Its glossy leaves were the color of winter waves breaking along the Cornish coast. She saw towering pines, much larger than anything she had ever surveyed in the woodlands at home or along the sweeping drive to the entrance of the turreted Barton Hall. And she saw wide, lush valleys and mountains thrusting their white-covered peaks like a woman's milk-filled breasts into a crystalline blue sky.

And then within her vision appeared a bubbling fountain spewing forth a gush of misty water that was taller even than the majestic pine trees cloaking the mountains that surrounded it. The geyser shot its torrent into the air like a fountain of the gods, steaming and hissing and throwing its scalding droplets exuberantly to the heavens.

And suddenly she felt at home. She was calmed by the certainty that this wondrous, magical place somewhere out west would be Max and William's home, just as surely as enchanted Cornwall had always been hers.

And now she knew she could sleep.

The labored sound of the Land Rover shifting into low gear outside the library window slowly penetrated Blythe's consciousness. Next came the hum of Mrs. Quiller's Ford Fiesta following along behind. But Blythe hardly heard either of them.

"I remembered . . . ," she whispered as tears streamed down her face.

A thousand shades of green.

She was part of Barton Hall, as her baby would be. She was a descendant of her tribe. Cornwall was in her bones and memory. She belonged here as surely as any of them. In her and Luke and Richard and the child she carried were the sum total of their ancestors' joys and sorrows that had burrowed into the antediluvian soil and clung, like lichen, to the ancient stone walls.

In the growing dusk the Land Rover continued past the kitchen and paused near the stable yard out back with its motor still running. She heard Richard's high voice shouting something and the sound of the dogs barking excitedly. Then the car revved its engine and headed toward the dirt track that skirted Hall Walk toward the sea, leaving Blythe to surmise that its driver was taking the back road to Painter's Cottage.

She wiped the moisture off her cheeks with the back of her hand and slipped into the wood-paneled powder room to splash cold water on her face. She flipped on the hall light as she walked past the portraits of Kit and the first Blythe Barton. Pausing a moment, she searched their frozen faces for the animating spark she knew once existed. However, they merely looked out across the entrance hall with unseeing eyes.

Suddenly she remembered her grandmother pointing to the base of the family's candlesticks. Their engravings were blurred beyond recognition by generations of hands that had polished their silver surfaces to a high gloss before replacing the pair in their customary position of honor above the fireplace at the Double Bar B.

"Your great-great-who-knows-how-many-greats-granddad was one of the first mountain men," Lucinda had been fond of declaring. "He came to these territories as a fur trapper and brought these beauties all the way with him," the old lady had said, pointing to the base of the candlesticks. "I think this, here, is the family crest! You can't make it out too well anymore, but your grandpa Barton told me his ancestors were landed folks . . . maybe dukes or earls or somethin'. The Double Bar B brand was based on it. See these two little ol' funny-lookin' things? They're supposed to be haystacks. They became the double bars, and the *B* was for Barton, of course," she chuckled. "Lucky for us, those ol' fur trappers had enough horse sense to homestead this beautiful land and raise cattle." Grandma Barton had gestured toward the window in the log living room that faced northwest. "They took one look at those mountains and that powerful big geyser up in Yellowstone, plunked down their bedrolls down-valley here, pitched their tents, and never took 'em down." Lucinda Barton had thrown back her shoulders and declared, "Y'come from hardy Cornish stock, m'girl, and don't you forget it!"

The door at the end of the hall leading from the castle's kitchen slammed open, and Richard was running toward Blythe, full tilt, with Derek and Beryl scampering at his heels.

"You're here!" he whooped with an amazed, joyful expression spreading across his face. Then he shouted over his shoulder, "She's here, Mrs. Q!" He laughed and added, "Poor Dad's gone to look for you at Painter's Cottage."

"I came here looking for *you,*" she laughed back. She hugged him tightly, reveling in the sensation of his short arms around her waist. "I thought you'd already left for Shelby Hall."

Richard pulled away and danced a little jig while the two Labs barked an excited accompaniment.

"I'm not going!" he said triumphantly. "We've just come from Mevagissey Day School. Daddy and I met the headmaster this afternoon. We were so lucky, Blythe," he confided in an awestruck tone. "One of the families with a boy in my form was moving up to London. They're allowing me to start there as a student *this* term. Isn't that super?"

"Super? That's wonderful!" Blythe cried, and crushed him in a second embrace.

Mrs. Q suddenly appeared in the doorway with a bag full of groceries in her arms. She firmly ordered the dogs back into the kitchen.

"Mr. Teague's gone down to the cottage to see how you be this afternoon," she explained, shutting the door to the hallway. "I saw him in the food shops in Mevagissey, and we followed each other t'home. Feelin' better, are you?" the housekeeper said worriedly.

"I'm fine," Blythe attempted to reassure her, as the significance of Luke's decision not to send his son away to boarding school began to sink in. "I feel absolutely super, to quote Dicken here!"

"Let's go find Daddy," Richard suggested.

Mrs. Q cast an odd look in the direction of her young charge and intervened quickly. "Ah . . . but, my fine lad. I'll need your help unloadin' the car and then it'll be time for your supper. Your father says you'd be wise to spend tonight havin' a look at the textbooks you'll be usin' at your new school."

"All right," Richard said resignedly. Then his face brightened and he turned to look at Blythe. "Now that I won't be away at school, I'll be able to help you dry the herbs this spring."

"Oh . . . absolutely!" Blythe nodded eagerly. "You'll be a help to me in ways you can't even imagine. . . ."

Blythe entered Hall Walk's verdant tunnel shaded by the murky shadows of dusk that dappled its mossy borders and wove through the thick canopy of branches arching overhead. As she headed toward the sound of the sea, she found herself groping for precise descriptions of the abundance of plants that lined her path. The colors of their leaves blended from sage to olive, from apple-green to deep emerald. There were splashes of jade and fern, teal and willow, and grasses tinted a rainbow of ivy tones, like the palette of a brilliant painter whose eye discerns an infinite variety of light and dark hues within a single pigment. Certainly a thousand subtle shades of green sheltered her passageway through the dark wood.

There were many ways to classify this vibrant color, a part of the natural world that signified life, growth, and renewal. Perhaps it was rather like the act of forgiveness, Blythe thought as a buoyant sense of joy invaded her chest. There were many ways to find the strength to pardon those who had done injury to their fellow humans. In her own case her means of forgiving Chris for his betrayal with Ellie had finally come when she had recovered her own sense of gratitude for the good parts of her life—her Wyoming childhood, her grandmother's love, her passion for flowers and plants, the Cornish legacy of pride and determination that had been handed down to her through the generations. All these things had ultimately provided her with the strength to release Christopher and Ellie with a kind of dispassionate love. Love—and keeping a safe distance from them both. And through that process had come true forgiveness.

Every lamp in Painter's Cottage was alight, bathing its granite walls in a warm, golden glow. Blythe closed the gate and paused to drink in the loden field dotted with the estate's ubiquitous sheep. The last rays of the autumnal sun glinted off the English Channel like a shimmering length of china silk. A pungent tang of seaweed tickling her nostrils signaled that the tide was out, as did the shrill, plaintive cries of the herring gulls searching for their supper among the glistening rocks exposed on the beach below.

The air was light and the dewy grass sweet with the smells of approaching evening. Her Wellington boots were cushioned by the moist, plump mounds of turf that sank beneath her feet as if she were treading on tufts of cotton.

Luke's battered moss-green Land Rover appeared to be part of the landscape, parked, as it was, a few yards from her front door. As she approached, she could hear the sounds of a deep bass voice singing with gusto. Blythe gave a chuckle as she recognized the tune from Gilbert and Sullivan's *Pirates of Penzance*.

The town of Penzance, some fifty miles farther west of Gorran Haven, had, indeed, been a pirate's lair. Luke had told her the story of how in 1772—the year of the first Blythe Barton's birth—a customs boat had been plundered and sunk by smugglers. Later the same year the cutter *Brilliant* had been seized, in full view of the customs authorities, by buccaneers with nefarious designs on the goods she carried.

Stealthily Blythe approached the large artist's window on the side of the house and peered inside. She stared, slack-jawed, at the sight that met her eyes.

A well-built fire burned cheerfully on the hearth. Near it the tapestry screen had been folded into a single, narrow panel and was leaning against the wall. In her ball-and-claw bathtub sat Lucas Garrett Barton Trevelyan Teague, up to his armpits in bubbles. He was bellowing at the top of his lungs.

Hurrah for our Pirate King!
And it is, it is a glorious thing
To be a pirate king, hurrah!

Blythe sprinted past the window and then crept toward the front door.

Hurrah for our Pirate King!
When I sally forth to seek my prey
I help myself in a royal way
I sink a few more ships, it's true
Than a well-bred monarch ought to do!

As Luke continued to warble in the background, Blythe paused to read a handwritten note that was taped to the latch.

September 9, 1994
Darling Blythe,

Thank God you refused to allow that rogue to kidnap you to Kenya. Will you pay Dicken and me the undying honor of marrying me?

I love you, and all the Blythes—past, present, and future—

Ever your Lucas

Blythe was about to open the door and announce her presence when Luke burst forth with a basso profundo rendition of yet another ditty from his favorite operetta.

Here's a first-rate opportunity
To get married with impunity
And indulge in the felicity
Of unbounded domesticity . . .

Without waiting for the second stanza, Blythe flung open the door and stood on the threshold, her hands on her hips in an attitude of mock dismay.

"Now, just a cotton-pickin' minute here!" she declared in her best Wyoming twang. "You may be the landlord in these parts, but this here's pretty outrageous behavior!"

"Come in here, wench, and shut the door!" Luke demanded. "The draft's becoming downright unhealthy."

Blythe obeyed and shed her Barbour coat, hanging it on its peg on top of Luke's. Then she turned to face her brazen intruder.

Luke was neck-deep in frothy bubbles. Beneath his shock of black hair he was gazing at her with alarming intensity. She suddenly felt self-conscious, as if she had already stripped off her clothes and were standing in front of him naked and exposed.

"Would you be a darling and bring that chair over to the bath so you can sit down next to me?" he commanded. "I want us to have a little talk before I invite you in here."

Wordlessly she followed his instructions.

When she had sat down, he reached for her right hand, which was resting on her jeans-clad leg. A clump of bubbles pooled on her knee.

"I know about the baby," he said quietly.

"You do?" she replied with astonishment. She wondered: How? Didn't patient confidentiality count for anything in Gorran Haven?

"Lindsay looked green about the gills at the beginning of both her pregnancies," he revealed softly. "Your hasty exits the last few days gave you away . . . not to mention your sudden passion for saltines," he added, pointing to a platoon of identical cracker boxes lined up like soldiers on her kitchen counter. Then he propped her chin in his fingers in an attempt to force her to meet his gaze. Instead, he succeeded only in leaving a blob of bubbles along her jawline. "It's absolutely wonderful news. I couldn't be more thrilled. You'll *have* to marry me now."

Blythe stiffened as Chloe's pronouncements earlier that day echoed in her head. *Lucas may think he's infatuated with you . . . but I guarantee that he's convinced himself of that because he's so terribly desperate to save Barton Hall from the Inland Revenue!*

"Resigned to making an honest woman of me, are you?" she replied evenly. Her heart sank at the thought that Luke might feel obligated to marry her after the tragedy he had revealed about Lindsay's aborted child. "You Brits are such an honorable lot."

Luke abruptly sat up in the bath, sloshing water onto the floor. "This has absolutely *nothing* to do with honor, my love," he objected, ignoring the pools of soapy liquid oozing across the floor. "I wrote most of that note asking you to marry me before—"

"Before what?" she interrupted.

It's only a matter of time before he realizes how unsuitable you are for his kind of life. . . .

"Before I had an interesting little session in the library with my cousin Valerie after lunch today."

"You did?" Blythe said, her eyes widening. "And . . . did anything . . . ? I mean, what happened? What did Valerie *say*?"

" 'Lucas, my dear,' " Luke mimicked his cousin's high-pitched tone of voice, " 'you've got to keep an *open mind*!' "

"Oh, my God," Blythe whispered, sinking against the back

of her chair. "She hypnotized you? I would have liked to see that! Well . . . what happened?" she demanded.

"She most certainly did *not* hypnotize me," he corrected her, "but she showed me several passages in Reverend Kent's diary. . . . One I particularly remember predicted that 'the Children of the House of Barton shall ne'er be lost. . . . Their path shall be lit by Silver Candlesticks into a land of misty waters and fertile ground.' "

"You're not serious," she breathed. "That's from Reverend Kent's diary?"

"Along with quite a collection of bizarre notations and predictions. What I'd like to know is what 'misty waters' can there possibly be in Jackson Hole, Wyoming?"

"Waterfalls in spring?" Blythe guessed. Then her dark-brown eyes lit up like roman candles. "Old Faithful! The big geyser in the national park! When it shoots up, it's misty as a dusty gulch in a sandstorm!" She stared at the candlesticks as if they might suddenly shout "Boo!", and then gazed at Luke once again. "Tell me exactly what happened!" she demanded. "What did Valerie tell you?"

"She told me those candlesticks arrived today," he replied, nodding his head in the direction of the table littered with brown paper wrappings and the two tall pieces of silverware. "Did Valerie have a look at them today?" he asked suspiciously. "Did you open the parcel in her presence?"

"Nooo . . . ," Blythe answered slowly, her puzzled look signaling she thought his question distinctly odd. She pointed to the pile of shredded packing materials plastered with a customs declaration and a crazy quilt of U.S. postage stamps. "I told her that the box contained the candlesticks and some other family stuff that my father sent from Wyoming when he moved out of the ranch. They've always been handed down to the eldest son—or the oldest surviving child. They're awfully heavy," she pointed out matter-of-factly, "so I thought it'd just be easier to carry them home from the village and open them here."

"And have you studied the crest engraved on the base?" he asked soberly.

"It's just a smudge now." She shrugged. "They're so scratched with age, you . . ." Her words drifted off as she scanned his face for a hint of what else Valerie might have told him—especially about the strange experiences she'd been having all summer.

"Have a look at them with the magnifying glass I brought with me," he directed.

Blythe rose from her chair and walked over to the table. As soon as she zeroed in on the objects in question, her hand holding the heavy brass-encased lens began to tremble.

"Grandma Barton always called them the 'Barton candlesticks,' " she acknowledged slowly as she squinted to get a clearer look at the magnified view, "though we could never quite make out the etchings on the base." Yet coming into focus beneath Luke's high-powered glass were two badly scratched, but delicately engraved, sheaves of wheat flanking the blurry letter *B* carved in Gothic script.

"See anything?" Luke asked, sitting absolutely still in his bubble bath.

"Oh, Lordy Lord . . . ," she said under her breath, "the Barton Crest . . . just like the one painted on your genealogy chart . . ." Blythe put down the magnifying glass and placed both her hands on the table for support. "What else did Valerie tell you?" she asked in a low voice, refusing to look at him.

"Not much . . . She seemed to enjoy making a guessing game of it all. I was the one who mentioned you'd told me you'd seen the vision of a baby during your little tête-à-tête at the village fair. What *other* things have you seen in my dear cousin's crystal ball?" he demanded.

"It's not just the crystal ball," Blythe replied, continuing to keep her eyes averted from Luke's penetrating gaze.

"Oh?" was his only response.

Blythe finally turned to face him and nearly laughed aloud at the sight of him frowning at her, awash in mounds of fragrant bubbles.

"Look, Luke," she began, "I went to see Valerie a few times during the summer because a lot of weird things kept happening to me from the moment I arrived in Cornwall."

"Such as?" he pressed, arching a black eyebrow.

"Such as," she continued, her eyes glinting with mounting amusement, "I probably know a hell of a lot more about your family than *you* do!"

"Such as?" he repeated, gazing at her steadily.

She returned to sit in the chair placed beside the bathtub. Then she extended her hand and, with the tips of her fingers, lightly smoothed his brow.

"My darling Lucas . . . if you remain a *very* good buckaroo," she teased him gently, "I might let you in on a few secrets concerning this ancient pile."

"When?"

"Oh . . . from time to time."

"And how, pray tell me, shall I earn your confidence?" he asked, his glance drifting lazily down the length of her body.

"You already have," she said quietly.

Lucas Teague had accepted her western origins. He'd taken her as his business partner. He wanted to marry her and be a father to their child. All she had to do now was trust that he would accept one more thing. The Barton candlesticks would, eventually, light their way.

"Did Reverend Kent's diary say anything else noteworthy?" she asked with a casualness she didn't feel. "Valerie offered to let me read it, but I've never gotten around to it."

"Oh, the usual claptrap about peering into the old boy's shewing stone and naming the succeeding generations."

Luke's skepticism seemed as ingrained as ever, Blythe thought as her heart took another sudden nosedive. Then she noticed that an evil grin had begun to spread across his face.

"Am I missing something?" she asked, and realized that she had been holding her breath.

"There was nothing much more in the diary," he replied nonchalantly. "However, I showed Valerie a note I'd found in something else—the 1794 Barton Hall inventory. I had pulled it off the shelf to prove something to her."

"Which was?"

"That the 1794 inventory recorded the fact that several pieces of family silver, plus a pair of silver candlesticks with ornate scrolls and the Barton crest, went missing that year. Foolish me." Luke nodded ruefully. "I thought the entry noting that the engraved candlesticks had been lost or stolen sometime in the eighteenth century proved your candlesticks *couldn't* have been from Barton Hall. I see now, thanks to my grandfather's old magnifying glass, that there might be some room for discussion on that point."

"Holy cow and Christmas!" Blythe moaned, and sank back against the back of the wooden chair. "It all fits."

"Might you know something about how my family silverware happens to be in your possession?" he asked with mock severity.

"What do you mean *your* family silver, Mr. Teague?" she replied tartly. "Whose last name is Barton around here?"

"Touché." Then he cocked his head to one side and asked, "But what do you mean by 'it all fits'? Valerie said the same thing to me."

"Well . . . now, lookee here." Blythe grinned, resorting to a special-edition version of Grandma Barton at her saltiest. "This here tale's a mighty long story. . . ."

"I'm listening," Luke replied patiently.

Blythe narrowed her eyes mischievously. "I just reckon one day I might tell you some interesting details I picked up from that genealogy chart of yours. That is, if you promise to listen *very* carefully," she announced with a veiled warning.

"Well," Luke countered with mock solemnity, "I promise—at the very least—to hear you out."

"Even if there's no 'rational' explanation for what I swear to you I've seen?"

"As Valerie says, I must do my best to keep an open mind," he said solemnly, and then flashed an unreadable grin.

"Promise me you won't think I'm completely crazy?" Blythe asked suddenly, abandoning her teasing tone as her gaze probed his for any serious signs of derision.

"At first . . . this afternoon . . . I-I very much thought one of us might be," he admitted with a wry look. Then he grew somber. "But soaking in the bath here . . . in this cottage . . . surrounded by Ennis Trevelyan's paintings . . . those candlesticks. I've had time to think," he continued, gazing at her with disconcerting intensity. "To be quite honest, I can't quite believe this business about the Barton silver isn't some strange sort of wild coincidence. Maybe it isn't. But whatever it is . . . it's certainly captured my attention." Smiling gravely, he grazed his thumb along her ring finger. "All I know for absolute fact is that after two hundred years the mistress of Barton Hall has returned to her home."

"Are you sure?" she asked, her eyes troubled. "Are you absolutely positive that this Blythe Barton belongs on a duded-up spread like this? Because Chloe"—she silenced Luke before he could interrupt—"Chloe believes it's only a matter of time before it dawns on you how 'unsuitable' I am for your kind of life."

"Chloe can be an utter ass on occasion!" Luke retorted, his eyes flashing with annoyance. "My old way of life . . . this relic of a place . . . had no purpose before you came. The notion of a grand seigneur living on the labor of others is dead! I've known that for quite some time, but I couldn't for the life of me sort out what to do about it."

"Then I arrived at your doorstep, kicking up dust," Blythe intervened, "and proposed the risky scheme of creating Barton Hall Nurseries. But there's no guarantee it will work, Luke," she added, "and if it doesn't, are you sure that I'm—"

"I am not proposing we spend a life together merely to form a business partnership," Luke insisted. "If we fail with the nurseries, it would be vastly disappointing to us both."

Then he grinned slyly and added, "However, the consolation prize of you and a new baby remains pretty spectacular, as far as I'm concerned." He reached across the rim of the bathtub and deposited a dab of bubbles on the tip of her nose. "Suitable? Who's better suited to my overheated sensibilities than you, my beautiful, talented, sex-crazed darling woman! There's not a house or garden or any figure one could name that equals the importance of having you in my life, Blythe."

"But, Luke . . . ," she protested, not quite sounding convinced.

"We're going to be a *family*. Do you have *any* idea how much that means to me after what Richard and I have been through?"

It was Blythe's turn to close her eyes for a moment and offer up a silent prayer of gratitude. Along with everything else, Luke had worked a miracle and restored the most important thing in the world to her.

"When my grandmother died," she said softly, "I remember staring at her face just before they closed the coffin. I thought to myself, 'I'll never have anyone again in my life who loved me so much.' " Blythe extended her hand again and brushed the back of her fingers along the contours of Luke's jaw. "Now I know . . . she was the one who prepared me for finding you."

Luke nodded, his smile now tinged with melancholy.

"I was thinking just before you came through that door that dear, kind Lindsay had taught me much of what I needed to learn before it would have been right with you."

He raised her right hand to his lips and kissed it. Then he added solemnly, "And now I must ask you to take off your jumper, please."

His seductive tone of voice made her flush with excitement.

"As Grandma Barton would say: Buster, you're mad, bad, and dangerous to know," Blythe countered, glancing at him sideways.

"How flattering. That's precisely how the poet Lord Byron was described by his admirers," Luke replied indulgently. "He was related to the original family who built Caerhays, you know . . . the next castle down the road."

"How bizarre," was all Blythe could reply as Luke arched an eyebrow expectantly.

"Now, do as I say, please," he commanded in a cool, authoritative tone. "That's a good girl." He nodded as she finally managed to stand up from her chair and pull her cable-knit sweater over her head. "Come, come! Shed your Wellies and knickers, if you don't mind."

Blythe kicked off her boots, shimmied out of her blue jeans and panties, and stood beside the tub that was overflowing with fragrant bubbles. Once again she felt awkward and shy. She found she was shivering and peered down at the goose bumps that were pimpling her flesh.

"Come closer," Luke said, his voice raw with an emotion she had never heard before.

In one graceful movement he rose out of the water and knelt on the bottom of the tub, pulling her body hard against his chest. He wrapped his moist arms around her backside as he laid his cheek against her abdomen and closed his eyes. After a long moment of silence Blythe cradled his head in her hands, threading her fingers through his blue-black hair. She nearly wept when he planted a tender kiss on her belly.

"Hello in there," he murmured against her skin. "Your mummy and daddy are very happy you're on your way."

Blythe then sank to her knees beside the bathtub as Luke studiously began to scoop daubs of foam and deposit them on her left breast, then her right. Then he shook the froth remaining on his hand into the snowy mass that seethed on the surface of the steaming bathwater.

Brazenly she leaned forward to kiss him in a manner that was designed to get her into serious trouble. Eventually he unclasped her hands from his various extremities and pointed to the bathtub's curled porcelain rim that separated their torsos.

"Got a problem, Englishman?" Blythe asked with feigned innocence.

"Actually, quite a big problem," he said, his blue eyes turning the color of smoke.

"Well, then . . . got any room in there for a close relative?" she inquired as a mischievous grin began to spread across her lips.

"Climb in, cowgirl . . . ," Luke commanded gruffly. "I want to get my hands on you before the water gets cold."

An Excerpt from

THE BRITISH-AMERICAN TRAVEL GUIDE TO CORNWALL'S HISTORIC HOUSES, CASTLES, AND GARDENS

MEVAGISSEY-TREGONY REGION (SW 94/SX 04)

1996 Edition

BARTON HALL GARDENS

Location:

The Barton Hall estate, with its splendid turreted castle, is situated on the south coast of Cornwall between Mevagissey and the River Luney, which rises near Hewaswater.

Hours:

April–September: 10:00–18:00 Tuesday through Sunday

October–March: 10:00–13:00 and 14:00–16:00 Wednesday through Sunday

Closed: December and selected Barton-Teague family anniversaries

A PRIVATE GARDEN BECOMES A PUBLIC TREASURE

In the autumn of 1994, Lucas Garrett Barton Trevelyan Teague, a widower, married an American descendant of the original Bartons of Barton Hall, Ms. Blythe Barton of Jackson Hole, Wyoming, and Brentwood, California. Upon their union, the couple joined their names, becoming the Barton-Teagues.

On Mothering Sunday (Mother's Day) 1995, Barton Hall Gardens and Nurseries, Ltd.—located on the castle grounds near Gorran Haven—was first opened to the public, along with a second location on the A390, St. Austell Road at the Charlestown crossroads.

The busy Barton-Teagues now have three children: Richard, aged twelve (whose mother was the late Lindsay Wingate of Mevagissey); Matthew, two; and Blythe Lucinda, born earlier this year during the March gale.

THE BARTON-TREVELYAN-TEAGUE LEGACY

Barton Hall and its properties were joined with the adjacent Trevelyan House lands through the marriage in 1789 of the heiress Blythe Barton to Christopher "Kit" Trevelyan. It was an unfruitful union, however, and the properties passed to Trevelyan's first cousin, Garrett Teague (1772–1848), in 1794, whose line has owned them ever since.

This first Teague owner prospered during the Napoleonic Wars when the demand for agricultural goods was high. His son, Richard Garrett Teague, was a member of Parliament for the region from 1827 through 1840, as was the current owner's grandfather, the Rt. Hon. Charles Garrett Teague, from 1940 through 1952. In 1995 Mr. Lucas Barton-Teague was elected president of the Cornwall County Council.

Among many distinguished members of this ancient Cornish family is Ennis Trevelyan, a well-regarded seascape artist in the late eighteenth century. His paintings still hang in the Hall and in Painter's Cottage and can be viewed during the Annual Fete when the house is open to the public (see below).

THE ORIGIN AND DEVELOPMENT OF THE GARDEN

The grandson of the first Garrett Teague developed a keen interest in gardening, and in 1850 began planting some of the thirty to forty species of azaleas and rhododendrons that were then being introduced to Britain from Northern India. Many of these plants thrived in the Cornish soil and climate and grew to be as high as forty feet tall.

The opening up of China to the West between 1850 and 1930 permitted the Teagues' descendants to gather dozens of new varieties of rhododendrons and transplant them to what is now considered to be one of the finest privately owned gardens in Britain.

Many economies in the management of Barton Hall were made in the wake of two world wars, government-imposed death duties, and various destructive gales. Trevelyan House, a derelict, was pulled down in 1955.

The Barton-Teagues have a great fondness for the writings of the local novelist, Daphne du Maurier (1907–1989). As a result, hybridized rhododendrons named in the author's honor have been developed here under the guidance of newly appointed head gardener John Quiller. Most spectacular are: the magnificent scarlet "Rebecca," "Frenchman's Creek" (purple), "Cousin Rachel" (white), and "Jamaica Inn" (coral). All are on display in the gardens and are available for purchase.

BARTON HALL EDUCATIONAL AND CULTURAL CENTER

Each Saturday morning at 10:00, Mr. or Mrs. Barton-Teague offers a slide presentation and morning tea to whet the novice gardener's appetite for more ambitious planning for the family garden. (Schedules of all events are available at both nursery sites.)

"Garden Chats" are held at 14:00 in the converted stables the first and third Sunday of the month. At these bimonthly lectures, visiting experts offer their insights on various aspects of gardening, with a question-and-answer period to follow.

The second and fourth Monday evenings are devoted to illustrated talks by representatives from such public institutions as The National Trust, The Cornwall Garden Society, English Heritage, Royal Horticultural Society, etc.

Mr. and Mrs. Barton-Teague's television series *In the Garden* was produced for BBC-TV and will debut on Public Broadcasting Service in America this autumn. Audio- and videotaped versions (recorded in both British and American VCR formats), in addition to their illustrated guide, are available for purchase in the shop. An interactive CD-ROM version will be released in 1997.

Barton Hall Nurseries and Shops

Both locations are renowned for the cultivation of rhododendron, azalea, camellia, hydrangea, and magnolia starter stock, along with selected examples of larger specimens.

The herb garden is now the sole responsibility of Master Richard Teague, who supervises the curing and packaging of the extensive selection of dried herbs and fragrant potpourri, also available for purchase.

Experienced local gardening staff are on hand to answer questions at both nursery locations. A large selection of quality gardening tools, garden furniture, statuary, paving stones, and other items related to gardening or country living may be purchased in the converted sheep shed. A shopping-by-post catalog is available near the register, along with the latest gardening videos and coffee-table books. The complete works of Daphne du Maurier are also kept in stock.

The Tearoom

Afternoon Cream Tea is served at Barton Hall from 14:00 to 17:00 hours on days when the nursery is open to the public. Prices are posted near the door of the tearoom, which can be found adjacent to the walled herb garden. Scones, bangers, Cornish pasties, and Barton Hall Brambleberry Jam are also available for take-away purchase. Private catering for local events may be arranged upon consultation with Mrs. Margery Quiller, proprietress.

The Annual Fete

The Barton-Teagues host an annual garden party to raise funds for the Search and Rescue Team the first Saturday in September. Featured are Cornish pony rides, special tours of the Hall, stall sales, raffles, a Punch-and-Judy show, teas, the Pet Parade, a demonstration of Wild West barrel-racing by Mrs.

Barton-Teague, a display of The Ennis Trevelyan Seascape Collection, and a psychic fair under the direction of psychologist Dr. Valerie Kent. Telephone Barton Hall (Nursery office, please) for information. Transport is available by arrangement. Children free. Dogs welcome.

For further information regarding Barton Hall Gardens and Nurseries, Ltd. (including a video press kit upon request), contact:

Mrs. Chloe Vickery
Vickery Public Relations
Shipwright's Loft
Rattle Alley, Gorran Haven

Author's Note and Acknowledgments

This book, a work of fiction, required a surprising amount of research and was ultimately accomplished thanks to many others besides its author.

As mentioned in the dedication, I am deeply grateful for the enthusiasm and hospitality extended by Edd and Gay North, who live in a charming Cornish village west of Plymouth. As soon as they read the proposal for the novel, they wrote to say they had found the "perfect location" to set the story and urged my husband and me to "journey across the Pond" immediately.

In May of 1994, during Cornwall's exuberant spring, we explored the region around Dodman Point, Mevagissey, and Gorran Haven. In the course of this heavenly excursion, we were treated to a delicious afternoon cream tea by Julian and Delia Williams, the owners of the magnificent Caerhays Castle, mentioned briefly in the story. (Yes, Caerhays has two secret doors.) The Williamses' sumptuous private rhododendron gardens and their family nursery business, Burncoose Gardens near Gwennap and Redruth, both provided the inspiration for "Barton Hall Gardens and Nurseries."

In August of that year, I returned to the Fowey region of Cornwall and rented a stone cottage next to a creek through The National Trust, a half mile from where Daphne du Maurier wrote her first novel, *The Loving Spirit,* in 1931. The real "Hall Walk," incidentally, is a National Trust path that begins at Bodinnick across the river from Fowey and ends—via Penleath Point—at the footbridge at Pont Pill. Revisiting many of the du Maurier novels during the previous year and a half has been a joy, and I envy anyone about to indulge in reading her work for the first time.

On this second trip to Cornwall I enjoyed the company of my pal, novelist Cynthia Wright, and was treated to the vast knowledge of local history, flora, and fauna provided by Dr. John Gask and his wife, Dilly, who made steak-and-kidney pie for us in their cliffside house in Cawsand and pointed out the sights around historic Plymouth.

Those interested in the lore of eighteenth-century smuggling activities should secure a copy of *Smugglers' Britain,* by Richard Platt (printed and published by The Ordnance Survey of Great Britain, Cassell Publishers, Ltd.), and visit the seaside village of Polperro. Colorful fishing boats still crowd the harbor, and following a tour of the small smuggling museum featuring items associated with the "Free Trade," don't miss the crab sandwiches at the riverside eatery, The Bakehouse!

I spent an entire day at Boscundle Manor, near St. Austell, learning about the rigors of running a small, first-rate country inn from owner Mary Flynt. Dinner there is just as delicious as described in the scene where Christopher Stowe and his ex-wife break bread together for the first time since their divorce. Reservations are a must.

En route from Dover to the village of Polruan, my dear friends Randolph and Valerie Kent offered their customary hospitality and did not object when I borrowed their names. As I returned to California via the Hampshire village of Stockbridge, Fiona and Bill Orde likewise warmly welcomed me to their home, where Bill provided the necessary background about his favorite vehicle, the British Land Rover.

In London, Suzannah and Anthony Jennens not only offered shelter and superb cuisine, but also—along with Lindsay and Cephas Goldsworthy—filled my head with the elegant cadences of the King's English. From them and other English citizens, I beg forgiveness for any slipups of British phraseology by citing George Bernard Shaw's epigram that Britain and America are two countries divided by a common tongue. I must acknowledge, however, the wonderful lexicon *British English A to Zed* by Norman W. Schur, a witty collection of nearly five thousand Briticisms and Americanisms (Harper Perennial).

In addition to my British friends already named, sculptress and Cornwall fanatic Hazel Court Taylor, now living in California, reviewed the manuscript for blatant "Yankisms" and was enthusiastic and knowledgeable about the "psychic" subject matter. From the first she had urged me to set the story in "enchanted Cornwall" in her native England and recommended a number of books on parapsychology. Works by Raymond Moody, Jr., Dick Sutphen, Bruce Goldberg, and Betty J. Eadie were particularly instructive. *Real Moments,* by Barbara De Angelis (Delacorte Press), provided intriguing insights regarding the journey of "a life, well-lived," and offered an effective plan for people faced with putting life back together after traumatic events.

During the course of my sixteen years as a health and lifestyle reporter for KABC Radio in Los Angeles, I had occasion to interview a number of experts engaged in cutting-edge research in brain chemistry at UCLA. I owe them thanks for my basic understanding of the "Mind-Body Connection" and the effect of stress on health. My personal speculations concerning wide-ranging scientific theories of "Genetic Memory," however, are entirely my own inventions.

My thanks must also go to "cowgirl" Kathy Brody, friend, horsewoman, and station manager of KJVI-TV in Jackson Hole, Wyoming, who set me straight on rodeos and bronc riding. Some of Grandma Barton's best quips came from Kathy's lips. I also put words in Lucinda Barton's mouth, thanks to inspiration found in *Never Ask a Man the Size of His Spread: A Cowgirl's Guide to Life,* by Gladiola Montana (Gibbs-Smith Publisher).

Ruth Bracken, who earned a master's degree in landscape design and is a production designer of feature films and commercials in Los Angeles, gave unstintingly of her time, and, as it turned out, offered inspiration to the process of developing the character of Blythe Barton. She spoke eloquently on the challenges that face professional women in the Hollywood entertainment industry.

My "Resident Reader," Ann Skipper, did her customary marvelous job giving me her reactions to early drafts of the work, and her husband, Peter, is my local expert on Gilbert and Sullivan operettas.

Among a long list of friends and colleagues, writer, teacher, and friend of many years Elda Minger allowed me to pick her brain at crucial moments and, as always, was perceptive and supportive. Barbara Thornburg, of the *Los Angeles Times Magazine,* and Alayna Grey of Rancho San Carlos in Carmel Valley, California, generously volunteered their knowledge of "western style." Carol Adams, of Adams World Cruise Specialists, arranged my lecture tour on board Holland-American Line's spectacular ship the *Statendam,* which docked in August of 1994 a mere day's drive from my beloved Cornwall.

Journalist and television news producer Tony Cook, whose grandmother was born in England (and whose cousins and friends are "mad, bad, and dangerous to know"—not to mention wonderful fun), cast his critical eye on a later version of the manuscript. His suggestions were gratefully received, as were the cups of tea he cheerfully supplied throughout the revision process.

As with my previous two historical novels, *Island of the Swans* and *Wicked Company,* I owe an enormous debt of gratitude to President Robert Skotheim, the staff and administration of the Henry E. Huntington Library, Art Galleries and Botanical Gardens in San Marino, California, where I have been a reader in British-American studies since 1983. The late William A. Moffett, director of the library, welcomed me into his office for chats about everything from smuggling to smallpox epidemics in eighteenth-century Britain, and I shall greatly miss his enlightened spirit. Fellow readers and authors

Barbara Babcock, Pat Barlow, the late Josette Bryson, Harriet Koch, Mary Fry, Karen Langlois, Karen Lystra, Martin Ridge, Elizabeth Talbot-Martin, Jeanne Perkins, Diane Worthington, Catherine Turney, and Paul Zall offered their scholarly expertise and encouragement during the researching and writing phases.

Computer whiz Sam Reynolds did a fantastic job helping to create the Barton-Trevelyan-Teague genealogy chart. Thanks, too, to my astute literary agent and dear friend, Jane Chelius, for guiding me through some choppy waters.

Beverly Lewis responded enthusiastically to the kernel of an idea for this "unorthodox historical novel," and then helped me make sense of it. I deeply appreciate and am indebted to her discerning observations, sage suggestions, and unflagging loyalty. Carolyn Nichols at Ballantine Books has my heartfelt thanks for having offered this novel—and me—such a wonderful publishing home.

And finally, it is with love and a sense of gratitude that I acknowledge the help and kindness that William E. Borah extended to me at a time when I needed it most.

Ciji Ware
The Old Farmhouse
Montecito, California

Don't miss these delightful Regency romances by Marian Devon

MISS ARMSTEAD WEARS BLACK GLOVES

When Miss Frances Armstead invented a secret betrothal to Lord Greville Wainwright to ward off her uncle's insistent matchmaking, she thought it was the perfect safeguard to a single life. After all, Lord Greville was a naval hero who—rumor had it—was consigned to a watery grave at sea.

But suddenly her faux fiancé returned very much alive! Would he tar and feather young Frankie's reputation all the way to fashionable London—or would Lord Greville exact an altogether more titillating vengeance?

MISS ROMNEY FLIES TOO HIGH

Lord Petherbridge had taken it into his head to leave his considerable fortune to his illegitimate daughter, Sarah Romney, with pious Lady Petherbridge none the wiser. So he laid down the law: whichever of his three nephews married the young lady would inherit a fortune with her.

Marry an *actress*? Two of the hopefuls had no choice: They would be penniless without the Petherbridge portion. Only Lord Graymarsh was wealthy in his own right. So how was it that the man with the least at stake should win the lovely lady's heart?

On sale now wherever books are sold.
Published by Fawcett Books.